A0295272

CW00632054

The Makeshift Marriage

It was Laura's first meeting with Augustine Townsend, and she tried not to tremble as that lady spoke.

'So, my *lady*, we meet at last,' said Augustine? in a voice as cool and mocking as her green eyes. 'Already I think you know how things will be here, don't you? There's no place for you at King's Cliff, and I advise you to leave now, before you suffer any more.'

'I have every right to be here,' Laura declared with all the firmness she could muster.

'You do not honestly imagine that *you* are capable of taking Nicholas from *me* and keeping him, do you?' Augustine's eyes glittered coldly. 'You are nothing here, as you will soon discover if you are ill-advised enough to remain. I am mistress of both this house and its master. And I shall see to it that every moment you spend here is a misery from which you will wish only to escape.'

In her heart, Laura knew that Augustine spoke the truth. To remain here in this mockery of a marriage was the height of folly – every bit as foolish as it was to fall so deeply in love with a man who clearly would never love her. . . .

The Makeshift Marriage

Sandra Wilson

ROBERT HALE · LONDON

© Sandra Wilson, 1983, 2009
First published in Great Britain 2009

ISBN 978-0-7090-8655-0

Robert Hale Limited
Clerkenwell House
Clerkenwell Green
London EC1R 0HT

www.halebooks.com

The right of Sandra Wilson to be identified as
author of this work has been asserted by her
in accordance with the Copyright, Designs and
Patents Act 1988

2 4 6 8 10 9 7 5 3 1

Typeset in 10/12½pt Classical Garamond
by Derek Doyle & Associates, Shaw Heath
Printed in the UK by the MPG Books Group

Chapter 1

The principal bedchamber of the Hotel Contarini was justifiably renowned as one of the most magnificent in Venice, for its windows afforded an unrivaled prospect of the Grand Canal. The guidebooks extolled its virtues, and during the season there was always an eager throng of fashionable souls eager to be privileged enough to occupy it. Once inside, it was obvious why the *beau monde* of Europe cherished this particular chamber, for its walls were hung with golden silk, the ceiling was festooned with gilded plasterwork, and the furniture was the ornate lacquered chinoiserie so peculiar to Venice. There was not a surface left undecorated, and that which man had adorned, nature beautified still further with delicate water reflections from the canal outside. The crystal droplets of the chandeliers shimmered in translucent light as the early spring sun rose higher in the sky above the city. A sea breeze moved the gauze curtains and only a few sounds penetrated the silence, but none of them disturbed the sleep of the young Englishwoman in the canopied bed.

She did not hear a maid calling softly to her that it was time to rise, nor did she hear the song of a passing gondolier. Her slumber was deep because she was exhausted after a long journey from England in jolting stagecoaches on roads which were badly rutted after a hard winter. Her long dark hair spread over the silk pillow in a cloud of tangled curls, and her demure night bonnet lay unused on a console table. Anyone looking at her as she slept in this royal room would have been forgiven for thinking she was a princess, for they would have seen a sweet profile, a flawless complexion, and a certain roselike fragility of which any princess would have been justifiably proud. But she was not of royal blood, nor even a titled lady. Her name was simply Miss Laura Milbanke and she was squandering what little fortune she had on this once-in-a-lifetime visit to the most romantic and beautiful city in the world.

Her arrival at the hotel the night before had been greeted with some degree of surprise, for it had been fully expected that she would have several servants to attend her – for only the very rich took the principal bedchamber. Her emergence from the gondola, completely alone, had caused not a few whispers. To her shame she had resorted to a mumbled fib or two about her maid having contracted a fever and having had to return to England, when the truth was that she was not, and never had been, in a position to employ a maid. Laura Milbanke was the epitome of that unfortunate class of creature – the poor relation. Her family was grand enough in its way, for on her mother's side she was connected to the Hazeldons of Sussex, but that meant very little when her own branch was impoverished due to poor investments and the somewhat dubious distinction of having lost everything on the turn of a card. For that her mother had never forgiven her father.

But the quarrels of unhappy parents did not concern poor Laura for long, for she was left an orphan at a very early age and had found herself being taken under the wing of her Aunt Hazeldon, a matriarchal dragon who always made absolutely certain that Laura 'knew her place.' And that place was very low in the varied and complicated pecking order at Hazeldon Court. Laura was above the servants, and below the family; she occupied a no-man's-land in between and knew the advantages and disadvantages of both sides. Not wishing to appear mean in the eyes of her peers, Aunt Hazeldon had seen to it that Laura had a considerable and fashionable wardrobe, and that she had enjoyed the services of one of the lesser maids – not a true lady's maid, one must understand, for that would not have done at all and would have puffed up Laura's head with undeserved importance! This, together with a comfortable room and all the comforts of a grand house, was the advantageous side of Laura's life.

On the side of disadvantage came the times when she was not permitted to dine with the family because an important guest was expected. She was not allowed to accept invitations which could have led to her meeting a young gentleman who might have offered for her hand and thus have elevated her above her rather dull and plain cousins who would have stood little chance beside Laura's outstanding beauty. But for all that, Laura was not ungrateful, for she knew well enough that without her aunt's protection, her life could have been so very dreadful. It was one thing to be grateful, however, and quite another to be happy. Laura had never known true happiness, and she sought refuge in dreams to compensate for this dreadful gap in her life.

She had found the guidebook, a relic of her late uncle's grand tour, in the library at Hazeldon Court, and Venice had filled her thoughts from the moment she had turned the first page. Over and over again she had read that little leather-bound book, and she felt she knew by heart everything there was to know about the city which was denied to her both by her impoverished situation and by the interminable war with Bonaparte's France. Europe had been effectively closed to travelers, and it was this last fact which had given her a little comfort over the years, for even had she been a wealthy woman she would still not have been able to see Venice; but then Bonaparte's final defeat at Waterloo had removed even that small consolation. She had dreamed on, however, imagining herself in the principal bedchamber at the Hotel Contarini. . . .

The change in her circumstances had come quite suddenly and had been totally unexpected. Early in 1816 Aunt Hazeldon was suddenly struck down by an ailment which had rapidly taken its toll, for by the end of January she had been laid to rest in the family mausoleum. Laura's cousins had lost no time in informing her that she was no longer welcome beneath their roof, and she was left with a small bequest in her aunt's will – and an uncertain future. She knew nothing of the outside world, and the only life she felt able to contemplate was that of being a lady's companion, for after all, was that not what she had been hitherto? Unfortunately, the only position that presented itself had been that of companion to Lady Mountfort, a dowager renowned for her mercurial temper and penny-pinching meanness. With her cousins insisting that she leave, however, Laura felt she had no option but to accept the position with Lady Mountfort.

Standing in the library at Hazeldon Court that dull winter afternoon, she had steeled herself to write the necessary letter. Outside the snowdrops were nodding beneath the hedges of the maze, and a little snow still clung to the ground. The library was always a dark room and she had lit a candle before sitting down to write. The light of the feeble flame had fallen across the guide book. The thought had suddenly struck her that Venice was within her grasp after all. She had immediately dismissed the notion, dipping her quill in the ink and beginning to write, but the thought would not go away; it insisted upon being heard. She had only a little money from her aunt's estate, but it was sufficient for a journey to Venice. She could, if it was available, occupy that room in the Hotel Contarini for several weeks, and thus she would have for the rest of her life memories to call upon whenever things seemed about to overwhelm her. Oh, it was a foolish, foolish notion, of course, but she could not put it out of her mind. How could she possibly contemplate squandering absolutely everything on a *vacation*? How? Only too easily, for she had dreamed of just this one thing for so long that the dream had almost become an ambition, and Laura Milbanke was not one to turn her back upon such a thing. Her mind was made up in a moment. She *would* go to Venice, and she *would* see all those fabled sights, and then she would return to England – and Lady Mountfort. And so she had penned two letters that afternoon, one to her future employer, postponing the moment of taking up the post, and one to the Hotel Contarini, on the impressive Hazeldon Court parchment reserved exclusively for important communications. She had smiled a little to herself, for what more important communication could there be than this?

A month later, when the catkins were yellow in the Sussex hedgerows, Laura had set off upon her dreamed-of adventure, leaving England's shores for the first – and probably the last – time in her life.

Some doves fluttered noisily past her windows now, and at last she began to stir, stretching her arms luxuriously above her head and opening her deep blue eyes. She looked slowly around the room. It was everything she had dreamed it would be. In such surroundings she would be able to forget her woeful circumstances and pretend for just a little while that she was as privileged and carefree as any fine lady.

Slipping from the bed, she crossed the crushed marble floor to the tall windows that opened on to the balcony. She had arrived the night before in darkness and had seen little of Venice from her gondola, and now she held her breath in anticipation as she drew the delicate curtains aside. Dazed by the sheer magnificence of the sight that greeted her, she stepped unwarily out on to the balcony where the window boxes were bright with grape hyacinths. Seagoing ships rode the Grand Canal, which winked and flashed in the spring sunshine, and there were smaller boats of all descriptions thronging the busy water. Black gondolas rocked at blue and gold mooring posts by the steps of the hotel, and the gondoliers stood talking together as they waited for custom. Their red sashes were a vivid splash of color against their white shirts, and the ribbons in their hats flapped in the breeze. They were laughing together at some shared joke, and Laura found herself smiling too, although she could not hear what they said. Across the canal she saw a fruit merchant's barge swaying by the walls of a house, and far above a maidservant lowered a basket to him on a rope.

The moment was broken suddenly by an intrusive martial sound that put an end to the gondoliers' laughter. An Austrian military band struck up somewhere nearby and the Teutonic music was a harsh reminder that Venice was no longer her own mistress but had been ignominiously defeated by Bonaparte and then bartered for Austria's territories in the Netherlands. After centuries of being the undisputed queen of the Adriatic, la Serenissima was now merely a slave. Although by the end of the wars, Austria had been Britain's ally, Laura's sympathies lay with Venice and she felt as instinctive a dislike for the military music as did the gondoliers.

Ignoring the music, she remained on the balcony, savoring everything she could see from her vantage point and unmindful still that she was plainly visible to all in her nightgown, her hair unhampered even by the night bonnet which was de rigueur for all ladies of quality. She was reminded quite sharply of her misconduct, however, when she found herself looking straight into the disapproving eyes of a very handsome and fashionable young gentleman seated in a gondola that was nosing its way toward the hotel steps. His very blond hair was startling as he lounged in the black craft, and the plain cut of his excellently tailored clothes marked him instantly as an Englishman. His top hat lay discarded for the moment on the seat of the felze beside him and he was toying idly with the thick frill of his shirt at his cuff. His face was very lean and bronzed, and he continued to look up at her until the gondola slid from sight beneath the balcony. Only then could she gather her scattered wits enough to hurry back into the safety of her room. How could she have been so utterly foolish and remiss? What must he think of her? Her cheeks flushed scarlet with mortification.

Thoughts of her *faux pas* and the unknown gentleman vanished a moment later, however, when her glance fell on the golden clock on the mantelpiece and she realized how dreadfully late she already was for breakfast. With a gasp she began to untie her nightgown, for if she did not hurry, she would surely be too late to take breakfast at all! She shivered as she bathed her face in the ice-cold water she poured from the porcelain jug.

In a short while she was very properly and demurely dressed in a pale green sprigged muslin chemise gown. Her dark hair was twisted into a Grecian knot at the back of her head, and wisps of dainty curls framed her face. A lace day-cap rested on top of her head and her only jewelry was a black velvet ribbon at her throat. A lozenge-shaped reticule swung at her wrist as she picked up her Kashmir shawl. There, she thought, she looked well enough even for Carlton House itself let alone the dining-room of the Hotel Contarini! Her blue eyes sparkled at the somewhat fanciful thought of the likes of Miss Laura Milbanke gracing the halls of the Prince Regent's London house! With a final pat of her hair she left the room. It was the first day of March, and her first day in Venice had commenced.

Chapter 2

Tiredness the night before had robbed her of any appreciation of the grand staircase or the echoing vestibule with its magnificently patterned marble floor, but now she gazed around in wonder as she descended. The Hotel Contarini was very splendid, and indeed had once been the most beautiful palace in this city of palaces. Two white-uniformed Austrian officers paused on the staircase as she passed, their eyes warm with admiration as they bowed, their heels clicking smartly together. She hardly noticed them beyond allowing them a polite inclination of her head.

As she reached the vestibule she heard once again the rousing military music she had heard earlier, and now she could tell that it came from the dining-room of the hotel itself. Dismayed at the thought of taking breakfast to such a noisy accompaniment, she approached the doors where the smiling *maître d'hôtel* waited to greet her.

'*Buon giorno*, Miss Milbanke. I trust you slept well.'

'Excellently, thank you.'

'If you will please follow me.' He led her into the vast red and gold room that had once been the ballroom.

A sea of white uniforms greeted her eyes. The hotel seemed to have been entirely taken over by the Austrian army; there were very few civilians, Venetian or anything else, and even fewer ladies. Her dismay deepened as she followed the *maître d'hôtel* past the long, fully occupied tables, and a flush touched her cheeks at the obvious stir her arrival was causing in this masculine stronghold. The sound of the band was louder than ever, for the musicians occupied a stand in the very center of the room, and the floor throbbed a little beneath her feet as she passed them and was conducted toward a very small table in a far corner, well away from the band and from most of the other tables.

'*Buon giorno*, Sir Nicholas,' said the *maître d' hôtel* politely.

Her head came up sharply and she looked with horror at the sole occupant of the table. It was the gentleman in the gondola! Her cheeks, already warm, now became uncomfortably hot. If she recognized him so swiftly, then he must equally as swiftly identify her as the immodest lady on the balcony!

Sir Nicholas rose to his feet with a polite, but silent, bow as the *maître d'hôtel* drew out her chair and muttered something about her being a *donna inglese*, before hurrying away to attend to her breakfast. Nervously, Laura sat down, glancing up at her table companion. He was tall and broad-shouldered, and his hips were slender – all in all, he was her ideal of masculine beauty. But his glance was witheringly cold, and her nervousness increased. She fumbled with her recalcitrant reticule, which seemed of a firm mind to tangle itself with the crisp, spotless tablecloth, and she knew that she must be going from bad to worse in his eyes.

He took his seat again and returned his attention to a small account book which lay on the table beside his untouched breakfast. She could not help noticing that a great many of the figures written in the book were in red, and that the letter, which also lay close by, was from Messrs. Coutts, the London bankers. He poured himself another dish of the thick Turkish coffee in the elegant silver-gilt pot. Instinctively she knew that his uneaten meal and the black coffee were not the result of over-indulgence the night before, but rather a consequence of the contents of the account book and the letter.

The *maître d'hôtel* brought her the light breakfast of toast and coffee she had requested the night before, not being accustomed to taking a large meal at the beginning of the day, and as she began to eat she stole another look at Sir Nicholas. He concentrated so fully on the book that he was unaware of the close scrutiny to which he was being subjected. Up close he was even more handsome than she had thought, and with his golden hair and tanned face could lead the fanciful to compare him with a Greek god. She sipped her coffee. Yes, maybe it was not so fanciful after all, for that was what he did remind her of – in particular of a statue in the grounds at Hazeldon Court, although that statue had certainly not been clad in Bond Street elegance! What *would* he say had he known the indelicate thoughts she was thinking at this very moment! What would *anyone* say! Laura hid a smile. Glancing around, she saw that she was not alone in admiring him, for the few ladies present looked frequently in his direction. His fashionable clothes would have set him aside in any London drawing-room, but here, among so many white-uniformed officers, he was outstanding, the more so with his pale hair and fine gray eyes. A diamond pin sparkled in the folds of his cravat and he wore a heavy signet ring on which she could make out a design of the sun with many curving rays. Now, as in the gondola, he toyed with the frill of his shirt cuff, and she knew that it was a habit resorted to when he had a great deal on his mind. It was no great feat of insight on her part, merely the fact that she had often seen her late Uncle Hazeldon do precisely the same thing.

As she watched he closed the account book and put away the letter. Then he took a miniature of a red-haired woman from his pocket. Who was she, wondered Laura? She was very beautiful. His wife maybe? But he wore no wedding ring. . . .

Suddenly he looked at her, and his voice when he spoke was soft and almost light. 'It would seem that we are thrust together as being the only two Britons in this nest of Austrians. Allow me to introduce myself. Sir Nicholas Grenville of King's Cliff.' He inclined his head.

'I – I am Miss Milbanke. I trust you do not find it too disagreeable having to share your table with me.' A vision of herself in her nightgown floated horribly in front of her eyes as she tried to meet his gaze.

'In view of the crowded state of this establishment, Miss Milbanke, I doubt if finding it disagreeable would have any practical consequences to justify the effort.'

It was not politely said and she was suddenly angry. She may have been guilty of reprehensible behavior a little while earlier, but her crime had not been deliberately committed and it ill became the likes of Sir Nicholas Grenville of King's Cliff to behave as if it had! 'I will endeavor to disturb your meal as little as is humanly possible,' she said coldly, turning her attention to her breakfast and, as she thought, ending the conversation with the last word.

The last word, however, was to belong to him. 'You will not disturb me at all for the moment, Miss Milbanke,' he said, getting to his feet, 'For I am about to leave you in sole possession of the table. Good day to you.'

She did not deign to reply or even to look up. He may have the looks of an angel, but his disagreeable manners damned him in her eyes! The word 'gallant' was probably not in his limited vocabulary! Still, no doubt his dear mama adored him! Laura spread marmalade on her toasted bread as if it

offended her. Then she took a long breath. This was foolish; she had not
come to Venice to be immediately put out by a toad like Sir Nicholas
Grenville! She had come to enjoy herself, and enjoy herself she would!

The marmalade had a pleasant sharpness that went well with the coffee.
Thoughts of Sir Nicholas receded over the horizon and she contemplated
instead the delights that lay before her. She looked around the room, the
ceiling of which was so high that it took up two whole floors of the building. Immense chandeliers glittered in the smoky atmosphere and the red and
gold decorations were elegant and pleasing. Gradually, however, she became
uncomfortably aware that she was being observed. It was a disturbing sensation, one which made the hairs at the nape of her neck prickle a little and
sent a cold shiver down her back.

She turned sharply in the direction of that steady gaze. Among all those
white uniforms there was one of a completely different hue, and she
wondered how she had not noticed the tall, dark hussar before. His jacket
was dark green, his tight breeches a bright crimson, and the fur-trimmed
pelisse fixed casually over one shoulder was of the same dark green as the
jacket. Black and gold braiding sparkled impressively and a red shako bearing the Austrian oak-leaf emblem lay on the table before him. He smiled at
her in a way she found offensively forward and she looked coldly away to
signify her disapproval. He continued to stare disconcertingly at her, a touch
of amusement on his thin lips. His face was dark, as were his peculiarly
intense eyes, and there was an ugly scar on his cheek.

Her heart almost stopped when he stood, for she thought he was about
to approach her, but instead he left the busy dining-room, his tall, imposing
figure drawing mixed glances from his fellow officers. He did not speak to
any of them, nor they to him, and the atmosphere in the room lightened
noticeably with his departure.

Soon afterward, Laura left the dining-room herself. She had forgotten the
hussar, but then suddenly he was in the doorway before her and she almost
collided with him. He must surely have been waiting there for her, although
he managed to make the encounter appear to be accidental.

With a gasp she stepped back from him, her blue eyes wide and startled.

He bowed, smiling at her. '*Entschuldigen Sie bitte, gnäddige fräulein,*' he
murmured.

'The – the fault was entirely mine, sir, for I was not paying attention.'

'Ah, you are English. . . . Forgive me, dear lady, for barring your way.'

His deep voice disturbed her as much as his burning gaze, and she
muttered something hasty and unintelligible before hurrying past him and
up the sweep of the grand staircase. As she went, though, she knew that he
was still watching her, and the conviction that he had lain in wait for her
grew with each step she took. Out of his sight, she halted at the top of the
staircase to look back down at him.

A sardonic smile touched his thin lips and he tossed a coin lightly into the air, catching it deftly in a way that suggested he had found the answer to some irritating problem. Then he turned on his heel and left the hotel. She heard him calling a gondolier before the doors closed loudly behind him.

She stood there a moment. She was afraid of him. There was something devilish about him and she knew instinctively that he was a man to avoid at all costs.

Chapter 3

The sun was high in the heavens when Laura emerged at last from the hotel to commence her first day of sight-seeing. Her green parasol twirled gaily and a floating veil of embroidered net was draped over her satin bonnet. The perfume of orange blossom was strong from the small trees in their terracotta pots on the hotel steps and she remembered how cold it had been when she had left England and how the catkins had been the only color in the hedgerows. Spring had barely begun at home, but here it was well on the way to summer—

An old man called a ganzier held a gondola alongside for her, and she was mindful of the guide book's advice and took care to drop a coin into his outstretched hand. Realizing that the zentildonna was English and not one of the loathed Austrians, the gondolier grinned broadly at her, waving away the guide book she held. In halting English he promised that she would not need it, for he would show her all the many sights of the most beautiful city God in all His wisdom had ever created!

Smiling, she sat back on the black leather seat beneath the gondola's curtained felze. The little wrought-iron holder, which the night before had held a little light, now held a posy of fresh flowers, and the gondolier was already humming to himself as he poled his craft through the crush by the famous hotel. She felt sure now that she was in a dream, as indeed she supposed she was, for had she not dreamed of this moment every day since finding the book in her aunt's library?

At last the gondola was out on the shining water and Venice began to unfold before her. The pale gold and ocher reflections of the marble palaces shimmered in the dazzling water and the continuous lap-lap of the small tide against the gondola served to make everything seem even more dreamlike. Not even the relentless decay that pervaded everything could detract from the city's unique charm. There was the infinite arch of the brilliant azure sky above and the mirrored shades of the water beneath – and in between the beauty that was Venice. . . .

She noticed incongruous things as well as the magnificent sights. The gondolier pointed out the Doge's palace, but she noticed as well the bright red valerian growing in crevices, the flower heads so heavy that sometimes they bent to touch the rippling water. She was shown the Rialto Bridge, but glancing up at an open window she saw a tiny canary hopping from perch to perch in its gilded cage. The gondolier pointed away into the distance where stood the white marble gazebo where the tyrant Bonaparte had liked to take his coffee, but in another window she saw a bowl of orange marigolds. Time passed swiftly, and even had this one morning been her only time here, she knew already that she had been right to squander her meager inheritance upon this journey. Saving it all would never have given her as much exquisite pleasure as this lazy excursion in a gondola.

It was almost three o'clock in the afternoon before she realized that she had not taken her luncheon, and so she asked the gondolier to take her back to the hotel. He gave a disparaging sniff and remarked that he could not understand anyone wishing to take an Austrian meal when there was good Venetian fare to be sampled.

She smiled. 'I am sure the Hotel Contarini serves excellent food.'

'Certainly. If you are an Austrian.' He removed his hat and placed it reverently against his chest. 'As I swear upon the Blessed Virgin. Contarini serves only sausages, pickles and cold cabbage.'

She laughed then, for she was certain that such mean fare would not find favor with the well-fed officers she had seen at breakfast. However, the hotel dining-room would undoubtedly mean that wretched band playing again, and that would surely jar upon her after having savored Venice all morning.

'Tell me then,' she said at last, 'if you were going to eat now, where would you go?'

'Fontelli's,' he said promptly.

She wondered slyly if he had an arrangement with the proprietor of Fontelli's but perhaps she was being a little unChristian. 'Very well, I too shall eat there,' she said.

He beamed at her and turned the gondola. Her conviction that he did indeed have an arrangement with this particular eating house deepened when he took a very circuitous route through a great many narrow side canals before at last poling his craft toward some steps by a bridge. Some women were opening shellfish there and a crowd of beggars swarmed forward as the gondola nudged the steps. The gondolier leaped ashore to help Laura disembark and then turned to wave the beggars away imperiously, singling one out, however. He was a tall, burly fellow who did not look in the least as if he needed to beg for his livelihood, and Laura guessed that he and the gondolier were well acquainted. Was this play reenacted time after time, she wondered? No doubt they had an interest in the prosperity of Fontelli's!

The gondolier assured her that her new guide would look after her and that when she had eaten he would conduct her to another gondola. Thanking him, she paid the not-too-exorbitant price he charged, and then left the steps with the beggar. She felt a moment's trepidation, for she did not know where she was going, but soon the uncertainty vanished as once again the magic of Venice folded over her. They walked up a narrow, busy street where there were stalls with colorful awnings, selling everything from stewed pears to grilled fish. Women sat on their doorsteps chattering loudly to one another as they peeled vegetables or mended garments, and there were children excitedly playing skittles down an alley. On the buildings that overlooked the street, there were strange carved heads. They had been much in evidence since she had left the hotel that morning, and now they seemed to watch her progress still, their lips drawn back in a snarl which should have been menacing and ferocious, but which in Venice was nothing of the sort.

At last her guide led her into a small square, one side of which seemed to be entirely taken up by an eating house. It was crowded and obviously very popular with the Venetians. The beggar ushered her into a seat, accepted the coin she gave him, and then retreated to a shady corner at the far end of the square to wait for her. She sat there a little uncertainly, glancing at the several dishes being consumed at other tables. She did not recognize any of them and so felt a little foolish as a smiling serving girl appeared by her side. Taking a deep breath, Laura pointed at the next table where a well-to-do gentleman was eating something with obvious relish. The girl beamed and nodded, and a short while later a bowl was placed before Laura. It contained a dubious-looking piece of meat floating in what appeared to be a thin black soup. Her appetite dwindled as she stared at it.

'*Fräulein*, I do not think you will enjoy what you have ordered.'

She knew the voice even before she looked up into the hussar's dark eyes. He stood there with his hands on his slender hips, his pelisse swinging as he placed one shining, spurred boot on a chair and leaned forward, smiling down at her. How could it possibly be coincidence that brought him to this very place at the same time as her? She believed in coincidence, but after her experience in the hotel that morning, she doubted very much that this was any such thing. It seemed only too likely that he had been following her, and as she looked up into his dark eyes she knew that her suspicion was correct. She felt cold suddenly, and more than a little frightened.

He glanced at the bowl. 'It will not be to your English taste, I think.'

'Why?'

'It is called *calamari* – squid cooked in its own ink.'

Horrified, she pushed the bowl away.

He smiled. 'Permit me to order anew for you, *Fräulein.*'

'Certainly not, sir! We have not been introduced and I know absolutely nothing about you.' Her words sounded prim and proper, but the last thing she wanted was to strike up any sort of acquaintance with this unnerving man.

'Ah, etiquette,' he murmured. 'Then I shall put matters right by introducing myself. Baron Frederick von Marienfeld of the Radetzky Regiment in the service of the Emperor of Austria.' He bowed smartly and clicked his heels together.

How she wished he would go away. He was forcing himself upon her and she was uncertain of how to handle the situation. For the first time since leaving England she really wished she had a companion, but she did not, and he was waiting for her to reply. She felt cornered, and loathed herself, and him, when she meekly gave in to the pressure he was putting upon her. 'My name is Miss Milbanke, sir.'

He drew her hand to his lips. 'I am charmed to make your acquaintance, Miss Milbanke. And now, I shall order something a little more palatable for you.' Without waiting for her reply, he sat down, snapping his fingers at the serving girl.

'I – I'm not hungry, sir,' said Laura lamely.

'Nonsense, you came here to eat, *Fräulein,* and eat you shall. Besides, propriety will not be offended by my assistance, Miss Milbanke. After all, we are allies, are we not?'

'Allies?'

'England and Austria.'

'Oh. Yes.'

'And so I will consider it a privilege if you allow me to order your luncheon for you.' He spoke briefly to the maid, who did not smile at him as she had smiled at Laura.

Glancing around, Laura noticed for the first time how suddenly quiet the square was. The crowd of Venetians had vanished, including her beggar guide, and she was now quite alone with the baron. The golden alyssum tumbling over a nearby wall stirred audibly in the breeze, birds sang in the garden behind the eating house, and the sounds of Venice continued beyond the square – but at Fontelli's everything was horribly quiet.

The baron removed his red shako and leaned back in his chair, smiling a little at her apprehension on seeing how deserted the square now was. 'I am not welcome in this city, and neither are any of my countrymen. The people of Venice are fools, are they not? With Austria as their overlord they are more prosperous than they have been in centuries.'

'The conquered never love their conquerors, sir.'

'It does not concern me what they think or why they think it. They are of no consequence to me.'

How arrogant he was, more arrogant even than Sir Nicholas Grenville, and that was saying a great deal! Was it to be her fate here in Venice to take her meals with disagreeable companions?

The silent serving girl brought the baron's order, which included a bottle of Tokay wine. He smiled at Laura. 'I trust, Miss Milbanke, that you like *risi e bisi*. It is rice sprinkled with vegetables and ham and Fontelli prepares it most excellently.' He poured the wine and then commenced to eat his meal.

'Do you like Venetian food, Baron?' she asked.

'It is passable. As is the wine, although it cannot compare with our hock.'

'No, of course not.'

He looked sharply at her, rightly suspecting her of sarcasm, but she met him with a bland, uninterested expression through which he could not see and which would have silenced a lesser man. The rice dish looked delicious and the wine was cold enough to chill its glass, but the last thing she was going to do was give him the satisfaction of seeing her enjoy what he had rudely insisted upon ordering. She did not want his company or his strange notion of chivalry; she found him conceited and swaggering and objectionable. Normally she would have left him in no doubt at all of her feelings, as she had done that morning with Sir Nicholas, but there was something about the Austrian that cowed her just a little, an air of menace of which she was constantly conscious.

He was aware that she had not begun to eat, but for the moment he chose to ignore it. 'I have only recently returned from a visit to England, Miss Milbanke,' he said conversationally. 'A town called Taunton. Do you know it all?'

'No. I come from Sussex.'

'Taunton is most charming.'

'Indeed?'

'You are not eating your luncheon, Miss Milbanke. You English have no idea how to enjoy your food.'

'Maybe that is because we are not renowned for our cuisine, sir.'

'Perhaps. You excel at roast beef and plum pudding, but beyond that. . . .' He shrugged. 'Some good Austrian food would fatten you up.'

'I have no wish to be fattened.'

'No, maybe that is because you are perfect as you are.' He spoke this last softly and his eyes glittered as he raised his glass to her. His gaze moved slowly over the low neckline of her gown and in such a way as to make her feel he could see right through the delicate sprigged muslin.

She flushed, wishing more and more that he would take the hint that he was not welcome. But he obviously had no intention of seeing what she made no attempt to disguise.

'Such a tiny appetite cannot be healthy, Miss Milbanke.'

'I did tell you that I wasn't hungry,' she reminded him.

'Ah, yes. So you did.' His eyes were half closed now and a smile played coolly around his lips. 'Tell me, Miss Milbanke, are you well acquainted with Sir Nicholas Grenville?'

She stared at him, taken aback by the change of subject. 'And how would that concern you, sir?' she asked.

'It was merely a pleasantry, Miss Milbanke, please do not think that I am prying.'

But that is exactly what you are doing! she thought, but she did not say aloud. Deliberately she did not answer his question, thus forcing him to either drop the subject of Sir Nicholas Grenville, or to contradict his own words about prying by asking her again. A flame of anger burned in his intense eyes for a moment at her stubborn silence, but then it had gone and he was smiling again.

'Will you dine with me tonight, Miss Milbanke?'

'I – I cannot, Baron, for I have already accepted an invitation to dine with Sir Nicholas,' she said swiftly, willing herself to meet his gaze as if she spoke only the truth.

'Then I must concede victory to Sir Nicholas. For the moment,' he said smoothly.

She stood, determined to bring the meal to a close.

'May I be of any further assistance to you?' he asked. 'I could procure a gondola for you perhaps. . . ?'

'Yes,' she said quickly, 'yes, that would be most kind of you.'

He stood, tossing some coins on to the table and putting on his shako.

The walk back to the canal seemed endless, with the baron determined to conduct a conversation with her. She answered in monosyllables. Drat the man, why did he not take the hint? His skin must be thicker than an elephant's!

At last she was free of him. The gondola nudged out into the canal and she looked back at him as he stood on the steps where people thronged the merchandise stalls on the quayside. She sat back beneath the felze with a sigh of relief. But what could she do now? She had got herself into a tiresome fix and somehow must now contrive to sit with the odious Sir Nicholas this evening. But how? She could not be certain that she would automatically be taken to the same table again – she could not even be certain that Sir Nicholas would take his dinner at the hotel!

Her problem seemed all the more insurmountable when she and Sir Nicholas happened to arrive back at the Hotel Contarini at the same time. He disembarked from his gondola without giving her a glance, even though she knew perfectly well that he was aware of her presence. He seemed preoccupied, however, and she noticed that the account book was under his arm as he went into the hotel. She could not forgive him, though, no matter how preoccupied he was. What a truly disagreeable fellow he was, quite the most rude and infuriating of men! Why, oh *why* had she been foolish enough to fib about dining with him? She could have invented something a little more easy to carry out, but instead she had resorted to this, and now must face the consequences. At all costs she wished to avoid the baron, whose company was just a little more unpleasant than Sir Nicholas's. Yes, Sir Nicholas Grenville was definitely the lesser of two evils as far as she was concerned.

Entering the hotel, she heard the band beginning to tune up in the dining-room, and as she glanced in she saw that the *maître d'hôtel* was there too. There was nothing for it but to brazenly ask him to see that she was seated at Sir Nicholas's table that evening and to then cross her fingers that that gentleman decided to take his meal there! She knew that she was blushing as she asked, and she knew too that the *maître d'hôtel* quite obviously thought she was pursuing her handsome countryman, but she did not really care what he thought. The object of the exercise was to convince the baron that she had been speaking the truth. The *maître d'hôtel* beamed and nodded. But of course she could sit with Sir Nicholas, nothing could be simpler to arrange. . . .

Or more hateful, she thought as she climbed the grand staircase.

Chapter 4

The chandeliers in the bedchamber glittered as Laura dressed for dinner. Outside it was quite dark and the room was warmed by charcoal burning in a little terracotta stove. With a sigh of relief she lowered her arms after painstakingly putting in the last little artificial flower in the carefully pinned curls piled high at the back of her head. Ringlets twisted down from the curls, and she surveyed herself in the mirror. Her arms ached. Enjoying the services of the maid at Hazeldon Court, she had not realized how very hard it was to achieve a fashionable evening coiffure. But she looked well enough now, and certainly no one would know she had labored this past hour to look as she now did!

She got up from the dressing table and shook out the skirts of her pale blue silk gown. The crossover bodice was trimmed with dark red and green embroidery, as was the hem, and the petal-shaped sleeves were tied with dainty golden strings that trembled against her naked arms. It was a gown she was very proud of, for it was very fine indeed, quite elegant and costly enough to grace the dining-room of the Hotel Contarini. She pulled on her long white gloves. She didn't really know why she had taken such pains with her appearance tonight; it wasn't as if she was ever likely to impress Sir

Nicholas, but somehow she had felt that she must look her best.

Outside, the satin waters of the Grand Canal shone in the darkness, and the lights of the palaces were reflected brightly on its surface. The bell of the church of San Giovanni de Rialto had long since sounded sundown. It was time to face the dining-room. For a moment she was chickenhearted. She could avoid all this by meekly taking her meal in her room. But that would be to give in, something she could not do.

The *maître d'hôtel* smiled knowingly at her as she entered the dining-room, where the tables were again completely full and the band was striving even harder to drown all conversation.

A flicker of annoyance crossed Sir Nicholas's handsome face as she took her seat opposite him, and he made a very poor show of getting to his feet. 'Good evening, Miss – er, Milbanke.'

'Sir Nicholas.'

The meal was indeed as Austrian as the gondolier had predicted, but no one could honestly have grumbled at the excellence of the fruit-stuffed goose that was the main course. It was certainly a far cry from sausage, pickle, and cold cabbage! And from calamari and *risi e bisi*! Thinking of her disastrous luncheon brought her thoughts inevitably to the baron, who was sitting at the same table he had occupied that morning. She could feel his dark, knowing eyes upon her. She was suddenly nervous, snapping open her fan to cool her face. She must at least attempt to engage Sir Nicholas in a conversation and make it appear as if they got on well enough for him to have asked her to dine with him.

'Are – are you in Venice for long, Sir Nicholas?'

He glanced at her in surprise. 'A week or so.'

'Is it your first time here?'

'Yes.' He was not at all encouraging.

She continued, undaunted as yet. 'Are you one of the Flintshire Grenvilles?' she asked, inventing a fictitious branch of his family.

'I beg your pardon?'

'The Flintshire Grenvilles.'

'No, my family comes from Somerset.' He sat back, looking steadily at her. 'I've never even heard of the Flintshire Grenvilles.'

'Indeed? How strange.'

'Am I to presume from your question that you come from Flintshire, Miss Milbanke?'

'No. From Sussex.'

'Ah, so you are not one of the Leicestershire Milbankes. I did not think that you could be somehow.' He spoke smoothly, and his words conjured up a reminder of her misconduct on the balcony that morning, just as he had intended they should.

She flushed, at once hurt and furious.

'And now, Miss Milbanke, could we please dispense with polite conversation, for I vow I find it tedious in the extreme.'

'I was not aware that either you or your conversation had been in the least bit polite, sir, so dispensing with both will be exceedingly easy,' she said acidly. His manner upset her, even though she knew it was foolish to expect anything else of a man who had obviously taken a dislike to her from the outset.

'I did not come to Venice to make small talk. I came to think, as I have a great deal which is of concern to me at the moment,' he said, as if belatedly thinking he needed to make some restitution for his gross ill manners.

'There is no need to excuse your appalling conduct, sir. I shall put it down to your ignorance of how to behave in polite society.'

His gray eyes darkened angrily, but he said nothing more, allowing her the privilege of the last word this time.

The conversation, such as it was, had served her purpose. The baron must have realized very swiftly that her appointment with Sir Nicholas was proving disastrous, but at least he could not possibly know she had fibbed about it all in the first place.

She continued silently with her meal, still smarting from her verbal duel with Sir Nicholas. From beneath lowered lashes she surveyed him, however. He was wearing a tight, dark blue velvet coat, which sported a handsome set of gilt buttons, and a white brocade waistcoat, its top buttons undone to reveal the frill of his shirt. The jeweled pin glittered in the unstarched folds of his cravat, which was tied in the loose style known as the Byron, from the poet's liking for it. He looked, she thought grudgingly, exceedingly excellent – and exceedingly attractive. Was he always as disagreeable as this, she wondered, or was there another side to him? What would it be like to be courted and flattered by him? She pondered the thought for a moment, and came to the reluctant conclusion that he could probably charm the birds down from the trees if he wished. No doubt the beautiful redheaded woman whose portrait he carried only saw that other side of him. Laura suddenly wished that she too knew that other side, for she had to admit to herself that in spite of everything she found him very attractive. Damn him. And damn her own appalling taste!

Coffee was at last served and not a single word more had passed between them. It was at this point that the baron chose to present himself at their table, his heels clicking loudly as he bowed.

'Good evening, Miss Milbanke.'

Her heart sank. 'Good evening, sir.'

Nicholas glanced curiously at her as he slowly got to his feet, waiting quite obviously for her to introduce him to the baron. She was a little surprised, for she had somehow assumed that they were already acquainted in some way after the baron's question earlier that day.

'Sir Nicholas,' she said quickly. 'Allow me to present Baron Frederick von Marienfeld. Baron, this is Sir Nicholas Grenville.'

Nicholas inclined his head, but his manner was decidedly chill.

The baron smiled, and it was a smile that did not touch his eyes. Laura felt an urge to shiver as he took her hand and raised it to his lips. 'I look forward to our next meeting, my dear Miss Milbanke,' he said softly. Then he turned and left them.

Nicholas sat down again. 'You keep poor company, Miss Milbanke.'

'I know,' she said coldly. 'I'm sitting with it.'

A glimmer of a smile touched his lips. 'I was referring to your friend the baron.'

'He is not my friend. I hardly know him.'

'He, on the other hand, would quite obviously like to know you a great deal better.'

'I assure you that those feelings are not in the least reciprocated.'

'Beware of him. He is a notorious and dangerous man – certainly not someone I would think suitable company for you.'

'Notorious and dangerous?'

'He is virtually a professional duelist; his services can be purchased and he is considered to be almost above the law here in Venice as he is a close friend and confidant of the governor.'

She stared at him, the coldness she had felt before about the baron returning now that she knew the truth.

'At least ten men have died at his hand, Miss Milbanke, six by the pistol and four by the sword. He is equally proficient with both weapons.'

'I did not know,' she breathed.

'I thought not. Have great care in your dealings with him, for his notoriety does not stop at dueling. His reputation with the fair sex leaves much to be desired.'

Her *dealings* with him? Once again she felt that she was being unfairly condemned for appearing on the balcony in her undress. Did he imagine she was a demimondaine, a Cyprian whose favors could be purchased as easily as could the baron's prowess as a duelist? An angry flush stained her cheeks as she got to her feet, folding her napkin. 'I thank you for your timely warning, sir, and I shall take care to conduct myself decorously in future,' she said stiffly.

'You would be wise to avoid the baron's company entirely, madam.'

'Why, Sir Nicholas,' she said with sugary sweetness, 'that is exactly what I have been endeavoring to do this evening. Why else would I wish to sit with you? Good night.'

Chapter 5

For the next week or so, Laura enjoyed Venice. Venice in the springtime was probably at its finest, for the burning heat of summer would take the edge off pleasure, and indeed the wealthy citizens of the city took themselves to the mainland during the hottest months when the canals could smell so unpleasant and the mosquitoes and other insects came to torment the unwary. In March, however, it was perfect – as warm as May in England, and as colorful, with its flowers and trees bursting into blossom. The glorious city and its treasures were a constant source of delight to Laura, never tiring her and never causing a moment's boredom.

The only clouds on her horizon were those which appeared at breakfast and dinner in the hotel when she shared Sir Nicholas Grenville's table. She continued to endure his presence, for to have asked to be seated elsewhere would be to risk the baron thrusting himself upon her again. But one thing became more and more obvious to her with each passing day, and that was that she was still annoyingly drawn to the blond Englishman. He paid her scant attention, but she yearned for him to be more pleasant. He was not, however, and she kept her self-respect by treating him in exactly the same way that he treated her. The result was that they conducted their meals in virtual silence, apart from a polite greeting before and after.

She was very careful to keep out of the baron's way, although that was very difficult when she was sure that he was still following her. She met him on the grand staircase and he begged her to attend the theater with him, but she declined, pleading a headache she quite obviously did not have. She became adept at waiting until there was a crowd of officers in the vestibule before entering or leaving the hotel, so that she could slip past him without him being able to stop her. She had disliked him at first sight, and now that she knew more about him she found him quite abhorrent.

When she was sight-seeing, she frequently felt that he was watching her, and when she glanced in what she thought was his direction, it was always as if he stepped from sight a bare second before she turned. It was unnerving, and she told herself that she was imagining things, but the feeling still persisted. In the hotel he stared quite openly at her and there was little she could do except ignore it, but outside it was quite different, for she felt alone and unprotected. The tall figure in green and crimson was always there, just on the edge of her thoughts – close and menacing.

The nervousness he wrought in her remained with her all the time, until one afternoon in the Piazza San Marco it erupted into sudden terror. In the shadow of the campanile she came face-to-face with him. He seemed to appear from nowhere to stand in her path, and although the square was crowded, she felt that she was alone with him. His hands were on his hips in the arrogant stance she had come to loathe, and there was something positively threatening in his silence. She froze, unable to move, and he reached out to catch her wrist, drawing her inexorably toward him, but as his other hand slid around her waist she at last could fight him. With a cry she pushed him roughly away, turning in wild panic to run across the square, setting a cloud of pigeons fluttering wildly into the air as she fled, and almost knocking some costly bales of cloth from one of the many stalls cluttering the open space before the cathedral. Her heart was thundering as she ran blindly toward the steps leading down to the water. She hailed a gondola and begged the gondolier to return her to the Hotel Contarini as swiftly as possible. She felt hot and frightened, and her wrist burned as if the baron still held it. When the gondola was well out on the waters of the Grand Canal, she dared to look back, but there was no sign of him.

She remained immured in her room for the rest of that day, trying to convince herself that it was all foolishness on her part. But she had been badly frightened now, and there was no mistaking the baron's actions as he had drawn her closer. He desired her.

The time to dine approached and she reluctantly began to dress. She must make herself go down, for she could not remain locked safely in her room for the remainder of her sojourn in Venice. Just as she was putting the final pin in her hair, however, someone knocked very softly at her door. She went to open it, but then her outstretched hand froze on the handle. Instinct told her that it was the baron. She remained absolutely still and silent, conscious of the thunderous beating of her heart. He knocked again and the handle turned, but she had taken the precaution of locking the door earlier and so he could not come in. At last he went away, and she leaned weakly back against the door, her eyes closed. Her mouth was dry and her hands ice cold.

She waited until she heard several people in the passageway before daring to emerge, and even then she felt compelled to glance over her shoulder in case the baron was there, but there was no sign of him again. Her silk skirts rustled as she hurried along, but then she halted as she passed the open doors of one of the many elegant drawing-rooms, for inside she caught a glimpse of the reassuring figure of Sir Nicholas Grenville seated at an escritoire.

Under any other circumstances she would never have dreamed of approaching him, but today was decidedly different and so she entered the green and gold room.

'Good evening, Sir Nicholas.'

He looked around quickly, the surprise plain in his gray eyes. 'Good evening, Miss Milbanke.'

'Are you about to go down to dine?'

'I am.'

'Then may I wait for you?'

He stared.

'After all,' she went on bravely, 'we are the only two Britons here and we should show a united front, should we not?'

His eyebrow was raised just a little. 'If you wish.'

She smiled nervously, toying with the strings of her reticule and opening and closing her fan with a flick of her wrist. She glanced back at the open doorway.

Nicholas watched her for a moment but he said nothing. Dipping the quill into the ornate ink stand, he put the finishing sentence to his letter. Laura could read what he wrote. *With all my affectionate and enduring love.* N. Folding the letter and sealing it with his ring, he addressed it to Miss Augustine Townsend, King's Cliff, Somerset, England.

For the first time she noticed that the miniature was lying on the escritoire nearby. 'Who is she?' she asked. 'She is very beautiful.'

'There is no one more beautiful. Her name is Miss Townsend; she was my late father's ward and is soon to be my bride.' He stood and offered her his arm. 'Shall we go down, Miss Milbanke?'

The baron sat in his usual place and had almost finished dining. The waiter brought him a glass of kirsch, which he raised to Laura as she happened to catch his eye. She did not smile at him and looked away again.

'Are you unwell, Miss Milbanke?' asked Nicholas.

'I beg your pardon?'

'You look a little pale.

'I – I'm quite well, thank you.'

The band, hitherto silent, began to play suddenly, and she started at a loud clash of cymbals and a drumroll. She was quite on edge now and had little or no appetite, even for the magnificent offerings of the Austrian chefs employed at the hotel. Austrian food, Austrian voices all around, Austrian music drowning out even thought – and one particular pair of Austrian eyes constantly upon her. . . . Her hands trembled and she pushed away her unfinished meal. How could she endure all this? It was too much and she did not know how to extricate herself from something she had unwittingly managed to get into.

Nicholas at last finished his coffee and seemed about to take his leave of her, and in desperation she spoke to him. 'Sir Nicholas, may I beg a favor of you?'

'A favor?'

'Would you please escort me to my room?' Oh, how shameless those innocent words could sound!

'I beg your pardon?'

'I – I assure you that I am not making advances,' she said, her face a miserable crimson, 'and it is not so very much to ask of you, is it?'

'I know that you are not and I know that it isn't,' he said, smilingly disposing of her anxiety on that score. 'But nevertheless I must wonder greatly why you ask me.'

Unwillingly she glanced at the baron. 'I wish to avoid any possibility of meeting with the baron,' she said at last.

'Has he been bothering you?'

'In a manner of speaking.'

'It is entirely your concern, of course,' he said, mistaking her reticence for unwillingness to divulge the true nature of things.

'I have not encouraged him in any way, in spite of what you think of me.'

'In spite of what *I* think of you? And what may that be?'

'I think we both know your opinion of me, Sir Nicholas.'

'Do we indeed? Well this half of us is greatly intrigued and very much puzzled. However, we digress. I shall, of course, be delighted to escort you to your room, Miss Milbanke.'

Relief surged through her as she rose to her feet and put a timid hand on his arm. She did not know how tightly she was holding him, her fingernails digging into his arm, until they were ascending the staircase.

He smiled. 'I realize that it is ungentlemanly of me to draw attention to it, Miss Milbanke, but you truly have a grip like a vise.'

She took her hand away immediately. 'Forgive me, I did not mean—'

She was covered with confusion. She was also embarrassed, afraid, anxious, and she felt very foolish all at the same time.

He spoke gently. 'I know that you did not mean it, but it seems to me that you are unduly upset. Why are you so distraught?'

'I believe that the baron has been following me since my arrival.'

'You believe, but you are not certain?'

She bit her lip. No, she wasn't *certain*, how could she be when it was more intuition than anything else. She was not imagining her encounter with the baron in the Piazza San Marco, but she could not say for certain that it had been him at her door earlier. . . .

'Miss Milbanke, I hope that nothing I have told you about him has brought on this agitation, for if it is, then I cannot apologize to you enough.'

'It has nothing to do with what you have said.'

They continued up the staircase and halted at last by her door. 'What will you do tomorrow?' he asked.

'Tomorrow?' She had not thought beyond tonight. . . .

'If it will help in any way, I can escort you to and from the dining-room. We can, as you so aptly put it, present a united front.' He smiled. 'And I can reap the benefits of escorting the most beautiful woman in Venice.'

The compliment was unexpected and oddly reassuring somehow. 'Thank you, Sir Nicholas.'

'For the offer or for the compliment?'

'Both.'

'As to the compliment, well I believe it is long overdue, considering my odious conduct until now. I apologize, Miss Milbanke, for I vented my anger upon you, and it is not your fault that my problems seem without satisfactory solution. You have stoically endured my heavy presence and must surely have wished me in Hades. Forgive me.'

'There is nothing to forgive, sir,' she said, for suddenly his crimes were forgotten as she smiled into his eyes.

'And you wish me to walk to the dining-room with you in the morning?'

'I would be most grateful.'

'Then I shall come at half-past nine.'

'Thank you.'

He took her hand and kissed it. 'Sleep well, Miss Milbanke.'

'And you, Sir Nicholas.'

She watched him walk away along the richly decorated passage toward his own room. His hair was very golden in the lamplight, and his figure, clad in dark blue velvet, looked very tall and impressive. How good it had been to see that other side of him, and how especially good to be flattered by him. If it were not for the unseen presence of Miss Augustine Townsend, it would be easy to read more into his change of heart, but Laura knew that that would be foolish. He was being kind because he thought she was frightened. No more than that.

Suddenly something made her turn sharply to look over her shoulder. It was that same uneasy sensation of being secretly watched. It seemed that a shadow moved swiftly out of sight by some velvet drapes. The baron. . . . He had been there, listening. She opened her door and went swiftly inside, locking it securely behind her. She listened, her breath held. But there was no sound. She relaxed a little then, tossing her reticule and fan on to the console table and teasing her evening gloves off finger by finger. Pulling her shawl more tightly around her shoulders, she stepped out on to the balcony.

The welcome night breeze ruffled her hair and whispered against the cool silk of her gown. In the moonlight the grape hyacinths in their window boxes were turned to silver and on the water below the lights of Venice flashed and twinkled on the moving surface.

On the steps below she heard the baron hailing a gondola. Leaning forward she saw his unmistakable figure climbing into a gondola which was then pushed away, gliding from the hotel steps as the gondolier poled it out into the center of the Grand Canal. Laura breathed out slowly. She was safe for the time being. So great was the comfort of knowing that Frederick von Marienfeld was not in the hotel that she began to hum a little tune as she undressed and prepared for bed.

Chapter 6

She was ready the next morning a quarter of an hour before she expected Nicholas to call. Once again she was wearing the pale green sprigged muslin gown she had worn on her first morning in Venice, and she stood on the balcony watching the fruit barges making their way to market.

Someone knocked at her bedchamber door, and she turned in surprise. Nicholas was early. She hurried to open the door, but the smile of welcome died on her lips as she saw not Nicholas but the baron standing there.

She could not speak. Her hand crept to her throat to finger the black velvet ribbon.

He smiled coolly and walked into the room without permission, closing the door behind him. 'Good morning, my dear Miss Milbanke.'

'Please leave,' she whispered, backing away from him. All the terror returned, and not even the brightness of the spring morning could dispel it now.

'Leave? But that would avail me of nothing.'

'Avail you?'

He nodded, still smiling as he came closer to her. She was aware only of the intensity burning in his eyes. 'I ask you again to leave!' she cried.

'How very beautiful you are, even when you are afraid,' he murmured, reaching out a gloved hand to touch her pale cheek. 'You have eluded me, Miss Milbanke, and your beauty almost led me astray from my main purpose. But now it is done, in a few minutes it will all be over and my purpose completed – well, almost completed.'

She stared at him.

'Even had you been as ugly as sin itself, Miss Milbanke, I should still have come here now. Fortune, however, has smiled upon me and made you so very beautiful that my task will be sweetly accomplished. Oh, how sweetly.'

'Please go,' she said, her voice barely audible, 'Please. . . .'

He reached out to her and she stumbled back against a small table as she tried to elude him. She wanted to scream, but as before in the piazza, her voice lost all strength. Please let Nicholas come soon! Please!

Moving with unexpected swiftness, the baron caught her wrist, his smile not wavering as he drew her into his arms. He was so very strong that she stood no chance. Pressing her body against his, he forced her face up and kissed her hard on the lips. It was a kiss that seemed to last a lifetime, during which the mute helplessness and revulsion swam over her again and again in sickening waves. Her mind screamed for help to come, but her voice was struck dumb, her strength drained so that she could not even struggle against her assailant.

Vaguely, almost from beyond consciousness, she heard some-one knocking at the door. It *must* be Nicholas! It must be! Please God. . . . With a supreme effort she summoned her poor strength to thrust herself away from the baron, and at last found voice enough to scream.

The door opened immediately and Nicholas came in, his eyes hardening with anger as he saw the scene. Instinctively he held out a hand to her and she ran to him, clinging to his fingers and almost sobbing with relief.

'I thought he was you,' she cried, 'I let him in. . . .'

The door remained open and Nicholas coldly inclined his head toward it. 'I think your presence is displeasing to Miss Milbanke, sir,' he said.

The baron smiled, not at all perturbed by the situation, indeed he seemed to be rather enjoying it. 'Yours is the presence which is displeasing, my dear Sir Nicholas.'

Two Austrian officers stood outside the door, their attention caught by, what was happening. 'Baron, I demand that you leave,' said Nicholas.

'But you heard what Miss Milbanke told you,' said the baron reasonably. 'She let me in. Do not let her protestations of innocence fool you, Grenville. She invited me in knowing full well what would ensue. She has played games with me since first she arrived, enticing me and playing the coquette. It was all leading to but one purpose, which as a man of the world you must know as well as I do. You have interrupted a tender consummation, sir, and it is *I* who must ask you to leave.'

Laura stared at him. How very convincing he was, how very plausible!

The baron smiled again. 'Keep your well-bred nose out of my affairs, Grenville, and you may take that as a timely warning, a warning to which you would be advised to pay good heed.'

Laura knew suddenly that he was doing it all purposely; he was deliberately trying to provoke Nicholas into a duel. But why? *Why?* Her fingers tightened over Nicholas's. 'Be careful,' she said urgently. 'Just let it pass, I beg of you.'

The baron's dark eyes swung angrily to her then. 'Whores should be seen and fondled, madam, but never, ever heard!'

'You go too far now,' said Nicholas in a cold voice.

'Too far? When I state the obvious – that the lady is a whore?'

'You are a liar, and have lost any claim to being called a gentleman.'

Again the baron smiled. 'I suggest that you retract that, my dear sir, for I do not take kindly to being insulted.'

'I retract nothing.'

Laura stared from one to the other in growing horror. The inevitability of it all was terrifying. They were moving toward an unavoidable confrontation, and she was the unwitting catalyst, the pawn the baron had chosen to employ. For some reason the Austrian had singled Nicholas Grenville out to be his eleventh victim, and he would be just that unless she could dissuade him now from allowing the baron to force him into a corner from which there was no escape.

'Sir Nicholas,' she pleaded, 'don't listen to him, don't let him have his way. He *wants* a duel, can't you see? Please, just retract and let it finish at that! Please.' She whispered the last word, almost in tears now, for she knew that she could not divert him.

Nicholas ignored her. 'I will not retract,' he said again to the baron.

'Then I consider my honor to be impugned and I demand satisfaction.'

'No!' breathed Laura desperately. '*No!*'

The baron smiled coldly at her. 'He will not listen to you, Miss Milbanke, for he is an English gentleman, a man of pride and honor. He would sacrifice both were he to step down from me now. Is that not so, Grenville?'

She lowered her eyes. This could not be happening. Only a short while ago she had been on the balcony in the sunshine, everything had been so calm and pleasant. . . . Now it was all a nightmare from which she could not awaken.

Nicholas spoke. 'Name your time and place and send your seconds to me.'

Laura's fingers slipped away from his. Blinded by tears she leaned her hands on the cold marble surface of a table, her head bowed. He was throwing his life away, and for what? For *honor*! What was foolish honor when set beside his life?

She heard little of the next exchange between the two men before the baron left the room, nor did she hear much of what the two Austrian officers said as they offered their services to Nicholas as his seconds. Then they too had gone and she was alone with Nicholas.

He closed the door and she turned to look at him, tears shining in her eyes. 'I'm sorry,' she whispered, 'I'm so sorry—'

'You have no reason to be.'

'If I had not involved you in my foolish anxieties, then he would not have been able—'

'I involved myself willingly enough, and I must remind you that you distinctly tried your best to avert the danger. I chose not to listen.'

'It's still all my fault.'

'No.' He took his handkerchief and gently wiped the tears from her cheeks. 'Please don't cry, for I cannot bear to see a woman weep.'

'He used me in order to force you into this duel.'

'Come now, that is a little fanciful. You underestimate yourself, Miss Milbanke, for you are an exceedingly beautiful woman, by far desirable enough to lure a man like the baron.'

But she could remember the baron's words only too clearly. *But now it is done, in a few minutes it will all be over and my purpose completed – well, almost completed. . . . Even had you been as ugly as sin itself, Miss Milbanke, then I should still have come here now. Fortune, however, has smiled upon me and made you so very beautiful that my task will be sweetly accomplished. Oh, how sweetly. . . .* Those were not the words of a man driven solely by desire to possess her, they were the words of a man who had an entirely different object in view. He had also said something about her beauty almost leading him astray from his main purpose. What else could he mean but that until this one time he would not have been able to successfully involve Nicholas Grenville? The baron had used her to achieve this duel with Nicholas, and nothing anyone could say would turn her from that opinion.

'Miss Milbanke, honor is a precious thing – in that the baron was correct. It cannot be set lightly aside if a man is to hold his head up among his peers, believe me.'

'Then I ask you to think of Miss Townsend. Can you lightly set aside her future happiness because of honor?'

'Do you honestly imagine Augustine would think better of me for taking such a cowardly course? She would scorn me, of that you may be sure.'

She stared at him, tears pricking her eyes again. '*I* would not scorn you,' she whispered, 'I would love you all the more for having the strength to refuse to be forced into something like this. No one questions your bravery, Sir Nicholas, least of all me. If Miss Townsend has an ounce of love for you, she will feel the same. If I were in her place I would thank God above for your safe deliverance from such a vainglorious and futile death!'

For a long moment he looked into her tear-filled eyes. 'But you are not in her place,' he said softly, 'And I am vainglorious enough to wish to continue with this. He said things about you which no man of honor, least of all myself, could allow to pass unchallenged.'

'Oh, how can you be so *calm* about it?' she cried, 'He'll kill you, he'll make you his eleventh victim – and for what? You hardly know me, you don't even *like* me very much – and yet you are about to die for my good name!'

He smiled. 'It is not true that I do not like you, Miss Milbanke; it is not true at all. Oh, I admit that my manner may have – *did* – give you that impression, and for that I have already apologized. I thought you knew that I meant every word I said last night. Perhaps it will convince you if I ask you to spend the rest of this day with me.'

'Now you jest—'

'It is hardly something to jest about. This may be my last day on this earth, and what better way to spend it than with you?'

There was nothing she would like more than to spend a day alone with him, but not like this – not with such a dark and terrible shadow hanging over them.

'If my past conduct weighs too heavily still . . .' he began, seeing her indecision.

'No. No, it is not that. Please believe me.'

'What then? Will propriety be offended?'

'Propriety is offended already. It was offended the moment I left England alone, without a companion or a maid, and it is offended each time I speak to you when I have no chaperon to watch over me. No, Sir Nicholas, it is not propriety. What of Miss Townsend? How will she feel if she discovers not only that I am the cause of your predicament, but that you also spent a day with me? How will she feel then?'

'She is not here, Miss Milbanke. You are. I do not see that under these circumstances there is anything else to consider, do you?'

She met his gaze. 'No, I suppose not,' she answered. Oh, dear God, how easy it would be to fall in love with this man. With a glance and a soft word he could melt her heart, make her forget everything but the pleasure of being with him. She had been drawn to him from the outset, and each moment with him now merely made her admit to herself that she was dangerously close to loving him already.

'Then it is settled. Shall we go?' He offered her his arm.

Slowly she slipped her hand over the rich stuff of his sleeve.

'Besides,' he murmured lightly, almost to himself, 'who is to say that this will indeed be my last day on earth? I am not exactly cross-eyed and palsied, you know, as many a Frenchman found out to his cost at Waterloo. It could be that the baron is *my* first victim – that would be a turn up for the proverbial book, would it not?'

She felt an absurd desire to laugh as they walked from the room.

Chapter 7

The gondola was pushed away from the hotel steps, sliding out from the shadows to the dazzling blue water. There was magic in the air; diamonds flashed in the wavelets and the sky was the color of pale sapphires; even a barge piled high with red apples seemed to be carrying rubies. Color was sharper, sounds more clear, and Laura herself more acutely aware of Venice, of Nicholas, and of life itself than she ever had been before.

He leaned back on the black leather seat beside her, smiling just a little. 'Did you know that in Venice the occupants of a felze are always assumed to be lovers?'

'No.' She hoped that she wasn't blushing.

He laughed. It was an easy laugh, quite unforced and natural. She looked away toward the Rialto Bridge. He was treating her with an intimacy that only the night before would have been unthinkable. It was as if they had known each other for a lifetime, not merely for a week or so, and the feeling was good. She had so longed to know him like this, but even now she knew that it was only circumstances that brought about this change. How he must be longing for his Augustine and wishing that she sat with him, not Miss Laura Milbanke.

He glanced at her. 'I hope that you do not really mind me asking you to spend the day with me, for on reflection it does seem rather a lot to ask of you.'

'No,' she said quickly. 'No, I don't mind at all.'

'I thought you seemed a little reserved—'

'I was only wishing that I could be your Miss Townsend for today.'

He looked away then. 'Well, maybe it's just as well that you aren't.'

'Why do you say that?'

'Because I came here to think about decisions I have to make, decisions which will not meet with her approval in the slightest.'

'Forgive me if I appear unduly inquisitive – but why will she not approve?'

'Do you really wish to be bothered with my financial adversities?'

'I shall not mind at all if you wish to talk about them.'

The breeze ruffled his hair as he removed his top hat and tossed it on to the seat. The wash from a passing barge made the gondola sway and he reached out to take Laura's hand, steadying her for a moment until the gondola was level once more. Studying her face for a moment, he released her hand. 'Perhaps you are right, Miss Milbanke; it would do me good to discuss my problems. My difficulties stem from one thing – my estate, King's Cliff in Somerset.'

'King's Cliff? When you introduced yourself to me the name meant nothing, but now it seems familiar. . . .'

'No doubt on account of the famed King's Cliff hunt.'

'Yes, of course, that is it! Even my Uncle Hazeldon extolled its virtues!'

'Oh, that damned hunt is quite the thing with the *beau monde*, from royalty down.'

'You do not like hunting?'

'It does little for me, I fear – is that not an admission from a gentleman? It is tantamount to high treason, I fancy. But I am no rakehell, no demon of the gaming hells, no devotee of luxurious vice, and certainly no hunter, shooter, or fisher! I believe there is more to life than that. Oh, do not think I wear a halo, for I have indulged in my fair share of riotous living and will never aspire to sanctity, but I will also never see the point of an existence which leads inevitably to ruin.'

'I don't understand.'

'I have but recently inherited King's Cliff, Miss Milbanke, and years of mismanagement and extravagance by my foolish father, Sir Jasper Grenville, and similar years of avaricious aiding and abetting by my disagreeable cousin, James, Earl of Langford, have left me with accumulated debts which put King's Cliff on the verge of bankruptcy.'

'Surely not—'

'The estate is vastly overstaffed; it has been run on a lavish scale which it cannot support; its farms are poor and mostly unproductive as they have been managed to suit the hunt and little else. And on top of all that, my father raised mortgages, acquired monumental gaming debts, and resorted to one of the most notorious moneylenders in London. In short, he has left me well up to my elegant neck in difficulty. With his shining example before me, it is small wonder I have no desire to emulate his ways.'

The gondola slid beneath a bridge and the water echoed around them in the gloom before they emerged into the brilliant sunlight again.

She smiled at him. 'So it is not like father, like son.'

'Most definitely not. To be honest, my cousin is more my father's son than I have ever been, and indeed he worked tirelessly toward that end – seeking to have me disinherited and taking my birthright. There is very little love lost between James Grenville and me, Miss Milbanke, very little indeed. We tolerate each other, and that is all. James is a very wealthy man, and his tastes ran parallel with those of my father; hence they got on extremely well together. But James was in a position to live as he did; his wealth supported him more than adequately; my foolish father could not, or would not, see that his own finances were so appallingly managed that he could not possibly hope to match James. I could see what was happening, and my continuous argument against what they did eventually left me in the cold where my father was concerned. I left King's Cliff and took a commission in the army, serving with Wellington in Spain and eventually at Waterloo. I fully intended the army to be my life, for I had little doubt that I would be disinherited and that my cousin would have King's Cliff.

'However, when my father died last year it immediately became apparent that James had not succeeded, for it all came to me after all. I resigned my commission and went home – to find that things had reached such a sorry pass that I was faced with either bankruptcy – or making such severe cutbacks and changes in order to put King's Cliff into profit once more that I could only be vilified in the county.' He smiled ruefully, the jeweled pin in his cravat glittering in the sunlight as he lounged gracefully back in the gondola. 'Venice is a luxury I can ill afford, but I decided to allow myself just one small extravagance before attending to the unpalatable task of confounding Somerset with my remedies for ruin.'

She smiled. How strange it was to hear him speak of his visit to Venice in words that could so easily have been applied to her. Was not she too guilty of unwarranted extravagance by coming here? 'Sir Nicholas, it seems to me that you have no choice, you *must* carry out whatever plans you have in mind. Why then do you believe Miss Townsend will not approve?'

'To explain that I must tell you a little of family history. Augustine's family were once the owners of King's Cliff; indeed it is named because one of their ancestors held the cliff on which it stands for the king at the time of Monmouth's rebellion. His reward was a grant of the land, and part of Sedgemoor which it overlooks. It remained in the Townsend family until they were in difficulties and my great-grandfather, Sir Henry Grenville, purchased it from them. Augustine still in her heart regards the estate as belonging to her family, and maybe she is not to be blamed too much for that, but she believes too that the house will go on forever as it now is, which has become an impossibility with me as its master. Throughout her life she has seen brilliance all around her, glorious wealth on a scale which even the Prince Regent could envy. There were endless house parties, the guests were royalty and nobility, and they stayed for week after week sometimes. The marsh at King's Cliff offers the finest waterfowl and good fishing; the hunting season meant more guests, expensive balls, routs, masques, and so on. As my father's ward she lived like a queen; she saw nothing of the huge debts accumulating.'

He took off his signet ring and handed it to Laura. 'My family emblem is "the sun in splendor", and by *God* did Father live the role of sun! The term *bon vivant* takes on new magnificence when applied to my sire. That is why Augustine will not understand when I tell her what must be done to her beloved King's Cliff. She will not understand that and she will not understand me. She wants things to remain as they are, and I cannot do that, not even for her. If my cousin had inherited, then King's Cliff would have continued—'

'But he has not.'

'No. He wanted to, though – and it was because he coveted the house, and he coveted Augustine. If he had owned the house, then he would have seen a chance of winning her.'

'So many *ifs*, Sir Nicholas? He hasn't won her; you have.'

'Yes, that is true – or is it? Has she accepted me because she loves me, or because through me she will gain King's Cliff?'

'Oh, surely you misjudge her—'

'I pray so, for I love her very much indeed. I am painfully uncertain, however, of how much she loves me.'

Laura could only look at him. How could any woman in her right mind not love him?

He gave a short, embarrassed laugh then. 'Dear God, I have confessed my innermost soul to you, and yet until yesterday I had not even granted you a kind word. I could not have told Augustine herself what I have just told you. Why am I so unguarded with you, Miss Milbanke?'

'Perhaps it is simply that I am not involved; I am not the object of your love.' *Would that I were. . . .*

'Whatever it is, you certainly seem to have a profound effect upon me.'

She smiled a little. 'Maybe it's just Venice.'

The gondola glided on to a stretch of silver water. The city shimmered all around, the atmosphere pale and tenuous, a gamut of greens and blues which turned the palaces and churches into a strange, miragelike fantasy. The air was still and yet it moved. Everything seemed so unreal, as if it would flee if touched.

'Miss Milbanke,' he said at last, 'can you even begin to imagine the shock which will greet the news that the King's Cliff hunt is to be sold? Can you imagine the noise in Somerset when I set about draining my portion of Sedgemoor, called King's Cliff Moor, thus depriving a vast army of poachers of their livelihood and another vast army of wealthy gentlemen of their shooting and fishing? I shall turn out tenants who will not comply with my new ways of things and I will rid myself of land which is useful only for hunting and cannot be turned into rich pasture or crop land. I am about to become notorious. That is, if I survive tomorrow—'

'Don't say that!' she cried. 'Please don't!'

He took her hand again, his fingers light but firm around hers. 'It must be faced.'

'No!'

He smiled. 'Very well, we will forget it.' The gondola rocked gently on the small tide and he pointed across to the distant Rialto Bridge. 'Did you know, Miss Milbanke, that it is said that no fewer than thirty thousand trees were required to give solidity to the foundations of that bridge? And hundreds of thousands for the construction of the church of Santa Maria della Salute?'

She blinked a little at the change of subject. 'No, Sir Nicholas, I did not.'

He grinned then. 'It never ceases to amaze me what snippets of useless, but interesting information I seem capable of remembering.'

The noon day sun was high in the flawless sky when Laura and Nicholas entered the cathedral of San Marco. There was surely no other building on earth as wonderful as this, she thought. Everything about it bespoke Byzantium, of times gone by – except that here in Venice Byzantium lived on in all its glory. The sun's rays brought out the color of the marble and porphyry and the radiance of the gold mosaics. The cathedral was encrusted from floor to ceiling with precious metals and jewels, and she was aware of a sultry opulence she had never before seen in a church. English cathedrals had their own magnificence, but it bore no resemblance whatsoever to this building, which seemed so like a medieval reliquary, so rich and ornate that it was almost too much for the eye to bear. The air was vibrant with the glimmer of gold and rubies seen through the flicker of a thousand candles, and the atmosphere was heavy with incense. Somewhere a choir of small boys was singing, and a shiver ran through Laura at the haunting poignance of the sound.

From the cathedral they walked awhile, wandering through the shadowy bustle of a high-walled, narrow street where they were accosted by a pretty flower girl who thrust her basket of bright red anemones in front of Laura, begging Nicholas to purchase some. Laughingly he obliged, pinning the small posy to the underbrim of her Leghorn bonnet where they made a vivid splash of color. In the same street they were accosted by a fortune-teller whose little dog was trained to pick tickets from a basket. The little dog leaped and danced around them both and Nicholas paid for Laura to have her fortune told. She could not read the words on the ticket the dog brought to her, but Nicholas translated it for her.

'You are assured of great future happiness and a grand marriage to a wealthy husband who will adore you.'

She laughed. 'Now I know why this fortune-teller is still plying his trade in the streets!'

'The prophecy could come true.'

'Not when I already know what lies ahead when I go back to England.'

He looked into her blue eyes, his smile dying away. 'You do not look forward to returning?'

'No. I am a church mouse, Sir Nicholas, and should not be luxuriating in the Hotel Contarini's grandest chamber.'

He drew her hand through his arm. 'Come, we will go to Florian's and take some coffee, and then you can tell me about yourself.'

'It is not an interesting topic,' she said quickly.

'Allow me to be the judge of that. Besides, I have willfully brought you to the edge of *ennui* with my tale of woe, and I owe it to you to hear your story.'

She said nothing more, lowering her eyes as they returned toward the Piazza San Marco. She did not really want to tell him the dreadful truth about Lady Mountfort. How would he feel when he learned that she was penniless and would soon be little more than a paid servant? Would he still wish to escort her then?

Chapter 8

Florian's, said to be the oldest café in Europe, lay behind an arcade in the piazza, affording an excellent view of the campanile and beyond it the cathedral itself. The tables were in the shade beneath the arcade, although soon the sun would move around and there would be no shelter from its heat. Across the piazza was the rival cafe, Quadri's, frequented by Austrians and therefore shunned by the Venetians, who thronged Florian's instead.

Laura and Nicholas sat at one of the tables and were immediately the objects of concerted attention by the various hawkers and beggars who waited in the famous square. They ignored this shameless importuning and were eventually left alone. Laura untied her bonnet and laid it on the table, glad to feel the cool air through her hair. The domes of the cathedral gleamed in the hot sun, its facade suddenly obscured by the flashing wings of a flock of pigeons that rose as one from the square. The noise of their flight was like the rushing of water as they soared high into the clear blue sky to circle the domes. There was color everywhere – on the cathedral, in the sky, and in the square where many stalls had been laid out to display costly clothes, which spilled over in streams of crimson, purple, emerald, and sapphire. It was a scene to remember forever, and just a tiny part of this day, which would never be forgotten. Laura lowered her eyes then. *Please, let tomorrow never come. . . .*

Nicholas watched her thoughtful expression. 'Now,' he said gently, 'tell me what it is that lies ahead of you in England.'

She braced herself. 'Lady Mountfort.'

'Forgive me, I don't quite understand. . . . You are related to her?'

'No. I am soon to be her companion.' She met his startled gaze. 'I have no money, Sir Nicholas, no family to provide for me, and so I shall have to take a position if I am to live.'

'I had no idea.'

'No.' She smiled a little wryly. 'Would you still have protected my good name if you had?'

'Now you do me an injustice.'

'Forgive me, it's simply that I am only too aware that I am masquerading as a lady.'

'You *are* a lady, Miss Milbanke, and have no need to resort to masquerade to prove it.'

'Whatever way it is put, I am still not what I appear to be. Oh, I have good clothes and my background is not lowborn, but the fact remains that I am impoverished and shall soon be reduced to working for my living.' She told him of her life with Aunt Hazeldon. 'So,' she finished, 'I do not think I am at all the sort of person you would normally associate with, am I?'

'And how would you know anything about that? I associate with those whom I like, and that is my only yardstick. You have far more quality in your little finger than many a fine and titled lady has in her entire body, that much I promise you. It is interesting, is it not, that you and I have both come to Venice under strangely similar circumstances – we neither of us should have come to this lap of luxury and we both know it. We are kindred spirits, it would seem.'

'Are we?'

'Yes. I salute you for having the sheer nerve to squander your inheritance on this, but as to the wisdom of going to Lady Mountfort, that is another matter. She is odious in the extreme, a female equivalent of my loathed cousin, and I cannot imagine you ever finding any morsel of happiness with her.'

'I have no choice, Sir Nicholas.'

'No.' He glanced away across the piazza. 'I had not thought how very fortunate I am; I was concerned only with my own problems. Maybe it is a salutary lesson.' He turned suddenly to her again. 'Do you ride, Miss Milbanke?'

'Ride? In *Venice*?'

'Oh, it is possible to enjoy an excellent ride – on the Lido. Shall you join me?'

She laughed. 'In this flimsy gown? What a sight I would be!'

'Then we shall return to the hotel for you to change—'

'I could return to the hotel until I go gray, sir, and still not find a riding habit among my personal effects.'

'Will you ride with me nonetheless?'

'If you will find an unconscionable amount of ankle acceptable.'

'Oh, I am sure your ankles are as exquisite as the rest of you, Miss Milbanke.'

She laughed. 'You will be able to judge that for yourself if I get up on a horse, sir.'

He took her hand and rose to his feet. He held her hand a moment longer, making her look into his eyes. 'Lady Mountfort is not for you,' he said softly, 'and you know that she isn't.'

The lagoon was hazy and the horizon vanished into a silver mist through which the gray silhouette of Venice could just be seen. Only one of the many islands could be seen clearly, its beautiful monastery rising high above the rocks where pale pink sea mallow was already in bloom and where a colony of cats basked lazily in the sun. The other islands had an ethereal look and only the drumming of the horses' hooves on the hard sand gave any substance to the long, dreamlike afternoon.

Riding had always brought roses to Laura's cheeks, partly from excitement and partly from the lingering fear that had remained from a childhood fall. She was by no means a brilliant horsewoman and now was really put to the test as she tried to rally her flagging mount to keep up with Nicholas. He seemed to have deliberately chosen the largest and most fleet-footed horse in the stables, and it carried him as if he were feather light. Laura's mount could not stay with him.

For another half hour they rode over the Lido, with Laura falling farther and farther behind, until at last Nicholas reined in at the very edge of the sand, the tiny wavelets creaming softly around his horse's restless hooves as he waited for Laura to catch up.

He laughed at her windblown hair and flushed cheeks, and the way the ribbons of her bonnet had become entangled and were now far from the pristine bow she had tied on leaving Florian's. Her parasol bumped against her leg and her reticule flapped like a wild thing as she thankfully reined in at last.

'My dear Miss Milbanke' – he laughed – 'what would they say at Almack's if they could see you now?'

'They would say that it was most ungentlemanly of you to ride off like that and put me to such a task,' she retorted.

He nodded. 'Aye, it was ungentlemanly; forgive me. I felt the need to push my mount to his limit.'

'And to push yourself too.'

His gray eyes showed slight amusement. 'You read me like a book, madam,'

'No, I don't, for if I did then I would be able to persuade you against meeting the baron tomorrow.'

'In that we must agree to disagree then.' He smiled at her. 'But what is your opinion of my other undertaking?'

'The alterations at King's Cliff?'

'Yes.'

'I think you are right, Sir Nicholas. I think too that Miss Townsend, who must surely love you, will be of the same opinion.'

'As you would be in her position?'

'Yes.'

'Then I must pray that she is more like you than I believe,' he said, swinging his leg over the cantle and dismounting. He helped her down and they left the horses by a windbreak of tamarisk shrubs and then walked along the sand together.

Out on the lagoon some heavily laden boats glided toward Venice, their prows painted with symbols to keep away evil spirits. Their ocher and red sails were brightly patterned with the sun, moon, and stars, and they made not a sound, their wash lapping softly against the shore as if trying to keep their passage a secret. The sun was beginning to set and the haze that had lingered through the afternoon was threading upward like wisps of gossamer to reveal Venice in a blaze of gold. The monastery bell on the island began to sound sundown and the mellow chimes drifted lazily over the still water. Laura and Nicholas walked in silence, each with deep thoughts that did not need to be put into words.

It was not until they at last returned to the horses that he spoke. 'We have shared many intimacies today, Miss Milbanke, and I feel that I have known you all my life. And yet I do not even know your first name.'

'Laura.'

'Thank you for today, Laura.' He drew her fingers to his lips.

*

The lantern on the prow of their gondola shone on the black water as they returned across the lagoon. The gondolier hummed lightly to himself, echoing the music from a water-borne barrel organ which accompanied a party of revelers in their elegant barge.

Laura was fighting back the tears when at last the gondola reached the hotel where the perfume of orange blossom hung heavily in the air by the steps. It was nearly over. This one magical day was at an end and tomorrow's dawn seemed suddenly so dreadfully near, a doom from which there could be no escape.

Nicholas helped her ashore, and as she wore no gloves, he must have known how cold her fingers were. The imminence of the duel was emphasized sharply as they walked into the hotel to find the two officers who were to be his seconds waiting.

The taller of the two bowed to them. '*Guten abend*, Sir Nicholas, *Fräulein* Milbanke.'

'Major Bergmann.' Nicholas bowed. Laura could not bring herself to say anything.

'All is arranged, Sir Nicholas; we will attend you one hour before dawn.'

'Thank you, Major.'

'Herr-Doktor Meyer will also attend, he is an army doctor-surgeon and very capable.'

'Again, I thank you, Major Bergmann.'

'*Guten nacht*, Sir Nicholas.' The Austrian's spurred heels clicked.

'Good night.'

'*Fräulein* Milbanke.'

Laura could barely manage a smile of acknowledgment. Her eyes were bright with unshed tears and her fingers coiled again and again in the folds of her gown.

At her door Nicholas put his hand gently to her cheek. 'Don't cry, Laura.'

'I'm trying so very hard not to,' she whispered, and then she caught his hand. 'Please don't meet the baron tomorrow. Please don't—'

'I must.'

She closed her eyes and the tears welled out. His fingers tightened around hers and he drew her into his arms, holding her close. She raised her face, her lips parting to speak again, but he put a finger over them to silence her.

'Don't,' he whispered. 'Don't ask me, for I cannot and will not grant you what you wish.' He hesitated a moment and then bent his head to kiss her on the lips.

She clung to him, holding him tightly as she returned the kiss. Her head was spinning, her pulse racing, and she could taste the salt of her own tears.

Slowly he released her. 'Good night, Laura,' he said softly.

'God be with you, Nicholas.'

Then he was gone. Her tears blinded her and she almost stumbled into her room. Bitter sobs shook her body as she flung herself on to the bed. Her heart was breaking. *Please God, please let him live! Let him live because I love him so!*

Chapter 9

The light in the room was the palest of grays. Dawn was almost upon Venice. Laura lay awake on the bed. The posy of anemones was in a small bowl of water, their bright heads upturned. They had been so wan, their stems bending and their flowers drooping, but they were refreshed now and as beautiful as they had been the day before.

She watched the pale light beyond the windows. She heard Nicholas's seconds passing her door, their spurred boots loud. They knocked at a door and she heard the low murmur of voices. The hotel was so still then that she could distinctly hear the hum of insects out on the balcony. The footsteps returned then, spurs jingling, and she clenched her hands tightly, willing herself to remain where she was. She wanted to call out to him, to rush out and beg him on her knees not to go, but he would not welcome that and it would not help him to face the ordeal. She closed her tired eyes. The footsteps passed from hearing and silence returned.

The limpid light softened and brightened with each passing minute now, but Laura's face was hidden in her pillow and she did not see. The only sound was the slow ticking of the clock as the moments passed relentlessly by.

'*Fräulein* Milbanke! *Fräulein* Milbanke!' Major Bergmann was hammering at her door.

Laura got up. Her heart felt like ice as she stared at the door. She could not move toward it, for to do that would be to hear that he was dead. . . .

'*Fräulein* Milbanke, come quickly please! Sir Nicholas is badly wounded, but he lives.'

With a choked cry she ran to the door and would have gone to Nicholas's room, but the major caught her arm. 'I warn you, *Fräulein*, it is very bad and the doctor does not hold out hope.'

She stared at him. 'No,' she whispered, 'No, I will not believe—'

'But you must, for it is true. Sir Nicholas was struck twice.'

'*Twice*? But how could that be?'

'It shames me to acknowledge that the Baron von Marienfeld is my fellow countryman and fellow officer, for today he behaved in a most craven and disgraceful manner. He discharged his second pistol when Sir

Nicholas was unarmed. It is always the baron's custom to take both pistols from the outset, for his aim is as true with the left hand as with the right. Sir Nicholas, as is the more usual custom, took only the one, meaning to replace it afterward before taking the second. Both men took up their positions and the first shots were discharged. The baron was wounded a little in his shoulder, but Sir Nicholas was hit very badly in his left arm. He was still standing at this point, however, although losing a great deal of blood and obviously faint. But rather than face him equally a second time, the baron discharged his second pistol immediately. It was an act of cowardice and callousness such as I did not ever think to witness, and only the fact that Sir Nicholas swayed on his feet at that moment saved him from certain death.'

'Where did the second shot strike him?'

'It grazed his temple. It was meant to strike his head a mortal blow.'

She closed her eyes weakly. So close, so very close. . . .

'The baron has been forced to flee from Venice, *Fräulein*. He may be close to the governor, but even that would not assist him under these vile circumstances. To fire at a defenseless opponent and to do so before witnesses is an act with consequences from which even he could not hope to escape. He will never be able to hold his head up here in Venice again, for all will despise him even more than they already do. He is an evil man, *Fräulein* Milbanke, the devil's henchman.'

She nodded. 'I must go to Sir Nicholas. . . .'

Still he detained her. 'Wait one moment more, *Fräulein*, I beg of you. I think it only right to tell you that the doctor wishes to amputate Sir Nicholas's left arm; he says that that is his only chance – and a very slender one at that.'

'If it is his only chance, then it must be done.'

'In my opinion he stands more chance *without* the attentions of a doctor-surgeon! On the field of battle I have seen more men die after treatment than I care to remember. There is another thing, however, and that is that before the commencement of the duel, Sir Nicholas took me aside and gave me specific instructions that on no account were any injuries he might receive to be treated by amputation. He was most firm on this and demanded that I gave him my word as an officer and a gentleman. This I did. I believe that I am right, both because I honor my sworn word, and because such chance as he may have will be eliminated by such savage surgery in his present weakened state. There you have it, *Fräulein* Milbanke, and I tell you because I know that the doctor will try to persuade you to give your permission for the operation to be carried out.'

'*My* permission? But I have no right—'

'You are Sir Nicholas's friend. He spent yesterday with you and he fought the baron because of you. I think you have the right to decide. If you wish the operation to be carried out, then I will not stand in your way. I may be wrong to stop the operation; I know only that I have done what Sir Nicholas asked of me. You are not bound by my promises if you believe the doctor is correct. Do you see what I am trying to say? I think Sir Nicholas is a brave and valiant man, and I do not want *honor* to deprive him of his life,'

She smiled a little. '*Honor. Honor* appears to be everything,' she murmured, walking slowly on towards Nicholas's room.

Dr Meyer was a sallow-faced man with graying hair. His white uniform outlined his lean, bony shape as he bent over Nicholas's still figure. Nicholas's valet, Henderson, stood at the other side of the bed, holding a bowl of water and some fresh dressings. The wiry little valet looked anxiously down into his master's ashen face. Nicholas did not move; his eyes were closed and the aura of death lay over him.

A bandage had been hastily applied to the wound on his right temple, but already a red stain marred its whiteness. There had not been time to remove his coat and the doctor had cut away the arm of the garment that a Bond Street tailor had labored over so long and lovingly. Such a sad end to a magnificent coat. . . . The blood from the shattered arm flowed freshly, staining the Hotel Contarini's expensive silk coverlet. At last the doctor succeeded in stemming the flow a little, and then he straightened, giving Major Bergmann a cold disdainful look before turning to Laura.

'Forgive me, *Fräulein*, for subjecting you to this ordeal, but I must beg of you to give your permission for me to remove Sir Nicholas's left arm immediately.' He wiped his bloody hands on a cloth.

'I have no right, Doctor.'

'There is only you, and I must turn to you because others present here would deny Sir Nicholas his chance of survival.' Again a disdainful look at the unfortunate Major Bergmann.

'Doctor,' she said, 'can you tell me exactly what the chance is?'

'He has lost a great deal of blood, far too much. I am afraid that the ball lodged in his arm will make the flesh putrid and that that will in turn lead to a terrible death. Therefore it is my opinion that such a possibility must be avoided by the removal of the arm.'

'But the flesh may not become putrid.'

'There is that possibility.'

'And it is certain that the shock of such an amputation may prove too much for him in his present condition.'

'I know my profession, *Fräulein*,' snapped the doctor, 'And I most certainly pride myself on my speed in such matters. Sir Nicholas would suffer the minimum of pain. I cannot emphasize strongly enough the necessity for the arm's removal.'

She hesitated. But what right had she to go against Nicholas's own expressed wish? She found herself looking into the hostile eyes of the valet. You are to blame, said those eyes, but for you Sir Nicholas would not be lying at death's door. You are the cause of it all. . . . *And he's right, he's right!* She forced herself to meet the valet's gaze, however. 'Do you know why Sir Nicholas was so particular with his instructions about amputation?'

'Yes. I do.'

'Tell me.'

'Because he believes in the work of his close friend, Dr Daniel Tregarron of Langford. Dr Tregarron believes that sometimes a bullet can be left in a wound without causing the patient any harm, and he's proved it on King's Cliff by tending a gamekeeper who got shot in the leg. The bullet is still in that leg and the gamekeeper as hale as the next man.'

Dr Meyer snorted disparagingly. 'This man Tregarron is a charlatan, and a lucky one at that. Centuries of medicine have proved that leaving wounds only results in putrefaction. *I* am the surgeon-doctor here, not this Tregarron, and *I* warn you all that unless I remove that arm swiftly, then Sir Nicholas Grenville will most certainly die.'

Everyone looked at Laura now. They forced the unwelcome decision upon her. She looked down at Nicholas. How dark his lashes were against his pale skin. Even now he was so very handsome, so beautiful, almost. . . . She raised her eyes to the doctor. 'I'm sorry, but I will not be party to any amputation.'

'Then, *Fräulein*, on your head be it.'

'I did not seek this responsibility, sir, but as it has been thrust upon me, I will act accordingly to my conscience.'

He nodded. 'Very well. I will do what I can for him within the limits placed upon me. I can only bind the wounds and make him as comfortable as possible.'

'Thank you, Doctor.'

He worked as swiftly as possible, applying fresh dressings, and fifteen minutes later he prepared to take his leave. 'If, and it is unlikely, he survives to this evening, then I am to be sent for again.'

'Very well, Doctor.'

He and the major left then, and Laura was alone with Nicholas and the valet, whose hostility was still very much in evidence. With a heavy heart she sat down on a chair beside the bed, thereby signifying that she had every intention of remaining in the room, whether the possessive valet liked it or not.

The room was very hot, for the doctor had ordered the kindling of several of the terracotta charcoal stoves and the closing of the windows against the ill humors present in the fresh air outside. She could hear the whine of mosquitoes in the stuffy atmosphere. She looked at the valet then.

'Would Dr Tregarron have closed the windows and had stoves lit?'

'No, ma'am.'

'Then, as we are following the gospel according to him, we will open the windows and extinguish the stoves.'

He smiled a little reluctantly. 'Yes, ma'am.'

The cool Venetian breeze whispered pleasingly and refreshingly over the room, moving the hangings of the ornate bed where Nicholas lay so still. Laura's eyes went to the table beside her.

Augustine Townsend's beautiful face stared at her from its dainty little frame. In front of the miniature lay a folded, sealed document the last will and testament of Sir Nicholas Grenville of King's Cliff in the county of Somerset.

Laura bowed her head, the tears stinging her tired eyes.

Chapter 10

The long, dark shadows of the Venetian sunset lengthened across the floor. Outside the sky was a dazzling gold as the day at last came to an end, but still Nicholas lingered uncertainly between life and death.

Henderson sat on a chair in a far corner of the room, his tired head nodding forward on his chest as he slept. Like Laura, he had not slept the night before, and the anxiety and uncertainty of the day had taken its toll. Laura remained at Nicholas's side. While he still lived and breathed, then there was hope. . . .

Major Bergmann had returned several times, but there had been nothing to tell him. Nicholas neither deteriorated nor improved. The *maître d'hôtel* had personally brought a tray of food to the room, but neither Laura nor the valet had had any appetite, although they had thankfully accepted the dish of tea he insisted they take. Henderson quite obviously still blamed Laura for what had happened, but he had managed a smile when she had remarked that the *maître d'hôtel* quite obviously believed that come what may, the British took tea!

Now she leaned her weary head back against her chair. Her thoughts returned to the moment she had embarked upon her journey to Venice. Little had she then thought events would take this disastrous and momentous turn. She held Nicholas's right hand and it seemed suddenly that his fingers stirred a little. She sat forward immediately, her heart beating like thunder. Now his lips moved, as if he was trying to form a word. She bent close. It was almost unintelligible, but to her it was only too clear. It was a woman's name, 'Augustine.'

But there was no time to give in to the heartbreak that single utterance brought her. 'Henderson!' she cried, 'Henderson, quickly! Sir Nicholas spoke. Bring Dr Meyer!'

The valet was rudely jerked from his slumber and without question he ran from the room.

Anxiously, Laura returned her attention to Nicholas. 'Nicholas? Can you hear me?'

There was no reaction.

'Please, my love, open your eyes!' She held his hand against her cheek. 'Augustine?'

'Open your eyes.'

His eyelids flickered a little and then he was looking at her. He seemed puzzled at first, as if he did not know her, but then a smile touched his ashen lips. 'Laura.' He was barely audible.

'I've sent Henderson for the doctor.'

'Doctor?' The puzzled look returned.

'You are badly wounded.'

Memory seemed to return then. 'The duel—'

'The baron broke the rules. Do you remember?'

'A little.'

'You wounded him,' she said, hoping to encourage him just a little. His voice was so faint and shaky that she could barely understand him. Her hands trembled as she poured him some water and held the dish to his dry lips. He drank only a small amount, and even that effort seemed too much for him. His dull eyes closed again and he slipped back into unconsciousness.

Almost in tears, she replaced the dish on the table. At that moment Henderson returned with the doctor, and they were accompanied by the portly, black-clad, and bewigged figure of a chaplain.

The chaplain bowed. 'The Reverend Xavier Smythe,' he said. 'Attached to the British consulate here in Venice. Your servant, ma'am.'

'Sir.' Laura rose slowly to her feet. 'But why. . . ?'

The doctor put down his bag. 'I took the necessary precaution, *Fräulein*, of sending for the chaplain as I think it only right that Sir Nicholas should have the comfort of a priest at this time.'

It seemed so very final. 'But Sir Nicholas spoke to me,' she protested. 'He spoke to me and drank some water!'

'Alas, *Fräulein*, that is often the case, a rally before the end. I have seen it too often to take false hope. I knew when the valet came to me that your hopes had been raised, but I cannot encourage you at all.'

The chaplain agreed. 'I fear the doctor speaks the unfortunate truth, Miss—?'

'Milbanke.'

'Miss Milbanke. From what I hear of today's regrettable incident, and from what I now see of poor Sir Nicholas's condition, I think that all we can do now is pray for his soul.'

'No!' she cried. 'No! He's isn't dead!' Praying would be to tempt Providence . . . or to give up a race before it was fully run.

The chaplain's gray-wigged head nodded gravely. 'I understand how you feel, dear lady, but truly there is nothing more to be done. He is in the gentle hands of the Almighty now.'

'I will not accept that statement until his heart no longer beats, sir. Dr Meyer may be the finest practitioner of his skills in the whole world, but even he cannot know for certain what will happen. I will not give up yet, I swear that I will not.'

Nicholas's faint voice broke into the ensuing silence. 'Why are you here, Chaplain?'

Laura turned sharply, reaching out instinctively to take his hand again. He was looking at the Reverend Smythe. 'I don't need you, my friend,' he murmured.

The bulky chaplain leaned over him. 'I fear that you do, Sir Nicholas.'

'Not yet. Not yet.'

'I admire your brave words, Sir Nicholas, but I think you know in your heart that they are indeed just words.'

The hollow eyes moved to Laura's anxious face. 'Do I need him, Laura?'

She couldn't speak. Just when she needed her own strength most, it deserted her. She should deny it now, she should give him encouragement, but her resolve evaporated and she could only bow her head to hide the tears that sprang to her eyes when she wanted them least.

'My poor Laura,' he whispered, 'You came to Venice to be happy and instead I have made you weep. You must forgive me for everything.'

'*I* forgive *you?*' She was almost overcome with emotion. 'There is nothing to forgive,' she said at last. 'Nothing at all. Maybe you should be forgiving me.'

He smiled a little. 'You need not be a church mouse, Laura, there need not be any Lady Mountfort.'

'What do you mean?'

He looked at the waiting chaplain. 'Your visit shall not be wasted,' he said, pausing a while because the effort of speaking exhausted him.

The Reverend Smythe leaned closer. 'How may I serve you, sir?'

'By making Laura my wife.'

Laura stared at Nicholas, her eyes wide as she was taken completely unawares. 'You can't,' she breathed. 'You can't possibly do that!'

'Why?' he asked.

'Because of Miss Townsend. You love her, not me.'

'Only a miracle can make her my wife now. Look at me, Laura. I would die happier knowing that I had helped you. As my widow you will be amply provided for and you would not have to go to Lady Mountfort. Please, Laura.'

She turned to search the others' faces. Henderson was weeping openly and the doctor looked compassionately at Nicholas. The chaplain's eyes were sadly downcast, but there was no shocked condemnation on his face.

Nicholas spoke again. 'Do this for me, Laura.'

Slowly she nodded her consent. 'I will marry you,' she said softly. *For I love you, I love you with all my heart. . . .*

Dr Meyer and Major Bergmann were witnesses to the brief ceremony that took place a little later when a special license had been procured from the British consulate. The passage outside the room was thronged with people; it seemed that everyone in the Hotel Contarini had come to see the strange wedding.

She could hardly say the words, speaking haltingly and clutching the little posy of pink and white wild cyclamen Major Bergmann had managed to find somewhere for her. The flowers were the only bridal token she carried. Nicholas's signet ring felt ice cold as it was slipped on to her finger.

The Reverend Smythe closed the prayerbook and Laura bent to kiss Nicholas on the lips. The flowers were bruised against the coverlet and their delicate perfume was released into the still air. 'I love you, Nicholas,' she whispered, unable to bear not confessing her feelings to him now, but when she looked she saw that he had slipped into unconsciousness. He had not heard her. She turned sharply to Dr Meyer and he shook his head.

'Maybe he will awaken again, Lady Grenville, but I cannot offer you any hope.'

The flowers slipped from her fingers. She felt drained of all strength, all resistance. She could hear some of the maids in the passageway whispering prayers, and tears blinded her as she went to the balcony where the air was cooler. Nicholas's room overlooked a small canal at the side of the hotel and she looked down to see one of the distinctive Venetian, red-draped boat-hearses gliding silently toward the steps at the hotel's other entrance. A coffin covered by a red pall was carefully taken into the hotel – Nicholas's coffin. . . . A shudder ran through her, she would *not* accept the inevitable, she would *not*!

Turning back into the room, she looked at Major Bergmann. 'Tell them to send the coffin away.'

'But—'

'I will not have the coffin here while he lives! I demand that it be removed!' She was trembling defiantly.

The major inclined his head and left the room.

She did not know when at last she was alone with Nicholas. She was lost in her thoughts and silent prayers. The chaplain had placed the certificate of marriage on the table next to Augustine Townsend's portrait, and the document shone very white against the black lacquerwork. Laura stared at the piece of paper that made her Nicholas Grenville's wife. She loved him so very much – and he would never perhaps know that. He had married her because he pitied her, not for any other reason – his heart was given to Augustine. . . . An incongruous smile touched Laura's pale lips. The fortune ticket had been partly right, for she had a rich, albeit encumbered, and titled husband. But there was no great future happiness ahead for Laura, Lady Grenville of King's Cliff.

Chapter 11

The brilliant sunshine that streamed into the room as Henderson drew back the curtains the next morning roused Laura from the exhausted sleep that had at last overtaken her before dawn. She was curled up on the sofa, still wearing her sprigged muslin gown. She had unpinned her hair and brushed it before falling asleep, and now it tumbled down over her shoulders as she sat swiftly up, her first thought of Nicholas.

'He's the same, ma'am,' said the valet, seeing the sharp anxiety leap into her eyes.

Relief flooded through her as she got up and went to the bed. Nicholas awoke as her hand brushed his. 'Laura?' His voice was a faint whisper and his eyes were lackluster. But he was alive, he was still with her. . . .

'How are you feeling?' she asked.

'Bang up to the mark.'

She smiled at the dry humor he still seemed capable of in spite of his condition. 'You must drink something.'

'Cognac?'

'Water.'

'Damned washy stuff.'

Her hands were trembling as she poured some water from the jug by the bedside. Henderson supported Nicholas's head as she held the glass to his lips. He succeeded in drinking most of it and Henderson laid him gently back.

Laura glanced at the valet. 'Go and find Dr Meyer.'

'Yes, ma'am.' She knew that the valet still resented her part in all this, but the hostility was not as keen this morning.

She looked down at Nicholas again. 'Does your head ache?'

'Abominably.'

'Maybe the doctor can give you something to help.'

He nodded, almost imperceptibly. 'What a very dull wedding night you've had,' he murmured. 'My apologies.'

'There is time enough.'

He smiled at the brave words, but said nothing more, for at that moment Henderson returned with the doctor. The Austrian made no secret of his amazement that Nicholas had survived the night. He put his leather bag down and looked at his patient. 'You should be a corpse, Sir Nicholas, by all the laws I know of.'

'Austrian laws?'

'Human laws,' said the doctor firmly, bending to look at the dressings. 'Your head wound looks well enough, but no doubt it gives you much pain.'

'Yes.'

'I will give you laudanum. As to your arm – it should have been amputated. I tried my best to persuade . . .' The doctor glanced at Laura.

Nicholas smiled at her. 'You refused?'

'Yes.'

He nodded.

'There is time yet,' said the doctor, still determined to have his way, if possible.

'No, Doctor.'

'But, Sir Nicholas—'

'No.'

'Very well, I cannot of course impose my wishes upon you. But this one thing I will ask, and that is that if, God willing, you survive another week, then you will permit me to operate to remove the ball which lodges deep in the wound.'

'If I survive another week,' replied Nicholas quietly, 'then I will not remain in Venice.'

Laura stared down at him and the doctor was aghast. `You cannot think of traveling, Sir Nicholas! Such a course would be tantamount to lunacy!'

'Then consider me mad.'

'You must listen to me, Sir Nicholas. You are lucky to be alive, but only a cat has nine chances. If you undertake to travel in your condition, I cannot give you any hope of surviving.'

'You gave me no hope of being here now.'

The doctor gave a grim smile. 'I was wrong about that, but I am not wrong about this.'

Nicholas glanced at Laura. 'Promise me you will do as I wish.'

'But Nicholas—'

'Your word, Laura. As my wife.'

'And if I give my word, will it be as your widow that I reach England?'

'Your word,' he insisted, moving his hand toward hers.

She took his cold fingers. 'I promise,' she whispered.

'Lady Grenville!' protested the doctor. 'You cannot know what you are doing!'

'My husband wishes to go home, Dr Meyer, and I will do all I can to help him.'

The doctor sighed heavily. 'I should wash my hands of everything, for all my advice goes unheeded.'

'Dr Meyer,' she said, 'please believe me when I say that we are both very grateful for all you have done.'

He smiled. 'The English are quite mad. I have always suspected it, now I it know for certain. As I said, I cannot impose my wishes upon you, and as a doctor I feel bound to do what I can. If Sir Nicholas is set upon this crazy return to England, I will, of course, do what I can to make the journey as comfortable as possible for him.'

'Thank you, Doctor.'

'And now I will leave some laudanum for the pain. I will first change these dressings, however.' He began to unwind the bandage on Nicholas's head.

Nicholas blanched at the sharp, raw pain, but he did not cry out.

'Shout if you wish, sir, for I realize that the pain is great.'

'It is nothing I cannot endure.'

'You fought at Waterloo, did you not?'

'Yes.'

'Then in my opinion it is small wonder Bonaparte was crushed, for if all Englishmen are as stubborn as you are, Sir Nicholas, then the French did not stand a chance!'

Over two weeks later Laura's baggage stood waiting by her bedchamber door to be taken down to the waiting boat which would shortly transport her and Nicholas to the waiting British barquentine. The journey was the height of folly, but nothing would move Nicholas from his decision. She had managed to delay him another week, but that was all, and she had insisted on making the journey by sea, and not overland in stagecoaches that would jolt over every rut on appalling roads. But the final morning had arrived, and in a few moments they would leave the Hotel Contarini for the last time.

She took two of the cyclamen which had been her wedding bouquet. The flowers had not yet faded entirely for she had rescued them and put them with the anemones in a glass of water. Now she put samples of the flowers between the sheets of her guidebook, pressing the book tightly together and binding it close with a green ribbon. She put the book into her reticule and drew the strings firmly. There, she was ready to go.

She looked at her reflection in the cheval glass. Her traveling pelisse of pale lilac wool with its three little capes usually became her very well, but now it seemed only to emphasize the paleness of her face and the shadows beneath her tired eyes. It was loose on her now, too, for she had lost weight over the past weeks. Rouge would color her cheeks, but nothing could disguise the deep anxiety and tension that pervaded her so constantly.

With a heavy sigh, she picked up her green satin bonnet and tied its ribbons beneath her chin, draping the embroidered net veil over its high crown. Nicholas's ring was so large on her finger that she had to wear it over her kid gloves, and now she glanced at the shining gold. He had married the wrong woman. He had thought he was dying, but he had survived. Maybe he would survive until they reached King's Cliff. What then? It was his home, but it was also Augustine Townsend's home. How could it ever be Laura's home? She would be an intruder, an encumbrance – maybe even an embarrassment. She would be completely unwanted and she would also be the object of Augustine's justifiable loathing. She lowered her eyes unhappily. Whatever the outcome of this voyage, there could never be any true happiness for her.

Two footmen came to take her luggage, and she picked up her reticule, taking a final look at the room she had occupied for the past month. A month. Was it possible that she had only known him for that short time? He was her whole life, and he always would be. . . . On the first of March she had left this room to commence her visit to Venice, and on the first of April she was leaving it for the last time. *April fool. April fool.* The words echoed in her head as she followed the footmen from the room.

Major Bergmann was waiting in the vestibule, as were many of the hotel staff, and some of the officers she had come to know over the past weeks. The major took her hand. 'Farewell, Lady Grenville, I pray that your voyage will go well.'

'I pray so too, Major.'

He lifted her hand to his lips. '*Viel Glück.*'

'Thank you.'

He walked with her to the steps where the boat was waiting. Nicholas lay on a pallet, drowsy with laudanum so that he did not really know what was happening. The orange blossom still bloomed, filling the air with its sweetness, and the warm water of the Grand Canal lapped softly as it broke into turquoise against the marble steps.

She didn't look back as the boat was rowed farther and farther away from the hotel.

Chapter 12

Almost a month later the barquentine *Cygnet* was in sight of England's shores, but a continuous storm prevented her from coming into the small Dorset town of Lyme Regis.

Laura steadied herself as the ship rose sharply on another mountainous wave, the boards creaking and vibrating with the force of the storm. The gimbal-mounted candles smoked thickly as they swung from side to side, making the already heavy atmosphere in the cabin even more heavy. Shutters had been nailed to the window, but a short while earlier she had gone out on to the heaving deck to stare miserably across at the shore through a maelstrom of foam and spray. Angry gray clouds scudded across the low heavens and the gale howled through the rigging, making the ensigns lash like whips. The storm had beaten the small ship since she had entered the Bay of Biscay, and it had followed her northward to England. When a calm voyage was what had been prayed for, Dame Fortune chose to inflict her most malevolent gales.

Nicholas tossed feverishly on the narrow, hard bed. An unhealthy flush brightened his pale cheeks and he deliriously muttered words neither she nor Henderson could understand. His skin burned with fever, but he shivered as if ice cold. An ague, the captain had said, contracted because of his weak condition and because of the ill humor in the Mediterranean air. . . . An ague. But which one? Was it fatal? Could a doctor cure it? Anxiously she paced up and down, her handkerchief twisted in her distraught hands. There was no doctor on board the *Cygnet*, and the only treatment available had been an infusion of vervain leaves. A sovereign febrifuge, the captain had assured her, but it had done little to help. It had not lowered Nicholas's temperature, nor had it soothed his discomfort in any way. He tossed again and she went to try to restrain him as best she could, for each time he moved she was terrified he would open the wound in his arm once more. As she looked now, though, she saw that her fears had been justified, for the clean dressing was stained with dark red. . . . *Please God, please calm the storm.*

Nicholas's dark eyes opened suddenly and he caught her wrist. 'Augustine?' He did not know her.

'I'm here,' she said soothingly, although it pierced her heart to hear another woman's name on his lips.

'You – must understand. I must do it. King's Cliff.'

'I know.'

'Do you understand?'

'Yes. Of course.'

He relaxed a little, releasing her hand. 'I love you,' he whispered. 'I don't want to hurt you.'

'I love you too.' Tears were bright in her eyes.

The moment of consciousness was over and a convulsive shiver seized him. The tears welled out and down her cheeks then. 'I love you, Nicholas Grenville,' she whispered, forgetting Henderson, who sat on a small stool nearby.

The valet watched her a moment. He blamed her, and yet was he justified? She had tried to make Sir Nicholas refuse the challenge, and she was obviously under great stress now. And she loved the man she had married, there could be no mistake about that. The valet got up.

'You should rest awhile, Lady Grenville.'

She turned swiftly. 'I had forgotten you were here.'

'Reckon I know that, my lady. Reckon too that I should ask your forgiveness. I've misjudged you and I had no place even having an opinion.'

She smiled tiredly.

'I'm glad he married you and not that Townsend she-devil.'

She stared at him, taken aback at his outspoken words. 'I beg your pardon?'

'I know I've no business saying anything, but she wasn't the wife for him. She'd have only made him unhappy.'

'You think I will not?' she asked drily.

'*You* wouldn't knowingly do anything to hurt him.'

'Meaning that Miss Townsend would?'

'She'd do anything to have her own way. She was a mean and spiteful child, and now she's a mean and spiteful woman. She's the most beautiful thing you ever saw, but she's evil and black inside. Reckon you won't find any of the servants at King's Cliff who won't welcome you, my lady, for you've saved them from her.'

'Oh, surely you exaggerate.'

'No, my lady. You'll see the truth for yourself soon enough.'

Her heart sank at his ominous prediction. She went to the shuttered window, trying to look out between the uneven wooden slats, but all she could see was the heavy sea. And all the time the howl of the gale in the rigging.

It was late evening when the storm suddenly abated and at last a boat could be lowered to convey Nicholas ashore. He was still burning with the ague, and yet he shivered as if frozen. She hoped with all her heart that there was a doctor in Lyme Regis, or an apothecary at the very least. The men rowed swiftly over the white-capped waves and the setting sun shone brightly on the cliffs, making the cottages and inns of the small town look very startling, their windows winking and flashing as the boat moved. Lyme Regis spread up a long, steep hill from a pleasant little bay and tiny harbor. Soon the bay would be thronged with bathing machines as fashionable society came to enjoy the sea air, but for the time being it was quiet still.

The boat came to a halt at the water's edge and the sailors jumped out to drag it further up the beach. Laura got out and stood looking at the stone steps leading up from the beach. A doctor. Please, a doctor. . . .

The waiter at the inn shook his head. 'I'm afraid Mr Harper, the surgeon. has been called away over Bridport way. He won't be back before tomorrow.'

'Is there an apothecary?'

'Not since old Mr French died two months back.'

She looked helplessly around the tap room with its stacked barrels and dusty floor. Through the bow window she could see the bay where the *Cygnet* lay at anchor. Dared she wait here for the surgeon to return? What if he was delayed?

She turned to Henderson. 'How far is it to King's Cliff from here?'

'Reckon about twenty-five miles.'

'And where does Dr Tregarron live?'

'Langford. About five miles from King's Cliff by road, but only one mile through Langford Woods.'

She looked back to the waiter. 'Do you have a chaise for hire? And a good saddle horse?'

'Yes, my lady.'

'Then have both made ready. Henderson, I intend to go on to King's Cliff. You must ride ahead and find Dr Tregarron, or any other doctor if he is not available. Be waiting at King's Cliff.'

'Very well, my lady.'

She seemed to have been waiting an unconscionable length of time, and the valet had long since ridden off when the waiter at last came to tell her that the chaise was ready.

She sat with Nicholas's head resting on her lap as the coachman whistled and cracked his whip to encourage the team to greater effort as the heavy old carriage lumbered out of the cobbled yard and turned slowly up the steep hill that led out of Lyme Regis. She steadied Nicholas as the carriage swayed, and she stared blindly out of the window. They were almost at journey's end and would reach King's Cliff before dawn. But what awaited her there?

The chaise came to a standstill again and at first she did not open her eyes, for the journey had involved many stops at tollgates and crossroads, but then she recognized Henderson's voice and looked out immediately. Lanterns moved by some immense wrought-iron gates and she could make out the windows and door of a lodge. Henderson came to the carriage door and opened it.

'Is all well, my lady?'

She nodded. 'He is the same.'

'Dr Tregarron waits at the big house. My lady. . . ?'

'Yes?' She caught the unease in the valet's voice.

'I had to wait here by the gates on account of the keeper not believing Sir Nicholas was alive. None of them would believe me at first.'

She stared blankly at him. But how could they think he was dead? How could they know anything of what had taken place in Venice? They could only know if someone had sent word – but who would do that? She certainly had not, and neither had the valet. Then she remembered the British consulate. Yes, that must be the answer – someone there must have written to King's Cliff when Nicholas was believed to be *in extremis*.

Henderson closed the door again and climbed up beside the coachman. The gates swung open, creaking loudly, and the chaise jolted forward for the last time as the tired team trotted along the gravel drive toward the immense silhouette of the house, so clear in the pale moonlight.

Her heart began to beat more swiftly now and she was suddenly afraid. Soon she would be face to face with Augustine Townsend. . . .

Lamps had been lit beneath the tall, marble portico, and as the chaise came to a halt the great doors of the house were flung open and some footmen in dark green and gold livery came out, followed by a dark-haired young man in a fashionable dove-gray coat and beige breeches.

Henderson jumped down to open the carriage door and the young man looked up at Laura. His long-lashed eyes were dark brown and the night breeze ruffled his hair and the rich folds of his silk cravat. 'Lady Grenville?'

'Yes.'

He bowed. 'Daniel Tregarron. Your servant, madam.'

'Sir.' She was surprised, for he was roughly of an age with Nicholas and she had expected him to be much older.

His eyes lingered on her face a moment more and then he turned his attention to Nicholas. 'How long has he been like this?'

'A week.'

'And before that?'

'There was not ague, he was just very weak from his wounds.'

He gestured to one of the footmen to hold a lamp closer. The bright light swayed over the drab interior of the coach, illuminating Nicholas's pale and yet fevered face quite clearly. The doctor said nothing, but took a long breath as he inspected the blood-stained dressing on the wounded arm. He glanced at Laura again. 'It does not look well, Lady Grenville.'

'You must save him, Doctor,' she whispered. 'Please, you must save him.'

'I will do all in my power, I promise you,' he said gently, nodding at the footmen. 'Carry him carefully now.'

She took the hand Daniel Tregarron held out to her and stepped down
from the carriage as they carried Nicholas into the house. The night air was
cool and she could hear the soft rustling of trees. An owl hooted somewhere
and she could hear the famous King's Cliff foxhounds in their kennels
nearby. She stared up at the ivy-covered walls and then back at the great
double doors at the top of the steps. She half expected to see Augustine
standing there, but she was not.

Slowly she walked up the steps with the doctor. Black-ribboned wreaths
had been placed on the doors and more black ribbons hung from the many
paintings lining the hall's pale green walls. Black and white tiles covered the
echoing floor, and high above, the gold ceiling shone dully in the light of the
magnificent chandeliers. Gilded plasterwork surrounded the doors and
there were elegant statues in the niches on either side of the immense black
marble fireplace where the remains of a log fire glowed. Some gun dogs lay
sprawled before the fire, sleeping on in ignorance of what went on around
them.

But Laura noticed little of this; she saw only the lines of servants, all
wearing black weepers on their arms, waiting to be presented to the new
lady of the house. All their eyes were upon her, at once curious and nervous
as they sought to gain the measure of her in those few seconds. There was
still no sign at all of Miss Augustine Townsend.

Daniel Tregarron bowed to her. 'Forgive me, Lady Grenville, but I must
attend to Sir Nicholas.'

'Of course, Doctor.'

'The Reverend Tobias Claverton is here, waiting in Sir Nicholas's room.
He is vicar of Langford parish and has long been associated with the
Grenville family. I felt duty-bound to send word to him the moment I
learned what had happened.'

'Naturally, Dr Tregarron.'

He smiled at her and then turned to hurry up the curved staircase that
rose between vast marble columns at the far end of the echoing hall. She
looked more assured than she felt as she turned to the man who stepped
forward from the lines of servants.

He bowed gravely. 'Welcome to King's Cliff. I am Hawkins, the chief
butler.'

'Hawkins.' She inclined her head in the way she had so often seen her
imperious aunt do in the past.

A sea of faces then passed before her, each one bearing a name she knew
she would not remember. The stiff formality of the occasion was almost
ridiculous under the circumstances, but she knew that etiquette demanded
that it be carried out to the letter. She wanted more than anything to go to
Nicholas, to hear what Daniel Tregarron's opinion was, but instead she must
stand here and endure a nonsensical ceremony. The chief butler bowed

again as the last maid bobbed a curtsy. Silence fell on the hall again, and they were all looking expectantly at her.

Somehow she must assert herself now. But how? What could she say? She felt so out of place, so inadequate. . . . A trembling panic threatened to well up inside her, but outwardly she remained as calm as ever. A maid hurried dutifully forward as she began to remove her gloves, taking off her wedding ring and resting it on the top of a long, white marble table in the center of the hall. All eyes went to the ring as if hypnotized. The weepers on the maid's arm fluttered as she took the gloves. Laura replaced the ring on her finger.

'I will have all signs of mourning removed from the house immediately,' said Laura to the butler. 'And all mourning cards returned from whence they came first thing in the morning.' She indicated a silver platter containing a great number of black-edged cards.

'Very well, my lady.'

'Where is Miss Townsend?'

A detectable stir passed through the hall. The butler cleared his throat. 'Mrs Townsend and Miss Townsend are not at home, my lady.'

'Mrs Townsend?'

'Miss Townsend's mother, my lady.'

'Oh.' She had two of them to face?

'Where are they?'

'Taunton, my lady.'

'Why?'

'They are attending a subscription ball with the Earl of Langford, my lady.'

She stared at him. Nicholas had been presumed killed, the house was in deep mourning, and yet Augustine and her mother saw fit to attend a ball with the man who had tried to usurp Nicholas and win the woman he was to marry? 'Very well,' she said after a moment, 'that will be all.'

'May I take this opportunity to say how very glad we are to learn that Sir Nicholas is not taken from us after all? And how very pleased we are to welcome you to this house?'

She was reminded of Henderson's words on board the *Cygnet*. The butler did indeed seem to mean his words of welcome, and the eyes looking at her from all around were not at all hostile as she had feared.

But her ordeal was over for the moment. With a hidden sigh of relief, she watched them all file out of the hall. A footman waited to escort her to Nicholas's room, but as she followed him up the wide staircase, she remembered that the last time she had heard Taunton mentioned had been at Fontelli's in Venice. By Baron Frederick von Marienfeld.

Chapter 13

The Reverend Tobias Claverton was waiting outside the master bedchamber.
He was a vast figure of a man, clad entirely in black, with two crisp flaps of
cravat standing out aggressively beneath his many chins. A dusting of
powder from his enormous wig lay on his broad shoulders, and he emitted
a strong smell of pipe tobacco as he bowed before her. Laura was to learn
with the passage of time that he was a keen scholar of Greek and Latin, but
that he knew more about Homer and Horace than he did about people.
Closely related to the very superior and high Tory Countess of Bawton, the
widowed owner of a neighboring estate, he hung on to every one of that
aristocratic lady's words as if they were the gospel itself. Where she led, he
followed, and he expected everyone else to do the same. To cross the
Countess of Bawton was to cross Mr Claverton.

But there was no real malice in him – he was just incapable of seeing
beyond the end of his bulbous red nose – and he was genuinely concerned
about Nicholas. Upon seeing Laura, he immediately took her hand –
although, despite this display of warmth, she could sense that he was a little
outraged at the obvious haste of the marriage in Venice and was just as obviously wondering if she and Nicholas had, as it were, anticipated nuptial bliss
and thereby been forced into a swift marriage.

'My dear Lady Grenville, we must offer our humble thanks to God
Almighty for preserving the precious life of our beloved Sir Nicholas. . . .'

'Indeed so, sir.'

'*Deo gratias. Deo gratias.*' He placed the tips of his fingers together,
almost as if about to pray. 'I trust, Lady Grenville, that we shall have the
pleasure of seeing you in church soon.'

She could only murmur that of course she would go, although the last
thing she felt like doing was braving the curious eyes of Somerset by going
to Langford church.

'I will take my leave of you now, and, *Deo favente*, Dr Tregarron will
have uplifting news for you.'

'Yes.' Thankfully she watched his enormous figure move away along the
portrait-hung passage toward the head of the staircase.

Daniel Tregarron was completing his examination as she entered the
room. The master bedchamber at King's Cliff was a beautiful room,
furnished with polished walnut, its walls hung with gold-and-white-striped
silk. A predominantly red Axminster carpet covered the floor and there
were gold-fringed red velvet curtains at the windows. Nicholas lay in a
cream-canopied four-poster bed. He still shivered violently and she could
see the feverish color on his cheeks. Daniel drew some warm blankets over

him and then extinguished most of the candles in the room.

He turned to Laura then, taking her hand and leading her to a comfortable chair by the pink marble fireplace with its elegant screen. 'You have seen the good vicar?'

'Yes.'

'I fear he finds his tasks onerous at times, especially when they impinge upon his scholarly and uninteresting dreams.' He smiled at her. 'About Nicholas . . .'

'Yes?'

'I will deal with the ague first. He has a temperature of one hundred and four degrees of Fahrenheit and his pulse is one hundred and twelve in the minute. That, together with his other symptoms, suggests to me that he has the disease we know as malaria. From its name you realize that many believe it to be caused by bad air, the miasma from stagnant pools, but I am of another opinion, and believe that it is caused by the bite of a mosquito. I know it is early in the year yet, but I would imagine that Venice and the Mediterranean have that insect in plenty already.'

'Yes, it was very warm there, much warmer and more advanced in season than this country. But malaria can be treated, can it not?'

'It can indeed, by the taking of Jesuits' bark, which I will prepare for him. As to the wound in his arm – well, there I am less sanguine.'

'Why?' she asked quickly, alarm creeping into her heart.

'It was well done to refuse the amputation, but I must warn you that I am concerned that the wound has opened again. That is not at all a good sign. As soon as he has recovered from the rigors of the journey and as soon as I have managed to bring down his fever just a little, I will have to operate to remove the ball lodged in his arm. It is not my usual practice unless I see no other course, but I fear that the danger of putrefaction is too great. The balance is delicate.'

She stared at him. 'But will not the shock of such an operation—'

'Do you trust me, Lady Grenville?' he interrupted.

She looked into his dark eyes. Trust him? She hardly knew him. And yet. . . . 'Yes, Dr Tregarron, I trust you.'

'Then listen to what I have to say and listen well, for it concerns an innovation which you will find hard to accept.'

'I am listening, Doctor.'

'Have you ever heard of Paracelsus, my lady?'

'No.'

'He lived in the sixteenth century. He was a physician of German-Swiss blood – he was also an alchemist and astrologer, but that does not concern us.'

'Of that I am glad, for if you were about to resort to reading the stars, I am afraid that I would indeed find your innovation difficult to accept,' she remarked drily.

He smiled at her. 'It is Paracelsus the physician who interests me, Lady Grenville. In my opinion he was one of the greatest doctors of all time. I have read his works and there is a great deal to which modern medicine would do well to pay heed. As far as Sir Nicholas is concerned, it is what Paracelsus wrote of a substance known as sweet vitriol, or sulfuric ether, which is of importance.'

'Is that not used in the treatment of coughs?'

'It is indeed, but it has another property of which you will not know. Paracelsus wrote of it that "it quiets all suffering without any harm, and relieves all pain".'

'And does it?'

'I fear that you find this claim to be of dubious character, don't you? I hear it in your voice. But yes, my lady, sweet vitriol does indeed have the effect I have described. I know it does because I have used it upon myself. I was standing by my desk when I inhaled the vapor, and I immediately lost consciousness. I came around a little later to find that I had a very bad bruise on my forehead, and yet I have no recollection of receiving that bruise. I must have struck my head quite forcibly as I fell, but there was no pain at all. I have since used the substance upon a cat with a broken leg. The creature felt nothing while I set the bone and now she is as whole as any other cat. I am convinced that sweet vitriol is indeed a sovereign remedy for the removal of all feeling.'

She looked at him in stunned silence and then slowly got to her feet. 'And you wish to use this sweet vitriol on Nicholas?'

'Yes.'

His words echoed in her head as she went to one of the windows, holding the curtain aside to look out. Everything was black and she could see only her own reflection looking back at her. Daniel came to stand at her shoulder.

'He will feel no pain and therefore no distress, which things are the cause of so many deaths on the operating table. Surgeons can pride themselves on their speed and dexterity, but such great and excruciating pain kills and there is no denying it. Believe me, I would not attempt to do anything if I did not consider it to be essential. The wound is angry and threatens to become poisonous – which in turn will mean amputation after all. If I can operate to remove the ball and thereby cleanse the wound, then I firmly believe all will be well.'

'You suffered no ill effects from this sweet vitriol.'

'None. I understand your skepticism. I felt the same way when first I read what Paracelsus had written, but I know it is correct and so ask your permission.'

She looked across at Nicholas. 'You have my permission, Doctor.'

'You love him very much, don't you?'

'Yes.' She thought of something then. 'Dr Tregarron, do you know how word reached King's Cliff that he had been killed?'

'I believe the Earl of Langford was told, and I presumed the British consul in Venice had relayed the tidings.'

'Nicholas's cousin, James Grenville?'

'The very same. God forbid that there should be two Earls of Langford!'

She smiled. 'You do not like the gentleman?'

'Nicholas is the only member of the Grenville clan I have ever felt any warmth for – and if he's a true Grenville, I'll be surprised. I'll warrant his mother had a secret to keep concerning his siring!' Daniel laughed. 'You have only to look at the Grenvilles, all dark and swarthy, and then to look at Nicholas to see that he bears no resemblance whatsoever to them. Incidentally, perhaps you should be warned that the earl will be beside himself with fury when he learns that Nicholas is alive, for at this very moment he happily believes that King's Cliff is about to fall into his greedy little hands. A totally unlovable fellow, is the good earl, I fear. Nicholas is as far removed from his cousin as chalk is from cheese, and that is probably why I like the man you married so much. I like him all the more for bring-ing someone as lovely as yourself to reside among us.'

She flushed at the compliment. 'You are too kind, sir.'

'Somerset will rattle about you for weeks. I'll warrant that even by midday tomorrow there will not be anyone from one end of the country to the other who does not know about Nicholas Grenville's Venetian match.'

'No doubt they will all whisper that I married a dying man so that I could enrich myself.'

'And did you?'

'I married him because I love him.'

'Then what does it matter what they say?'

She smiled, liking him a great deal.

'Your appearance on the scene will cause quite a stir in other quarters,' he said.

'You refer to Miss Townsend?'

'Yes.'

'I can hardly expect her to be pleased. I know that he loves her and would have married her.'

'Maybe he did love her, but the fact that he married you must surely mean that you have his heart now.'

'I fear not, Dr Tregarron. He married me because he thought he was dying and he was sorry for me. He did not for one moment imagine that he was still going to be alive over a month after the duel or even that he would be back here at King's Cliff.'

'I know it is none of my business, but I know Nicholas Grenville very well indeed. Henderson told me a little of what happened in Venice, and I suggest that if Nicholas felt only sorry for you, then all he needed to do was make financial provision for you; he did not need to go as far as marrying you. If he was well enough to put his name to a marriage certificate, he was well enough to sign a deed of gift.'

'I wish I could believe what you say, but I think that a deed of gift simply did not occur to him.'

He smiled then. 'Perhaps it is more of a love match than you believe, Lady Grenville.'

'Oh, on my side it is. I love him with all my heart.'

'I could almost envy him.'

She blushed again. He was very liberal with his compliments. She glanced at him. He was a very good-looking young man, and no doubt well able to set the feminine hearts of Somerset all aflutter whenever he wished.

'Lady Grenville, I imagine that you are far from looking forward to your first meeting with Augustine Townsend and her equally disagreeable mother.'

'Equally disagreeable?'

'I make no secret of finding both ladies decidedly abhorrent.'

She stared at him. 'But you are Nicholas's friend—'

'That does not mean to say I have to like Augustine Townsend. She and I loathe each other and always have done. Oh, I assure you I do not speak out of pique because she spurned me.'

'Henderson told me that she was not liked.'

'He spoke truthfully. She will do nothing to make your life here easy; she will do all in her power to hurt you. Never trust her, Lady Grenville, and if you need reason, then wonder only how she, who was expecting to marry Nicholas and who ordered the house into mourning, has still togged herself up like an altarpiece to go dancing with the odious Earl of Langford. The king is dead, long live the king. She will give her hand in marriage to whoever owns this house, *her* house as she so firmly believes. Nicholas is well out of a match with her.'

'Is he well out of such a match? His marriage to me is unconsummated, and therefore is a marriage in name only and can be set aside. We both know that, Dr Tregarron. When he is well, he will want her, not me. How can I expect it to be otherwise? I am the intruder here, and soon there will be no place for me. He loves her, he told me that in Venice, and whatever anyone else may say of her, he obviously does not agree.' She felt very tired suddenly, but she did not know that she had swayed until Daniel suddenly put his arm around her waist to steady her.

'When did you last eat or sleep?' he asked.

'I don't really know.'

'As the only doctor present, I recommend that you remedy both failings immediately.'

'I cannot leave him—'

'Rubbish, you have me to do the worrying for you for the time being.'

'You will stay here?'

'I am at your command, Lady Grenville. I may be *persona non grata* with Miss Townsend, but you are mistress of the house now. I will stay for several days if you wish me to.'

'I wish that very much, Dr Tregarron.'

'Then I will do so – provided you promise to follow my prescription of taking some food and then sleeping.

'I promise.'

He led her to the door, and on opening it she saw that a maid was waiting outside.

Daniel smiled at the girl. 'Kitty Roberts, isn't it?'

'Yes, Dr Tregarron.' The girl looked adoringly at him, and Laura hid a smile. The handsome, dashing doctor did indeed have a way with him!

'Well, Kitty, I imagine that you are to be Lady Grenville's maid.'

'Yes, Dr Tregarron. With your permission, my lady.' The girl curtsied to Laura, her mobcap trembling on her neat, light brown hair.

'Show her ladyship to her room then, Kitty.'

'My lady?' The maid waited, her hazel eyes very wide and anxious. She knew as little about her new mistress as Laura did about her.

Laura managed a smile. She followed the maid along endless passageways carpeted in deep green. Hazeldon Court had been a large house, but it was a small dwelling compared with King's Cliff.

The room that had been hastily made ready for her lay at the front of the house, but it was not one of the principal bedchambers. She supposed that those would be occupied by Augustine Townsend and her mother, which was natural enough. However, even though it was less grand that it might have been, it was still a charming room, furnished with gold and white Louis Quatorze chairs and tables, and with a beautiful bed hung with green and white floral curtains. A fire had been kindled in the hearth, for the room was a little damp still after the winter, and Kitty had laid Laura's nightrobe over a chair to warm.

Beyond learning that Kitty was Langford born and bred and that her father was one of the many gardeners employed at King's Cliff, Laura did not engage the maid much in conversation. She felt too tired for small talk and was now quite beyond anything but a long, deep sleep. On reflection she was glad to have been spared meeting Augustine Townsend and her mother, for she no longer felt up to such a confrontation. She thought about Augustine for a moment. What was she really like? From Daniel Tregarron and Henderson she had heard similar accounts, but was it possible for Nicholas to be so mistaken about her?

Before retiring, she sat in a comfortable chair to eat the light supper Kitty brought for her. She had just finished when she heard the crunch of carriage wheels on the drive. Going to the window, she stepped behind the shelter of the curtains to look down at the elegant landau drawn by six magnificently matched white horses. It was a breathtakingly expensive and handsome drag, that much was plain even in the darkness. The carriage lamps arced as the coachmen tooled the team around in front of the portico steps and two blue-liveried footmen jumped down to lower the iron rungs and open the door. Laura's heart sank. It must surely be the Earl of Langford bringing Augustine and her mother home. . . .

A short, portly man in evening black emerged first, tucking his cocked hat beneath his arm as he turned to dashingly hold out his hand to the next occupant. Her graying hair and tightly laced waist marked her as being of an older generation than the man, who for all his paunch was only in his thirties. The earl and Mrs Townsend, thought Laura, waiting with baited breath for her first glimpse of Augustine.

In a dainty flurry of shimmering silver gauze, Augustine stepped lightly down, her hair very red in the light of the carriage lamps. She was as beautiful as her portrait suggested. Her skin was pale and clear and her figure quite exquisite, and Laura could hear her tinkling laughter as she leaned coquettishly toward the adoring earl. She tapped his hand with her closed fan and moved away as he tried to seize her fingers and kiss them.

Laura felt only loathing as she watched them. How they had enjoyed themselves tonight! Dancing the hours away and making merry when they were supposed to be in deep mourning for Nicholas! There was not the slightest hint of grief or sorrow in their manner. The earl's attitude she could understand a little more – he and Nicholas had never liked each other and Nicholas's death could only be to the earl's advantage. But Augustine was quite another matter. She was to have married Nicholas, and yet so swiftly she encouraged the earl's advances. What had Daniel Tregarron said about her? The king is dead, long live the king. Yes, and that was precisely how the beautiful Miss Townsend was behaving now. Nicholas was dead, the earl very much alive.

'Oh, Nicholas,' she murmured sadly, 'you do not deserve such a hollow creature as this.' She felt a savage pleasure at the thought of their faces changing when they learned what had happened in their absence. But the earl was spared the rude discovery, for he did not go into the house, but climbed back into his carriage and drove away. Augustine and her mother went up the portico steps and vanished into the house.

Stepping back into the room, Laura glanced at Kitty. 'I shall not need you anymore tonight.'

'Very well, my lady.'

'And I do not wish to be disturbed unless I am needed by Sir Nicholas or Dr Tregarron.'

'Yes, my lady.'

'Sleep well, Kitty.'

The maid smiled shyly. 'I shan't sleep a wink, my lady, not after all that's gone on today. Good night.' She curtsied and was gone.

Laura went to the door and locked it. She did not want to see Augustine; she wanted to hide away now. She extinguished the lamps and climbed into the bed, lying there listening to the silence. By now Augustine would know.

She distinctly heard the light, angry footsteps approaching, and the rustle of silver gauze as Augustine halted by the door and saw no light shining beneath it. The handle turned slowly, but the door would not open.

Laura made no sound at all and at last the footsteps went away again.

Chapter 14

The much-needed sleep refreshed Laura, but her spirits were still desperately low when she awoke the following morning. Her first thought was of Nicholas and she slipped from the bed, pulling on her wrap and telling herself that the fact that Daniel Tregarron had not sent for her during the night must surely be a good sign.

She forgot Augustine as she hurried through the many galleries and passages she had memorized the night before when following Kitty. Her bare feet made little or no sound on the highly polished floor of the main gallery overlooking the magnificent gardens, and she didn't even glance at any of the statues or portraits lining the paneled walls.

At his door, however, she stopped abruptly, for it stood ajar and thus afforded her a clear view of the room beyond. Augustine was seated on the edge of the bed, Nicholas's hand held lovingly in hers as she leaned tenderly over him, the very picture of loving concern and care. The contrast between her behavior the night before and this sweet anxiety now was almost obscene. She looked so very lovely in a yellow muslin gown which became her striking coloring so very well. Her shining red hair was piled with apparent abandon of the top of her head, but the almost negligent effect must have taken her maid an age to achieve. There were yellow ribbons looped around the light curls, hanging down to the nape of her neck at the back, and a choker of creamy white pearls was her only jewelry. She was almost too beautiful, perfect in every possible way. Gently she ran her cool fingers over the scar the baron's bullet had left on Nicholas's temple, and his eyes flickered and opened. In spite of the malaria which still held him in its grip, he smiled up into Augustine's loving green eyes, and the smile twisted like a knife in Laura's heart.

Augustine must have known the very moment Laura had appeared, for she turned now to look at her, a malevolent smile playing around her lips. Still smiling then, she bent to kiss Nicholas on the lips, lingering over the caress. Laura was unable to move, she could only watch in misery. The nightmare was real; she could only lose him to this woman.

Augustine stood then, still holding his hand. 'I will leave you now, *cher ami*,' she murmured softly. 'For you must sleep, but I promise that I shall come again soon. I cannot tell you how glad my heart is that you are safe after all and have come home to me.'

Laura felt rooted to the spot as the other emerged from the room and slowly closed the door, leaning back on it as if to emphasize her superiority by placing herself so firmly between Laura and Nicholas.

'So, my *lady*, we meet at last, and already I think you know how things will be here, don't you? There's no place for you at King's Cliff and I advise you to leave now, before you suffer anymore.'

'I have every right to be here.'

'Because he is your husband?' Augustine gave a mirthless laugh. 'Oh, come now, do you honestly imagine he will want to keep you as his wife when he recovers? Your so-called marriage can be set aside the moment *I* wish. Yours is a *mariage de convenance*, an empty contract. That ring you wear means nothing. No doubt you thought yourself so very clever, trapping a man on his deathbed into marrying you, but your plotting will come to nothing. I will see to that.'

Laura was gallingly unable to think of anything acid enough to say; her wits seemed to have deserted her, leaving her totally at Augustine's mercy. 'I do not think my marriage is any concern of yours,' was all she could manage.

Augustine laughed. 'It isn't worth anyone's concern, my *lady*, I'll grant you that. How Nicholas must be regretting his mesalliance.' The cool green eyes swept over Laura, at once scornful and triumphant. 'Dear *God*, how he must be regretting it.'

'You hope. You can't be sure, though, can you?'

'Oh, I think I can. You do not honestly imagine that *you* are capable of taking him from me and keeping him, do you? If you do, then you obviously dwell in the realms of fantasy.' Augustine straightened then, her eyes glittering coldly. 'No tawdry adventuress with an eye to doing well for herself is about to turn my world around, or intrude upon my existence in any way whatsoever. You are nothing here, as you will soon discover if you are ill-advised enough to remain. *I* am mistress of both this house and its master. You are not welcome and I shall see to it that every moment you spend here is a misery from which you will wish only to escape – I will see to that, I promise you.'

Laura said nothing, turning to walk away. She heard Augustine's low, mocking laughter following her, and tears of anger and unhappiness filled her eyes. Oh, why had she not stood up for herself? She should have given as good as she got, but the words had simply failed her and her lips remained foolishly and weakly closed. She had allowed the first victory to Augustine, and it must have been a sweet victory indeed, for it showed the new Lady Grenville to be painfully unsure of herself and therefore a rival of little consequence.

'Oh, you fool, Laura Milbanke,' she whispered to herself, 'You *fool!*' She pushed open the doors of the main gallery.

Daniel Tregarron was standing by one of the windows, and he turned as he heard her enter. 'Good morning, Lady Grenville, I trust that the night's sleep was agreeable.'

'G-good morning, Doctor,' she replied, praying that she sounded brighter than she felt. 'Yes, I do feel a little better, thank you.'

His dark, shrewd eyes rested on the unshed tears for a moment. 'You have been to see Nicholas?'

'That was what I set out to do.'

'I take it that you have met Miss Townsend.'

'Yes.' She looked away.

'I am afraid that she means to reassert her place in his affections.'

'She has no need, sir, for I do not believe she has ever been out of them.'

'That is defeatist talk.'

'I have nothing with which to fight an opponent like her.'

'With all due respect, my lady, that is poppycock. In my opinion your beauty far outshines hers, and you have more than your fair share of charm – she has none at all!' He smiled at her. 'Forgive me if I seem a little forward in my praise, but I think you are wrong to hold yourself in such low regard.'

She returned the smile. 'You flatter me, I think, sir.'

'No. I don't.'

She changed the subject. 'How – how is Nicholas? Is there any change in his condition?'

'He is awake occasionally, but he is not aware a great deal of what goes on around him. I have administered the Jesuits' bark for the malaria and have given him a little laudanum to lessen the pain he is in. I am reluctant to administer both treatments together, as in my experience laudanum is a very uncertain substance and it can sometimes react badly with other medicaments. However, at the moment I feel Nicholas's condition warrants the application of both. I trust that soon there will be sufficient improvement for me to go ahead with the operation to remove the bullet from his arm. Perhaps I should warn you that Miss Townsend does not wish me to operate; she would prefer a more eminent London man.'

'But I want you to attend him, Dr Tregarron, and I am sure that he would wish that himself.'

'That is all I need to know.' He smiled at her. 'Thank you for your confidence in me.'

'You are a man to inspire confidence, sir.'

'If that is so, let me inspire you now to stand up for yourself where the Townsend cats and the Langford rat are concerned. You will not be alone, for you and I are both natural allies against them. You have a friend in me, Lady Grenville.'

She smiled at his neat description of the opposition. 'Thank you, Doctor, I will certainly endeavor to improve on my first performance.'

'It was that bad?'

'It was appalling. I was so ineffective that I might as well have not been there. She, as they say, wiped the floor with me. My late Aunt Hazeldon would have been aghast that a kinswoman of hers could be so utterly useless!'

'Maybe Miss Townsend won the first battle, Lady Grenville, but she has not won the war yet.' He took out his fob watch. ' 'Now it is time for me to go to Nicholas. Shall you come with me?'

'Yes.' With Daniel there it would be easier to stand up to Augustine – if she had returned.

To her relief, however, Augustine was not there. Nicholas was awake, but very, very drowsy, and his hand was burning when Laura took it. 'What a poor husband I am to you, Laura,' he whispered, his voice very weak. His face was still deathly pale, the flush of fever confining itself to his cheeks, and there were heavy shadows beneath his eyes. Those eyes, once so penetrating and bright, were dull now and almost lifeless. 'I'm so cold,' he murmured, 'So very cold. . . .' His eyes closed as the laudanum drew him back into unconsciousness.

Chapter 15

An hour or so later Laura left her room to go down to breakfast. She had screwed up her courage, with not a little assistance from the comforting thought that Daniel Tregarron would be there to support her. As she descended the staircase, she noticed that her instructions about removing all signs of mourning had been carried out. The footmen wore no weepers and the bowl of black-edged condolence cards had been taken away. She paused for a moment to look up at the gold ceiling of the vestibule. The Grenville sun in splendor spread its magnificent rays into every corner. . . . 'You're a Grenville now, Laura,' she said softly to herself, 'Act the part!' Then she turned to the double doors of the breakfast room, and the two footmen standing on either side immediately flung them open to admit her.

To her dismay, the first thing she noticed was that Daniel Tregarron had not come down yet. Augustine and her mother presided alone at the table.

They sat at the white-clothed table and they did not even glance around as she entered. Augustine was leaning confidentially toward her mother, although the loud tone she employed was anything but confidential.

'The dreadful creature looked as if she had just emerged from her bed! *Such* a ridiculous sight; she is quite obviously not *au fait* with polite society. No one of consequence would appear in public in her undress. It was quite disgraceful. She can only ever be an embarrassment to King's Cliff and I cannot imagine what Nicholas can have been thinking of in Venice!'

Laura felt the hot stain of red spreading across her cheeks as she went to her seat. Sunlight streamed in through the windows and she could see the beautiful gardens and the cedar trees. Red tulips swayed in the gentle breeze and gardeners were tending the plants around an ornamental pool where a fountain was playing. In the breakfast room, refreshingly decorated in blue and white, there was a pleasant smell of toasted bread and crisp bacon. Hawkins, the chief butler, drew out Laura's chair for her to sit down. Augustine stopped talking and the atmosphere immediately grew heavy.

Mrs Townsend's eyebrows were raised just a little and her face bore an expression that suggested she could detect a disagreeable odor. Laura glanced curiously at her. At one time she must have been almost as beautiful as her daughter, but now she was plump and had lost her looks. Her graying hair was powdered and her ample form tightly laced into a full-skirted gown of dull red and green brocade. A capacious mobcap rested on her head and a fichu of white muslin was tucked into her bodice. She had not moved with the times at all and was still firmly in the eighteenth century of her youth.

The silence continued and was so obviously calculated to be as insulting and hurtful as possible that Laura felt provoked. 'Good morning Mrs Townsend, Miss Townsend.'

No one answered. Mrs Townsend applied herself with great vigor to a plate of sausages, and Augustine nibbled neatly on some toast. Like a rabbit, thought Laura savagely – a very supercilious rabbit!

'I said good morning,' she said, determined to draw a response of some sort.

Mrs Townsend's knife and fork were put down with a clatter. Her pale blue eyes swung at last to Laura. 'I do not think we have anything to say to you, madam. Your presence here is decidedly *de trop*. I see no necessity for any communication with you, for you are beneath contempt and I hardly

dare hazard a guess about your background. Until dear Nicholas is himself
again, however, we are forced to endure you. Apart from taking our meals
with you, which unfortunately cannot be reasonably avoided, we wish to
have nothing whatsoever to do with you. Is that quite clear?'

Laura was astounded that anyone could without provocation be quite so
rude. The woman's arrogance verged on the ridiculous. Laura was determined not to repeat her mistakes of earlier and now could not resist the
temptation of pricking the woman like the balloon she was. 'Oh, it is
perfectly clear to me, madam,' she said sweetly. 'And it is also perfectly clear
that if anyone's background must be questioned, it is surely yours. Only a
very vulgar person could have manners as frightful as yours would appear to
be.'

With an outraged gasp, Mrs Townsend stared at her, every fiber of her
body quivering with fury. Augustine's cool, elegant eyebrow twitched just a
little. 'Ignore the creature, Mama, for to do otherwise would be to lower
oneself to her level. Now then, where were we. . . ? Ah, yes, the court.
Gossip has it that the Princess Mary is to marry the Duke of Gloucester. Of
course, it cannot be a love match, for who could love the duke, and it is said
that she'll marry simply *anyone* to escape the queen, who is so ill-humored
of late. I feel certain we will be invited, which will be some compensation
for having to turn down the invitation to dear Princess Charlotte's nuptials.
If only we had known that Nicholas was not dead after all, we could have
accepted. . . . However, *c'est la vie*, and these things cannot always be
avoided.'

Mrs Townsend threw a last venomous glance at Laura before returning
her attention to her daughter. 'The marriage of the duke and Princess Mary
is hardly adequate compensation for missing out on the marriage of the
future Queen of England, Augustine.'

'I am truly miffed about Princess Charlotte's wedding, I had such a capital notion for a new gown – I was going to have it of that very finest silk and
simply covered with pearls. It would have cost a fortune, but it would have
been so exquisite. However, I will go ahead and order it from that dolt of a
dressmaker, and I shall pray that she makes a finer fit of it than she did of
the mauve wool.'

'She isn't exactly a *court* dressmaker, my dear. I do not know why you
use her. You should go up to London more regularly and order everything
there. The quality always do; I know that I do.'

'She is more convenient.' Augustine smiled. 'I shall be able to wear the
gown at the summer ball. Oh, I'm so looking forward to it, for it will be
quite the most impressive and lavish entertainment ever. We shall invite
simply everyone, *tout le monde* – well, the *beau monde* anyway.' She smiled
coolly. 'I was thinking of being bold enough to write to Prinny himself; after
all, he adores coming here for the shooting, does he not? And what a feather

in our cap he would be – the dear Countess of Bawton will be positively *pinched* if we snap him up.'

'She would indeed, but my dear, if we invite the Prince Regent there will be so many other people who will have to come too. The work will be simply too much.'

'Too much? My dear mama, how can you say that? And if there are many others who accompany him, then what does it matter? King's Cliff has always thrown open its doors to the *ton* and will continue to do so.'

Laura had listened in silence, but now she could not hold her tongue anymore. 'Miss Townsend, I do not think that you should issue any invitations to anyone, for I happen to know that Nicholas intends to cut—'

'I think, Mama,' interrupted Augustine smoothly, 'that I shall ride Lieutenant over to Langford Place this morning.'

'Do you think that wise, my dear? After all, he is such a willful beast.'

And will be ridden by another one, thought Laura, gritting her teeth. This odious pair were far, far worse than she had ever imagined.

'Oh, I am well able to control Lieutenant,' went on Augustine airily. 'There are few horses I cannot manage. Besides, he is a good ride, and will take less time to convey me to the dear earl, who simply must be told what has taken place here. If only he had come into the house last night with us. . . '

'It must have been a shock,' said Laura lightly, 'to come back from all that junketing to find that the man you thought was dead had survived after all. Your light-hearted happiness must have increased tenfold.'

Augustine's mask dropped just a little at the taunt, and fury flashed in her green eyes. 'How *dare* you—!' she began.

'Have a care now,' said Laura, delighted at having drawn blood at last, 'or you will sink to my level, and that would never do.' From the corner of her eye she saw the butler gaping that anyone could dare to speak in such a manner to the imperious Augustine.

With a tremendous effort, Augustine overcame her momentary lapse. The mask slid back into place and she turned back to her mother. 'I believe that we must celebrate dear Nicholas's salvation. I know, we will have the very *grandest* assembly possible. A masquerade! Yes, a masquerade is the very thing!'

'A capital notion,' agreed her mother, taking up her knife and fork again to finish the sausages.

'We can have those hothouse lilies all over the ballroom, and the golden lanterns in the trees in the park, just as we did when dear Sir Jasper was alive. I will have that excellent orchestra from Bath to play for us all and the iced champagne will flow like water!' Augustine's hands were clasped in rapture as she gave her extravagant imagination free rein.

Laura watched the two women in disgust. Were they totally unaware of the dire straits Nicholas was in, she wondered, or did they simply not care? They spoke as if he was the most wealthy landowner in England, not a man facing ruin unless he made some totally devastating changes to the estate he loved so much. Either they were foolish and empty-headed, which she doubted very much, or they were simply callous beyond belief. Yes, she decided, they were callous, for what other conclusion could she come to after having witnessed their behavior the night before. They loved only themselves, attended only to their own advancement and own desires; nothing else mattered. But for all that, she felt she must try again to tell them that their extravagance could not go ahead. 'Miss Townsend, Nicholas will not be able to agree to a masquerade such as you describe, he—'

Augustine's expression was withering. 'Come, Mama, I find the atmosphere in here disagreeable in the extreme.'

Their napkins were flung in unison on to the table, and Hawkins hurried to draw out their chairs. They swept past Laura without another word, the very picture of superiority as they rustled out in a flurry of brocade and muslin.

Laura sipped her coffee in silence. There had been many an uncomfortable meal over the past months, but none so unpleasant as this first breakfast at King's Cliff. Augustine had promised to make her every moment a misery, and that was exactly what she had done so far.

'I'll warrant your thoughts are worth a ha'penny or two.'

She looked up in surprise to see Daniel Tregarron smiling down at her. 'I did not hear you come in, Doctor.'

'I am afraid that I was cowardly enough to wait until the two sourpusses had gone. My digestive system is very delicate and is quite put out at the least hint of fur and claw.'

'There was a little fur flying, and a great deal of claw, I fear.'

'I trust you unsheathed your own claws this time, Lady Grenville,' he said, sitting down.

'I did. It seems, however, to be the order of the day to treat me as if I crawled from beneath a particularly grimy stone – which as far as they are concerned, I suppose, I did.'

'No doubt, but then they consider anyone without an inherited title to be beneath them – which attitude I fail to comprehend as they have not a whisker of title between them.'

She smiled and waited as Hawkins poured her some more coffee. 'Dr Tregarron, how friendly are you with Nicholas?'

He looked at her in surprise. 'I suppose you could say that we are very good friends. Why?'

'Then he must have told you about the financial plight he is in.'

'I know that he was left considerable debts – mortgages, loans from Coutts—'

'Considerable would not seem to be the correct word under the circumstances. Mountainous is more apt. He feels that in order to deal with them he must make swingeing changes here at King's Cliff.'

'*Swingeing*? Surely not—'

'The hounds are to go, and any land which cannot be made profitable. He is also going to have King's Cliff Moor drained and made into farming land.'

A silver platter crashed to the floor as the startled butler fumbled. He was obviously shocked by what he had heard, although he tried to retrieve his composure.

Daniel, too, was shocked. A low whistle escaped his lips. 'The devil he is—'

'He told me in Venice, and he meant every word.'

'Such changes will cause a storm of protest. I cannot think of one neighbor who will not throw up his hands in horrified condemnation. And I'll warrant that Miss Townsend will not receive such tidings at all well. I had no idea things were as bad as that here. Oh, I knew that old Jasper was living beyond his means, but even so I had little notion of the true extent of his debts.'

'I do not know the exact sums involved, Doctor. I only know what Nicholas told me. I saw an account book he had with him, and there was an uncomfortably high number of entries in red ink.'

'Such worries will not speed his recovery,' said Daniel slowly, 'and I fear that they are worries which will weigh him down for some time yet as he is in no condition to attend to them.'

'The situation is pressing, Dr Tregarron.'

'It will have to wait, Lady Grenville. He is by no means over all the hurdles yet.'

'I believe it to be urgent.'

He studied her face for a moment. 'In that case all I can suggest to you is that you see his land agent, Mr Charles Dodswell. He was Sir Jasper's agent too, but do not let that deter you, for he did all he could to dissuade Nicholas's father from his extravagances. He also tried, unsuccessfully, to interest him in the new high farming methods which are so much spoken of these days, but Sir Jasper would have none of it. I know that Nicholas listened a great deal, however.' Daniel smiled. 'As a boy he spent a lot of time with the agent at Home Farm, and indeed I suppose it could be said that Mr Dodswell was more a father to him than Sir Jasper ever was. There is a lot of warmth and understanding between Nicholas and Charles Dodswell, and he was quite devastated by the news of Nicholas's apparent death abroad. He came to the house late last night, the moment he heard what had happened, but Nicholas knew nothing of it.'

'Did Mr Dodswell mention anything to you about Nicholas's problems?'

'No. But he was most insistent that the moment Nicholas was able to see him, he be sent for without delay.'

Laura thought for a moment. 'I think that you are right. Dr Tregarron, I must indeed go to see Mr Dodswell.'

He nodded. 'Would you like me to accompany you, Lady Grenville?'

'I would like that very much.'

Chapter 16

A short while later, Daniel and Laura emerged from the house. Her parasol frills fluttered as the breeze caught them, and the ribbons of her bonnet streamed behind her as she walked. She wore her sprigged muslin gown and a tight green spencer with a fashionable ruff, and she looked as fresh and beautiful as the spring day. There was a smile on her lips, but inside she felt only anxiety and unhappiness; the anxiety was on many scores, but the unhappiness came solely from her unrequited love for Nicholas Grenville. It was Augustine he wanted, and it was Augustine who even now kept a vigil at his bedside.

They walked past the front façade of the house. The grounds were truly magnificent, and looked particularly fine on this warm spring day. The lawns, tended by an industrious line of gardeners, stretched smoothly away to the woods on one side and to the Taunton to Langford road on the other. Some more men were digging over a gravel path, while others pulled a heavy roller to flatten the new surface. Laura wondered idly if one of them was Frank Roberts, Kitty's father. There were flowers everywhere, a blaze of color that dazed the eye with its glory. Red deer browsed by the woods and a skylark tumbled in the blue sky, its trilling song rippling over the countryside in a clear portent of summer. Someone was playing Mozart at the piano in the music room and they caught a glimpse of Mrs Townsend through the opened windows. She played skillfully, and there was not a note out of place. . . .

The sound of the nearby hounds in their impressive kennels made Laura halt. Daniel smiled. 'Would you like to see them?'

'Yes, I believe I would as I have heard so much about them.'

The cluster of low buildings that comprised the kennels was built around a house which, Daniel told her, was occupied by the chief huntsman. The kennels were fairly new and had obviously been built at no small cost, for there seemed not a single convenience lacking. There was no sign of the hounds, for they were shut away in three lodges at the rear of cobbled yards. A number of men and boys went about their business, cleaning the kennels and preparing the feed, but the moment Laura and Daniel entered she became aware of a change in the atmosphere. News of what she had said at the breakfast table had obviously already reached the kennels, and it was not liked, both for the destruction of the hunt and for the uncertainty that now hung over the future livelihoods of those employed to look after the hounds.

She knew all this as she stood by the fence that screened one of the yards listening to the hounds in the lodges, their paws scratching and pattering on the floor. The sound left her cold. She felt no sense of excitement at hearing these famous creatures and the thought of hunting did not arouse her in the slightest.

Daniel noted her unenthusiastic expression. 'Am I to presume that the new mistress of King's Cliff is left unmoved?'

'Completely.'

'For shame,' he teased. 'This is probably the finest pack of hounds in the realm and yet you, Lady Grenville, are on the verge of a yawn.'

She smiled. 'Have you ridden to them, Dr Tregarron?'

'It has been my privilege.'

She looked at him. 'Do you approve of Nicholas's plan to sell them?'

'If his financial predicament is as you say, then he has no choice. They *are* a very expensive plaything, very expensive indeed. As you can see, Sir Jasper spared no expense on the building of these kennels, only the finest materials were used, but the real cost comes from the social side of hunting. The lavish house parties held at King's Cliff are a byword with the *beau monde*, and half the aristocracy of England has at one time lodged here, enjoying the breakfast meets where barons of beef were as numerous as days in the week and venison pies were of a legendary succulence. When the gentlemen hunted, their ladies remained behind, and so entertainment had to be provided for them. The cost of King's Cliff hospitality must have been as astounding over the years, and there was not a penny of subscription to meet the bills. The estate shouldered the entire burden and from what you tell me, it was bowing beneath the weight. Yes, Lady Grenville, I approve of what Nicolas wishes to do and can well understand his fervent desire to be rid of the encumbrance.'

Laura gazed at the lodges, built so excellently, emulating the style of the big house. . . . Whether it was by accident or design, she did not know, but at that moment the lodges were opened and the blue-mottled hounds bounded out, yelping and snapping excitedly as they rushed to the fence. Standing on their hind legs, their forepaws on the wood, they set up a howl for their daily feed. Startled, and not a little frightened, Laura stepped hastily back from them.

Daniel took her arm swiftly. 'Don't be afraid, they cannot come out.'

'I know. It's just. . . . Oh, I don't know.' She glanced across at a group of unsmiling men.

'Come; enough of mere canines. We have Mr Charles Dodswell to beard in his den.'

'Yes.'

They left the kennels and walked on, taking the gravel path which led beside the lodges toward a high box hedge that screened what lay beyond. Daniel pushed open a wicket gate where the purple spikes of lilac swayed in the breeze and the heady perfume of wallflowers filled the air. The wicket gate led to a path flanked by more high hedges, and Laura looked back at the house before proceeding. She could see the window of Nicholas's room.

Her eyes downcast then, she accompanied Daniel along the path. Thoughts of Augustine, sitting so adoringly at Nicholas's side, filled her head. Laura had remained in the room for only a little while, for she had been unable to endure watching Augustine's masterly performance as she wilted just a little as she leaned over him, weeping bravely if he happened to awake, and whispering her undying love. . . .

'I trust the hounds have not upset you, Lady Grenville,' said Daniel, seeing her withdrawn face.

'No.'

'Then perhaps I have said something . . .'

She smiled at him. 'No, Dr Tregarron, it isn't anything you have said. I was merely thinking of Nicholas and Miss Townsend.'

'It is within your power to order her from his room.'

'Possibly, but I do not think that will help – it certainly will not help him to recover, for I know that it is her he wishes to see, not me.'

'If you believe that, why do you remain here?'

'Because I am his wife and I love him. Until I hear from his own lips that he does not want me here, I will stay and I will do all I can to aid and uphold him. Can you understand that, Doctor?'

'I understand that you are a very remarkable woman, as well as a very beautiful one, and that if Nicholas is fool enough to prefer Augustine Townsend, then the bullet which grazed his head must have affected his intelligence!'

'You are very kind to me, Dr Tregarron.'

He glanced at her but said nothing more. They walked on in silence toward a thick copse of trees that darkened the path ahead. The hedges ended abruptly and they were in a small wood where bluebells were in bloom and the wild flowers nodded their delicate heads as the gentle breeze whispered over them. Suddenly they were in the sunshine again, standing on the edge of the escarpment on which King's Cliff stood, and Laura halted in surprise on seeing Sedgemoor itself for the first time.

Three hundred feet below, at the foot of the escarpment, the marsh's silent acres led away to an indistinct haze by a line of hills that struck out from the west. Enclosed by hills on two sides, the triangle of the moor owned by King's Cliff was smooth and green, broken here and there by trees and by the flash of sunlight on water. The tall marsh grass undulated in long, rhythmic waves, as if the sea itself had gradually turned from water into this lush vegetation, which harbored waterfowl and provided some of the finest shooting in the land. The comparison with the sea was accentuated by a small hill that rose like an island in the distance. She could make out a line of cows on the hill and a man driving them slowly toward a small farm by some elm trees.

Pollarded willows were the only trees of note on the marsh itself, growing by the sometimes seen, sometimes unseen water which was almost everywhere beneath the screen of grass. She stared, spellbound. It was a landscape to bewitch the beholder, for after the rolling hills, it was so completely, so hauntingly different. And yet if Nicholas went ahead with his plans, it would all be changed. . . .

Daniel pointed away to the north. 'The marsh is said to shelter the spirits of the dead from the battle of Sedgemoor in 1685. The Duke of Monmouth's army met its end not far from here.'

She followed the line of his finger, and her gaze fell on a stark monument built on a spur of escarpment that struck out like a headland over the sea. 'Does that commemorate the battle?'

'No, that is the Townsend memorial. It was erected by Nicholas's great-grandfather, Sir Henry, the first Grenville to own King's Cliff, in honor of his predecessor, James Townsend.'

'Oh.'

'It is a very handsome edifice, is it not?'

'It is. It is also a constant reminder of their grievances to the present members of the Townsend family,' she said tartly.

'I suppose it is.'

'How very foolish of Sir Henry,' she remarked, her parasol twirling as she followed the path down the hillside toward the marsh far below. She could see ahead the roofs and barns of the Home Farm, dwelling of Mr Charles Dodswell. The farm looked out over the marsh, and the garden of the farmhouse stretched up the escarpment behind.

They were shown into the agent's office, where they were greeted by a thin, stooping man who was, she guessed, somewhere in his fifties. His gray wig was askew, as she was to learn it usually was, and he had pushed an ink-stained quill behind his ear as if their arrival had interrupted his work. He hastened to remove a pile of seal-hung documents from a chair, dusting the seat with his spotted kerchief so that she could sit down.

The room lay at the back of the house and was consequently away from the sunlight. It smelled damp and there was a slight chill in the air. A map of King's Cliff hung on the wall above the small fireplace and the window overlooked the garden, although the escarpment rose so sharply that very little but grass could be seen. The room was as dusty as the agent himself and was littered with ledgers and legal documents, for like many land agents, Mr Dodswell was a lawyer too.

Now he positioned himself behind the untidy desk, which was the room's principal item of furniture, and waited. 'How may I be of service to you, Lady Grenville?' he asked at last.

She could tell that he did not quite know what to make of her. Being as close to Nicholas as he was, her arrival on the scene and the circumstances under which it had occurred must obviously be somewhat bewildering. Did he, as would others, believe she had married Nicholas simply to enrich herself?

'Mr Dodswell, I wish to acquaint myself with the financial affairs of the estate.'

'But, I don't understand—'

'I know that all is not well, sir, and I know that you wish to see my husband as soon as he is able. Therefore I wish to learn as much as possible myself in order that I may see if there is anything I can do while my husband remains so ill.'

The agent looked ill at ease, glancing at Daniel and then back at her. 'Forgive me, Lady Grenville, but I gave my word to Sir Nicholas before he departed for Venice that I would say absolutely nothing to anyone until he returned and had decided what exactly to do.'

'Charles,' reproved Daniel, 'it is Nicholas's wife to whom you speak.'

'I am well aware of that, Daniel Tregarron, but a man's word is his bond.'

Laura glanced sharply at him. 'And a man's wife is his right hand, sir.'

'I did not mean to suggest—' the agent began hastily.

'My first responsibility and duty is to my husband and therefore to this estate too. He saw fit to confide in me, telling me of the troubles besetting him and what he wished to do about putting things right. Maybe he did not expect to survive and maybe there was no thought in his head that his marriage to me would last beyond one night, but the fact is that it has. I am his wife and I am proud to be so, and I have nursed him and brought him home to the house he loves so much. You surely do not imagine that I think my duty is done now and that I will sit back and twiddle my thumbs? That is not how I am made, Mr Dodswell, and I think that you should realize that.'

A ghost of a smile touched the agent's thin lips. 'I begin to, my lady.'

'Do you still feel bound by your word?'

'How can I, when you obviously know a great deal already, and you know it from Sir Nicholas's lips? I will tell you all you wish to know, but I do not think there is anything anyone can do about it until Sir Nicholas is well again.'

'Maybe not, but I still wish to be *au fait* with everything.'

'Sir Jasper, as you know, left mountainous debts, some of which Sir Nicholas has been able to meet.'

'How?'

'By selling items of value from the house. There is one particularly alarming debt still outstanding, however, and that is to a certain moneylender in London whose reputation is not at all savory.'

'How large is the debt?'

'Twenty thousand guineas.'

She stared at him. 'So much?'

'Sir Jasper had been living well beyond his means for some time. At first he resorted to the usual practice of falsifying his returns to the Treasury, raising mortgages here and there – and finally everywhere – and so on, but gradually he came to need more and more to sustain the white elephant which was King's Cliff and to sustain his own wildly impractical way of life. He went frequently to London with the Earl of Langford, simply to visit the gaming hells, where he proceeded to lose vast sums night after night. The estate could only support this for a short while, for it is not productive enough to maintain such extravagance. In the end Sir Jasper was foolish enough to fall into the clutches of a moneylender.'

The agent sighed. 'And all the time something could have been done to make King's Cliff more profitable, but the land is turned almost entirely to the needs and pleasures of fox hunting. The farms are let to tenants who are, like Sir Jasper, enthusiastic about hunting, and vast stretches of good land are simply left – or cleared to provide long rides. There is no sign of the new methods of high farming here, Lady Grenville, no sign at all. Even King's Cliff Moor, which could be so fertile, is left undrained. Most of Sedgemoor has been drained, but not here. The medieval drainage system, built by monks back in the mists of time, has been allowed to fall into disrepair, with the result that here you will find the finest shooting in the county. Waterfowl and fish abound, and it is quite the thing to come down to King's Cliff for a stay. The only persons to benefit financially have been the considerable horde of poachers who inhabit the town of Langford. King's Cliff eels and birds find their way to tables where they have no right to be found. And all I can do is stand by and watch it all happen, because until now the master of the house has seen fit to allow it all. Sir Jasper was blind to everything but the glorification of both himself and King's Cliff, and he was encouraged in every way by the Earl of Langford and, I am sorry to say, by Miss Townsend and her mother. They wallowed in that reflected glory, and could not see it for what it truly was – the ruining of a fine and ancient estate. The heedless extravagance went on and on, and neither my voice nor that of Sir Nicholas was listened to. Being land agent to a man like Sir Jasper Grenville was a bitter, frustrating, and unrewarding experience, my lady, but how much worse must it have been for his son?

'Forgive me for speaking my mind, Lady Grenville, but Sir Jasper was an unnatural father, making his preference for his brother's son only too plain. In Sir Nicholas he had so very much, but he chose to forfeit it. I love Sir Nicholas; indeed I have come to look upon him as the son I never had, and I see in him the will and determination to bring this estate, which is his birthright, to its feet again. I admire him greatly and will willingly stay here to assist him. I endured here because of him, and when I thought he had been killed. . . .' The agent's voice died away, his glance falling on some neat piles of papers on a shelf.

They were too neat for Mr Dodswell, she thought, and then realized quite suddenly that they were like that because he had been setting everything in order. He had been intending to leave King's Cliff, because without Nicholas the estate did not matter. 'Mr Dodswell,' she said gently, 'I too endure because of him.'

He smiled at her. 'Of that I have no doubt, my lady.'

'Tell me, Mr Dodswell, how long will it be before the debt to the moneylender falls due?'

'Unfortunately it is overdue now, and that is why I was so anxious to see Sir Nicholas.' He smiled again. 'Until yesterday I believed the estate to have fallen into the clutches of the Earl of Langford, and so could not have cared less about the debt – I feel very little but dislike for the Earl. However, with Sir Nicholas alive still, the matter changes dramatically. I must see him, to have his permission to sell something of value in order to stave off the duns. Mr Peterson of London is the most notorious and most pitiless of all his tribe, and he will show no mercy at all. Sir Nicholas must be made aware of how dangerous the situation is.'

Daniel looked sharply at him. 'He cannot be worried, not in his present state. The calmer and more relaxed he is, the better for his recovery—'

'I understand, Daniel, but you must understand my anxiety. However, until I actually receive a communication from Peterson, no doubt things can be left in abeyance. One thing is for sure, the Earl of Langford will not give his permission for anything that might yet come to him to be sold, no matter what the reason!'

'The Earl of Langford?' asked Laura. 'But what has it to do with him?'

'Unfortunately,' said the agent, 'there is a long-standing arrangement within the Grenville family for each head of a household to come to the aid of a kinsman or kinswoman at time of distress, such as illness as in this case. Sir Nicholas is obviously not in any state to run King's Cliff for himself, and so the responsibility falls upon the earl. There is nothing which can be done about it – for the moment the earl is in command of King's Cliff's affairs. Legally, that is. As to the moral aspect, well that is quite another matter. James Grenville was quite openly delighted to learn of Sir Nicholas's apparent demise, and he has already been making preparations for taking over here – indeed, his intention was to quit Langford Place, which is not so fine a dwelling, and to live here. No doubt with Miss Townsend as his bride.' The agent's face told volumes of his low opinion of both the earl and Augustine, for distaste and dislike twisted his thin lips for a moment.

They were silent for a while, and then Laura spoke again. 'So, Mr Dodswell, for the moment there is nothing we can do?'

'Nothing – unless Sir Nicholas himself expresses his wish.'

'And he must not be told anything which will cause him stress.' She looked at Daniel, who immediately nodded.

'Mr Dodswell, is the debt to this Mr Peterson the only one now outstanding?' she asked.

'The only one of any urgency. Coutts, the bankers, are awaiting payment, but they will not press while Sir Nicholas is so very ill. It would be infinitely better to implement any changes Sir Nicholas wishes to make here immediately, but obviously that cannot be helped. The changes must wait.' He picked up a small sheaf of notes. 'Before he left for Venice, he asked me to draw up a list of every parcel of unprofitable and useless land, every item of unnecessary equipment, every surplus hand employed by the estate – and there are a considerable number – in short, everything which can be dispensed with. I have completed that list. I know that he intends selling the hounds, draining the marsh, and so on, for he had come to that conclusion before he left and went away merely to put everything into perspective in his own mind. I know what must be done and what he wishes to have done, but without his hand at the helm there is absolutely nothing I can do about it. The Earl of Langford holds sway here for the time being, and he will not agree to anything at all which will change King's Cliff.'

'And there is nothing at all which can be done?'

'The man in me wishes there was, but the lawyer tells me there is not. The law upholds the earl in this.'

She nodded. 'Then I must accept the situation, must I not? But at least I can learn a little about the running of an estate like this. There are estate books which will inform me?'

'There are a great many books, Lady Grenville, but I must warn you that although I find them most interesting and informative, you may find them decidedly dry. Informatiion about the valuing of tithes, stock, and crops, the marking, measuring, and selling of timber, complaints from tenants, and guidelines for the taking on of new tenants are hardly enjoyable reading for a lady.'

'We do not all read only Gothic novels, I promise you. I will try my best to find them interesting, Mr Dodswell,' she said with a slight smile, getting to her feet and preparing to leave.

'We have kept you from your work for long enough. Will you have some ledgers and books sent to me at the house?'

'I will, Lady Grenville. Lady Grenville. . . ?'

'Yes?'

'I have not welcomed you to King's Cliff, but belatedly I do so now. I see that Sir Nicholas has been very fortunate in his bride.'

'He would have been infinitely more fortunate had I been wealthy, Mr Dodswell, but I bring nothing to King's Cliff, nothing at all.'

'Except yourself,' he said gallantly.

'Well, that is not a very great contribution on my part, is it? Good day, Mr Dodswell.'

'Good day, Lady Grenville.'

He watched her go out and then looked at Daniel, who was putting on his hat and gloves. 'I was guilty of grave prejudgment where she was concerned, Daniel, for I believed that she could only be a scheming adventuress. I quickly perceived how wrong I was, for she is every inch a lady of quality, and she is so obviously in love with her husband.'

'But is he in love with her, that is the question?'

The agent nodded sadly. 'His wife is worth a thousand Augustine Townsends.'

'I'll drink to that,' said Daniel softly.

'Remember that she is another man's wife, my friend. I know you well enough to recognize that look in your eye when you watch her.'

'What man could not desire her? As to remembering that she is Nicholas Grenville's wife, I do not see how I can damned well forget it. Oh, but it would be good to suffer a little amnesia!' Daniel grinned at the agent. 'Good day to you, Charles.'

'Good day, Daniel.'

Chapter 17

As Laura and Daniel came within sight of the house again, they saw immediately that Augustine's ride to Langford Place later that morning would no longer be necessary, for word had already reached the furious earl who had immediately driven over to see for himself what was happening on an estate which only the night before he had believed to be his own at last.

Laura looked with some trepidation at the landau with its fine team of

whites, and Daniel reassuringly put his hand over the small fingers that
rested on his arm. They entered the house and Hawkins immediately came
forward.

'My lady, the Earl of Langford expects you to attend him in the library at
one o'clock.'

'Thank you, Hawkins.' She glanced at Daniel. 'He expects that *I* attend
him? Oh, he does indeed regard this house as his, doesn't he?'

He took out his fob watch. 'You have half an hour in which to fume.'

She smiled. 'And fume I will. I will also take myself to my room to
change. Shall you go to Nicholas now?'

'Yes.'

'I will come there directly my ordeal is over.'

He watched her ascend the staircase. How small and lost she looked, and
how desperately vulnerable, for all her brave talk. Charles Dodswell's words
came into his head again. 'Daniel, my laddo,' he admitted to himself, 'You
do indeed begin to covet that which is not yours.'

Laura's route took her past the red saloon, and as its door was not properly
closed she heard low voices inside. She stopped, recognizing Augustine's
voice.

'But I beg of you, James—'

'I will not be made a fool of, madam; nor will I allow you to forget that
which you are party to.'

'That was uncalled for!'

'Was it? I think not, and it would seem that a timely reminder is quite in
order under the circumstances.'

'You are only saying these things because you are angry that Nicholas is
alive.'

'Angry? I am damned well furious! And your decision now, madam, does
little to soothe that anger.'

Mrs Townsend spoke then. 'My lord, I do not think you are at all fair
with my daughter.'

'What has being fair to do with this? Is she fair with me? Well – is she?
There, you cannot give me an answer, because you know that she is not. I
am not fool enough to think that over the past weeks she has encouraged
me because she has miraculously fallen in love with me! She has welcomed
my advances simply and solely because of this house – oh, and maybe also
because of my wealth and title. But it is the house which sways her, isn't
it? I have accepted that, because I cannot expect anything else, for I have
not the looks and charm of my elegant cousin! What I cannot and will not
accept, however, is her return to his side after what has passed between
us.'

'But I have not returned to his side,' protested Augustine, with an air of innocence Laura could only admire. 'How can I when he has a wife now?'

'An unconsummated marriage can be set aside, as you and I both know full well. So I think we may forget this so-called wife, don't you? It is quite obvious to me that the moment he is well enough, he will wish to rid himself of an unwanted marriage, and that he will then take you as his bride.'

'James, how can I convince you that I am true to you now? I have every intention of becoming your wife the moment your two years of mourning for your first wife are over. In six months' time your ring will be on my finger, but in the meantime I must ask you to allow me to conduct my affairs as I see fit.'

'Would to God I could believe you. . . .'

'You *can* believe me.'

'Prove it then by agreeing to let our former agreement stand.'

'It would not look well.'

'Since when has that concerned you? Augustine, I swear that unless you do as I demand now, then I will work against you, and believe me, that is no idle threat.'

'Against me? In what way?' Augustine's voice was suddenly very wary.

'By openly and warmly welcoming the new Lady Grenville. By effecting introductions for her, by generally signifying my approval and thus making it very difficult indeed for Nicholas to cast her off.'

'You would not do that!'

'But I would, Augustine. I love you and have done so for longer than I care to mention, for my wife was certainly alive when first I wanted you. It is my desire for you which drives me so far – why else do you imagine that I sought to—?'

'Don't!' she cried. 'Don't say it aloud, not here in this house!'

'Why not? Because it offends you? Come now.' He gave a short, cold laugh.

At the door Laura felt the mirthless chill of that laugh, and she shivered. Her mind was racing. What was he referring to? What had he done that so frightened Augustine now?

He spoke again. 'I mean it when I say I will work against you, my dear, and I urge you to think carefully on it, for if Nicholas's marriage remains intact, then what will there be for you? I promise you that you will not be able to turn to me. You will have nothing, Augustine, absolutely nothing.'

She was at her most persuasive and convincing then. 'James, you have no need to threaten me or to doubt me. Your fears are not justified, for I promise you that when the time comes I will become your wife.'

'If I have fears, they are of your causing. Allay them now once and for all by allowing the arrangement made yesterday, before all this happened, to go ahead as originally planned.'

What arrangement? Laura could not even begin to guess what they were talking about, but she did know that all that she had overheard in the red saloon was of great moment.

Augustine still hesitated over her answer, and the seconds ticked leadenly by as the earl waited. 'Very well,' she said at last, 'I will come to Taunton, but I will need to make a very convincing excuse—'

'You will succeed in that, my dear, I am sure.'

'I do love you, James, please do not think that I do not.'

'With the answer you have just given me, Augustine, how can I doubt you?'

'Will you take some more coffee with us, my lord?' inquired Mrs Townsend, and Laura distinctly heard the chink of a silver coffeepot against a porcelain cup.

'I fear I cannot, dear lady, as I have to see my cousin's upstart of a wife shortly, and before then I wish to see that damned valet Henderson, to find out exactly what did happen in Venice. Something is very wrong somewhere, as I think both you and I know only too well. I will not be tricked by anyone, not by *anyone*!' His heavy steps approached the door and then stopped again. 'By the way, I fear I have something to tell you which will not please you at all. You will not receive an invitation to the Duke of Gloucester's marriage ceremony.'

'Not?' Augustine's disappointment was evident. 'Why?'

'Because of your recent connection with me, my dear. The duke and I have never seen eye to eye, and the last time I was in London I am afraid that I crossed him severely, something the duke is not a man to forgive. However, you will soon have your own wedding arrangements to make, will you not? I promise you a wedding as grand as the duke and Princess Mary's, and I promise you guests of as great consequence.' He came toward the door again.

Laura glanced fearfully around. Where could she hide? She saw a small adjoining passageway and gathered her skirts to hurry to the shadows there, just as the door opened fully and the earl emerged. She did not see him, however, for he turned in the opposite direction, his slow, careful steps echoing as he walked along the main gallery.

In the red saloon, the two women continued to talk, and the door remained just that little bit open so that once again Laura could hear what they said.

Mrs Townsend's voice was decidedly anxious. 'I think, Augustine, that you would do better to stay with the earl—'

'And lose this house and Nicholas Grenville? Never!'

'The house is not more important than your own future, my dear.'

'My future will always be connected with this house; nothing else matters to me. Except perhaps Nicholas. I swear that I did not know how much I wanted him until I thought him dead.' Augustine's voice was soft.

'He has taken another woman as his wife, and if he survives his present setbacks, there is nothing to say he will not wish to keep her.'

Augustine was scornful. 'You think she is capable of taking him from me? *No one* can take from me that which I wish to keep – and I wish to keep Nicholas Grenville.'

'And if he dies? The earl may see through you yet, Augustine, for you play a dangerous game with him. We both know how far he will go, don't we?'

There was a silence then and Laura knew that her mother's words had had an effect on Augustine. But the moment was short, and Augustine's supreme confidence and vanity returned. 'I know what I am doing, Mama. Believe me. Whatever happens, if Nicholas lives or dies, I will have this house. I want to live here as Nicholas's wife, but if that is not to be, then I will live here as the Countess of Langford. But now, enough of this, let us turn to more cheering and immediate matters. . . .'

They began to talk about arrangements for the masquerade they intended holding, and Laura walked on, turning over and over in her mind what she had heard. What dark secret of the earl's had Augustine and her mother decided to condone? And what arrangement was it that would take Augustine to Taunton? But all the questions remained unanswered as she reached her own room and called for Kitty.

Chapter 18

The earl was alone in the galleried library when she arrived, and he looked oddly out of place among the sedate shelves of leather-bound volumes, for the room was elegant and tasteful, which James Grenville, Earl of Langford, most certainly was not.

His corpulent shape was unfortunately emphasized by his fashionably tight turquoise coat and by the Apollo corset he quite obviously wore beneath. The corset attempted unsuccessfully to draw in his vanished waist and to puff out his chest, but the effect was alarming, as if at any moment his restrained figure would burst free of the confines which held it. He wore cossack trousers, a fashion he had eagerly adopted in 1814, two years previously, when the czar had visited England. Their loose, baggy style was decidedly at odds with his tightly corseted upper half, making him look as if everything that was squeezed so much above his waist had somehow sagged beneath to fill out his posterior and his legs. What hair he had was arranged in hyacinthine curls through which gleamed a great deal of pink scalp, the backs of his hands were blanched, there was rouge on his cheeks and lips, and he surveyed her critically through a quizzing glass. He looked quite ridiculous, although she knew he was far from being that in actual fact.

His shrewd, sharp eyes moved slowly over her, his lips curled disagreeably, and he did not offer her any civility, neither greeting her cordially nor asking her to be seated. They stood facing each other.

'Madam, I wish to make things abundantly clear to you from the outset. In your husband's incapacity, *I* am legally the master here.'

'I am aware of that.'

'I'll warrant you are. By God, madam, you astound me. You come here, no doubt expecting to be treated like a lady, and then you subject Miss Townsend and her mother to a quite appalling display of ill humor and vulgarity!'

Laura stiffened, not bothering to hide the loathing she felt for him.

'A *lady*!' he went on. 'When it is quite obvious that that is the *last* thing you are.'

'And what do you mean by that remark?' she asked coldly, loathing him more and more with each passing second.

'I mean that your actions hitherto have hardly been those of a person of quality, have they? You brazenly contrived to marry a man who was believed to be on his deathbed, and who may yet die, simply to ensure for yourself the comforts of a wealthy life!'

'How *dare* you, you of all lamentable creatures, dare to point a finger at me when your own conduct is far more iniquitous! You made no secret of your delight when you heard that Nicholas was dead, which fact is a clear indication that you are a very base coin, sirrah! As to my conduct with Miss Townsend and her mother, all I can say is that when it comes to vulgarity, they leave me at the post! All three of you are the most despicable insects it has ever been my misfortune to encounter, for I swear that I did not believe anyone could be as low as you.'

'Hold your tongue!' he cried, his rage erupting viciously as he raised his hand to strike her.

She held her ground. 'Strike me if you wish, for that would be further proof of your cowardly nature.'

His whole body trembled, gripped by powerful, barely controlled emotion, and his small eyes were very bright and dangerous, but he did not strike her; instead he vented his wrath upon a vase, sweeping it from the table so that it shattered against the shelves.

She was frightened, but she did not move or show that he had any effect upon her. Looking into his eyes at that moment, however, she knew that he was capable of sinking to any depth, of committing any crime in order to have what he wanted. She found herself wondering again what it was that he had done that so frightened Augustine and her mother now.

After a long, tense moment, he recovered, assuming his former arrogant stance. 'This interview is at an end, madam. Remember only that although you bear my cousin's name, as far as I am concerned, and as far as Miss Townsend and her mother are concerned, you have no rights at all.'

She said nothing, turning on her heel and leaving the library without a backward glance.

She had not reached Nicholas's room before she found her way barred by Augustine. A cool smile touched the perfect lips. 'I trust you enjoyed your interview, my *lady*.'

Laura did not deign to reply, she was so filled with disgust still after her encounter with James Grenville. She began to walk on.

Augustine's yellow muslin gown hissed a little as she turned, and the ribbons moved against the shining red hair. 'You cannot hope to succeed, you know; any plan you may have is doomed from the outset. I already know from Nicholas's own lips that he doesn't want you, that he wishes he had never, in a moment of great stress, taken you as his wife.'

Laura halted, hiding the pain that stabbed through her. 'You seem certain that he will remain ignorant about you, Miss Townsend. It could be that you underestimate him.'

'It is you who underestimates me. I play my cards with great skill, I assure you, and I simply cannot lose with the excellent hand I have. If Nicholas survives, then he and this house are mine. If he dies, then there is the earl, who wants me so very much and who is also providentially Nicholas's heir.'

'You are sure of the earl, are you?' asked Laura, not daring to be too clever, for that might convey to Augustine that she had maybe overheard something she should not.

'I am sure of my ability to gain whatever end I wish, whether it be your husband, or his cousin.'

'Are you not fearful that you may be overheard?'

'Who is there here but yourself, *my lady*? And of what consequence are you? None whatsoever. Good day, my *lady*.' With a swish of costly muslin, she continued on her way, leaving Laura to gaze after her.

Unbidden, Augustine's taunting words returned. *I already know from Nicholas's own lips that he doesn't want you, that he wishes he had never, in a moment of great stress, taken you as his wife. . . .* She bit her lip, fighting back the tears. Let it not be true that he had said that, please let it not be true. . . .

Slowly she walked on What else could she in her heart expect, though? It was Augustine he loved, and it was Augustine he would want at his side. She hesitated at his door, dreading that she would see in his eyes that he had indeed said those words. Taking a deep breath then, she forced herself to go inside.

Daniel was inspecting the dressing on Nicholas's arm. 'I will endeavor to cause as little distress as possible,' he said, beginning to undo the bandage.

Nicholas nodded slightly, turning his head to look at Laura as she went to the bedside. She saw how he shivered still, but not as violently as before. His eyes were so very tired and dull, but although they bore witness to the great strain he had been under over the past weeks, she could read nothing else in them. Carefully, Daniel tried to remove the final portion of bandage, but he inevitably disturbed the wound so that Nicholas gasped as an excruciating pain washed over him, draining his face of what little color it had and bringing the perspiration instantly to his forehead.

Daniel worked as swiftly as possible, putting on a fresh dressing and fastening it firmly. He straightened then. 'Forgive me, I did my best.'

'I know.' Nicholas began to shiver again, and his voice was a whisper.

'You must take some more bark.'

'I'm awash with the stuff.'

'You won't drown, I promise you.' Daniel smiled as he poured some liquid from the jug and held the cup to Nicholas's pale lips. 'The fever is down a little, and in a day or so it will be gone.'

'And then?'

'Then we consider removing the ball from your arm. You know that I would not attempt anything unless I thought it vital.'

Nicholas nodded a little, looking at Laura. 'Is all well?'

She felt Daniel's warning look and smiled. 'Yes, Nicholas.'

He seemed to relax then, and Daniel took up a phial of laudanum. 'I think that I should administer some more of this, Nicholas.'

'Do your worst.'

Nicholas closed his eyes when he had taken the laudanum, and a little later Daniel drew Laura out into the passageway, closing the door.

'How was the noble earl?'

'Odious in the extreme.'

'What had he to say?'

'That he was master of the house for the time being and that I had no rights whatsoever as far as he was concerned.'

He nodded. 'From what Charles Dodswell says, he is within his rights to say that.'

'And there is nothing which can be done about it?'

'Only if we risk telling Nicholas how bad things are, and as his doctor I cannot allow that to happen. You do understand, don't you, Lady Grenville?'

She smiled up into his dark eyes. 'Of course I do.'

He kissed her hand. 'I wonder if Nicholas Grenville knows how lucky a man he is?'

She drew her hand away slowly. 'You do my bruised pride much good, Dr Tregarron.' She turned then as Hawkins approached. 'Yes?'

'My lady, the ledgers and books you requested from Mr Dodswell have arrived. Where do you wish them to be placed?'

'In my room.'

'Very well, my lady.'

Daniel looked at her. 'Charles was right, you know, you *will* find them dry reading.'

'Maybe.'

'Positively.'

She smiled.

'You are too pale, Lady Grenville; I prescribe an invigorating ride this afternoon. And as your doctor, I will ride with you to make certain the treatment works.' He held up a strict finger. 'No, I will not hear any argument. We ride together this afternoon.'

'But—'

'This afternoon.' He left her, going back into Nicholas's room.

'But I haven't a riding habit,' she said to the closed door.

Luncheon in the presence of the earl and the Townsend cats was too much, and any doubt Laura may have had about the advisability of riding in a gown fled out of the window. At the appointed time, she presented herself on the portico steps. Daniel was waiting for her, and a groom held the reins of two horses.

Daniel's eyes swept over her. 'A gown for riding?'

'I tried to tell you, but you wouldn't listen.'

'Doctors never listen to stubborn patients who argue with their diagnoses.' He took her hand and then lifted her lightly up on to the saddle of the smaller horse. 'Maybe we should be discreet and ride only in Langford Woods – the teacups would positively thunder if word of your delightful ankles should get out.'

She smiled. 'After that odious luncheon, I could not care less.'

'That's the spirit.'

The ride did indeed do her good. There was something so satisfying about riding a good horse on a fine, warm afternoon, in woods where the bluebells made a carpet of color beneath the fresh green branches.

They said very little as they rode, and she was glad of his companionable silence. She felt very easy in his company, had from the outset, and she wondered about his private life. Surely there was a sweetheart, for a man as good-looking as Daniel Tregarron would not be without female admirers.

They returned to the house, and to her relief she saw the earl's landau departing. How good it would be if the Townsend cats were with him, but that was not to be, for they were waving from the steps.

They had gone inside when the two horses were reined in by the portico and Daniel dismounted, then helped Laura down. His hands remained on her waist for a moment as he looked at her. 'There are roses in your cheeks, my lady, and I do believe my prescription has proved a sovereign remedy for your melancholy.'

'I do feel a lot better, it is true.'

He removed his hands then. 'We must ride together again.'

'I would like that. Thank you.' She turned to go up the steps into the house.

He watched her until she passed from sight. Holding her waist like that had brought forth damnable temptation, for it would have been so easy to draw her close and place a kiss upon those sweet lips. After a moment he handed the reins to a waiting groom and then followed her into the house.

Chapter 19

A week passed, and for Laura it was a desperately miserable time, for she was completely at the mercy of Augustine and her mother. She was also forced to suffer at the hands of James Grenville, who saw to it that he made frequent visits to King's Cliff. His impotent fury at having the estate plucked from his clutches was a terrible thing, and Laura found him quite abhorrent. Had he said aloud that he wished Nicholas dead, he could not have been more plain. Augustine's attitude was scarcely palatable either, for she made every opportunity to be with Nicholas, but if the earl should come to King's Cliff, then she was most careful not to raise his suspicions about her activities. Between them all, they did everything they could to make Laura's position untenable, and it was obvious to her that nothing would suit them more than that she should bow beneath it all and leave King's Cliff. Had it not been for Daniel Tregarron's comforting and uplifting presence, she felt she would indeed have sunk beneath it all. At the worst moments she called upon her memory of that one day in Venice when everything had been so very good and when it had seemed so right that they should be together.

Nicholas's progress was slow but steady. The malaria seemed to have almost faded, although Daniel warned that it was an ague that recurred when least expected – particularly at times of stress. And so nothing was said to Nicholas about the estate's problems, and when he asked Laura about such things, she was careful to reassure him. He still had a slight temperature, and from time to time the shivering returned, but it was nothing like the first attack on board the *Cygnet*. The Jesuits' bark was no longer being administered, and Daniel only gave him laudanum now, to deaden the immense pain from his badly wounded arm. The wound itself remained blessedly clean, although Daniel was fearful that it would after all become putrid before he felt Nicholas was ready to endure the operation. Where the baron's bullet had grazed Nicholas's temple, there was only a scar now, a scar which would remain with him for the rest of his life.

With Augustine guarding him so closely, there were few opportunities for Laura to be alone with him. She was reduced to seizing her chance the moment the earl chose to call, and to creeping to his bedside during the night. Sometimes he was awake on these occasions, but mostly the laudanum made him sleep. Sleep, said Daniel, was a great healer. . . . Haunted by Augustine's revelations, Laura sought desperately to discover if indeed it was true that he wished their marriage to be set aside as soon as possible, but there was nothing in his manner to tell her anything. He said very little, but when he smiled at her and inquired about her own health and well-being, she simply could not believe that Augustine had been telling the truth. Always mindful of Daniel's warning, Laura made herself appear cheerful and buoyant, but inside she felt far from either emotion.

Each day she saw Mr Dodswell, fearful that the post would produce the dreaded communication from Mr Peterson, the moneylender, but so far there had been nothing. It was a sword of Damocles hanging over them, a sword made all the more sharp and quivering by the senseless extravagance, which still continued unabated, of James Grenville and the two Townsend cats.

Taking her meals with them had proved far too unpleasant, and so Laura now took her meals in the library, and there, to her great pleasure, she was joined by Daniel, who still remained at the house while Nicholas was so ill. They had repeated their afternoon ride several times now, and on each occasion she had to admit that she felt better on her return to the house than she had at the outset. The heavy atmosphere in the house, the hatred of the two women, the vitriolic spite of the earl, and the constant fear that Nicholas would take a turn for the worse took its daily toll on her. The roses in her cheeks gained by the rides had faded again after an hour or so back in the house. She told herself that she was a fool to remain, that she would receive no thanks when it was all over, but she could not bring herself to desert Nicholas. In spite of all the barriers she could see rising all around her, she still felt far too much for him to be able to go.

Mr Dodswell's estate books and ledgers proved heavy going, but she labored each night in her room, and the consequence was that she found herself discovering more and more about the house over which she was titular mistress. One thing she learned immediately was that Augustine Townsend's family had no claim whatsoever to King's Cliff, for they had sold it quite legally and finally to the Grenvilles. This one fact was very satisfying, and Laura had dwelt triumphantly upon it, for it proved beyond a doubt that Augustine had no right at all to behave the way she did. She studied too the agent's list of everything considered to be dispensable – and a vast list it was. If Nicholas did carry out all these changes, King's Cliff would never ever be the same again, that much was for sure. . . .

It was the final day of April and Laura and Daniel rode down the escarpment, passing beneath the soaring pinnacle of the Townsend monument. King's Cliff Moor stretched away beneath them, and then they were on the levels, the horses picking their way on to a small, barely detectable causeway, built hundreds of years earlier by the monks of a nearby monastery. The marsh grass swayed as the breeze whispered over the lowland and, apart from that small sound, there was a serene silence everywhere. The shining water flashed in the late April sunlight, and the deep gold of kingcups shone at the rim of the ancient rhines, which once had drained the marsh but which were now so dilapidated and untended as to be useless. Pollarded willows grew along the rhines, their delicate foliage drooping lazily over the still water. The riders brought their horses to the largest of the trees.

Daniel dismounted and helped Laura down. They stood for a moment, listening to the soothing silence, and Laura looked back toward King's Cliff where it straddled the escarpment some two miles away. The Townsend monument pierced the sky like a gigantic needle, and the house itself looked magnificent, a veritable Versailles in such a setting.

Daniel tethered the horses to the willow and then came to stand beside her, looking at the house. 'That place has a strange effect upon all those closely connected with it. They either love it completely, or despise it; there does not seem to be a half measure.'

'And what do you feel, Dr Tregarron?'

'I am not closely connected with it.'

'Nevertheless, you must have an opinion.'

'I despise King's Cliff.'

She looked at him in surprise. 'Such vehemence? Why?'

He shrugged. 'I don't really know, but I've always felt that somehow that house would one day bring me great sorrow. I know that I shall not be sorry to leave it and return to my own dwelling, modest though that dwelling be.' He smiled at her. 'One thing I will be sorry about, however, is that when I leave, I will no longer be so frequently alone in your sweet company, Lady Grenville.'

'You are very gallant, Doctor.

Gallant? He looked away from her. Gallant was the last thing he felt toward her, for each time she smiled at him he was seized with a desire to crush her in his arms and bruise her lips with his kisses. No, *gallant* was far from the real Daniel Tregarron.

She knew nothing of his thoughts as she looked back at King's Cliff again. 'It's a very beautiful house, is it not?'

'It is, but beauty alone cannot make you, of all people, feel gently toward it, surely? Your life there is intolerable in the extreme.'

'Maybe.'

Daniel hid his feelings. That single word spoke several volumes of her love for Nicholas Grenville. *God help me, but I begin to wish Augustine Townsend success with Grenville, for that will leave his wife with no one to turn to – except maybe to me. . . .*

A dog whined somewhere close by, and Daniel turned sharply in the direction of the sound. Abruptly he caught Laura's hand and drew her safely beneath the canopy of the willow, pressing his finger warningly to his lips. Startled, she obeyed by remaining silent, but her eyes were wide with unspoken questions. He caught the reins of the horses, soothing them softly so that they too made no sound. His dark eyes searched the waving marsh grass, already very tall and concealing, and Laura followed his gaze across the rippling expanse of the rhine.

A small boat nosed through the reeds at the edge of the open water, almost entirely concealed from sight by the vegetation. Had it not been for the excited gun dog in the prow, they would not have known there was anyone there. Two men were in the boat, one poling it carefully and silently along, the other watching with sharp eyes.

'Poachers,' whispered Daniel.

The craft slid on its way, the reeds and grasses folding over so completely that there was immediately no sign of its passing.

Daniel relaxed then, releasing the horses. He smiled at Laura. 'It is better to be safe than sorry.'

'Sorry?'

'Poaching, as you well know, is against the law, my lady, and some of the men of Langford make a tidy living by stealing Grenville waterfowl. I recognized that pair, the Tibdale brothers, and a more rascally family I have yet to meet. Advertising our presence here would have been an unnecessary risk.'

'But you and I have every right to be here!' she protested.

'We are unarmed.'

She stared then. 'You do not mean that they would – ?' She could not finish the sentence.

'They have a great deal to lose if they are arrested, too much for them to stop to consider the niceties of allowing us to toddle along as if nothing had happened. Shooting wildfowl and taking fish is against the law, and that is what the Tibdales and many others like them excel at. Already they will know what is planned for this marsh, my lady, and that will make them your implacable enemies, for you take away their livelihood, even if that livelihood is illegal.'

She gazed at the grass and reeds where the boat had been that short time earlier, and she felt a little cold in spite of the warm spring sunshine.

Daniel saw her fear. 'Come now, they have gone and there is no danger. Think instead of seeing those same brothers done up in their best togs at church tomorrow for the May Day service.'

She had almost forgotten church, having several days earlier received a reminder from Tobias Claverton.

'The world and his wife will be there waiting to catch their first glimpse of the intriguing new Lady Grenville,' he continued.

'Are you trying to make me feel nervous, for I swear that if you are you are succeeding, Doctor.'

He smiled. 'Why should you be nervous? You are beautiful, poised, and charming.'

'Your compliments do not work this time, I fear. To begin with I must drive to the church with the Townsend cats—'

'Why?'

'What else am I to de?'

'Drive with me.'

She stared at him. 'With you?'

'I am expected to attend the Reverend Tobias Claverton's atrocious sermons as much as you are, my lady. There is absolutely no need for you to endure the Townsend cats if you do not wish to.'

'Maybe not, but it would surely not look well in the eyes of the county.'

'Because you choose to ride with me rather than with those of your own sex?'

She flushed. 'Something like that.'

'You are alone with me now and it has not concerned you.'

'This does not seem the same, somehow.'

'It is exactly the same – do you imagine that the neighborhood is unaware of our rides together? If you believe that, then you seriously underestimate Somerset gossip mongers. Lady Grenville, if you would prefer to drive to church in my carriage, you have only to say so, for it would give me great pleasure to have your company.'

She searched his face. 'I *would* prefer to be with you,' she admitted.

'Then it is settled, we go together.'

'Perhaps we should return to the house. . . .'

'Of course.' He lifted her lightly on to her horse.

They rode back along the causeway, and although she searched the marsh, she saw nothing more of the Tibdale brothers and their gun dog. As they rode up the escarpment toward Langford Woods, however, they saw a group of young people from the nearby town, laughing and chattering together as they picked branches from the spring trees.

'What are they doing?' asked Laura.

'Birching.'

'What is that?'

He pretended to be shocked. 'You mean to tell me you've never heard of *birching*? Sussex must be a very dreary county, my lady. It is May Eve today, or had you forgotten?' He smiled. 'In these parts it is the custom on the last evening of April to gather branches from various trees and bushes, and tonight those branches will be put on neighbors' doors, the particular branch chosen denoting the opinion held of the occupant.'

'What do the various different trees mean?'

He laughed. 'Oh, the list is too long for me to state it with any accuracy. I only know a few.'

'Tell me.'

'Well, flowering hawthorn, if it can be obtained so early, is always a compliment, but any other thorn means that someone in the house is the object of scorn and derision. Lime and pear are also a compliment, and rowan is a sign of affection. Gorse in bloom means that a woman in the house is of doubtful character.' He thought for a moment. 'The worst thing to find on one's door is elder, for that is a strong sign of censure and unpopularity.'

'And what do you usually find on your door, Doctor?'

He smiled, a little embarrassed then. 'Unfortunately, I find a rather alarming number of willow fronds.'

'Why unfortunately?'

'Because each one means that some lady in the neighborhood would like to receive more than medical attention from me.' He spurred his horse on a little more.

Laura laughed then, urging her own horse after him, and they rode swiftly through the woods and across the park toward the house. But once there, their lightheartedness soon evaporated, for Mr Charles Dodswell was waiting for them.

The moment she saw the agent's serious and anxious expression, she knew that what they had most feared had come about at last – there had been a communication from Mr Peterson in London.

'I fear it is so,' admitted the agent on her immediate question. 'There was a letter, but it did not come by the usual channels. It was delivered in person by two rather large and surly fellows whose manner can only be described as threatening. The moneylender calls in the debt immediately. I was left in no doubt that serious consequences would result from any delay.'

Laura's heart sank and her face paled. What could they do? They were in a cleft stick. On one side there was the earl, who would refuse point-blank to allow the sale of anything to meet the debt, and on the other was

Nicholas, who would be seriously worried if he was told the truth. . . . She looked helplessly from the agent to Daniel. 'What can we do?'

'Sir Nicholas must be told immediately,' said the agent firmly.

Daniel shook his head. 'No, I cannot permit it.'

'Daniel, we *dare* not put this off. . . .'

'He has progressed, but something as alarming as this will surely set him back, perhaps irreparably. It will of a certainty bring on the ague again, and that is something I wish to avoid. I am his doctor, and it is my duty to protect him as I see fit. Damn it all, Charles, you are a lawyer, is there *nothing* to be done to circumnavigate James Grenville?'

'The only thing which will dispose of the earl would be a document, signed by Sir Nicholas himself, designating someone else to act for him. Power of attorney will have to be obtained, Daniel, and to do that Sir Nicholas *must* be told.'

Daniel considered a moment. 'Would his wife be suitable for such a responsibility?'

Laura stared. '*Me?*'

'Who better? You are surely the one person James Grenville will not be able to honestly object to, for legally you stand closer to Nicholas than anyone else.'

Mr Dodswell nodded. 'That is true, Lady Grenville.'

'But in order for power of attorney to be granted to me, Mr Dodswell,' she said, 'Nicholas will have to be informed of the situation – which is something which must be avoided.'

Daniel smiled then. 'He need be told *something*, but not the truth necessarily.'

The agent looked sharply at him. 'You have something in mind?'

'Possibly. Charles, it is true that the good earl departs for Taunton tomorrow, isn't it?'

Taunton. Momentarily Laura remembered the overheard conversation between the earl and Augustine Townsend. Augustine was to go to Taunton. . . .

But the agent was answering Daniel's question. 'Yes, he leaves after morning service.'

'Then he will be suitably out of the way for our purposes. With him absent, we could inform Nicholas that some trifling matter has come up which Laura could attend to – if Nicholas puts his name to the necessary document granting her permission. Could you produce such a document, Charles?'

'Of course.'

Laura's anxious eyes flew from one earnest face to the other. 'But how can you expect Nicholas to sign his name? The laudanum makes it difficult for him to remain awake let alone hold a quill in his hand. . . .'

Daniel took her hand quickly, raising it to his lips. 'Hush now, my lady, and continue to have faith in me. I propose, God willing, to operate on Nicholas soon, and maybe this present situation forces me to bring the date forward to tomorrow or the day after. In order to operate I believe that I must discontinue administering laudanum, which, as I have told you, I have found does not always act well with other substances. I do not propose to endanger his life by giving him both laudanum and sweet vitriol together. While I wait for the laudanum to disperse from his body, he will be far more conscious than he has been until now – and, unfortunately, in a great deal more pain, but I do not feel that that can be avoided. During this time, Lady Grenville. he will be capable of signing his name.'

'If he wishes to.'

Daniel studied her pale face. 'My lady, why should he not? He entrusted you with his life when he asked you to bring him back from Venice, now he will think he is merely entrusting you with some relatively unimportant matter concerning the estate. Of course he will give you the necessary authority.'

'What if he would prefer Miss Townsend to act for him?'

Daniel smiled then. 'Nicholas may wear blinkers to some extent where she is concerned, but not to *that* extent! He has told me in the past that her extravagant ways appal him, and what reason have we to believe he feels any differently now? Be assured that he will agree to sign the document Charles here presents to him.'

She nodded. 'Very well.'

He put his hand momentarily to her chin, raising her face a little. 'Charles and I will be with you; we will help you all we can. Between the three of us we will stave off the moneylender, I promise you.'

She gave a weak smile. 'I pray you are right.'

'And we will stick an almighty pin in the overweaning arrogance of the Earl of Langford – that surely will bring a warmer smile to your lips.'

It did indeed, for she almost laughed. Oh yes, how very good it would be to thwart the odious James Grenville again.

Chapter 20

Later that day the Earl of Langford paid one of his more fleeting visits, and Augustine was thus forced to relinquish her well-guarded place at Nicholas's side in order to placate her fiercely jealous suitor. Laura waited until she saw them strolling in the gardens before hurrying along to Nicholas's room.

He gave her a weary smile, and the influence of the laudanum was evident in his lethargic, drowsy voice. 'Your visits are too few, Laura,' he murmured.

'I do not like to tire you, and one visitor at a time is surely better for you,' she replied. Oh, how glibly the words slipped from her lips, but she could hardly admit to him that she found it almost impossible to see him without Augustine being there.

His gray eyes were penetrating. 'Is all well with you? You seem pale.'

'I positively glow compared with you,' she said lightly, sitting on the edge of the bed and hesitantly taking his hand. The past week had left her feeling she had no right to approach him, and apart from that, Augustine's scornful, hurtful words echoed in her head as she looked at him.

But he did not take his hand away. 'Do you think of Venice at all?'

She was surprised at the question. 'Yes,' she replied honestly, 'I think of it a great deal.'

'Do you regret. . . ?' But his question was never completed, for at that moment, her timing immaculate, Augustine swept into the room. The earl's visit must have been very brief indeed. . . .

'Ah, there you are, Laura dear,' she said brightly, 'I was wondering where you had got to.' The green eyes glittered unpleasantly, and then Augustine turned, placing herself on the other side of the bed. 'Nicholas, dearest Nicholas, I have something to tell you and I do so hope you will understand my dilemma.'

'What dilemma?'

'You surely remember my old nurse, Edwards. Well, I have received a communication from her.' Augustine held up her hand, in which there was a crumpled sheet of parchment. 'I fear she is gravely ill and wishes me to go to her. You will understand if I desert you for a few days, won't you? Please, my dearest, say that you will understand.' The beautiful green eyes pleaded with him, and the long white fingers touched his forehead gently, as if wanting to openly caress him but unable to do so in front of Laura.

Laura felt sickened, releasing his hand and turning away, but she looked swiftly back at Augustine's next words.

'Edwards has a cottage in Taunton, so I will not be far away if you need me.'

Taunton. This could only be the arrangement Laura had overheard the earl press for, and the nurse's no doubt mythical illness was Augustine's excuse.

'I wish to go tomorrow, Nicholas, for poor Edwards seems in such a frail way . . .'

'Of course you must go.' said Nicholas, 'Stay as long as you wish.'

'Thank you, my dearest love.' Augustine's cool lips brushed his cheek.

Laura watched. What a truly consummate performance it was; one would need to know the truth about Augustine Townsend in order to see through it, for it was perfect in every way and the innocent could not even begin to guess how false it all was.

Nicholas glanced at her. 'Laura—?'

'I – I must go, I have much to do,' she said, hating herself for lying to him but unable to bear watching Augustine exert her undoubted power over him.

Tears pricked her eyes as she hurried away, and over and over again Augustine's mocking voice seemed to follow her. *I already know from Nicholas's own lips that he doesn't want you, that he wishes he had never, in a moment of great stress, taken you as his wife. . . .* The question Augustine's arrival had interrupted could be finished easily enough. He had been about to ask if his wife regretted their marriage as much as he did. . . .

Some footmen were approaching in the opposite direction, and rather than have them see her in such an obvious state of emotion, she thrust open the library door and hurried inside.

But the library was already occupied. Daniel Tregarron had at that moment returned from visiting some other patients. His leather case lay on a table and his top hat and gloves were beside it. He was pouring himself a glass of cognac, and he turned in surprise as the door opened and closed so hastily. As soon as he saw her face, he put down his glass and hurried to her.

'What is the matter?'

Dismayed, she stared at him. Confusion overtook her then. 'N-nothing.'

He took her face in his gentle hands. 'Tell me.'

The kindness in his voice and the concern in his dark eyes proved too much, and the tears began again. 'Please, Dr Tregarron—'

'You told me that you regarded me as a friend, and so I am. So tell me why you are crying.'

'He doesn't want me,' she whispered then. 'He told her that he wished he had never married me.' The hot, desperately unhappy tears welled down her cheeks, and she shook from head to toe with misery.

She affected Daniel greatly in that moment, too greatly for him to restrain himself from pulling her into his arms. He offered the comfort she needed so very much, and she thought nothing of turning to him, hiding her face in his shoulder as she wept. She meant no encouragement by her action, for although she knew he found her attractive, she had no real idea of what she had awakened in him. He could feel her body trembling, and he closed his eyes. Sweet Jesu, this woman stirred emotions in him over which he had hitherto been in strict control. Now those emotions were perilously close to the surface. . . . Just holding her to soothe her sorrows made him realize anew how very much he desired her. The perfume of her hair was warm and seductive, and a stray curl tumbled down from its pin, resting darkly against her smooth, bare shoulder. The temptation was almost unbearable, and he moved away slowly. He had admired her from the outset, but now it went far beyond that. The mixture of strength and fragile femininity he found in her, the uncertainty and then the determination which made her so different, so fresh and intriguing, had conspired to keep her constantly in his thoughts since first he had seen her barely a week ago. Had it only been a week? She seemed to have been on the edge of his consciousness forever. . . . She was Nicholas Grenville's wife and she loved her husband with all her heart – but she had come into Daniel Tregarron's life and stolen his love within days.

She looked at him. 'I know that I am not the wife he would have chosen under any other circumstances,' she whispered, 'and I know that I cannot ever have his love – but I still did not think he would be cruel enough to say something like that to her, not to her of all people. . . .'

'Is that what Augustine Townsend told you?'

'Yes.'

'And you would believe her before you would believe the Nicholas you know?'

'But I don't know him, do I? All I really know is that one day in Venice. For that short time he was everything I could have wished, and I *did* wish it so very much. But I know that he behaved as he did then simply and solely because of what lay ahead of him the next day. I cannot ignore the truth, or delude myself that I mean anything to him, but I still cannot help myself from behaving in this foolish way now.'

'You aren't being foolish. Why is it foolish to love and wish to be loved in return? That is human nature; it is what sets us beyond all other creatures.'

She smiled through her tears. 'I am sorry to burden you with all my problems. Your life must have been blessedly uncomplicated before I came into it.'

'My life was decidedly dull, and you do not burden me at all, I promise you.' He hesitated. He wanted to put their friendship on a more intimate footing, but maybe that would be to force the pace. . . . 'I – I was thinking that it is unnecessarily formal for us to address each other by title when we know each other so well. I would dearly like to have the privilege of calling you by your first name.'

'My name is Laura.'

'I know.' He took his handkerchief and brushed the tears from her cheeks. 'Never let Augustine Townsend or her ilk even begin to reach you again, Laura, for that way lies inevitable defeat.'

Neither of them heard the door on to the gallery open softly, and neither of them glanced up to see Augustine Townsend looking secretly down at them.

Laura spoke again. 'I'm so glad that you have such a magical way with

words, Daniel, for time and time again you give me strength. Thank you.'
She reached up shyly to kiss his cheek, wanting to show by that small gesture
how much she appreciated his friendship.

Augustine watched in delighted silence. She saw the desire written so
plainly in Daniel's dark eyes, and she saw too that the desire was not reciprocated, but that did not matter – a plan stirred in Augustine's cold, calculating heart. A rumor concerning Laura and the handsome, dashing doctor
could only serve to drive a final wedge between Nicholas and his bride. . . .
Stealthily, Augustine left the gallery, but she would have remained had she
known what would be said next.

To hide the effect the kiss had upon him, Daniel changed the subject.
'Everything has been put in hand with regard to our plan. You do not need
to concern yourself at all, Charles and I have plotted everything most carefully. There is something else which now works to our advantage –
Augustine and her mother are also going to Taunton tomorrow.'

'I know.'

'One ponders how much of a coincidence *that* is.' He smiled a little.
'However, it serves our purpose in that it removes the Townsend cats from
the scene of the crime as well, particularly since Charles is of the opinion
that the items which must be sold to meet the moneylender are in Miss
Townsend's possession.'

'What items?'

'Some of the Grenville jewelery. Oh, they are no longer fashionable
pieces, and Miss Townsend doesn't wear them, but the precious metals and
stones are particularly fine and will fetch a good price. Rest assured that by
selling them we do not do anything Nicholas would not do himself, for he
told Charles that they must go.'

'But they are Miss Townsend's.'

'No, they are simply in her possession – in a secret cupboard in her room,
I believe. They are a fortunate choice for another reason, for it is known that
they will have a ready buyer in Flaxton's, the fashionable Bath jeweler.' He
smiled at her. 'Everything has been thought of, Laura, all you need do is act
your part in front of Nicholas.'

She nodded. 'I pray only that I am up to it.'

'You are. Just think that by doing all this, elaborate as it may be, we are
snatching Nicholas from the duns.'

'I will.'

'So, it is all set to commence the moment church is ended tomorrow,
when the cats and the rat have departed for whatever it is in Taunton.' He
raised her hand to his lips. 'No more tears now, Laura.'

'No more tears.'

'That's better.' His lips brushed her skin again, and then he released her
fingers.

*

The hours of the May Eve night ticked slowly away, and Laura lay sleepless in her bed. She awaited the morning with great trepidation. What if the
earl did not go to Taunton after all? *What if – if – if – if. . . .* She closed her
weary eyes, listening to the distant moaning of the wind in the trees. So
much was to happen tomorrow. She must face Tobias Claverton's congregation, the people and landowners of Langford and its surrounding district,
people who would hold her in little esteem. She must obtain those jewels
and then playact that it was a matter of little importance, when it was in
truth of the greatest consequence. And her playacting must be convincing
enough to fool Nicholas into believing her, for he must not be worried,
especially not if Daniel was to operate in the evening. As if that was not
enough, there was the operation itself, with all its attendant dangers and
uncertainties. . . .

There was a stealthy sound at her door and her eyes flew open as she
distinctly heard something rustling. A cold fear touched her as she slowly sat
up, staring across the shadowy room toward the door. Who was it? Why
were they so furtive? Light footsteps receded and gradually silence returned.
Her heart was still pounding as she slipped from the bed and went to the
door. The passage was deserted and the house silent. Then something made
her look down, and she saw the small branches of spring foliage lying there.
Elder and walnut, their leaves barely unfurled.

Still shaking, she stooped to pick them up. The May birchers had left
their condemning mark, the elder for dislike and unpopularity – but what
did the walnut signify? The unmistakable smell of the elder pricked her
nostrils, but it was unpleasant now where once she had found it attractive.
In her imagination she could hear those light footsteps again, and she knew
to whom they belonged. This was not the work of the May birchers; it was
the hand of Augustine Townsend.

Still holding the branches, she retreated into her room, closing the door.
Then she hurried to the open window, thrusting the greenery out into the
blackness of the moonless night. She did not hear them fall on the gravel
drive far below.

Chapter 21

Laura dressed slowly for church the next morning, hoping that by delaying
her departure she would avoid encountering Augustine and her mother,
who had already announced that they intended driving to Langford alone.

Augustine had made a great fuss earlier about discovering a wonderfully complimentary bunch of greenery outside her door. Lime, hawthorn, and pear, she had cried delightedly, although her pleasure was dampened a little by Laura's silence concerning her own leaves. That Augustine had placed the leaves outside her own door too, Laura had no doubt, and she wished now that she had had the forethought to find a twig of gorse to lay at Augustine's door. Yes, that would have been a sweet revenge, for gorse would suggest that the occupant of the room was of doubtful character. However, she had not thought of it in time and Augustine's spite had gone woefully unchallenged.

Kitty dressed her mistress in silence. The maid had discovered a telltale elder leaf by the window, and on looking out had seen the discarded branches far below. Elder and walnut. The maid said nothing, for she knew well enough the meaning of those particular trees. The elder condemned Laura, and the walnut proclaimed her a whore. Kitty's hands shook, for she had that very morning heard from Betsy May Jenkins, Miss Townsend's maid, the rumors about Lady Grenville and Dr Tregarron. And it was true that they spent a lot of time together, and that they were very friendly, but Kitty did not believe that her mistress was unfaithful to Sir Nicholas, and she had firmly told Betsy May as much. Betsy May refused to speak to her now.

The rumor had not fallen on stony ground entirely, however, for there were many servants at King's Cliff who had reason to fear that the changes planned for the estate would mean the loss of their livelihoods, and those servants had little reason to like Laura or to wish to protect her good name. Kitty had not worked for Laura for long, but in that short time she had come to love her sad, beautiful mistress, and it made the little maid unhappy to think that someone had been unkind enough to place those leaves at her door.

Laura's thoughts at that moment were not of the leaves, however, for although they had not been forgotten, they were of secondary importance. Today was so very crucial, and the tasks to be accomplished and ordeals to be got through seemed legion. She glanced at her reflection in the mirror. She had chosen to wear the same clothes she had worn on leaving the Hotel Contarini, her caped lilac wool pelisse and green satin bonnet. On the first day of March she had commenced her visit to Venice, and on the first day of April she had left again. Now it was the first day of May, two months exactly since she had first met Nicholas Grenville. Oh, how very, very much had happened to her life in that short, fateful period. The guidebook lay before her on the dressing table, and she picked it up. The pressed flowers fell out and Kitty immediately retrieved them.

'How lovely they are, my lady.'

'Yes.'

'I know flowers, for my father is a gardener, but I don't recognize these.'

'The red ones are anemones, the pink ones wild cyclamen.'

'Why have you kept them?'

Laura gazed at the flowers. 'Sir Nicholas bought me a posy of the anemones in Venice, and the cyclamen I carried when I married him.'

Kitty glanced sadly at her before carefully replacing the flowers in the guidebook. Laura stood, picking up her prayerbook.

'Kitty, what is the meaning of walnut as far as May birchers are concerned?'

'I don't really like to say, my lady.' Kitty flushed uncomfortably.

'Tell me, for I wish to know.'

'They are only left outside a woman's door, my lady, and they accuse her of – of being a harlot.'

Laura flinched. 'I see.'

'No one takes any notice of it,' said Kitty, but she knew that she did not sound at all convincing. People *did* take notice of what the birchers said, and there was no getting away from that fact.

Laura managed a thin smile before leaving the room. Oh, Augustine had done her unpleasant work very well indeed, but at least she wouldn't have the satisfaction of knowing how deep her action had struck into Laura's defenses.

She hurried along to Nicholas's room, wanting to see him before she left, and praying that Augustine had already departed for church. Daniel was there, putting the final touches to a fresh dressing on the wound. As yet the laudanum still pervaded Nicholas, and there was little change in him. The pain was dulled, but so were his senses, and his voice still lacked any strength. He looked up at Daniel as he worked deftly with the bandages. 'I shall be glad when this operation is done, my friend.'

'And so will I, my friend.'

'Damned quack.'

Daniel grinned. 'That remark will cost you dearly when I present my fees.'

'Damned expensive quack.' Nicholas's eyes moved slowly to Laura, and he smiled a little as he recognized the clothes she wore. 'Venice,' he murmured, raising his hand a little. She took it, and returned the smile.

'Do I look well enough for Langford church?' she asked.

'Too good.'

Daniel straightened. 'There, you are tidy for the rest of the day, Nicholas. Be prepared for a great deal of pain when the laudanum leaves you, but I do not feel able to approach this operation in any other way.'

Nicholas nodded. 'I know.'

'By this time tomorrow it will all be over.'

'Keep a steady hand, quack, or I swear I'll return to haunt you.'

'That I am quite prepared to believe.' Daniel glanced at his fob watch. 'I fear it is time to go and weather Tobias Claverton.'

'Thank God I'm ill,' murmured Nicholas with some feeling.

Laura put his hand gently back on the coverlet, and left with Daniel. She glanced sideways at him as they descended the sweeping staircase. He looked very handsome in a dark gray coat and pale gray trousers. His taste was impeccable, from his blue brocade waistcoat and frilled shirt to his formal cravat, which was very excellent and complicated. He looked every inch a gentleman of fashion and quality, and was most certainly a man to turn many a woman's head. She wondered how many fronds of willow had been placed at his door this year.

Hawkins flung the doors open for them and they stepped out beneath the portico. May garlands had been put on the outside of the doors, and their gaily colored ribbons fluttered in the light breeze. The garlands were composed of the brightest spring flowers, cowslips, wallflowers, tulips, and even some early roses that had been found blooming in a sheltered part of the walled garden.

Daniel looked at the garlands. 'Miss Townsend was vastly pleased with the birchers' work during the night.'

'She birched all by herself,' retorted Laura acidly.

A landau waited at the foot of the steps, and Daniel handed her in, sitting next to her. As the carriage drew away, however, Laura's apprehensions returned, for this would be the first time she had ventured away from King's Cliff land, the first time she would have to face neighboring landowners and the people of Langford, none of whom would view her with any friendliness.

Daniel drew her hand through his arm reassuringly. 'Be easy now, for none of them will dare to actually bite you.'

She smiled. 'No, but they will certainly scrutinize me from head to toe.'

'If they do they will find only perfection.' He paused a moment.'Laura, I am afraid that I have to tell you of a slight obstacle in the way of our obtaining the jewels on our return from church.'

'Difficulty?' she asked quickly, 'What is it?'

'Only that unfortunately for us, Miss Townsend's garrulous maid, Betsy May Jenkins, is not to depart at the same time as her mistress, but will leave later. It could be that the wretched girl will remain in her mistress's rooms and that will make it very difficult for us to remove the jewels without being discovered. The last thing we want is publicity concerning our actions, for the more stealthily we achieve our aims, the better.'

'Wouldn't it be even better to wait until the maid has gone too?'

'Time is of the essence, Laura, for we do not know the duration of the earl's stay in Taunton. Everything should be over and done with before he returns, for that way he will not be able to do anything about it. In my opinion Charles Dodswell must be well on his way to Bath by tonight.'

Tonight. Fleetingly she thought of the operation, and the dangers to which Nicholas would be exposed.

Daniel read her thoughts. 'Everything will be all right, Laura, I promise you.'

'You can only promise to do what you can, Daniel; you cannot promise to keep him safe.' She looked at him. 'What are you going to do about the maid?' she asked, returning to the previous subject.

'Ah, well, I have thought of a way of occupying her time.'

'Daniel Tregarron!'

'Oh, not *personally*!' he protested with a laugh. 'I had rather thought that Henderson was the man for the task.'

'*Henderson?*'

'He may not be an oil painting, Laura, but as Nicholas's valet he is a fellow of some importance belowstairs. A good many of the maids would be only too pleased to lord it over the others by walking out with him. Anyway, Henderson has undertaken to do what he can to distract young Betsy May while we remove the jewels.'

The landau turned out of the King's Cliff gates and drove east toward Langford. The Somerset hills rolled down to the flat valley where the River Parrett cut through them from Sedgemoor. The river flowed westward toward the sea, wending its way across the marsh, and Langford town nestled on its banks, the main street stretching up the gentle slope toward the tall spire of the church, crowning the hilltop. The river was wide and shallow at this point, and it was spanned by an impressive stone bridge with four arches.

The coach descended toward the bridge, and Daniel frowned. 'This fool of a coachman goes too fast.' The landau swayed alarmingly over the bridge and Laura caught a fleeting glimpse of the long, green weeds waving to and fro in the clear water, and then the wheels were on cobbles as the team strained up the hill toward the church. Laura could hear the bell ringing as it summoned everyone to morning service, but there was another, more jarring sound, which vied with the bell.

'What is that?'

'May horns. Cow horns, to be precise.'

'What a dreadful noise.'

'It is the children; they always blow the horns on May morning. It is a tradition in Langford. They start at daybreak and go on all day, if they have the wind, which they usually do.'

She smiled, gazing out of the window at the passing houses. There were May garlands on most of the doors, and sometimes she saw evidence of the May birchers' activities. The church stood at the side of a square, in the center of which stood the maypole, painted in red and white stripes like a barber's pole. Ribbons twined with spring flowers hung from it in readiness for the dancing, but as yet there was no one by it, for it seemed that most of the township was gathered by the church gates, waiting for their first glimpse of the already notorious Lady Grenville.

A great many fashionable carriages had been drawn up along the wall of the churchyard, and Laura recognized both Augustine's barouche and the Earl of Langford's landau.

Daniel squeezed Laura's finger briefly. 'Courage,' he murmured. The carriage lurched to a standstill and as the footman flung open the doors, the sound of the bell and the more distant droning of the May horns leaped in. She distinctly heard the buzz of interest pass through the gathered crowd as Daniel climbed down, but she did not see the glances that were exchanged. It was true then, the glances said, about Lady Grenville and Doctor Tregarron. . . .

Daniel held his hand out to her, but uncertainty seized her, making her hesitate. He reached in then to take her hand firmly, and so she climbed down. The sunlight was very bright after the enclosed carriage, and she did not glance around at anyone. If she had, she would have seen a sea of unfriendly faces, for in their view she was an adventuress – a meddling, interfering temptress whose activities threatened their future and whose morals were already proved to be virtually nonexistent by her immediate commencement of a passionate affair with Daniel Tregarron.

The gathering remained silent as she and Daniel passed beneath the lych-gate and walked up the cinder path beneath the overhanging yew trees toward the church.

The church was crowded, and everyone turned as one as they entered. After the dazzling sunlight, the church was as dark as the landau had been, the only brightness coming from the magnificent stained-glass window behind the altar. There were flowers everywhere, filling the musty air with their perfume, and golden vessels shone on the altar. A tall, jeweled cross rose in the center, glittering beautifully in the rainbow light from the window behind, and Laura kept her eyes on that cross as she and Daniel walked down the aisle toward the second of the two Grenville pews, the first of which was already occupied by James Grenville.

Whispers spread through the congregation, and she knew that her cheeks were flaming as Daniel opened the low door to the pew and handed her inside. Augustine and her mother were already in their allotted places, but they moved still farther away along the wooden seat as Laura knelt to pray, thus ensuring that there was a suitably noticeable gap between their persons and those of Lady Grenville and her paramour. Augustine smiled with great satisfaction as she glanced around and saw the raised hands and fans, behind which the whispering condemnation went on. Yes, it had been such a simple exercise on her part, merely a matter of dropping a word in the ear of the likes of Betsy May Jenkins, and already the whole of Langford and the surrounding area was aware of what was apparently going on between Laura and Daniel Tregarron. Laura herself gave no hint that the rumors could be true, but one only had to look at the doctor's warm eyes to know that he would bed the new mistress of King's Cliff if he could. The smile still played around Augustine's perfect lips, for soon the rumor would be imparted to Nicholas himself, and that would see an end to any faint hope Laura may have had of retaining her empty marriage.

James Grenville sat stiffly in his pew across the aisle. He glanced neither to the right nor to the left, his plump hands clasping the carved ivory handle of his cane, and behind him, in her pew, the Countess of Bawton, influential and domineering matriarch of the family to which the Reverend Tobias Claverton was proud to belong, raised her quizzing glass to survey Laura closely. The Countess of Bawton resembled a crow, for she always wore black, her nose protruded in a way that unfortunately recalled a beak, and her voice when she spoke was deep and croaking. Now her lips were pursed sourly and disapproval registered in every fiber of her bony body as she lowered the quizzing glass and sniffed audibly.

At that moment the service began, and Tobias, in his flowing vestments, announced the first hymn. His sermon was up to his usual dismal and lengthy standard, for he seemed quite incapable of choosing an interesting text. When he had been preaching for an hour, almost the entire congregation was shifting uncomfortably, and only the Countess of Bawton remained motionless, her attention fully on her blundering kinsman. But everyone's attention was caught when suddenly they heard him mention Laura by name.

'And may I take this opportunity to welcome among us Lady Grenville, wife of our dear Sir Nicholas, who we so recently thought lost to us forever after a dastardly attack upon his life in a foreign land. We all pray constantly for his recovery.' The vicar's eyes slid uncertainly toward the Earl of Langford, for everyone knew that that was the last thing *he* would pray for! 'A-and now to happier things,' he went on, 'May God send His blessings upon our dear Princess Charlotte, our future queen, and her new husband, Prince Leopold. May He grant them long and fruitful lives, and much happiness. And may God grant too that the forthcoming nuptials between Princess Mary, sister of our beloved Prince Regent, and the Duke of Gl—'

Abruptly Tobias fell silent, and a ripple of amusement passed through the congregation, for everyone knew of the bitter rift between the Duke of Gloucester and the Earl of Langford. James Grenville scowled blackly at the unfortunate preacher, whose nervous glance went beyond him to the Countess of Bawton, whose face was similarly black, but for another reason. Her nostrils flared and she tapped her cane once upon the stone-flagged floor, commanding her relative to continue or it would be the worse for him.

Tobias cleared his throat miserably, for whatever he said now he would offend one of them, and better the earl than the dear countess. 'Between Princess Mary and the Duke of Gloucester,' he continued, 'who is so soon to be a guest of the Countess of Bawton and who will, I earnestly hope, be a worshiper at this very church during his stay.'

The countess sat back with great satisfaction at the stir of interest that went through the church. James Grenville's fury was evident as he turned to glower at her, but she ignored him. The Duke of Gloucester was a prize infinitely superior to James Grenville, Earl of Langford, for the dear duke was a prince of the royal blood, cousin of the Prince Regent. James Grenville was just a Grenville, and thus of little consequence when set beside her illustrious visitor.

Daniel smothered a smile as he witnessed the various silent exchanges, and for his pains received a look from the earl that would have annihilated a lesser man. Daniel merely returned the glance, allowing his mirth to show openly then, which infuriated James Grenville all the more. Snatching up his top hat, gloves, and cane, he stomped from the church, leaving a ripple of chatter behind, and the unfortunate Tobias to stare, openmouthed.

But if there was little love lost between the countess and the earl, that certainly did not mean that the countess would either accept or approve of Laura in any way whatever, and that much was made quite clear as they left the church afterward. Tobias made a further blunder by choosing to engage Laura and Daniel in conversation by the porch, thus affording everyone the chance of snubbing them as they passed. Not a word was uttered, skirts were flicked aside, heads averted, as the entire congregation filed out. Laura remained miserably where she was, her eyes downcast, her hand on Daniel's arm, as Tobias Claverton stumbled from pleasantry to pleasantry, all the time wishing the ground would open up and swallow him – or them.

Augustine and her mother had already left by the time Laura and Daniel at last escaped from the vicar. They had added to the insults by deliberately sweeping out without a word, and they had not glanced at the other occupants of their pew throughout the service. Their disapproval could only be noted.

The gathering of Langford people was still by the lych-gate as Daniel and Laura left the churchyard, and now for the first time she looked around at them all. Their unfriendly eyes looked back and she saw the accusation there. She saw in particular the Tibdale brothers, the poachers of the marsh, now resplendent in their best clothes, their faces pink and scrubbed, their shirts neat and ironed. As she looked, one of them spat contemptuously on the ground before turning to walk away.

Daniel helped Laura into the carriage and then climbed in himself. As the door closed, the children in the crowd began to blow their May horns, and the discordant sound jeered and mocked as they ran after the moving carriage, following it down the long street toward the bridge. Laura hardly heard them, however, for now her thoughts moved on to what must be done on their return to King's Cliff – the carrying out of their plan to relieve James Grenville of control of the house and the estate. She closed her eyes nervously, and Daniel took her hand, drawing it soothingly to his lips as he mistook the gesture for reaction to what had happened at the church.

'Don't let them hurt you,' he said gently, 'for they are not worth your pain.' But then his attention was snatched away as the coachman put his team at the bridge again, coming dangerously close to touching the wheels against the stone parapet.

Angrily Daniel lowered the window and leaned out, his words snatched by the wind as the carriage sped up the hill. 'You damned fool! You almost feather-edged then!'

'I'm sorry, Dr Tregarron, I didn't mean—'

'You're paid to drive this damned drag, not to aim and fire it!'

'Yes, Dr Tregarron.'

Daniel sat back again, looking anxiously at Laura. 'Are you all right?'

'Yes.'

The carriage drove on toward King's Cliff, and she swallowed as it turned in through the gates. Her stomach was beginning to churn now, for there was so much that could go wrong. At the very least Nicholas could be caused anxiety. . . . Her hands were ice cold.

Now Daniel knew the reason for her pallor. 'Soon it will all be over,' he said gently. 'The operation, the sale of the jewels, the ending of the threat from the moneylender.'

She managed a smile, but her heart was not in it. At the door of the house, however, something happened to restore a little of her shaky confidence and depressed spirits.

A gardener stood there, his hat removed and held against his chest as he shyly approached her. 'My lady?'

'Yes?' She thought he looked a little familiar.

'My name is Roberts, Frank Roberts.'

'Kitty's father?' She smiled at him.

From behind his back he drew an enormous bunch of red and yellow tulips which he held out to her. 'From my own garden, my lady, to say thank you for your kindness to my daughter.'

Her eyes shone with pleasure as she accepted the flowers. 'Why, thank you.'

'They aren't much, and they certain sure aren't a match for your beauty,

Lady Grenville, but I grew them myself and I'm proud of them. I hope you don't mind me being so bold.'

She smiled. 'I don't mind at all; in fact I'm very pleased to be given such a beautiful bouquet. Thank you.'

He bowed and then hurried away down the steps, his boots crunching on the gravel drive.

Daniel glanced at her. 'He's right, you know.'

'About what?'

'They aren't a match for your beauty.'

Chapter 22

Laura anxiously paced back and forth across the library floor, her hands clasped nervously in front of her and her eyes lowered to the richly patterned carpet. The smell of books was all around, and through the slightly opened windows she could hear the hounds whining and yelping in their kennels. Glancing out she saw the fresh wheel marks in the newly raked gravel. It was over an hour now since Augustine and her mother had departed for Taunton, and yet Henderson had still not come.

She turned to Daniel, who stood by the fireplace. 'Something has gone wrong. I know that it has!'

'Give him time. The pursuit of the fair sex is not something to be accomplished in seconds!' He smiled a little as she resumed her restless pacing.

There was a quiet tapping at the door and the valet's face peered around it. Seeing they were alone, he came in. 'My lady.' He bowed.

'You have seen the maid?'

'I have, Lady Grenville. She took some persuading, I can tell you, for she's mortal afraid of Miss Townsend, who's no easy mistress, but in the end she agreed to meet me. She'll be well away from Miss Townsend's room at three o'clock.'

She glanced at the clock on the mantelpiece. One hour from now. . . .

Daniel nodded. 'Thank you, Henderson.'

The valet hesitated, glancing from one to the other. Should he mention the rumours about them, which were rife belowstairs? After a moment's hesitation, he thought better of it, for if the rumors were true, then he would be making a sorry mistake with his revelations. With a slight bow, he retired from the room, but outside he paused again. He could not believe that Laura would so easily turn from Nicholas to Daniel Tregarron. In Venice it had been so very obvious that she loved Nicholas with all her heart.

Even so, the valet walked on, unable to bring himself to tell her what was being said of her and the doctor.

As the hour of three approached, Laura and Daniel strolled along the passage, to all intents and purposes engaged in admiring the various paintings on the paneled walls. Their route took them past Nicholas's room – for Augustine's rooms lay beyond it – and at the closed door, Laura halted.

'May I see him?'

'He is sleeping, and it is best that he does so while he may, for soon the pain will prevent any such rest.'

'He will survive the operation, won't he?' she asked suddenly, putting her hand on Daniel's arm.

'I will do all in my power to see that he does, Laura, but no doctor can state categorically that his patient will endure through such an operation. It is my honestly held opinion that the judicious use of sweet vitriol will ensure his safety throughout, but much as I would dearly like to, I cannot promise you anything.'

Her eyes were filled with doubt and fear and Daniel put his hand to her cheek, making her look at him again. 'It must be done, Laura,' he said softly. 'There is no alternative, for if that bullet is left any longer it will of a certainty make the wound putrid. I have delayed as much as I dare, for he was severely weakened by both the ague and the journey from Venice. Now is the time to do what must be done, and I sincerely urge you not to turn back at the eleventh hour.'

After a moment she nodded. 'I will not fail you, Daniel.'

'You do not fail me, Laura. Indeed, had you not doubted, I would have been surprised. Everyone doubts; it is natural to be wary – especially when you are concerned with the man who is dearest to you in the world.'

Somewhere a clock struck three, and Laura turned to look along the passage toward Augustine's room, but there was no sign of Betsy May. Perhaps she had changed her mind. Perhaps she had already gone to meet Henderson. How could they know for sure?

Augustine's door was of imposing gold and white, the gold repeating over and over again the Grenville sun in splendor, and Laura's pulse was racing as Daniel listened carefully for a moment before slowly opening the door. The sunlit room beyond was deserted; there was no sign of Betsy May. They went quickly inside, closing the door behind them again.

The room was very beautiful, its walls swathed with pale gray silk, and the plasterwork was so heavily and ornately gilded that it reminded Laura of her room in the Hotel Contarini. The bed's rich drapes were of royal blue velvet, and on the floor was a carpet picked out in a delicate blue and cream pattern. The Grenville emblem was everywhere, the sun's rays reaching magnificently over plasterwork, carvings, friezes, and doorframes.

Daniel wasted no time. He went to one wall where a large painting of an Italian landscape had been hung, and he lifted it carefully down, revealing that the wall was false and that a small cupboard was concealed there. He smiled at her. 'I gather that the key rests in a secret drawer somewhere in the dressing table, but I do not know exactly where.'

As he began his search something caught Laura's eye in the empty fireplace. She picked it up. It was a sheet of crumpled parchment and she had seen it before, in Augustine Townsend's hand as she had spoken of her nurse's tragic illness. Laura flattened the parchment and stared at its blank surface. There was no trace of ink, not a word – it was further proof that Augustine had gone to Taunton for purposes other than those she had stated to Nicholas. Tossing the parchment down in disgust, Laura went to help Daniel search for the secret drawer.

They had been searching for only a very short time when they suddenly heard voices at the door. Laura gasped, and Daniel moved swiftly, taking her hand and drawing her behind the heavy drapes at the windows. He pulled her close and she hid her face fearfully in his coat, her eyes closed tight and her heart beginning its wild beating again.

The door opened, and Daniel glanced in dismay at the painting, so obviously resting against the wall beneath the secret cupboard.

Betsy May stood with her hand on the door, her back toward the room. 'Listen here, Johnny Henderson, I just can't go with you, not when I've got so many things to do for Miss Townsend. I must have been mad to say I'd meet you.'

The valet glanced past her and saw to his relief that there was no one to be seen. 'Can't your tasks wait just a while?' he asked. 'Just a little while, eh?'

'No.' The maid pouted, pleased by his flattering attention. 'Come on,' he urged. 'You've plenty of time to do what your mistress wants afterward.'

'No, I haven't.'

'All right,' he said suddenly, 'Do your tasks, there's plenty of other wenches I can take my pick of.'

'That's not fair. . . .'

'You may be the handsomest of them all, Betsy May Jenkins, but I don't have to wait around on the likes of you.'

She hesitated, torn between her duty and her desire for glory belowstairs. The glory won the day. 'All right,' she said at last. 'All right, I'll come with you.'

To the immense relief of the two behind the curtains, the maid went out again, closing the door behind her. They remained in each other's arms for a moment, absolutely motionless until everything was completely quiet again.

Laura began to draw away then, but he held her a moment more. 'You are all right?'

She nodded, suddenly very conscious of his closeness. His eyes were very dark as he released her. He didn't say anything, but she was aware of him in a different way now, recognizing the strength of his desire for her. The realization came as a shock, and her hands were shaking a little as she went to continue searching for the drawer.

It was Daniel's questing fingertips that discovered the drawer's whereabouts behind the dressing table. Something clicked and suddenly the drawer was protruding a little from an apparently solid expanse of polished satinwood.

The key turned gratingly in the cupboard's rusty lock, proof that the Grenville jewels were indeed never used by Augustine Townsend. A silver-gilt casket was revealed inside, and they took it to a table and opened it. Emeralds flashed with green fire in the sunlight, and pearls glowed soft and creamy white. There were sapphires of the darkest hue, turquoises, opals, and most of all, diamonds. Laura held her breath as she took out one of the necklaces, its diamonds glittering like the sun on water, the bright reflections shimmering on the gray silk walls just as the water of the Grand Canal had shone on the walls of her room in the Hotel Contarini. . . .

The diamonds were fashioned in the Grenville emblem, many tiny suns linked together by golden chain. Daniel took the necklace and set it on a piece of soft cloth he had brought with him, but Laura retrieved it.

'Not this one,' she said.

'Why?'

'Because it carries his family's badge.' She replaced the necklace in the casket. 'I do not think he would sell this particular piece, do you?'

He smiled at her. 'Possibly not, but it would certainly fetch a tidy sum.'

'So will all the rest.'

'Very well, the diamond necklace remains.'

A little later a lot of the jewelery was safely wrapped in the cloth and hidden away in Laura's reticule. The casket was replaced in the cupboard, the door locked, and everything put back in its place. As they left the room nothing looked as if it had been disturbed, and unless Augustine returned unexpectedly and happened to open the cupboard – which seemed very unlikely – no one would be any the wiser. Unless something went wrong.

Charles Dodswell was waiting in the library when they returned, and the moment the door was closed behind them, he took a rolled parchment from his pocket and laid it on a table.

'I have done everything necessary for our purposes, my lady. If Sir Nicholas signs this, it will give complete power of attorney to you; you will be able to act in his name in whatever way you wish, exactly as if you were Sir Nicholas himself. The Earl of Langford will not be able to overrule you on anything, nor will Miss Townsend and her mother. Anything pertaining to King's Cliff and its estate, anything belonging to Sir Nicholas – all will be under your jurisdiction until such time as Sir Nicholas himself states otherwise. You will be mistress of King's Cliff in fact as well as in name.'

She gazed throughtfully at the document's neat lines of even handwriting. 'Does that mean that I will be able to implement the plans my husband has for King's Cliff? I could sell the hounds, and the unwanted land and possessions if I wished?'

Startled, they both looked at her. 'Laura—' began Daniel.

'I have thought about it, Daniel,' she interrupted, 'and I believe I know what I am asking.'

The agent nodded. 'Yes, Lady Grenville, you would indeed be able to do those things, but I do not know if I would recommend you commencing such a mammoth undertaking. You will meet with much resentment in the neighborhood, and your enemies will be legion.'

'Mr Dodswell, as land agent here, you more than anyone else must be aware of the danger this estate will still be in after the threat from the moneylender has been removed. My husband's health is such that he cannot do anything for himself, but if he were well, I *know* that he would immediately commence these sales.'

Charles Dodswell smiled at her. 'He would indeed.'

'Then so must I.'

'But you are a woman—'

'Does that make me less able to carry out his wishes?'

'That is not what I meant.'

'If Nicholas puts his name to that document, I fully intend doing all I can to implement the changes he desires here.'

Daniel watched her, and he could not keep the admiration from his eyes. She was so splendid, seeming to be so certain and determined, but it was all a fragile shell hiding the doubts and unhappiness beneath, and as always with her, he was affected profoundly. In that small moment he went beyond mere desire and into love itself.

She picked up the document. 'What must we do, Mr Dodswell?'

'Sir Nicholas must sign it before two witnesses – Daniel and myself – and then you too must sign it, as proof that you accept the responsibilities catalogued in the text.'

She nodded. 'Then let us see to it.' *Before my bravery falters. . . .*

Nicholas was awake, striving to hide his pain from Laura in a smile, when he noticed with some surprise that Charles Dodswell accompanied Daniel. 'A physician and a lawyer – all I am lacking is a damned minister of the church!' His voice was quite clear now, free of the laudanum, although it was not strong. He winced a little as a shaft of pain pierced his body from his arm, and he leaned his head weakly back against the silk pillows as he tried to conquer it. His eyes were closed and beads of perspiration started on his pale forehead. His face, already drained of so much color, seemed to take on a more ashen hue as waves of pain washed over him.

Anxiously she hurried to him, and he seized the hand she held out, crushing her fingers as another stab of pain passed jaggedly through him. 'It will pass,' he gasped. 'It will pass.' She felt each spasm as his fingers tightened and then relaxed, but then gradually the pain did indeed seem to go from him, for he breathed more easily and opened his eyes again. 'Forgive me,' he whispered, 'I did not mean to hurt you.'

She smiled a little. 'We are even, Nicholas, for I recall talk of viselike grips in Venice.'

His eyes acknowledged the humor. Oh, how impossible it was for her to believe he had said those things to Augustine. She looked away, afraid that he would read her thoughts too clearly. 'My poor Laura,' he murmured, 'How very tedious married life has proved for you.' His gaze went past her then to Daniel. 'I shall welcome the moment you begin your butchery, my friend, for this torment becomes too much.'

'It will not be long now, I swear. I believe that the laudanum will have dispersed in an hour or so.'

'If there is the merest trace of it in me now, I shall be damned surprised,' said Nicholas, wincing again as the pain returned. The air was sucked shudderingly through his clenched teeth as he sought not to cry out, and Laura could not bear it. She took his hand firmly, knowing that it would help him, if only a little. She almost cried out herself as his fingers tightened cruelly over hers, his nails almost drawing blood. The spasm held him for a long while, and then gradually it released him again. He leaned weakly back, breathing heavily for a moment.

Then he looked at the agent. 'Why are you here, Charles?'

'Only a small matter, Nicholas.'

'Let us hear it then.'

'There is a fellow in Langford buying horses for the army, and he is prepared to pay top price for your animals.'

'I'll warrant he is, they are top horses.'

'Before you left for Venice, you said that you wished to sell some of them, and unfortunately this fellow can only see them tomorrow as he has to travel on. As you know, your cousin the earl is away in Taunton, and would probably not wish to conduct such a sale anyway.'

Nicholas smiled at that. 'That goes without saying, my friend.'

'So, the sale could still be accomplished, if someone else could act for you in his absence. Lady Grenville is prepared to take the responsibility.'

Nicholas's eyes swung shrewdly to her face, and she knew that already he was suspicious.

The agent took out the document. 'If you sign this—'

'Charles Dodswell,' interrupted Nicholas, 'I know when I am being humbugged. The army is *always* sniffing around for good horseflesh, and this fellow would be only too willing to return at a later date. You know that, and I know it, and yet you have gone to the extraordinary trouble of having a legal document drawn up authorizing Laura to act on my behalf. That is a humbug if ever I saw one. I may be weak and indisposed, but I am not in my dotage yet! What is all this really about?'

'Merely horses—'

'The truth, damn you! Something is wrong, isn't it? Something connected with the estate?'

The agent could not meet the intense gaze, and Daniel glanced away too, shying away from breaking such a truth to a man in Nicholas's fragile state. He could sound sharp and alert, he could joke a little, but he was still very ill indeed, and a shock could do irreparable damage.

It was left to Laura. 'I will tell you, Nicholas,' she said at last, 'but first I will also tell you that you must not worry because I can attend to everything, I promise you that.'

'With the help of this bright pair?' The humor returned momentarily.

'Yes.' She sat on the edge of the bed, smiling a little.

'Tell me then.'

'Mr Peterson, the moneylender, has called in your father's debt.'

'Dear God above—'

'But it can be met easily enough if the Grenville jewels are sold.' He said nothing and so she continued. 'The earl will obviously not countenance such an act, and so I need your authority, Nicholas, if I am to keep the duns away.'

He gave a short laugh at that. 'St. George is to be rescued from the dragon by the damsel? But you are right about the jewels, and about needing my authority. My cousin would stand in the way of anything which would take from what he obviously still hopes will one day be his.'

'I do not like your cousin.'

He smiled. 'I do not know anyone who does; he has none of my immeasurable charm.'

'You are vain, sir.'

His smile died away a little as he put his hand over hers. 'You realize the implications of this document, don't you? The short glimpse I have had of it tells me that you will be able to do far more than just sell the jewels.'

'I know.'

'Laura, I don't want you to feel that you must – that you have to—'

'I will not do anything I do not wish to.'

The pain threatened to engulf him again, and he closed his eyes, his head falling back again. She shared every second of his agony, wanting to hold him in her arms, to stroke his golden hair and tell him how much she loved him. But she could do none of those things. . . .

At last he relaxed again and looked at her. 'You are sure you wish to embark upon this?'

'Yes.'

'I have no right to expect anything of you.'

'I am your wife, Nicholas, you have every right.'

'Maybe, but the circumstances of our marriage would hardly . . .' He did not finish.

'I made vows and I will honor them.'

He smiled at her then, his tone light and teasing. '*Honor*, Laura?'

'Yes.' She smiled too, remembering.

He nodded at Charles Dodswell, who brought a small writing stand. As the agent prepared the document and dipped the quill in the ink, Daniel helped Nicholas into a position from which he would be able to write. The movement caused great pain, and it was some time before he was able to complete his signature.

When Laura had put her own name to the document too, Nicholas drew her attention quickly. 'About the jewels—'

'Yes?'

'Do not sell the diamond necklace.'

'I have already set it aside, for I knew you would not wish it to go.'

Daniel watched them. Maybe it was a marriage of convenience, maybe Nicholas was fool enough to be in love with Augustine Townsend, but there was no mistaking the special rapport he shared with his beautiful wife. He had guessed immediately what her intentions would be once she had the authority, and she had known instinctively about the necklace. Their thoughts seemed to move side by side, and they had only infrequently to explain anything to each other. Jealousy stabbed Daniel, and he turned away, unable to bear watching them even glance at each other. He lowered his eyes then, for as Nicholas's oldest and closest friend, he knew him very well – well enough to realize that Laura possessed far more of her husband's affection than she knew.

Chapter 23

Laura watched as the footmen carried more lighted candles into Nicholas's dressing-room, spacing them so that their light fell to the best advantage across the scrubbed table that now dominated the little room. Daniel placed his case of surgical instruments upon a chair and then took out a small, dark brown bottle and a neat pile of small cloths.

She twisted her handkerchief over and over again as she watched the footman go to stand with his companion by the door. Everything was ready now; it only needed Henderson's arrival. . . .

The window by which she stood was open and the scent of honeysuckle was very heavy from the shrub growing against the wall outside. Twilight had faded into the inkiness of a starless night, and a breeze stirred the curtains. By now Mr Dodswell would be well on his way to Bath, lodged overnight in some wayside inn.

There was a hint of damp in the draught from the window, and she knew that there would be rain before dawn. The sun had set behind a thick, impenetrable cloak of dark clouds, clouds which had crept over the horizon just a short while after the agent had departed on one of King's Cliff fleetest horses. The cold air touched her warm skin through her flimsy muslin gown, ruffling the dainty ribbons on its puffed sleeves, and she drew her shawl more tightly around her.

Daniel emerged from the dressing-room as Henderson at last arrived. She turned then, her heart tightening. It was time. . . . She looked at Nicholas. He was still for the moment, exhausted by the almost constant pain, and he knew nothing of the touch of her lips on his as she prepared to leave.

She glanced at Daniel. 'You will come to me directly after it is finished?'

'You know that I will.'

'Let me stay.'

'No, Laura.'

'Please.'

He held her gaze firmly. 'No. I will work alone but for Henderson, Laura; on that I stand firm.'

She accepted then. 'I – I will be in the library.'

'I promise that I will come to you as soon as I can.'

'Save him for me,' she whispered, her eyes filling with;, tears. 'I beg of you that you save him.'

He nodded, and then she was gone, gathering her skirts as she hurried away. He stood where he was for a moment, and then went to the bed, touching Nicholas's shoulder. 'Nicholas?'

The glazed, tired eyes opened immediately.

'It is time.'

'I pray your blade is sharp.'

'None sharper.'

'Where is Laura?'

'I have sent her away. This is no place for her now.'

There was an almost imperceptible nod. The footmen came to carry him to the table and the pain increased sharply, washing over him so severely that he thought he would lose his sanity. A cry escaped his tight lips, but he made no other sound as they laid him carefully on the table. The candles flickered wildly in the draught as the footmen left to wait outside in the passage as they had been instructed.

Henderson remained nervously by the table, his face almost as pale as his master's.

'You are up to this?' asked Daniel swiftly, seeing the valet's pallor.

'I served with Sir Nicholas with Wellington in Spain, Dr Tregarron. I've not worked with a surgeon before, but I've seen enough blood and pain to know what to expect.'

'There will not be any pain,' reminded Daniel, 'not with sweet vitriol.'

'What must I do?'

'Sweet vitriol exerts its influence through its vapor, so it is important that neither you nor I inhale it ourselves. To that purpose I have improvised these masks. They are but cloth and strings, but they will serve to keep the vapor at bay for long enough for me to complete the operation. The liquid must be administered very sparingly, only one or two drops at a time on one of these cloths, and then the cloth must be placed so that he breathes deeply of the vapor. Are you clear on all that?'

'Yes, Dr Tregarron.'

The valet's hand were shaking as he opened the bottle and carefully allowed two drops to fall on a cloth. Daniel stared down at Nicholas for a moment. Laura's husband's life was in his hands. . . . Without this man, she would be a free woman, and Daniel Tregarron – oh, so eager to capture her.

Henderson lowered the cloth, and slowly Nicholas's pain-racked eyes closed. Daniel waited awhile before pinching the motionless hand, but there was no reaction. He took up his scalpel. But it was Daniel Tregarron the surgeon, the disciple of Paracelsus, who looked down at his patient then, not Daniel Tregarron, the man who would be Laura Grenville's lover. . . . The blade flashed in the candlelight before cutting deep into Nicholas's flesh. There was no cry of pain. No movement at all. Nicholas felt nothing, knew nothing.

The rain was falling heavily; she could hear it on the library windows. The ticking of the clock was the only other sound she heard as she sat in a deep leather chair, staring without seeing anything. How slowly time passed, she seemed to have been waiting for hours, and yet it was not all that long. Her thoughts returned to Venice, recalling Nicholas as he had been then, so virile and strong, so very attractive. She could see him now, lounging elegantly in the gondola, laughing at her with his eyes. And on the lido, riding like the wind on that black horse toward a break of tamarisk shrubs. And most of all at the end of that perfect day, when his lips had been so warm and soft as he had kissed her. . . .

'Laura?'

Daniel was there, and immediately she started to her feet, but he put out a reassuring hand. 'He sleeps now and is as well as can be expected. The operation was more complicated than I realized, for the bone was much splintered by the ball and I could not at first even locate the cause of the damage.' He tossed a tiny lead ball into a dish on the table beside her. 'But in the end I succeeded.'

She stared at the ball as it rolled in the dish. It was so very small, and yet it had caused so much pain, brought death so very close. . . .

'I must credit Nicholas with great courage, Laura, for he must have been in far more pain than I guessed. The wound was still clean, however, and I think there is no danger now of him losing the arm. With God's will, he can only begin to recover from now on.'

'And the sweet vitriol?'

'Worked as I said it would. I must be honest, Laura, I do not think he would have survived that operation without it.'

'How can I ever thank you?' she whispered, blinking back the tears of relief.

'You have nothing to thank me for,' he said, a little more curtly than he intended, for he could recall only too clearly those fleeting thoughts that had passed through his mind before he had commenced the surgery. He felt very tired suddenly, drained by his own emotions and by the sheer intricacy and novelty of the operation he had just completed. He went to where the decanter of cognac stood, pouring himself a large glass and draining it swiftly, not pausing to savor the bouquet. The fiery liquid warmed him. He smiled at her. 'Forgive me, I did not mean to snap at you.'

'You must be exhausted, it is more fitting that *I* should be asking *you* for forgiveness for not thinking of the strain you have been under. I thought only of myself and of Nicholas.'

'One does not expect the anxious relative to think of the doctor. Besides, the strain was of my own making. I *chose* to experiment with sweet vitriol.'

'And your theory is more than vindicated.'

He nodded. 'But for all that, it will not be made public.'

She was astonished. 'Why ever not? You have discovered something which kills pain and enables an operation to be carried out without any distress to the patient.'

'Pain is necessary, pain is God-given and it is our duty to suffer it.'

'Those aren't your words, Daniel.'

'No, they are not, but they are words which were spoken to me when I was foolish enough to take my theory to a senior and famous surgeon in London. His reaction was typical. Medical science appears to be more concerned with moving swiftly from the beginning to the end of an operation than with attempting to make that operation more safe, and it is certainly not ready for my dastardly innovation. Maybe the time will come soon; I pray that it does, but I will not risk what reputation I have again.'

'Oh, Daniel—'

'Man is a stubborn beast.' He poured himself another cognac, swirling the liquid for a moment. 'But maybe the American beast is more enterprising.'

'American?'

'Our former colony showed great insight by striking free of us, Laura, and it is my belief that my future lies across the Atlantic. I have had an offer, a most interesting one, from the man who once taught me what I know. He lives in New York now and he wants me to become his partner.'

'Will you?'

His dark eyes rested briefly on her face. 'I don't know.' *I was sure until you came into my life. . . .* He flung himself wearily into a chair, lounging back with one long leg swinging over the arm. He rested his head back. 'I am tired and yet am still screwed up to such a pitch that I know I will not sleep.'

'Shall I sit with you?'

'I know full well that you wish to fly to Nicholas's side. Besides, I am poor company tonight, and am therefore best left by myself to contemplate the ironies of life.'

'I do not think you could ever be poor company.'

He smiled. 'That shows how little you know me. I am capable of being decidedly dull. Good night, Laura.'

'Good night.'

Her skirts rustled a little as she left him. He drank the cognac, and then with a deep breath discarded the glass. That must be the last, for the mood that now seized him would see the emptying of the decanter and the commencement of another.

'Daniel, my laddo,' he murmured to himself, 'the sooner you quit this house, the better it will be for your peace of mind.'

Henderson had fallen asleep in the chair beside Nicholas's bed, and he did not awaken as Laura entered the room. A solitary candle illuminated the bed where Nicholas lay in a calm, deep sleep. She could hear the rain falling outside, and the smell of honeysuckle was stronger than ever as the rain bruised the delicate yellow-gold flowers which now and then caught the feeble light as the night wind swayed them by the window.

Nicholas lay quietly, his breathing soft and regular, and she knew that the blinding pain had gone. She bent to put her lips over his, lingering over the kiss. 'God speed your recovery, my darling,' she whispered.

Kitty waited in her mistress's room. The maid's hands were clasped nervously in her lap, for she had decided that she must tell Laura about the rumors that were circulating about her and Doctor Tregarron. But as Laura at last entered the room it was immediately clear that now was not the time for such unwelcome revelations.

For Laura, this important and harrowing day was almost at an end, and throughout she had remained as taut as a bowstring, but now the many conflicting emotions were perilously close to the surface. Slowly she went to the dressing table and sat down, her head bowed. The tears stung her eyes and her lips quivered as she tried not to cry, but her whole body was shaking now.

Kitty stared at her in dismay. 'My lady?'

Blindly Laura put out a hand to the maid, who immediately hurried to her. 'Oh, Kitty,' she whispered, her voice broken, 'I love him so much. If he dies I think I will die too, for I will not want to live without him. . . .'

The maid's own eyes filled with tears as she put her arms hesitantly around her sobbing mistress. Laura wept away the pent-up emotions of the day, but nothing could wash away the heartbreak her love for Nicholas had brought her.

Chapter 24

The ravages of a night spent weeping were only too evident in Laura's tear-marked eyes the following morning, and she did not feel able to face the household in such a sad condition. Anxious to learn how Nicholas progressed, she immediately sent Kitty to inquire, and Daniel sent back the reassuring word that his condition had not deteriorated and that he slept for most of the night, which was the best possible tonic.

Laura sat on the window ledge of her room, clasping her knees as she gazed out over the rain-swept park. Low clouds scudded dismally over the gray skies and the trees swayed wildly as the wind gusted over the escarpment. The hounds were disturbed by the change in the weather, and even though the window was closed, she could hear their noise from the kennels. Thoughts of the hounds brought her inevitably to the document she and Nicholas had put their names to the night before. She had his authority to act for him and she would not fail him. Maybe she was a makeshift wife, a temporary bride whose unconsummated marriage would soon be discarded, but for the time being she was still Lady Grenville of King's Cliff, and she would play her part to the best of her ability.

By the early evening she felt up to leaving her room. The judicious application of powder had done something to disguise the effects of her tears, but nothing could completely mask the reddened rims and dark shadows of her eyes. She looked lovely, wearing her blue silk gown, her Kasmir shawl draped lightly over her arms, but an air of sadness surrounded her even though she smiled at Daniel as she entered the library.

He saw immediately that she had been crying and he knew that it could only be because of her love for Nicholas Grenville. Had he not loved her so very much himself, he would have attempted to ease her heartbreak by telling her he believed Nicholas to have an affection for her, but to do that would be to risk bringing husband and wife together, and that was something Daniel had no wish to see happen. He had never loved as he loved now, never desired anyone as fiercely as he desired this one woman, and it was this that drove him now. Winning her from Nicholas was all that mattered, and the fact that Nicholas was his oldest friend was immaterial – as was the fact that he suspected Nicholas to hold her in a far greater regard than she herself could ever imagine. The ends justified the means, and so Daniel remained silent, determined to press his own suit as and when the time seemed appropriate. But the time was not appropriate just yet, not when the tears were still so fresh.

He smiled at her, taking her hand and raising it to his lips. 'You look very beautiful tonight, Laura.'

'And you are as chivalrous as ever, sir,' she replied.

'I am also a little remiss, for I did not think you would join me this evening and have therefore ordered only a cold supper.'

'I have little appetite anyway.'

'You must look after your own health, Laura.'

'Oh, I will probably eat like the proverbial horse once I know that he is better.'

'I am well pleased with his progress thus far. His temperature remains steady, and is only a little too high. His pulse is regular, and his sleep not at all restless. The dressing I removed this evening was more than satisfactory, and all in all I cannot see anything to cause me too much concern. He will be weak for some time, of course, and must therefore be prevailed upon to remain in bed, and I still advise against worrying him unduly with anything pertaining to the estate. He received last night's tidings well, but only, I believe, because you were able to immediately reassure him that the matter could be attended to. It would not be wise to assume that another occasion would go as well.'

'Of course not.'

'Actually, I am more concerned now with the malaria.'

'But surely it has gone!'

'It is merely in abeyance. There is always the possibility of its return, for such is the nature of the disease. However, when I leave in the morning, I will see to it that you have an adequate supply of the bark in case it is needed.'

'Leave?'

'I think I must, Laura, for I have a great many other patients who need my attention, and my medicines and books are at my own house.'

'Of course, I had not thought. It will not be the same here without you, though.'

'Ah,' he said theatrically, 'she will miss me. By my troth, she hath made me a happy man.'

She laughed. 'I *will* miss you, that is true enough.'

'For my engaging personality, or because I will leave you alone to face the rat and the cats?'

'That is an unfair question, but I will answer it. Now that I have Nicholas's authority to overrule them, I do not particularly fear them. So that must mean that I will miss you for your engaging personality, sir.'

'That is a sweet salve for my pride.'

'It was very good of you to stay here as long as you have, Daniel. Thank you.'

His dark eyes swept her face for a moment. 'It was no hardship to enjoy your company, Laura.' The atmosphere changed subtly.

She was aware of him again, and she moved away a little, glancing out of the window at the stormy evening. It was early, but already the candles had been lit. 'Do – do you think Mr Dodswell will return tonight?'

'Possibly. But it will be an arduous journey and he is not in the first flush of youth. I think it more likely that tomorrow will see his return; after all he has to go to Flaxton's, then to the moneylender's fellow, who I understand lodges in Taunton. And then he has to return here.'

'Yes, you are probably right. Oh, I do hope everything goes well, Daniel.'

'There is no reason why it should not.'

'No.'

Hawkins brought the cold supper, placing an elegant tray on the table. He inquired if she wished him to bring something for her too, but there was already more than enough provided, and Daniel remarked that it would appear the King's Cliff cook believed him to be in need of considerable nourishment!

The cold roast beef was particularly succulent, and the bread still warm from the oven. Daniel poured her a glass of the red wine, and she sat back in her chair, sipping wine and thinking. 'Daniel, how should I go about selling the hounds? And the land Mr Dodswell has listed?'

'Christie's.'

'The auctioneers?'

'There is no better way of selling, and no better way of reaching the *beau monde*. Notices of such an auction would appear in all the publications, and therefore a great deal of attention would be focused on King's Cliff.'

'There will be a fuss, won't there? I mean, when fashionable society learns what is to take place here. At the moment only this neighborhood is really aware, and already they condemn the changes out of hand. . . .' Somehow the thought of the highest circles learning of Nicholas's plans was not a pleasant one.

He put down his napkin. 'Did Nicholas seem perturbed at the thought of high society when he told you of his plans?'

'No.'

'Then why should you be?'

She smiled. 'No adequate reason, I suppose. I think I am merely of a cowardly disposition.'

'As we all are, Laura. The trick is in masking the fact.' He smiled then. 'Present a confident face to the world and it will not succeed in harming you.'

'Is that your philosophy?'

'One of them.'

'How many do you have?'

'Enough to suit each situation.'

'How very enterprising.'

He picked up his glass. 'It is strange you should apply that word to me, for it is the same one used by my friend in America.'

'You have decided to go there?'

He shrugged slightly. 'Possibly. There are pros and cons. However, I do not need to decide that just yet. I must await another letter from New York and then I will know exactly when he would like me to go there. Until then I shall remain undecided – one day remaining in this green and pleasant land, the next determined to go to the land of fortune.'

'If you go, America's gain will certainly be England's loss, Daniel.'

He lowered his eyes to his glass. She was the only reason he was undecided, for while there was a chance of taking her from Nicholas, then nothing on earth would make Daniel Tregarron leave England. . . .

She gave a short laugh. 'So, we both expect to leave here soon then, for one reason or another.'

'Come with me,' he said lightly. 'Be my companion instead of some doddering old dowager's.'

'What a very improper suggestion.'

'It was a thought. Improper – but exceeding agreeable.' He smiled at her. She thought he teased, but he meant every word.

Hawkins returned to the room. 'My lady, Mr Dodswell has returned.'

She could hear her own heartbeats. *Please let it be good news.* . . . 'Show him in, Hawkins.'

'Very well, my lady.'

To her relief there was a smile on the agent's travel-worn face, and she knew that everything had indeed gone as planned. His coat was mud-spattered and soaked through by the rain, and his boots left a damp mark on the carpet as the moisture trickled down. Droplets of water dripped as he removed his hat and gloves.

'Forgive my odious state, my lady, but I thought you would wish to hear my news as quickly as possible.'

'I do indeed.'

'The jewels fetched the necessary sum. Flaxton's made no protest about the price asked, and I was saved from having to ride back to Taunton as the duns were having me followed. One of Peterson's fellows was waiting for me outside Flaxton's, would you believe! He relieved me of the sum owed, and gave me a receipt.' He put a piece of grubby paper on the table.

'Nicholas is free of them?'

'He is, Lady Grenville.'

She exhaled slowly. 'Thank God,' she whispered.

'I have something else to tell you, my lady, a happy coincidence which I believe will be of interest. I lodged last night at the White Hart on the Bath road, and I shared a table with a certain young Scottish gentleman, a Mr Alistair McDonald, who by good fortune happened to be a surveyor and engineer. He had until recently been assisting the eminent engineer Sir John Rennie in a scheme to drain part of the Fenlands in Cambridgeshire. He knew a great deal about the drainage of such marshy places, and so I took the liberty of requesting him to come to King's Cliff to give his opinion of what might be done here. I realize that I overstepped my authority, but it seemed too good an opportunity to let pass.'

'When is he coming?'

'As soon as he can. He has several other minor matters to attend to first.'

She looked at Daniel. 'It is so sudden—'

'Don't bite off more than you can chew, Laura,' he warned.

She laughed a little. 'I shall not be going out personally with my spade to dig drains, Daniel.'

'Possibly not, but you will still be taking on responsibility.'

'No one is forcing me against my will.'

He said nothing more.

She looked at the agent. 'Please sit down and take some wine.'

'No, my lady, if I sit down, you will never get me up again. But I thank you, all the same.'

'You have done very well, and I will be most interested to meet Mr McDonald.'

'He is a very shrewd young man and I believe you will be able to rely on his opinion.'

'As I can rely on yours?'

'I trust so.'

'Then what would you say if I told you that I have decided to conduct the sale of the hounds, the land, and everything else through Christie's?'

The agent nodded. 'I would say that that is a capital idea, my lady.'

'Good. Then when you have recovered from your exertions in Bath, will you please communicate with them and make the necessary arrangements?'

'So soon?' He seemed taken aback.

'What reason is there to delay?' She smiled. 'You still have reservations because I am a woman, don't you?'

He shifted uncomfortably. 'King's Cliff is a very large estate, Lady Grenville, and you have no experience—'

'But you have, sir, and I shall be relying upon your help.'

'You may call upon me in whatever way you wish, my lady.'

'Thank you, Mr Dodswell. You will write to Christie's then?'

'I will, and I will inform you the moment I hear from them. And now, with your permission, I would dearly like to return to the farm.

'Of course. And thank you again, sir.'

'For you and Sir Nicholas, my lady, I would attempt to move heaven and earth.'

She smiled. 'I don't know about heaven, Mr Dodswell, but I sincerely hope you will shortly move a little earth, to say nothing of a good few pairs of hounds, and sundry other items.'

She did not disturb Nicholas, but stood for a moment by the bed looking down at him as he slept. Even when his health was brought so low, he was still very handsome, and so very arresting with his pale, clear complexion and golden hair. She touched his hair now, her fingertips so gentle that he felt nothing. She became aware of Augustine's portrait at the bedside, and slowly she removed her hand.

The wind howled eerily across the park, flinging rain against the window, and she crossed the room to look out. A draught moved through the house, making the solitary candle in the room sway a little. Shadows loomed over the pale gray walls and the gilded plasterwork glowed momentarily before the light settled into an arc which fell across the bed. Laura's reflection was broken by the rain, and her distorted face was that of a stranger seen in a nightmare.

She glanced back at Augustine's portrait. She had spoken bravely enough to Daniel about not fearing to face her opponents now, but inside she was not at all confident. She had right on her side, but employing it successfully was another matter. And right would not keep her marriage intact, it would not win Nicholas's heart, and it would not bring happiness.

He stirred a little then and she went to him. He heard the movement and opened his eyes. 'Augustine?'

She stepped into the arc of light. 'No, it's only me.'

'*Only* you?' He smiled a little. 'My poor Laura, have I been so neglectful a husband that you feel like that?'

'How are you feeling?'

'There is not so much pain.'

'You have Daniel to thank.'

'I know. I know too how much agony I have been saved by his interest in sweet vitriol.' He paused, remembering other things. 'I have seen field operations during battle; I know only too well what it could have been like.'

'You will soon be well. Nicholas, I have good news for you. The jewels have been disposed of and so has the danger from the moneylender.'

'It went well?'

She nodded.

'For which I have you to thank.'

'I did nothing.'

'That is not true. Laura, there are things that must soon be said between us.'

'Yes.' Her voice was very small. *Please don't say it, please don't tell me now. . . .*

He watched her for a moment. 'Has Augustine returned?'

'No.'

'I must see her first.'

'I will see that she is told when she returns.'

'Laura, I want to tell you—'

'You must rest,' she said quickly. 'You need all the rest you can get. I only came to tell you Mr Dodswell's news.' She backed away from the bed. If she wasn't in the room, then he couldn't say it; he couldn't destroy the little dreamworld she sought so desperately to cling to.

When she had gone, he thought he could still smell her perfume. So sweet a perfume.

Chapter 25

Daniel had departed the next morning when Augustine and her mother returned, their carriage arriving simultaneously with that of James Grenville, a coincidence which strongly suggested that they had been together while away.

Laura waited in the red saloon. She had left instructions with Hawkins that Augustine and her mother were to be informed that she wished to see them as soon as they returned, and if the earl was with them, so much the better, for Laura could get the confrontation over with in one fell swoop. She felt strangely collected and calm, her hands not shaking at all as she clasped them before her. She could hear their voices now, and the stunned, disbelieving silence as Hawkins duly delivered his message.

'Lady Grenville requests your presence in the red saloon.'

The earl demanded an explanation for such impudence, and was informed that Lady Grenville was the mistress of the house.

Her heart began to beat a little more swiftly as they began to come up the staircase, the earl muttering furiously, the two women whispering together. Laura swallowed, her chin raised just a little as the doors were flung open to admit the bristling figure of James Grenville. He was followed more sedately by Augustine and her mother. Augustine looked exquisite in mauve velvet and white muslin, and the tall feathers in her little beaver hat streamed proudly as she walked. There was a mocking smile curving her lips and it was obvious that she expected the earl to dispose of Laura in a matter of moments.

James Grenville halted before Laura, his hands on his hips, his jaw jutting out truculently. 'How *dare* you leave orders for me, madam!'

'I have every right to request something of someone who is in my house, sir.'

'*I* am master here while Nicholas is—'

'I must correct you, sir. You are not master here, for Nicholas has given me power of attorney to act for him. You have no rights here, which I am at pains to point out just as you once did to me, only I believe that I am being a little more polite about it.'

'What damned nonsense is this?' he growled, his face pinched with anger and an expression in his eyes that told her he would dearly like to strike the smile from her lips.

'It isn't nonsense, sir; it is a legal and indisputable fact that my word is a command here now, not yours.'

Augustine no longer looked quite so sure of herself and she glanced at her mother. Something in Laura's attitude suggested that she was not bluffing. Slowly Augustine teased off her dainty white gloves. 'So, my *lady*,' she taunted, 'once again you have tricked Nicholas into something foolish.'

'It is no trick; Nicholas was perfectly aware of what he did.'

'As he was when he married you?' The scorn was not disguised.

'He was hardly unaware.'

'I will go to him immediately—'

'Do so, by all means, but you will find that everything I say is true.'

Augustine's green eyes darkened. 'He would not trust you with anything as vital as this!'

'Go to him then,' said Laura smoothly. 'No doubt you are anxious to hurry to his side anyway.' She could not resist this last pinprick, and was gratified to see the uneasiness in Augustine's manner as she glanced swiftly at James Grenville. His whole body stiffened as he waited for her reaction.

Augustine turned to her mother. 'Mama, will you go to see Nicholas for us?'

Mrs Townsend nodded, gathering her cumbersome brocade skirts and sweeping from the room.

The moments passed silently, as if on leaden feet, as they waited. Augustine's eyes glittered with hatred as she looked at Laura, a fact Laura pretended to be unaware of. At last they heard Mrs Townsend returning.

Her face was pale as she appeared in the doorway. 'He confirms what she says,' she said. 'He has given her power of attorney.'

Augustine turned in amazement. 'He wouldn't!' she cried.

'He is most definite, Augustine.'

A vein throbbed at James Grenville's temple, and his face went pale and then dark again. He was impotent, and he knew it, but still he would not accept until Laura's claim was backed by more than words. 'I demand to see proof,' he snapped, 'absolute proof.'

She placed the parchment on the table before him and he almost snatched it up. 'I warn you,' she said, 'that that is but one of two identical copies.' *And may God forgive me for my lie. . . .*

Augustine came to read the document with him. 'Tregarron! And that fool Dodswell!' she cried. 'I might have known!'

James Grenville lowered the document at last. 'You have been very clever, madam, for this gives you *carte blanche*, does it not?'

'You certainly do not have such powers here anymore.'

'For the moment.'

'Before you leave I have something to impart to you.'

'I leave in my own good time.'

'You will leave directly I have finished speaking to you.' She held his gaze, and he said nothing more. 'I wish to inform you,' she went on then, 'that I am about to implement Nicholas's own plans for his house and estate. Those plans include the selling of the hounds, the—'

'No!' cried Augustine. '*No!*'

'The selling of the hounds, the shedding of much unwanted land, and the eventual draining of King's Cliff Moor to provide farming land.'

'It's damned madness,' spluttered the earl. 'Damned lunacy!'

'It is exactly the opposite, given the circumstances pertaining here at this time. What madness there has been has been of your doing, sir, and of Miss Townsend and her mother's. Oh, and that reminds me . . . Miss Townsend, about those invitations and plans you have set your heart on – I am afraid that as I warned you, they cannot possibly be contemplated. I have issued orders that everything is to be canceled.'

'You've *what*?' breathed Augustine.

'I believe you heard me. There will be no masquerade, no foolishly extravagant summer ball, and no guests who expect to wallow in King's Cliff's lavish hospitality. The belt, in short, has been tightened more than a mere notch or two; it has been drawn in a very great deal.'

'How dare you speak to me like that,' whispered Augustine, not trusting herself to speak louder her fury was so great.

'Oh, I dare, Miss Townsend, I dare. My only concern is Nicholas, and I intend to see that his plans are carried out. I don't much care for you, and I certainly do not care what you feel or think. I find you quite odious, Miss Townsend, as odious as the noble earl here, and that is odious indeed.'

James Grenville snatched up his hat and strode from the room. When he was gone, Augustine's lips curled into a snarl as she looked at Laura with all the venom she could muster.

'You'll pay for this, you'll pay for every word! Nicholas has done this to outwit James, and that is his only reason! You mean nothing to him, for he is in love with me! What little trust there may be between you now will soon be shattered, that I promise you!'

'Because you will tell him lies?'

'Because he will believe what I say.'

The poisonous hatred was chilling and Laura could all but feel it reaching out to touch her. Her own smile did not falter, however. 'I think this disagreeable interview is at an end, Miss Townsend, for I have no desire to be dragged into a low demeaning contest of words with you. Good day to you.' With a slight inclination of her head, she walked past both mother and daughter.

Augustine watched her. Soon that smile would be gone forever from the lips of Laura, Lady Grenville. Augustine looked at her mother. 'Do you think the rumors I so providently set in motion have spread sufficiently far yet?'

'That she and Daniel Tregarron are lovers? Yes, I would imagine that they had spread the length and breadth of the county by the end of the first day.'

Augustine smiled. 'They are about to reach Nicholas's ears. I'll destroy her for her impudence. I swear that I will trample her so low that she will never again claw her way up. He's mine, and this house is mine; nothing and no one is ever going to alter that!'

Augustine's skirts whispered coolly as she entered Nicholas's room, and her beautiful face was a study of anxious concern. She hurried to the bedside, taking his hand and raising it softly to her lips, kissing the palm. 'I have missed you so,' she whispered. 'Each moment I was away seemed like an hour.'

'How is your nurse?'

'I am more concerned to know how you are.'

'Better, as you can see.'

Her fingers moved against his face, their touch gossamer light and full of aching love. 'I love you so, Nicholas. I love you with all my heart.'

'Augustine, I wish to speak to you—'

'And I with you.' She stood abruptly. 'I don't know how to tell you this, Nicholas, but I feel that someone has to and the unpleasant task seems to have fallen to me.'

'Tell me what?'

'About your wife and – and—' Her voice shook as if she could not go on.

His eyes sharpened. 'And what?' he demanded.

'It isn't what, my dearest, it's who.' Augustine exuded unhappy consternation as she turned reluctantly toward the bed again. 'She and Daniel Tregarron are lovers, Nicholas. Oh, I know yours is a marriage of convenience, that there is no love, but it is still not something I willingly impart to you. The whole of Langford rattles about them, they have been seen riding together almost every day. They go to Langford Woods.' She paused to allow the implication of this information to have full effect. 'Ask anyone. Ask Henderson.' This last was her trump, for Henderson, so faithful and trusted, could only confirm the carefully orchestrated rumors. But she did not expect Nicholas's reply.

'Leave me, Augustine.'

'But – but you wished to speak with me!'

'No, not anymore. Please leave me for a while.'

'Do you blame me for telling you?' She had expected his anger, but not somehow quite like this. He was obviously much affected by what he had been told.

'In God's name will you go away?' he cried then.

She flinched a little and hurried out of the room. In the passage she paused. A marriage of convenience it might be, but it meant a little too much to Nicholas for Augustine's comfort. But it was over now. She had driven the final wedge between husband and wife, for Nicholas was not a man to tolerate his wife's infidelity, least of all with his best friend.

Nicholas closed his eyes, and in spite of the warmth of the day, a shiver passed through him. Laura. How pliable and honey sweet her lips had been when he had kissed her the night before the duel. And how that kiss lingered with him even now.

Henderson came as soon as he was sent for. A coal boy was busy stoking up a roaring fire and the windows were tightly closed. Soon the room would be unbearably hot, but Nicholas only felt the cold. The valet saw with dismay that his master no longer looked quite as well, and yet only that morning before breakfast he had seemed to be making excellent progress. The shadows beneath his eyes were once again pronounced and he was oddly restless as he beckoned the valet toward the bed.

'Come here, Henderson, and I want the truth now.'

'The truth?' Uneasiness began to spread through the valet.

'About my wife and Dr Tregarron.' Nicholas suddenly remembered the coal boy. 'Get out of here!' he snapped.

The boy dropped his shovel and ran out. Henderson glanced in surprise at his master, for it was not like him to be short with a mere child. 'Sir Nicholas?'

'How close are my wife and Daniel Tregarron?'

'Th-they know each other, how could it be otherwise when until today the doctor was a guest here.'

'That isn't what I mean.'

'I don't know anything more, Sir Nicholas.'

'Are they lovers?'

The valet's eyes widened. 'I don't know, Sir Nicholas,' he muttered unconvincingly.

'But you have heard rumors?'

Miserably Henderson nodded. 'I've heard them, Sir Nicholas, but I don't believe them. I don't think that her ladyship would ever—'

'You aren't certain, though, are you?'

'How can I be, Sir Nicholas? Everyone's talking about it; it's the constant topic belowstairs and everywhere else.'

'Have you ever known there to be so much smoke before without there being a fire to cause it?'

The valet slowly shook his head. 'No.'

Nicholas looked away. It must be true. What else could he believe? 'That is all, Henderson.'

The valet went to the door, pausing there. 'I don't in my heart believe any of it, Sir Nicholas. Not of her.'

Nicholas said nothing, and the door closed slowly behind the valet. The new fire crackled in the silence, but Nicholas was aware only of the empty cold that was setting over him. In Venice he had thought he had found the only woman he could ever know true happiness with, but it was quite evident now that she had not felt the same. The marriage was meaningless, for already someone else enjoyed her embraces, someone he had thought he could trust above all others . . . Daniel Tregarron.

A burst of glittering sparks spiraled up the chimney. Nicholas closed his eyes. He had come so close to confessing his love to her, so very close that had she remained in the room after telling him of the sale of the jewels, he would have told her. The words had remained unspoken, and now he could salve his shattered pride by pretending he felt nothing for her.

Dear God, how cold it was. He was conscious of an uncontrollable urge to shiver again. As before.

Chapter 26

Daniel was preparing to visit Nicholas at King's Cliff when his housekeeper came to see him. She entered the clean, whitewashed room where he kept his medicines, and she smoothed her hands nervously on her starched apron.

'Yes, Mrs Thompson? What is it?'

She said nothing at first and he turned to look at her. Her plump, country face, usually so ruddy, was a little on the pale side, and he noticed how her tongue passed swiftly over her lips. 'Mrs Thompson?'

'Sir, I don't know how to begin. . . .'

He smiled, closing his leather bag and crossing to gently take her arm and usher her into the room's only chair. He leaned on the edge of a table, his arms folded. 'Now then, what's all this about?'

'Dr Tregarron, you know that I've served you well for some time now.'

'Exceedingly well.'

'And I've no wish to cause trouble, but I reckon as how someone's got to tell you what's being said.'

'Being said? About what?'

'About you and Lady Grenville.'

His smile faded and he unfolded his arms. 'And what exactly is being said?'

A swift flush stained her cheeks then. 'Please, I don't like to say it outright—'

'Then how an I to know?'

She clasped and unclasped her hands, and then the words came out in a rush. 'It's all over Langford that you are Lady Grenville's lover.'

'Is it, be damned?' He straightened then. 'And how did this wondrous tale come about?'

'Oh, I don't know, Doctor, how does any rumor start? It just seems to appear from nowhere. Anyway, I thought I had to tell you, for *everyone's* talking about it. I've not known a rumor so strong for a goodly time now.'

'Thank you for telling me, Mrs Thompson.'

Slowly she stood. 'I didn't want to say anything, Dr Tregarron.' She searched his face for a moment, wondering how much truth there was in the tale, for he had not denied it.

He smiled then, knowing what she was thinking. 'My dear Mrs

Thompson, I only wish the tale was true, but unfortunately it is not. I am not Lady Grenville's lover.'

She smiled with relief. 'I'm sorry, Doctor, I didn't mean—'

'I know, Mrs Thompson. I know.'

When she had gone, he thoughtfully drew on his gloves. Rumors like this could only damage Laura's fragile marriage if they should reach Nicholas's ears, but it was not consideration of this that had prompted Daniel to be honest with his housekeeper. The only reason he had denied anything was a fear that at some time in the future Laura might discover that he had been guilty of aiding the rumors to gain strength. That, and only that, swayed him now.

As Daniel was preparing to leave his house, Laura heard for the first time that there was beginning to be concern over Nicholas's condition, that as before when he had had malaria, he was complaining of feeling cold when it was obvious that if anything he had a temperature. In some alarm, and still totally unaware of the rumors that had mushroomed all around her, she hurried to Nicholas's room.

Augustine was already there. She had been patiently waiting for the first confrontation between Nicholas and Laura since he had been apprised of his wife's alleged *affaire de coeur*, and now at last the moment had come. A little gloating smile of anticipation lightened Augustine's face as she sat neatly by the bedside.

Laura went to him. 'Nicholas, is it true that you are less well?' It was a foolish question, for she could see for herself that there had been a deterioration since earlier in the day. Thank goodness Daniel would soon be here. . . . Instinctively she reached out to touch Nicholas's hand, but he pointedly moved it away.

'I am only fractionally less well,' he said coldly, 'and it is certainly nothing which warrants your presence.'

She stared at him. 'Is something wrong?' she asked slowly.

'Nothing of importance.'

Augustine slipped her hand into his and this time he did not move away. 'Nicholas,' she murmured, 'I think it long overdue that Laura should meet the ladies of consequence in the neighborhood. It does not look well that she apparently snubs them.'

'*I* snub *them*?' gasped Laura, staggered that such a complete reversal of the facts should be presented as the truth.

Augustine ignored the outburst. 'She should take tea with them here at King's Cliff, as propriety and custom demand. The Countess of Bawton in particular—'

'No,' said Laura. 'No, I will not meet them.'

'You will do as I tell you,' snapped Nicholas, holding her gaze.

'Nicholas, why are you like this? What has happened?'

'Is the onus always to be on me to be pleasant, madam? Augustine is right; you have a duty to receive the ladies here and that is exactly what you will do.'

Numb with dismay, she met his cold gaze. For Augustine it was the sweetest of moments, but for Laura it was humiliating and painful. He was a stranger suddenly, changed and remote, and she did not know him at all. And the change, she sensed, had not solely to do with the setback in his health. There was more to it than that. Far more.

Nicholas was relentless. 'You may go,' he said.

She was trembling as she turned to go, and the tears were very close. She hurried blindly along the passage and down the staircase to the hall, ignoring Hawkins's startled gaze as she passed him without a word. Thankfully she emerged from the front door and breathed deeply of the fresh air.

The sun had faded behind a cloud and the breeze had risen a little in that way that presages a shower, but she went down the steps, holding her shawl tightly around her shoulders. She had to escape from the house for a while, escape from the pain Nicholas had so deliberately inflicted.

She halted at the foot of the steps, for Daniel Tregarron was riding toward her. He reined in by her, his capricious horse dancing impatiently around as he dismounted. His cloak flapped wildly in the wind, and his dark hair was ruffled as he removed his hat. 'Laura?'

'Daniel.'

His smile faded. 'What is it?'

'I don't know, and that is the truth.'

'Tell me.'

She gave him a wan smile. 'Burden you with my problems again?'

'If that is the way you wish to put it.' He handed the reins to a groom who hurried out, and then he drew Laura's hand through his arm. 'Come, we will walk together for a little while, and you shall tell me all about it.'

At first she couldn't bring herself to say what had happened, and they strolled slowly across the grass where the thick-leaved laurels rustled as they swayed.

Suddenly Daniel halted. 'Well? Did something go wrong? Was it the confrontation with the cats and the rat?'

'No. No, it was the confrontation with Nicholas.' Her voice almost broke and she was forced to look away.

'With Nicholas?' His mind was racing then, coming as he did so fresh from Mrs Thompson's revelations. 'What about?'

'I don't know. He was just completely changed, almost as if he despised me. He had been kind, he showed concern and even a little tenderness, but that is all gone now. He looks at me as if he dislikes me.' Her voice shook. 'And it is not only his changed attitude toward me which worries me so. I fear that the ague has begun to return, for he complains of the cold and yet his temperature I am sure has risen.'

Daniel took a long breath, convinced now that Nicholas had indeed somehow heard the rumors, for a devastating shock such as that could indeed work to cause the malaria to flare up once more. 'I will go to him,' he said, although he wondered what sort of a reception he would receive.

'Yes,' she whispered. Her voice was so small and lost, end Daniel could not help but pull her into his arms, his cheek resting against her hair.

'Don't cry,' he murmured.

His cloak flapped around them both and the dampness of rain was in the air now.

'I'm sorry, Daniel, I do not mean to lean so heavily on you all the time. It isn't fair of me.'

He put his gloved hand on her cheek and raised her face toward his. 'Laura,' he said softly, 'I welcome each time you come to me, for I swear that I curse the fact that you are Nicholas Grenville's wife and not mine.'

She stared at him. 'Daniel—'

'No, don't say anything, for I rather fancy that I have said more than enough for both of us.' He released her. 'And now I think it time I performed the professional duty which brought me here in the first place.

He walked away toward the house, and there was only the wind in the laurels and the touch of cold rain upon her face. Slowly she followed him.

Augustine watched from Nicholas's window. She had seen everything that had passed between Laura and Daniel and could hardly believe that they played so easily into her hands.

She turned to the bed. 'Their meeting is over and they come toward the house now.'

'I do not think you need be present, Augustine.'

She inclined her head and left, and a few moments later Daniel entered.

The moment their eyes met, Daniel knew that the rumors had indeed reached Nicholas – and that he believed them. Slowly Daniel put his case down. 'How are you, Nicholas?'

'You are no longer welcome in this house, Daniel.'

'If that is what you wish.'

'Stay away.'

'Very well.'

'From this house and from my wife.'

'That last I will not promise.'

The years of friendship slipped away in those few seconds, and Daniel sacrificed them willingly. He admitted nothing to Nicholas, and he denied nothing. He had not uttered a single lie. Let Nicholas believe the rumors, let him believe them and then cast off his wife – Daniel inclined his head briefly and then picked up his case. He had been there barely one minute.

Laura saw him leaving and hurried out into the rain after him, catching the reins of his horse, her face wet as she looked anxiously up at him. 'Daniel, why are you leaving so soon?'

'Because Nicholas declines to have me here.'

She stared. 'But how can that be? Why?'

'He did not say.' That much was the truth.

'He cannot have meant it!'

'I don't know or care if he did, his manner was such that I am content for it to be this way. My friendship with him is at an end, and I shall not come to this house again.'

Slowly her hands slipped from the reins. 'And your friendship with me?'

'Is constant.' He reached down to put his hand to her cheek, and then he was gone, spurring his impatient horse away along the drive.

Laura lay awake in the bed. The candle trembled in the draught from the slightly open window and she could hear the rain falling heavily. Her spirits were as low and damp as the weather. Sleep was far away. She stared up at the shadowy canopy of the bed, her eyes wandering over the embroidered suns she had hardly noticed before. An emptiness filled her. The change in Nicholas was too much to bear, for he spurned her now, and it was this that had brought her to a sad and difficult decision before she had retired for what she intended to be her last night at King's Cliff. A letter to Lady Mountfort lay upon a table, and the future that had stretched so unenviably before her at the beginning of the year now stretched before her again. It was as if nothing had happened in between.

In the distance she heard Augustine calling, and at first she took no notice, but then the note of fear in those far-off cries made her sit up. Augustine was with Nicholas! In a moment she was out of the bed, drawing on her wrap as she ran from the room and along the passages and galleries that separated her from Nicholas's room.

Augustine's frightened calls grew louder, and Laura's heart began to pound in dread. *Let him not be dead, oh, please let him not—* But as she reached the room, she saw that although he was alive, all was certainly not well with him. The malaria had returned with as much force as before, and he was as feverish as he had been on board the *Cygnet*, although not quite delirious, for he recognized her as she approached the bed. His face was flushed with unnatural heat and his eyes burned, but shivers racked him. She heard him say her name though. Just once.

Mrs Townsend was trying to calm her almost hysterical daughter. 'Hush now, you will not help at all, Augustine.'

'I f-fell asleep,' gasped her daughter, her face ashen with shock. 'And when I awoke he was like this!'

Laura poured some of the prepared bark and held it to his lips, and he drank most of it. His skin felt as if it was aflame.

'Nicholas,' she said urgently, 'we must send for Daniel.'

'No!'

'But he must see you. This is the height of folly—'

'Never. Never again!' he cried, his eyes darkening.

'But you must see a doctor, Nicholas,' she pleaded, 'for you are very ill again.'

'N-not Tregarron.' His breathing was heavy and his forehead damp.

'Please—'

'No!'

She saw again the rejection in his eyes, and resignedly she turned away to Mrs Townsend. 'Is there another doctor nearby?'

'No one is closer than Dr Brown in Ilminster.'

Ilminster was hours away, Daniel merely a few minutes, but she knew that nothing would prevail upon Nicholas to allow Daniel to examine him. She glanced at the door where some of the servants had gathered, brought by Augustine's cries. She beckoned to Hawkins. 'See that a man is sent to Dr Brown immediately, and make certain that the urgency of the situation is made known to him.'

'Very well, my lady.'

She returned slowly to her own room, going to the window and opening it fully. The wind and rain swept in and extinguished the candle. Her hair whipped across her face as she removed her night-bonnet, and the rain was cool against her skin. She felt so very tired. So very hollow.

Dr Brown of Ilminster was a stooping man, much given to the wearing of unrelieved black, which gave little comfort to his patients. He favored a white wig, so liberally dusted that it powdered his angular shoulders. He drank a large glass of Nicholas's finest cognac before turning to Laura, who stood waiting patiently by the fireplace in the red saloon. The pale, clear light of a fine dawn lightened the room.

'Lady Grenville, I confirm that Sir Nicholas is indeed suffering from a recurrence of the ague. As my colleague, Tregarron, informed you, this malady unhappily progresses in this manner, it being difficult for the body to rid itself of the ill humor which causes the condition. Were it not that he has already lost a great deal of blood due to the wound and the surgery he has undergone, I would recommend that he be bled. But his weakness, and the presence of the ague together, make circumstances exceptional, and so I cannot apply such treatment.' He gave a thin smile. 'It is not often that a West Country doctor is faced with a patient suffering from both a bullet wound and malaria at the same time. Nevertheless, I am acquainted with malaria, for it is common in parts of this country – I speak now of London and the Essex marshes – and it is my practice to administer syrup of poppies.'

'Dr Tregarron prescribed Jesuits' bark.'

He cleared his throat. 'Maybe so, but I prefer poppy. Oh, I am well aware that the cinchona tree for some reason produces a substance which combats the ill humors of malaria, but I still find syrup more of a remedy.'

She glanced at him. She detected the scathing tone of his voice at the metion of Jesuits, and she knew that it was religious intolerance that made him condemn the bark, not medical wisdom. 'I will continue with the bark, Dr Brown, because it proved efficacious when administered before.'

'Very well,' he said stiffly.

'How serious is this relapse, Doctor?'

'Considerable in a man as weakened as Sir Nicholas. It is absolutely essential that nothing worrying is mentioned in front of him. He must be kept calm at all costs. Has anything upsetting occurred recently?'

She thought of his strange and dramatic change toward her, and toward Daniel. 'Yes, Doctor, but I am afraid that I do not know exactly what it is, for he will not tell me.'

He nodded. 'Well, we must pray then that the crisis passes soon. I will return in a day or so, and in the meantime continue with the bark. I must leave now, as I have an important patient to attend to in the morning.' He glanced at his fob watch, 'Or should I say in several hours' time?'

'You will not take some refreshment?'

'Alas no, I have little enough time as it is. I will see you in a day or so then, when I trust there will be a substantial improvement in your husband's condition.'

She nodded. 'Good day, Dr Brown.'

'Good day, Lady Grenville.'

She stood there when he had gone. Yes, she would see him in a day or so, for how could she leave now? She would stay until she knew that Nicholas was out of danger again.

Chapter 27

And so it was that the letter to Lady Mountfort remained on the table in Laura's room the next day. There was no significant change in Nicholas's condition when the household awoke, which fact Laura communicated to Mr Dodswell before breakfast by hastily writing a note and sending a boy with it to the Home Farm.

Augustine, fully recovered from her initial shock, now remained limpet-like in Nicholas's room, and Laura made no attempt to go to see him. She did not know if she even wished to see him, for after the complete change in his disposition toward her, she felt that any contact would be painful in the extreme as far as she was concerned. She was at a loss to understand what had gone wrong, both as far as his dealings with her were concerned, and with Daniel.

She took a lonely breakfast, Mrs Townsend remaining in her bed, and Augustine ordering her own meal to be taken to her in Nicholas's room. Laura sat in silence, sorely missing Daniel's company, and deeply unhappy at having lost what little of Nicholas's affection she had ever laid claim to.

Hawkins entered. 'Mr Dodswell has called, my lady.'

'Show him in here, Hawkins.'

The butler bowed, and a moment or so later the agent was bowing before her. 'Good morning, Lady Grenville.'

'Good morning, Mr Dodswell. Will you take coffee with me?'

'That is most kind.' He sat down in the chair she gestured him to. 'It was also most kind of you to think of informing me about Sir Nicholas.'

'I knew that you would wish to know, for you are close to him.'

'I am. I understand there is still no improvement.'

'Not as yet, but then the bark must have a little time.'

'What is all this about him refusing to have Daniel Tregarron attending him?'

She poured the coffee and handed him the pink and white cup and saucer. 'I don't know, Mr Dodswell. I know only that something has happened to turn him against both myself and Daniel.'

The agent shifted a little uncomfortably in his seat, for he too had heard the rumors, although he gave them no credit. 'No doubt, Lady Grenville, his moods are caused by his state of health and we must make allowances—'

'Yes. Of course.'

'It is unfortunate that he has been set back like this, for I was hoping to be able to speak with him. I have received a visit from Christie's man, and the arrangements are well in hand, but I need Sir Nicholas's signature.'

'I do not think he is able to deal with anything at the moment, Mr Dodswell.'

'Then I must ask you.'

'Me?'

'You still have power of attorney, Lady Grenville.'

She nodded. 'I suppose I do.'

'There is more than the matter of Christie's and the auction, my lady. There is also the matter of cutting back on the number of staff employed here. There are already far too many, and when the hounds have gone and the surplus land sold – well, there will be an army where a mere company will suffice.'

'But where will they go? They must have employment, Mr Dodswell.'

'That is not my concern. Oh, do not think me heartless, but my duty is to King's Cliff, not to every man, woman, and child employed here.'

'How many must go?'

He took a paper from his pocket and handed it to her. She stared at the list of maids, grooms, gardeners, and so on.

'So many?'

'I fear so.'

Her glance fell on one particular name: Frank Roberts, Kitty's father. She folded the paper again. 'Is there no way we can keep them all, Mr Dodswell? I will find it very difficult to do this to them.'

'If I thought it practical, my lady, then of course I would not come to you like this, but it simply isn't practical. Or sensible. King's Cliff is in difficulties and those difficulties are too great to be foolishly lenient. Costs must be cut.'

She handed him back the list, thinking of the shy gardener handing her the bunch of red and yellow tulips. 'I don't want Frank Roberts to have to leave, Mr Dodswell, because he is my maid's father and because he has shown kindness to me.'

He nodded. 'I understand your feelings, my lady, but in Roberts's case there will be no difficulty. He is already assured of employment with the Countess of Bawton, whose penchant for tulips and other spring flowers is well known.'

'You are sure?'

'Positive. There is a position for Roberts with the Countess of Bawton.'

'Very well. But what of the others?'

'Some of them will naturally have difficulty finding work, but there are others who will step into other posts.'

'We must do what we can to see that they all have posts to go to, Mr Dodswell.'

He stared at her. 'But that is not possible.'

'I cannot go ahead with this unless I do all I can to place them elsewhere.' She was thinking of her own terror at having to find a position, of the desolate and humiliating knowledge that unless she found work she would starve. . . .

'If that is what you wish, Lady Grenville, then of course I will do all in my power to see that your wishes are carried out.'

'I will speak to the servants myself; I at least owe them that. I must explain as best I can why all this must be done.' She smiled a little. 'They probably know already, but it is only right that they should be told properly.'

'You will be taking on more responsibility, Lady Grenville, and this time there truly is no need.'

'But there is, Mr Dodswell, there most certainly is. I know only too well the importance of finding employment. They are not merely names on a sheet of paper, they are people.'

He smiled. 'You have a soft heart, Lady Grenville.'

'So, I must sign the whatever it is for Christie's and I must speak to the servants. Is there anything else which requires my attention?'

'Nothing urgent. Arrangements for the auction will go ahead, notices will appear in the major publications, and soon the whole realm will know what is about to happen at King's Cliff. There will be a considerable stir.'

'And, I trust, considerable interest – sufficient to bring them here intent upon paying a goodly price.'

'I trust so too. Oh, there is another matter. Mr McDonald, the engineer I spoke of, will be here either today or tomorrow.'

'How long do you think he will need to stay?'

'Possibly a week, my lady.'

'I will see that a room is made ready for him.'

The agent nodded and stood. 'If you will just sign these papers for Christie's, I will be on my way.'

'Of course.' She went to the escritoire in the corner and put her name to each one, while the agent held sealing wax to a candle flame and dropped a blob on each sheet. She pressed Nicholas's signet ring into each one. As she handed him the completed papers, she decided to tell him that she intended leaving King's Cliff. 'Mr Dodswell, I think I should tell you that I do not expect to be here for much longer.'

'Not be here?'

'No. It must be as obvious to you as it is to me that my marriage to Sir Nicholas is one of convenience. Until yesterday it was bearable, but now my position has become intolerable. I have decided to take up my life again, as if I had never met him and so as soon as he is out of danger, I shall go.'

'Does he know?'

She smiled a little. 'Mr Dodswell, I do not think he will particularly care.'

'I am sure you are wrong.'

'No, sir, I am not. My husband wished all along to marry Miss Townsend, and that is still his wish.'

'But where will you go?' he asked, half expecting to hear her say she would go to Daniel Tregarron, but her reply surprised him.

'I hope to take up a position as companion to Lady Mountfort, if that position is still open to me.'

His eyes widened. '*Companion*? But you are Lady Grenville!'

'Not for much longer, I fancy. Now perhaps you will understand my anxiety about the servants who will lose their posts here, Mr Dodswell. Uncertainty about employment is a terrible thing. I speak from experience, not from soft-heartedness.'

He took her hand, raising it to his lips. 'I do not know what to say, except to beg you to think again about leaving this house. Please wait awhile and reconsider.'

She did not answer, and he sadly took his leave of her. His heart was heavy as he rode away. She had not been at King's Cliff for long, but in that time she had impressed him a great deal. She was everything an estate like King's Cliff needed in its mistress, and she was the wife Mr Dodswell would himself have chosen for Nicholas Grenville. But it was not meant to be. As he rode down the escarpment, however, he wondered how much Daniel Tregarron had had to do with it all. And Augustine Townsend.

The vestibule was filled to capacity as Hawkins assembled the entire staff to hear what Laura had to say. They whispered anxiously together, for word had spread and they already knew that many of them had to leave King's Cliff. They fell silent as she appeared at the top of the staircase, a slender figure in pink muslin, her dark hair almost hidden by a dainty lace day-cap. Her hand trembled on the handrail as she descended, stopping halfway so that they could all see and hear her. They wondered, as they watched her, how much of it was true about her affair with Daniel Tregarron, but this took second place to their own anxieties now. Some of the maids were almost in tears, and the men were pale and tense. Very few of them felt secure.

She looked at Hawkins. 'Is everyone here?'

'Yes, my lady.'

Her mouth felt very dry. 'I – I suppose that my purpose in calling you all here is already known to you, and I want to tell you that I do not find this task at all easy, for I understand only too well how you must be feeling. I *do* understand, believe me, probably more than you can realize. I want therefore to reassure those of you who are to lose your posts here and who do not find employment elsewhere that I will do everything in my power to secure positions for you in the neighborhood. I cannot promise miracles, but I can promise to do what I can. I am deeply sorry that I have to face you like this, especially as I have been here for so little time, but King's Cliff is in great financial straits and I do not feel that I have any choice. I know what Sir Nicholas's wishes are and I am trying to carry them out to the best of my ability. Great changes are about to take place here, so that what existed in the past will never exist in quite the same way again. It grieves me, as I know it grieves Sir Nicholas, that you must suffer, but be assured that I will do my best, such as it is, for you. Hawkins has the list prepared by Mr Dodswell. That will be all.'

Her heart was pounding as she turned and went slowly up the stairs again. She had been sincere, but did they know that? Did they know that she would indeed do as she promised? She smiled ironically to herself, for her own conscience was keeping her at King's Cliff; she felt responsible somehow, and maybe she was, for she had Nicholas's authority to act for him. Until he withdrew that, the responsibility for King's Cliff and its employees rested solely with her.

Chapter 28

For Laura the atmosphere in the house continued to be oppressive, for although Nicholas's fever began to abate, his manner toward her did not soften at all; he was still an ice-cold stranger. She found herself wishing that Daniel was there, for he could always lighten her mood and make her feel good – and above all make her feel desirable. Riding with him in the afternoons had been such a pleasure, but now she felt totally alone, and although she still rode, it was not the same by herself. She confined her rides to King's Cliff land, particularly to Langford Woods where she did not feel so exposed, for she still had no riding habit and she knew that she did not present a creditable appearance.

Three days later she received a brief note from Mr McDonald, informing her that he would arrive by mid-morning. That same morning Dr Brown returned to see his patient and expressed his satisfaction that the crisis was over and that he would not need to come again. The doctor had not long gone when Augustine and her mother sallied forth to visit the Countess of Bawton, in the secret hope that the Duke of Gloucester would already have arrived for his visit, and so for the first time Laura had an opportunity of speaking to Nicholas alone.

It was not easy to go to his room, but she wanted to tell him what she was doing about the estate, particularly with regard to the servants. She found him much weakened, the recurrence of the malaria having obviously set his progress back, but any hope she may have had that his attitude would change was immediately dashed by his cool greeting. The only way she could salvage her own crushed pride was by adopting the same attitude, and so she was as icily correct as he was. He had expressed his approval of what she had told the servants, for Henderson had already conveyed the content of her speech to him, and he had also approved of the arrangements with Christie's. He expressed an interest in the arrival of the engineer, and inquired about several minor matters. He did not ask her about herself once; he showed no interest whatsoever in her well-being. And so, the interview limped to an end, the distance between them as great, if not greater, than before her visit.

Mr Alistair McDonald arrived with his three assistants in time for luncheon. He was a sandy-haired, young man with a long, pale freckled face and slender figure. His hands were small and beautifully cared for, he wore fashionable clothes which would not have disgraced Bond Street, and all in all he looked like anything but an engineer. He did not seem robust enough for the long, arduous hours he undoubtedly worked, and his manner was gentle. He spoke with a soft Edinburgh accent, choosing his words carefully, and she liked him immediately. After her uneasy confrontation with Nicholas, she was determined to ride out with the engineer and Mr Dodswell, for that would take her away from the house for a while. Mr Dodswell had protested that a lengthy, uncomfortable ride across King's Cliff Moor was hardly a suitable activity for a lady, but she had been adamant. Various instruments, including a theodolite, were attached to the saddle of the engineer's horse, and his assistants rode respectfully behind him as, with Laura and Mr Dodswell on either side of him, he rode across the park toward the escarpment.

Augustine lowered the curtain when they had passed from sight. She had returned from a fruitless visit to the Countess's house to learn that Laura had been to see her husband. Determined not to risk any patching up between them, she had immediately idly mentioned that Laura still rode in the afternoons. To Langford Woods. The implication was quite obvious, and must to Nicholas appear only too apparent. But he had said nothing.

She went to the bedside now, looking down at him as he slept. His reactions to Laura's supposed infidelities did not please Augustine at all, and she knew that that was because he was deeply hurt. He could only be hurt if he liked and trusted his wife. Augustine's eyes moved over his face. He was so very handsome, a flame to draw all moths, a man no woman would ever tire of. She knew that she wanted him. She would endure James Grenville's bed if that was the only way, but it was Nicholas she desired, the more so since she was no longer so certain of her hold over him. Jealousy stirred through her as she looked at him. He was *hers*, hers alone! But even as she stood there, it was James Grenville's evil face that she saw, and she was afraid.

The wind blew freely over King's Cliff Moor, rattling the stiffly upright reeds and rustling through the delicate fronds of the willows. An old man was gathering reeds and withies for baskets, and neat bundles lay ready nearby. He paused in his work as the horses passed and his gaze was cold as he watched them move up to one of the narrow, raised tracks that had been there since the misty times long ago when the monks had first attempted to drain the lowlands. The rhines and ditches were still now, choked with mud and weeds. The dissolution of the monasteries had seen the end of centuries of work, and now the water had begun to claim its own again.

There were tall spikes of wild iris growing on the edge of the water, and otter tracks crossed a smooth expanse of mud. Laura saw pure white swans and a flight of geeze winging northwards across the clear sky. She did not look back at King's Cliff once, looking only ahead as Mr McDonald began his work.

He seemed to know exactly what he was looking for, dismounting frequently to clamber down a bank, muttering to his busily scribbling assistants about dikes, rhines, sluices, and cuts. He measured distances with great accuracy and apparently for no reason, but everything was meticulously entered into a book, and a map was beginning to take shape.

They rested in the shade of some trees, and Laura settled herself comfortably, leaning back against a trunk. 'What do you think so far, Mr McDonald?'

'It is too early to say, my lady. I believe that I will not be able to tell you anything for a week. One thing I can say, however, and that is that by my calculations it would take a lowering of the land level of only ten to fifteen feet to turn these lowlands once again into a shallow bay of the Bristol Channel.'

'But the sea is twenty miles away!'

'Nevertheless, I believe that that is all it would take. Where we are seated now was undoubtedly once beneath the sea, and it would not take much for it to return to that state.'

She shivered a little.

He smiled. 'Do not take fright, my lady, for it was not a warning twinge in my big toe which prompted my remark; it was merely an idle observation. In 1703 there was a great flood here, a terrible storm which breached the sea defenses and killed many people as it washed inland. It came as far as King's Cliff, Lady Grenville, so that I can only warn you that whatever plan I may be able to present to you at the end of my survey, it cannot possibly keep back the sea should it return.'

Their progress across the marsh did not pass unnoticed. The poachers watched them from the secrecy of the reeds, and although she could not see them, Laura knew they were there. She could tell that Mr Dodswell was aware of them too, for he kept glancing around. It was an uneasy feeling, not at all pleasant, but not once did they see anybody, although once they saw the Tibdales' large black gun dog.

A week later Laura was working in the library. Working was the only way to describe what she did, for it was certainly not an idle passing of the time. Her head ached with reading the household accounts. Not only had King's Cliff been grossly overstaffed, it was also wasting money very unnecessarily. What point was there in sending to London for the best tea, when there was undoubtedly excellent tea closer in Taunton? And why pay for the services of a fellow from Essex to come to examine one of the brood mares? Surely there were skilled men in Somerset too? Why have this fellow simply because it was fashionable, for that was nonsensical in the present climate. She dipped her quill in the ink again and made another note. Jesu, the list seemed endless. . . . She put the quill down and wearily stretched her arms above her head, wishing that she was out riding with Daniel Tregarron now instead of sitting inside poring over figures and entries that were fast becoming a blur. Maybe she had worked too long. She glanced at the clock. It was half-past four; Mr McDonald would return soon from what he had informed her would be his last piece of surveying. Today he would tell her what, if anything, could be done.

Her glance fell on another sheet of paper on the escritoire before her. Already there were several servants who were unable to find new positions, and Hawkins had brought their names to her earlier. She had given her word and she stood by that, just as she stood by the word she had given to Nicholas. Now she was set to begin writing some letters to surrounding landowners, asking them to consider employing Bridget Donovan, Frederick Hartley, Joseph Bride, Benjamin Cruickshank, and so on, and so on. . . . Maybe some would respond favorably, for the servants employed at King's Cliff had always been the very finest, but there would be many landowners who would tear up her letter simply because it came from her.

Hawkins announced Mr McDonald and she looked up quickly. 'Good afternoon, sir.'

He gave a graceful bow and she hid a smile. His elegance never ceased to surprise her. He would never look like an engineer; he was formed for the drawing-room, not for ditches and drainage schemes. 'Good afternoon, Lady Grenville. I am happy to tell you that I have completed my survey and so am able to tell you my findings.'

'Please sit down, sir.'

He obeyed. 'First, I must tell you that in my opinion it will be reasonably easy to drain King's Cliff Moor.'

'Easy?'

'Most of the medieval workings are still there, and those which aren't can be made good speedily enough. None of it requires such major work that things will become complicated or difficult. It is merely hard work, if you follow me. The rhines do not at present carry away the excess water, but that is because they are choked and virtually useless. If they were dredged and maybe widened a little, then the water would begin to move again. I have studied the system's outfall into the River Parrett and believe it is adequate still for the volume of water involved. With five hundred laborers, the work could be commenced and well on its way by this autumn. By this time next year it could be complete and King's Cliff Moor well on the way to becoming fertile farming land, as Sir Nicholas wishes.'

'Five hundred men?' she gasped, taken aback.

He smiled. 'The projects I have worked on with Sir John Rennie in the Fenlands have employed upward of a thousand men, Lady Grenville.' Something caught his eye outside and he looked out to see Augustine and her mother mounting their horses for a ride. 'They will be sorry, I fear, for it will rain in a few minutes, and quite heavily too, if I'm not mistaken.'

I sincerely hope it pours down and leaves them like drowned rats, she thought. 'You can read the weather, Mr McDonald?'

'I have learned to take note of all the signs – being stranded out in the middle of a marsh when a downpour happens along is not exactly a pleasant experience, I assure you, and it has happened to me more than once.'

She smiled at him. 'Thank you for coming here, Mr McDonald, your helpfulness has been much appreciated. I realize that the cost of what you suggest will not be low, and for that reason I cannot give you any instructions to go ahead until after the forthcoming auction, of which you have no doubt heard.'

'I saw the notices in today's newspapers.'

'As will the rest of the land.'

'It will come as a shock to many. The King's Cliff hunt in particular is practically an institution.'

'Well, I trust that someone with a bulging purse wishes it to continue so somewhere else. Mr McDonald, will you tell Sir Nicholas what you have told me?'

'I will indeed.' He stood. 'Lady Grenville, I must decline to dine here tonight, for I am already overdue at my aunt's house in Bath. She is a little crotchety at the best of times, and tardy newphews appear to bring out the very worst in her.'

She smiled. 'I quite understand, sir. I have enjoyed your excellent company at dinner this past week.'

He inclined his head. 'You are most gracious, my lady.'

She wondered how much he was aware of the situation in the house? Could he have missed the fact that Sir Nicholas Grenville and his wife hardly ever saw each other? Could he have missed the fact that Augustine Townsend appeared to be too often with the master of the house? No, thought Laura, he could hardly have missed any of it, but there was nothing in his manner to hint that he noticed anything. She held out her hand to him. 'I trust, sir, that you will hear from us in the not-too-distant future.'

He kissed her hand. 'And I hope, Lady Grenville, that the auction goes well and thus lifts the weight from Sir Nicholas's shoulders.'

She sat down to work again when he had gone, and she had been writing for some time when she heard the first heavy drops against the window. A rumble of thunder spread across the skies and the rain began to fall more heavily with each passing second. She sat back, smiling. Let the heavens open, and let there be no shelter for Miss Augustine Townsend and her mother!

Chapter 29

Mr McDonald was still engaged with Nicholas when the thunderstorm at last ended and the sun came out. The birds sang their hearts out in the park and the leaves dripped, their colors more vibrant and fresh now. Augustine and her mother had not returned, and Laura had inquired of Hawkins where they were, only to be told that their destination had been the Countess of Bawton's house. Their purpose had been twofold, first to meet the Duke of Gloucester if possible, and second – and more important as far as Laura was concerned – to arrange the reception at King's Cliff at which Laura was expected to receive the ladies of the neighborhood. Her heart had sunk on hearing this, for she had been praying that Augustine would let the matter drop, but obviously that was not to be. Augustine was hardly likely to let such an ideal opportunity of making her rival's life more miserable slip away.

With the sun came Mr Dodswell, intent upon seeing Nicholas, but when he was informed that the engineer was with the master, the agent found himself shown instead into Laura's presence.

She smiled, putting down her quill. 'Why, Mr Dodswell, how good it is to see you. Please sit down.'

'I – er, came to see Sir Nicholas.'

'Mr McDonald is with him. Can I help in any way?'

'I – no.'

She looked at him in surprise. 'Is something wrong, Mr Dodswell?'

'No, my lady.'

'Does it concern the estate?'

'Yes.'

'Then please be good enough to tell me.'

The agent cleared his throat uncomfortably, for the last thing he wanted to do was speak to Laura about this particular matter. But she waited, and he had no choice but to tell her. 'It appears that a certain portion of Langford Woods, at present due to be auctioned, should in fact be offered to Dr Tregarron first. I found a paper signed by Sir Jasper to this effect, as apparently the doctor had once expressed an interest in the land, which adjoins his own property.'

'And is the paper legally binding?'

'Yes, my lady.'

'Then the land must of course be first offered to him.'

Mr Dodswell knew his cheeks were flaming now. 'I am anxious not to cross Sir Nicholas in any way, my lady.'

'Of course.' She thought for a moment. 'I will see Dr Tregarron, and thus you will be spared any involvement.'

'*You?*'

'Why not? I have no quarrel with the doctor, indeed quite the opposite, for in him I have found a good friend. I will go to see him this afternoon.'

The agent was inwardly aghast that his visit should have produced this result, but outwardly he showed nothing but a polite smile. 'There is no need, Lady Grenville—'

'Nonsense, someone has to see him about the land and I am quite capable of performing the task.'

The agent stood, and she looked curiously at him again. He seemed very odd today. 'Are you sure that there is nothing wrong, Mr Dodswell?'

'Quite sure, my lady.'

'You are not unwell?'

'I am perfectly well.'

'I hope you are not working too hard, sir, for I realize that you have had a great deal to do of late.'

He smiled then. 'I believe I work no harder than you, Lady Grenville.'

'I have nothing else of importance to do.' She lowered her eyes then.

'If anyone should be asked if he is feeling unwell at the moment, Lady Grenville, I believe that person to be the Earl of Langford.'

'Oh?'

Mr McDonald smiled again. 'He saw the notices in the newspapers this morning, and I believe Mount Vesuvius gives a poorer show of fireworks than our noble earl.'

'Good, I hope he bursts with rage.'

'From what I heard, my lady, that seems a distinct possibility.'

She walked to the main doors with the agent, her shawl trailing a little on the top step as she watched him ride away. How very strange his mood had been today. Something was on his mind, that much was for sure, but what could it be? It seemed so very odd that his own close friendship with Daniel Tregarron could stand in danger simply because Nicholas and Daniel had parted so acrimoniously. As the agent rode out of sight someone else approached King's Cliff. For the second time that morning her heart sank, for the carriage bowling swiftly along the drive now belonged to no other than James Grenville, Earl of Langford.

Swiftly she went back into the house, determined to face Nicholas's cousin in a place of her choosing, not his. But she had hurried up the

staircase and along the passage toward the library when not far from
Nicholas's room she encountered Mr McDonald. Dismayed, she halted, but
she smiled warmly enough at him.

'You are about to leave us, sir?'

'I am indeed, Lady Grenville. Sir Nicholas was good enough to tell me
that if the auction proves successful, then he will send for me to commence
the work on the marsh.'

'I'm so glad, Mr McDonald.'

At that moment the earl's angry voice echoed in the vestibule. 'I *demand*
to see her!' he shouted.

Mr McDonald was shocked, and Laura turned slowly as she heard the
earl hurrying up the main staircase. He saw her immediately, and with his
face red and his short plump figure bristling with rage, he stomped toward
her, waving a newspaper furiously as he did so. 'How *dare* you stoop to
vulgarly advertising what may yet be my property at an auction!'

'Please, sir,' began Mr McDonald, quite appalled at such conduct in front
of a lady.

'You keep out of this!' snapped the earl. 'This has nothing whatsoever to
do with you!'

Laura's glance was withering. 'Nor, sir, has it anything to do with you!
What takes place on this estate is none of your business!'

'On the contrary, madam, it is entirely my business when I am heir to it!'

'Please leave.'

'Not until you agree to withdraw these abominable advertisements and
cancel the auction.'

'If you do not leave, sirrah, I will have you forcibly removed.'

His eyes narrowed unpleasantly. 'How dare you presume to adopt that
insolent tone with me, madam!'

Another voice broke into the argument then. 'Do as my wife says, James.'

With a gasp, Laura whirled about to see Nicholas leaning weakly against
the door of his room. His face was ashen with the effort of rising from his
bed, and his breathing was heavy and uneven. She hurried to him, drawing
his arm around her shoulder and slipping her other arm around his waist as
she called to the startled Scot to assist her.

James Grenville could only stare at his cousin.

Nicholas leaned slightly against Laura, holding the earl's gaze. 'Leave this
house, James. You have no right to be here and no right to address my wife
in that disparaging manner. She is my wife, and if you insult her, then you
insult me. Never speak to her like that again, or so help me you will regret
it. You will never inherit this house. I would as soon will it to the Langford
smithy, for he would no doubt make a better fist of it than you! Now get
out, and be warned that you will never be allowed to set foot over my
threshold again.'

The enmity flowed evenly between the two Grenville cousins, and this time James knew he had met his match. It was James who backed down from further confrontation at that moment, turning away to walk quickly back toward the staircase. They heard his heavy steps descending, the main doors were closed loudly, and then there was silence.

Laura and Mr McDonald helped Nicholas back into his bed, and when he was made comfortable, she looked anxiously down at him. 'You should not have done that, you are not strong enough yet—'

'What he said to you could not pass unchallenged, Laura, for you *are* my wife.' He smiled a little wryly. 'For better, for worse.'

Until your choice us do part, Nicholas. Your choice. . . .

She alighted from the landau outside Daniel's house. For a moment she stood there, looking up at the elegant red-brick façade. The house had been built at the time of Queen Anne, and it was small by King's Cliff standards, but nevertheless it was a spacious and pleasing building, its raised main doors approached by a double flight of stone steps set against the wall. The formal grounds had been laid out after the Dutch fashion, a long canal stretching away before the house with symmetrical beds of flowers and herbs. Behind the house spread the green expanse of Langford Woods – but for which she would have been able to see King's Cliff, some one mile away as the crow flew.

She mounted the steps then and Mrs Thompson, the housekeeper, opened the door. Her eyes widened when she saw the identity of the visitor, but she stood aside and politely asked Laura to enter.

Laura waited in the red-and-white-tiled hall. A beautiful vase of dark red peonies stood on a highly polished table, and several paintings which she judged to be by the very talented Mr Turner hung on the wall opposite. A tall grandfather clock stood in a alcove, its slow pendulum swinging. Its mechanism began to whir and the delicate, melodious chimes echoed out in the silence.

Mrs Thompson returned to the hall. 'If you will come this way, my lady, Dr Tregarron will receive you in the drawing-room.' The housekeeper's keys chinked together as she led Laura up the black marble staircase.

Daniel stood by the window, his tall, slender figure bright in the shaft of sunlight that streamed in. The room was one of easy elegance, its chairs and sofas upholstered with bright tapestries and its walls hung with more of the landscapes and seascapes he seemed to favor so much.

He turned as she was shown in and she saw that he was wearing the same dove-gray coat he had worn the first time she had seen him. His dark eyes went to the housekeeper, who remained by the door.

'That will be all, Mrs Thompson.'

The housekeeper's eyes were reproachful, but she left them then, although Daniel knew that she did so against her own better judgment. He smiled at Laura. 'Good afternoon, Laura, I see that you are as beautiful as ever.'

'Good afternoon, Daniel.'

'Does Nicholas know you are here?'

'No.'

'Then you risk his wrath.'

'I come on King's Cliff business, which cannot offend him.'

'You think not?'

'I have not quarreled with you, Daniel,' she reminded him.

'To be sure you have not.' He came toward her then, taking her hands and raising them to his lips.

Slowly she drew her hands away. 'How are you, Daniel?'

'As you see, I am well. But you look tired, Laura.'

'That is not what you should tell a lady when she has spent hours at her toilet, sir.'

'It is the doctor in me which speaks now, not the gentleman – the gentleman sees only that you are quite the most lovely of creatures, Lady Grenville, not least because you are so original.'

'Original?'

He went to a table and picked up a newspaper. 'I refer to the auction, so loudly proclaimed in today's publications. I know of no other woman who would have embarked on even half the projects you have undertaken in your husband's name. The odds are stacked against you, your position is hopeless, and yet you go determinedly ahead with all this. Yes, Laura, you are very original. And to me you are devastatingly attractive.'

She stared at him. 'Daniel—'

'Don't embarrass you? Very well, I will behave. You say that you are here on King's Cliff's behalf?' He spoke lightly, but he was very close now to confessing his love. Was now the time? Would there ever be a *better* opportunity than this?

His words had disturbed her, but she collected herself. 'Yes, I understand that you have first refusal on the portion of Langford Woods adjoining this house.'

'That is so.'

'Why have you not said anything? The first I knew of it was when Mr Dodswell came to me today.'

'There seemed little point in saying anything when I shall shortly be selling this house.'

'You – you are going to America then?'

'Yes.'

'When?'

'I hope to be gone within a month.'

'So quickly?'

'Yes.'

'Oh.'

He watched her for a moment, and then came a little closer. 'Am I to hope from your reaction that you will miss me?'

'You know that I will – I miss you now when you are but a mile away. You will be so much farther if you go to America.'

'There need not be any distance between us at all, Laura,' he said softly, taking her face in his hands.

'Don't, please—'

'I love you,' he said quietly, 'As I believe you know well enough.'

'No!'

'Why did you come here today? Charles Dodswell could have done it, but you came in person. Why?'

She could only stare at him.

His thumbs caressed her cheeks. 'I offer you the love Nicholas denies you, Laura, and you are not indifferent to me, are you?'

'Please,' she whispered, 'please let me go.'

He held her still, bending his head to kiss her on the lips. He took his time, his lips moving softly but firmly over hers, and to her shame she found herself clinging to him, returning the kiss. The shame overwhelmed her then and she pushed him away. 'No!' she cried. 'No, it's wrong!'

'Why? Why is it wrong? Laura, I love you and I know that your marriage is empty. I am a man, not a mouse, and I want you even if your fool of a husband doesn't. Maybe you think yourself in love with him, bound to him by marriage vows, but a moment ago I felt a flaw in that love, I felt your lips meeting mine as sweetly as I could ever wish. Maybe you think it is sinful, for I break one commandment in coveting another man's wife, and I would break another by committing adultery if I damned well could! Do these protestations shock you, Laura? Well, they should not, for my heart is exposed to you now; I confess a love which has burned in me from almost the first moment I met you. I love you but your husband doesn't, I can give you the warmth you are made for, but he never will. He has made his rejection of you quite plain, and now I make my love for you equally as plain. Come with me, Laura, and I promise you enough love to wash away the hurt and pain he has caused you.'

'I will never love you in the way you seek, Daniel,' she whispered.

'No? Your kiss tells another tale.'

She flushed and turned to pick up her reticule.

'I have a month in which to win you, Laura, and win you I shall.'

Mrs Thompson hurried to open the doors for her, noting Laura's flushed face and hurried departure. As the carriage drew away, Laura glanced out and saw Daniel at the drawing-room window. Their eyes met for a long moment.

The carriage took her from his sight then and she sat back. The shame still lay over her. How could it have happened? How could she have wanted him to hold her like that? She didn't love him, she loved Nicholas, but she had returned Daniel Tregarron's kiss.

Chapter 30

Now that Mr McDonald had departed, there was no reason for Laura to go down to dinner, and so she once again ordered her own meal to be served in the peace and seclusion of the library, where she could afterward do a little more work. But as she dressed for dinner, thinking about her afternoon meeting with Daniel Tregarron, she became more and more aware of how unusually silent Kitty was. The maid's little face with withdrawn, and if Laura was not mistaken, it was also tearstained. 'Kitty?' she asked at last. 'What is wrong?'

Tears sprang immediately to the maid's eyes. 'Oh, my lady, it's my poor father. He fell down the stairs two days back and broke his leg, and today the Countess of Bawton's land agent came to say that she no longer wishes to employ him. We live in a King's Cliff tied cottage, my lady, and I have a little brother and sister. There's only me working, and we'll have no roof over our heads – I just don't know what to do, and my mother's fair out of her mind with worry.'

Laura was horrified. 'Oh, Kitty, I'm so sorry. Please don't cry, for you know that I will do all I can. First of all I must reassure you that you will not be turned out of your home. Maybe I cannot reassure you about work as well, but I will do all I can. Please tell your parents.'

The maid smiled through her tears. 'Oh, Lady Grenville, I don't know what to say.'

Laura went slowly toward the library a little later. Allowing Frank Roberts's family to remain in their cottage was all very well, but it was work he sought, for only if he worked would he have his pride and self-respect. The memory of Kitty's tears lingered thoughout her solitary meal and she hardly touched her dinner. The plight of Frank Roberts, more than that of the other servants, touched her personally and made her feel sad and responsible.

She had been working for some time by the light of candles, sifting through the maze of facts and figures concerning various acquisitions during the lifetime of Nicholas's father when she distinctly heard the gallery door open and and the rustle of taffeta. She looked up as Augustine leaned gracefully over the rail. She was splendid in turquoise, diamonds sparkling in her red hair and at her pale throat. A flouncy ostrich feather curled down from the bright comb holding her hair up, and her white, fringed shawl dragged lazily along the floor as she slowly approached the spiral steps to the lower level of the library.

Laura sat back warily, mindful of the purpose of Augustine's visit to the Countess of Bawton earlier. 'Good evening, Miss Townsend,' she said sweetly.

'Good evening, my *lady*.' As always, there was the sarcastic emphasis on Laura's title. 'My, my, are we working hard again? Your complexion will suffer if you labor by candlelight all the time. Indeed, now I come to look more closely at you, I fear my warning is too late. You look positively *ill*, my *lady*, and not interestingly so, I fear.'

'Really.'

'Yes – really.'

'Have you some purpose in coming here, Miss Townsend?'

'Why does one normally frequent a library, unless it is to choose a book – or to labor pathetically upon wifely tasks which will receive no thanks in the long run.'

Laura ignored the latter part of the statement, getting to her feet and going to a shelf where she had noticed a particular book. She took it down and held it out to Augustine. 'This would appear eminently suitable for you, Miss Townsend.'

'*A History of the Borgias*? How very droll, to be sure.'

'Very apt, I think you will agree.'

Augustine's eyes flickered and then she too selected a book, handing it to Laura. 'This is what I would choose for your nightly reading, my lady. *The Life of Catherine of Aragon* would appear so pertinent to your own situation.'

'That presumably places you in the role of Anne Boleyn and we all know her fate, don't we?'

Augustine casually tossed the books on to the table, but the action was not as casual as it appeared, for the force of the books' landing caused several papers to flutter to the floor. A smile touched Augustine's lips then, an unpleasant, triumphant smile, which made Larua feel cold inside. 'How is Dr Daniel Tregarron?' asked Augustine softly.

Laura stared at her. 'Well, I believe.'

'Yes, well you would know, wouldn't you? After all, you did visit him alone this afternoon, didn't you?'

Laura said nothing.

'So handsome and charming, is he not? And so very different from dear

Nicholas. Nicholas is a golden god; Daniel Tregarron is dark and interesting. A very intriguing gentleman, I think you will agree.'

Laura felt the guilt staining her cheeks and was glad that the candlelight would serve to disguise her color.

But Augustine missed nothing. 'Yes,' she murmured, 'no doubt you have decided to cut your losses and settle for Daniel when Nicholas casts you off. The world has remarked the good doctor's obvious partiality for you.'

'I don't know what you mean.'

'No? Oh, come now, don't be obtuse, my dear, for you surely don't expect anyone to believe that you have no inkling of the handsome doctor's feelings.'

To Laura it was as if Augustine had witnessed everything that had passed between herself and Daniel that afternoon. She recovered swiftly, however, returning to take her place at the escritoire and dipping her quill in the ink. 'If you have nothing agreeable to say, Miss Townsend, then I suggest that you leave me to my work.'

'But, of course, who am I to stand in the path of the lady who has power of attorney in this house? Your word is law, my *lady* – except when your husband overrules you. As in the matter of taking tea with the ladies of the neighborhood.'

'Am I to presume that you have something to impart to me, Miss Townsend? Or are you merely wasting both my time and your own?'

'I waste no one's time. The necessary invitations have been issued, my *lady*, and it is set for you to receive the ladies in the red saloon tomorrow morning.'

'I will endeavor to remember.'

'You would be advised to be prompt, for Nicholas will not be pleased if you let him down, would he? Oh, and do try to dress well, at least try to *appear* to be a person of quality. Appearances are so important, are they not?'

Laura toyed with the quill, stroking its shaft very slowly. She could not win this particular skirmish, but she would fire the last salvo. 'I trust your presentation to the Duke of Gloucester went excellently,' she purred, knowing full well that it hadn't. His Grace had remembered Augustine's unfortunate connection with the Earl of Langford and had therefore virtually snubbed her when she had been presented. Augustine had suffered extreme mortification and her cheeks flamed scarlet now as Laura reminded her, thereby intimating that she knew all about something Augustine would much have preferred to keep secret.

Augustine leaned her hands on the escritoire and her voice was a snake-like hiss. 'I will make you sorry you ever heard Nicholas Grenville's name!'

'So you keep promising me, Miss Townsend. I do not believe you have succeeded yet.' They were brave words, uttered in defiance of the truth.

Augustine's slippers tapped angrily on the floor as she left the library.

Laura put the quill down. She was disturbed by Augustine's hints about Daniel Tregarron, hints which after this afternoon were a little too close to the truth for comfort.

Before retiring to bed, Laura went to see Nicholas. She chose her time carefully, so that the moment Augustine went to take chocolate with her mother, Laura slipped swiftly along to his room. More than anything else at the moment she wanted to avoid meeting the Countess of Bawton and her friends, and maybe Nicholas would relent just a little. . . .

He was not in his bed, but for the first time was sitting in a chair by the empty fireplace. He wore a rich brocade dressing gown and his hair gleamed very pale in the candlelight. He looked up as she entered and there was no encouragement either in his glance or in his tone when he spoke. 'Good evening, Laura.'

'Good evening.' Hesitantly she went closer. 'Nicholas, I have something to ask you, to *beg* you.'

'And I have something to demand of you, madam – an explanation for your visit to Daniel Tregarron this afternoon.'

'A – an explanation?' Augustine's words rang in her ears.

'You know full well that I have severed all relations with him, and yet you flout my wishes by going to visit him. I wish to know why.'

'I went about the sale of part of Langford Woods.'

'Indeed.'

'Yes, Mr Dodswell came to me today and told me that he had discovered there to be an agreement between your father and Daniel Tregarron, whereby if a particular portion of Langford Woods, that adjoining Daniel's property, was ever to be sold, then Daniel was to have first claim.'

'It was hardly your place to attend to such a matter,' he said coldly. 'It was Charles Dodswell's place; he is my land agent.'

Her anger stirred a little then. 'Maybe it wasn't my place, but I am mindful that but for Daniel Tregarron's care, you might not be alive now, Nicholas. I don't pretend to know why you and he now hold such bitter feelings for each other, but I do know that *I* haven't quarreled with him. He has proved a good friend to me, probably my *only* friend since I came here.' *You aren't my friend, Nicholas, you whom I love more than anyone. . . .*

He ignored what she said, choosing instead to revert to the matter of Langford Woods. 'And what does he wish to do about the land?'

'He is no longer interested, as he intends leaving England shortly.'

The gray eyes searched her face. Would Daniel Tregarron be leaving alone? He looked away from her then. When his cousin had insulted her that morning, his own rage and confused emotions concerning her had driven him to defend her, but since then she had been with Daniel Tregarron again. What had taken place in Daniel's house Nicholas could only surmise, but when taken with the rumors which were so rife, it could only point to one thing – a lover's tryst. Jealousy and hurt urged Nicholas on now, making him cold and distant when he wished to win her, making him wish to deal to her the hurt he felt she had dealt to him.

His silence prompted her to think again of her purpose in coming to see him. 'Nicholas, I wish to ask something of you.'

'Yes?'

'Allow me the right to stay away from this so-called reception tomorrow.'

'It is your duty to attend.'

'I do not entirely agree, not given the circumstances pertaining here. They do not come to greet me as friends, they come to—'

'You will meet them.'

She looked into his cold eyes. It was hard now to even remember how different it had been in Venice, how different it had been at first even here at King's Cliff, for now there was no trace of the man she had fallen in love with. And yet he was still Nicholas, and try as she would, she could not conquer the feelings of love he always aroused in her.

'Very well,' she said, her chill matching his, 'I will do your bidding, sir.'

Chapter 31

For over an hour now the fashionable carriages had been arriving, and there was a long string of them drawn up along the drive in front of King's Cliff. Laura had delayed as long as possible, but now she walked slowly toward the red saloon. An icy calm settled over her, even though her anger and resentment had not lessened overnight. She did not feel at all nervous, as Augustine no doubt hoped she would; instead she felt defiant, and more than prepared to give as good as she got.

The footmen at the doors of the saloon waited for her signal as she paused, rearranging her shawl, and then she nodded to them and they flung the doors open to admit her. The room was loud with female chattering, which was immediately silenced by her appearance. Many pairs of critical eyes swept over her, scrutinizing the quality of her sprigged muslin gown, gauging the cost of the delicate lace in her day-cap, and noting the degree of fashion in her coiffure. Not one small detail of her appearance missed their eyes, from the black ribbon at her throat to the neat satin slippers peeping from beneath her hem. Teacups clinked and some throats were cleared expectantly as she crossed the floor to where Augustine stood.

Augustine's eyes shone. 'Good morning, Laura.'

'Good morning, Miss Townsend.' Gasps greeted this, for Laura quite deliberately denied Augustine the intimacy that had apparently been expected.

Augustine's smile went out, like an extinguished candle flame. 'Will you not introduce me?' asked Laura, the epitome of calm politeness.

A succession of limp hands were extended to her, and an impressive succession of names succeeded them. They were stiff and formal; she was unreadable as she gave a small smile to each one, but then at last the moment they had been anticipating came, and she found herself face-to-face with the Countess of Bawton, the lady who had so pointedly snubbed her at Langford church.

Augustine's voice was sweet. 'Allow me to present you to the Countess of Bawton. Lady Elizabeth, this is Laura, Lady Grenville.'

'How do you do, Lady Grenville.' The crowlike voice was cold, the tone calculated to distance the recipient.

'How do you do, Lady Elizabeth.' Laura sensed the room closing in, the faces eager to savor the confrontation between their senior member and the upstart mistress of King's Cliff.

The countess's smile was cool. 'Do tell us how long you have known Sir Nicholas, my dear; we're all simply *dying* to know all about it.'

'I met him on the first of March this year, Lady Elizabeth.'

'Indeed? So short a time. How very intriguing. One does not often encounter such – er, haste, does one?'

'Doesn't one?'

'Why no, surely it is more usual for both parties to be acquainted over a number of years before taking their vows.'

'How very dull a picture you paint, Lady Elizabeth.'

'I paint a proper picture, my lady.'

'It is still very dull.'

Glances were exchanged now, and Laura knew that they did not like her impertinent attitude.

'You are entitled to your opinion, of course,' murmured the countess, her fan tapping her lips for a moment as she pondered her next move, 'as I am entitled to mine. The circumstances of your nuptials are of course very unusual – very romantic, but also unworthy.'

'Unworthy?'

'What else is it but unworthy to the name of love to rush so precipitously into wedlock? You know the saying – marry in haste, repent at leisure.'

'Do you speak from experience, Lady Elizabeth?'

The room was very quiet now. The countess's lips were pursed into a rosebud, albeit a withered one. 'My dear Lady Grenville,' she said at last, 'you simply must show us your wedding gown. That is one of the delights of meeting a new bride, inspecting her wedding toggery. Do show us yours, my dear.'

'I am wearing it.'

The countess's nose positively twitched with disdain as she surveyed the sprigged muslin. '*That* is your wedding gown?' she asked faintly.

'Oh, come now, you know as well as I do, Lady Elizabeth, that precipitous haste such as was involved in my marriage would of necessity preclude the acquisition of elegant attire. None of the dressmakers I have ever frequented had such garments immediately to hand, but then maybe out here in the wilds of Somerset things are different. Oh, how quaint, how very provincial that you should believe I would be able to instantly acquire a dazzling creation from some Venetian *couturière*!' Laura gave a short, vaguely amused laugh. 'I declare I am tolerably diverted. And now, if you will excuse me, I will leave you all to scratch my character to your hearts' content.'

The numbed silence was broken by the sound of Laura's footsteps as she swept regally from the scene of battle.

The countess was very pale, weakly putting out a hand to a neighbor for support. 'What a very – disagreeable woman,' she muttered faintly, reaching for her sal volatile.

Augustine trembled from head to toe. This had not gone at all as she had planned, for the biters were themselves bitten! Nicholas should hear of this; he would hear every detail of his wife's disgraceful conduct! But for the moment Augustine must consolidate opinion to her side. 'You see what I must endure?' she asked them all. 'She is quite beyond all polite society!'

'My dear,' said the countess, recovering a little, 'she is too low to be commented upon.'

Laura did not return to her room, but sent Hawkins hurrying to the stables to see that a horse was saddled for her immediately. She felt choked with emotion now that she had faced the ladies, and the icy calm left her, the resultant void being filled with a fierce desire to escape from the house, to hide herself away somewhere and weep in private. There was no privacy here. . . .

She waited impatiently in the vestibule, and the moment she heard the horse being brought around, she hurried out and down the steps. The footmen, postilions, and coachmen waiting by the line of carriages that had conveyed the ladies to the house, watched in amazement as the new Lady Grenville hitched up her muslin skirts to mount the horse. With an inordinate display of dainty ankles and petticoats, she turned the horse toward the park, urging it faster and faster until its hooves drummed as it galloped to Langford Woods.

Her hair was snatched from its pins, but she did not care. Nor did she care that her progress had been witnessed not only by the visiting servants but also by the shocked ladies from the windows of the red saloon. Such was the tumult of emotion released in her now that she thought only of escape into some sort of oblivion for a while. The woods were cool and fresh, and the leaves so thick overhead that the sunlight did not penetrate them. On and on she rode, going further than she had ever ridden before, and at last she allowed the sweating horse to slacken its pace.

She looked around to find herself in a clearing she did not know, and slowly she dismounted, dropping the reins and leaning her forehead against the horse's damp neck for a moment. Nearby there was a mossy bank, a secret place overhung with low, protecting sycamores. She sat down on the soft moss, drawing her knees up and bowing her face as she allowed the tears to come at last. They were tears of rage and humiliation, of frustration and unhappiness, and beyond them the ever-present tears caused by her hopeless love for Nicholas Grenville.

A bird fluttered in a tree, the horse's ears twitched nervously to and fro, and then a jay burst chattering from the branches, dipping so low in flight that it almost touched the horse. Startled, the horse's head came sharply up and in a moment it was gone, bolting into the relative security of the woods and leaving Laura lost and alone.

She closed her eyes in misery, for now her day was complete. Having flown defiantly in the face of criticism and propriety, she would now be reduced to walking ignominiously back to King's Cliff and the undoubted storm that awaited her, for by now Nicholas would have been informed of his wife's disgraceful conduct in polite society.

Someone was calling her nearby. 'Laura?' It was a man.

Horrified, she searched for her handkerchief, but she could not find it and so her tears were hastily wiped on the hem of her gown. Nor could she find any pins with which to put up her hair so that she looked tolerably presentable. She could only sit there, bedraggled and in tears, wishing the ground would open and swallow her.

'Laura? Are you all right?'

It was Daniel. But of course, who else could it be who would address her by her first name? Relief swept over her. 'Daniel?'

He heard her and a moment later was riding into the clearing. He dismounted, approaching the bank immediately as he saw how miserable and upset she was. 'I saw you riding, and then your horse bolted past me. . . . Oh, my poor Laura, you are in a state, aren't you?'

She blinked back the tears, again absently searching for her nonexistent handkerchief. He smiled, the reins swinging in his gloved hand for a moment before he tethered his horse to a branch and then sat beside her, removing his top hat and dropping it to the moss. He took out his own handkerchief, and as once before, he gently wiped away the tears before putting his arm around her trembling shoulders and drawing her close so that her head rested again him. Gently he stroked her untidy hair. 'Was it Nicholas?'

'Partly.'

'Don't you want to talk about it?'

She shook her head.

'Did riding so recklessly help?'

'I don't know.'

'You could have killed yourself. At any moment an overhanging branch could have swept you from the saddle.'

'I didn't think of that; I just wanted to get away, to be by myself somewhere.'

'You would not weep if you were mine,' he said softly, still stroking her hair, 'for I would never give you the pain he gives you.' He knew that he was being very unfair to her now, pressing his suit at a time when she was least able to resist. But even in the face of her abject misery, misery he knew he could with a few words remove, he did not lift a finger to lessen her pain.

'I am a fool, am I not?' she said with a thin smile. 'I could have a man like you, but I want only Nicholas.'

'That is what you *think* you want.'

'I will never love you, Daniel.'

'Am I to believe you feel nothing for me?'

'You have proof to the contrary, haven't you?' She raised her eyes to look at him. 'How could any woman be indifferent to you, least of all me, for I have reason to be so grateful to you.'

'I don't want your damned gratitude!'

'I know. I also know that what I feel for you cannot be compared with the feeling I have for the man who is my husband. I am being honest with you, Daniel. I find you very attractive, both as a man and as a friend, and it would not be at all displeasing to have you make love to me.'

'Then let me make love to you,' he whispered, his eyes warm and dark as he pushed her gently back on the moss, leaning over her, his lips only inches from hers. 'Let me love you as I know you were meant to be loved, my dearest Laura, my love. . . .'

She closed her eyes as he kissed her, but the darkness only brought Nicholas to her. It was Nicholas she held in that moment, and it would always be Nicholas. She pressed her hands against Daniel's chest. 'No,' she said, gently but firmly. 'No, Daniel, for it is wrong, both to myself and most of all to you. You would always be second, all the time, and in the end you would not be able to accept that. So I will not let it happen; I will not give in to feelings which I admit to be there when you kiss me. It would be so easy now to turn to you, for that way I would salve my pride and would know the sweetness of being desired, but you deserve better than that, Daniel. Much better.'

Do I deserve better? Do I deserve anything at all for the way I have conducted myself of late? I have allowed lie and innuendo to thrust between you and Nicholas when I could have prevented it. . . . He looked down into her lovely, flushed face, and saw that her love for Nicholas was unshakable. Gentle wooing and the burning desire of his own love would not win her; it would take a moment of the deepest hurt to her, an undeniable realization that she was once and for all rejected by the man she loved. That moment had not come yet, but it would, and then she would turn to the love Daniel Tregarron offered, to the love she already half acknowledged and he had tasted in her kiss.

'I will pursue you, Laura,' he said softly, 'and in the end I will have you.' He bent his head to kiss her again.

'No, you will not.'

'I will not accept your answer.'

'You must.'

Their eyes met for a moment more and then he stood, holding out his hand to her. 'When I leave for America, Laura, you will be at my side, and if you could see but clearly for a moment, you would know that that is the way it must be. He doesn't want you and he makes it daily more plain to you. You suffer pain and hurt – that pain and hurt would be chaff in the wind were you to look closely at your life. Your future happiness lies with me, not with Nicholas Grenville.' He smiled a little. 'And now I think perhaps it is time I conveyed you back to that place you think is your home.' His hands were warm on her waist as he lifted her on to the horse. Then he mounted behind her, his arm steadying her as he kicked his heels and the horse moved swiftly away from the clearing.

From her window later that day, Laura saw Augustine and her mother at last saying farewell to their guests. Her return to the house had, to her mortification, been closely remarked. But it could not be helped; she had been seen riding before Daniel, her hair tumbling carelessly about her shoulders, her ankles once again revealed and her underskirts catching on the shining leather of his boots. She must have looked very immodest, and her conduct could only be construed as improper. As she had taken her leave of him at the main steps, she had known that her face was crimson with embarrassment, but there was absolutely nothing she could do about it. No doubt the good ladies of Somerset had picked the bones of her shaky reputation, leaving not a morsel of flesh upon the poor skeleton.

She turned from the window and sat before the dressing table. Kitty picked up the brush and the bristles made the dark curls crackle pleasingly. Laura glanced up at the maid's pale face. 'Kitty, I have decided that when the auction is done, and if it goes well, then I will ask Sir Nicholas if he will take your father on here again.'

The maid's eyes brightened hopefully. 'You would do that, my lady?'

'You know that I will, both for your sake and for your father's. I will not easily forget that bouquet of tulips.'

The clock struck three, and Laura bit her lip. She had been back in the house for several hours now, and she had known all that time that Nicholas wished to see her, but she had refused to go. Until now.

Kitty tied her hair back with a red ribbon and Laura stood. 'How do I look?'

'Lovely, my lady.'

Laura smiled. 'Do I look ready for battle, that is the question?'

Kitty said nothing and Laura did not expect her to.

He was by the window of his room, leaning against the opened shutter. He turned as she entered, and she saw immediately that he had to put a hand on a chair to steady himself. He was very weak still and she could see by his face that he found every effort tiring.

'You wished to see me?' she asked, facing him, her attitude one of defiance still.

'How good of you to eventually deign to come.'

'I saw no reason to rush to hear myself criticized.'

A light passed through his eyes. 'Indeed? And what makes you think I am bent solely on criticism?'

'Aren't you?'

'No, Laura, I am not. That I have some criticisms is natural enough, under the circumstances, but that is not all I wish to say to you. Why did you behave as you did in the red saloon?'

'Hasn't Miss Townsend informed you?' she asked acidly.

'I want your explanation, Laura.'

'Very well. I did not take kindly to being toyed with by those human felines. I am not a mouse to cower before them, not even before an arch-tabby like the Countess of Bawton. I would behave as I did again, if forced as I was today. I must remind you that I asked you to free me from that so-called duty, but you refused. I did what you demanded of me, Nicholas, but I gave no promise as to how I would conduct myself. I will not abase myself, not for you or for anyone else.'

'That much I gather, madam. I am fully aware of how the situation went, but not only from Augustine, whose account I will admit was bound to be colored against you. I know what happened, and was interested to know exactly what prompted your reaction. Now that I know, I will apologize to you for having, as you say, forced a situation upon you which went against your every grain.'

'You – you apologize?' She stared at him.

'For that one thing, yes.'

'But now we come to the criticisms?'

'You surely cannot expect me to condone your *every* action today?'

She lowered her eyes then, unable to reply.

'To begin with there is the matter of your riding out like a hoyden, in full view of the most inquisitive eyes in the county!'

'It once pleased you well enough to have me ride like a hoyden, Nicholas Grenville. I do not recall you finding fault on the Lido in Venice.'

'I do not need reminding,' he said quietly, 'for I doubt that I will ever forget that day. But it is in the past now, never more so, and you are in England, madam. A certain standard of behavior is expected, and from what I understand of today, you most certainly do not meet that standard. I forbid you to ride again until you have acquired a riding habit, is that quite clear?'

'Yes.' She looked rebelliously at him.

'Don't think to defy me,' he warned, 'for you are my wife and—'

'And you are my husband!' she cried. 'But it pleases you to forget that.'

His face paled. 'Which brings me inexorably to my next point. I forbid you to have anything to do with Daniel Tregarron. Absolutely and finally.'

'Because you dislike him?'

'Because your conduct with him has given rise to rumors which touch my honour, madam!'

'And what of your conduct with Miss Augustine Townsend? What of *my* honor?'

'What I do has nothing to do with this, Laura. I do *not* forget that you are my wife, whatever you may choose to think, and so I order you to sever all contact with Tregarron. I want your word, Laura.'

She pressed her lips firmly together and did not answer.

'Your word, Laura.'

'Very well.' She looked reproachfully at him. 'And I am mindful of my word given as your wife, Nicholas. But when I look into your eyes I do not see that I can expect the same from you. I promised that I would do all I could for this estate, and I still stand by that promise. In return you deny me any kindness, and you separate me from the one friendship I have enjoyed since coming to this house. That ours is a marriage of convenience cannot be denied, but I do not deserve to be made so obviously a temporary and unwanted bride. You sarcastically reminded me yesterday that I was your wife for better or for worse. Where is the better, Nicholas? All I have known is the worse.' Her eyes were bright as she turned to go, and she did not see the hand he put out to her. But he could not call her back. He heard her light, hurrying steps recede along the passage.

He bowed his head, his eyes closed momentarily. He could not say her name because he was silenced by his knowledge of her love for Daniel Tregarron.

Chapter 32

The day of the auction dawned to the sound of hammering as the auctioneers' laborers prepared a suitable stand from which to conduct the momentous occasion. The constant and unexpected noise excited the hounds, and they yelped and whined, occasionally breaking into a fuller cry as they milled around in their confined space. Sleep was impossible in the house and Laura sat in her window, watching.

Tendrils of mist still clung beneath the trees as the men from Christie's supervised the work. Some heavy wagons were drawn up on the grass and men carried planks of wood to the platform which was rising beneath a large, overhanging oak. The sun had risen slowly in the east, blurred by the haze of moisture in the cool air, but she knew that the day would be fine and warm – perfect for the business to be conducted at King's Cliff, business that was spoken of the length and breadth of the land.

Kitty thoughtfully provided her mistress with a dish of tea, guessing that the noise would have disturbed her sleep. It was good to sit on the window ledge, just watching, and wondering how the day's proceedings would go. Interest was at a fever pitch, and the neighboring landlords and farmers would come if only to see what happened. The Earl of Langford, however, would stay away, for he had made his anger and disapproval common knowledge. She sipped the tea. Yes, everyone would come, but would they dare to flout the earl by making bids? He was a force to be reckoned with, and she could only pray that the notices in the newspapers would attract interested parties from beyond Somerset.

As she watched she saw a woman on horseback riding slowly across the park. It was Augustine; Laura recognized her distinctive maroon riding habit. Laura watched her for a moment and then put down her tea. 'Kitty, I believe that I shall christen my new riding habit.'

'Now, my lady? Before breakfast?'

'Yes.'

The maid hurried to bring the new garment from the dressing-room, and Laura pulled a face. It was a disagreeable garment, disagreeably washy in color, being somewhere between gray and sage, and the haste with which a barely adequate Langford dressmaker had put it together was only too evident in its lack of grace or style. It would never even remotely match Augustine's for excellence, but it was all Laura had, and it did at least make her look proper. It would also allow her out of the house for a while. For once, Laura admitted to herself, Augustine Townsend had had a good idea, an early-morning ride would be just the thing.

She rode the same mare she had ridden when accompanying Mr Dodswell and Mr McDonald, and she confined her ride this time to well-remembered parts of the estate – the edge of Langford Woods, the escarpment, and the outer limits of the Home Farm.

She was on her way back, riding slowly up the escarpment a little to the north of the Townsend monument, when she saw Augustine waiting. Augustine could not see her, for a thin scattering of trees hid her, but there was something about the figure in maroon that made Laura halt. Augustine looked for all the world as if she was waiting for someone.

Curiosity got the better of Laura and she dismounted, leading her mount slowly through the sheltering trees until she was reasonably close. She saw the pinnacle of the monument stretching up into the heavens and heard the grass rustle over the hillside. She saw the feather in Augustine's black beaver hat flutter, her formal skirts flapping around her long legs, and the impatient way Augustine tapped her riding crop against the foot of the monument and glanced frequently at her fob watch.

Hoofbeats sounded at last, and Laura parted the leaves of a bush to watch as the Earl of Langford urged his black horse up the hillside toward the monument. For a moment she was afraid that he might see her, but the bush hid her and anyway he did not even glance in her direction. They were so close that she heard his leather saddle squeak as he dismounted. Laura's eyes widened immediately with surprise and distaste as he took Augustine in his arms and kissed her. Augustine submitted, there being no other way to describe her limp acquiescence as she allowed him to embrace her.

'Jesu, Augustine, I have missed you,' he said, his voice carrying quite clearly to Laura's hiding place.

'It is not easy to steal out like this.'

'But you are here now.' He smiled. 'Meeting you is the one solace I shall know on this blackest of days.'

'It is a black day for me too. King's Cliff will never be the same again. It is being destroyed.'

'By your former love.'

Augustine met his eyes quite blandly. 'Yes.'

'I cannot remain from you for much longer.'

'I told you that I would marry you when your mourning was over—'

'That is not what I meant.'

She looked sharply away. 'James, I do not think it sensible. What if we are discovered?'

'What difference will it make?'

'I will have no reputation.'

'We were discreet before and we will be discreet again. The same adjoining rooms—'

'We were lucky before.'

'And will be lucky again. I must go to Taunton at the end of the week. I want you to come there again too. Please, Augustine. Or must I once again resort to reminding you of what secret we both share?'

'It wasn't my doing!'

'It is now, as much as if you had plotted it all yourself, my dear. I go to Taunton at the end of the week. Be there.' His face had lost its warmth now, his eyes were cold, and his mouth had become a thin, cruel line. He turned to remount, urging his horse away down the slope until the curve of the hill took him from sight.

Augustine was very pale as she watched him go, and Laura saw how nervously her tongue passed over her dry lips as she gathered the reins of her horse and prepared to mount. Laura sensed the fear James Grenville had aroused in the woman he professed to love, but she felt no sympathy for Augustine, whose own greed and ambition had brought her to her present unenviable position.

The sun was high in a clear sky when the carriages at last began to arrive. There were elegant drags with coats of arms emblazoned on their panels, postchaises hired by farmers who had no fine carriage of their own, and wagons bringing the hundreds of lesser beings who flocked to King's Cliff. One and all, they were intent upon witnessing the day's events, the passing of an era that had glittered so dazzlingly and for so long.

Near the platform, the crowds jostled together, all eager for the finest positions, while the aristocracy gathered in a separate enclosure, sipping the iced champagne that was served by footmen in the impressive Grenville livery. The iced champagne was an extravagance, Laura knew, but maybe it would help to bring forth more generous bidding. . . .

She dressed as the hour approached for the auction to commence. She had chosen to wear her apricot lawn gown and her most colorful Kashmir shawl. The black ribbon graced her throat again and a particularly attractive lace cap rested on her carefully pinned hair. It was a warm, fine day, but she shivered as she descended the staircase, for she did not know what reception she would receive.

Mr Dodswell waited for her in the vestibule, and Augustine and her mother sat stiffly on a sofa, their faces grim and unsmiling. Laura ignored them, giving Charles Dodswell her undivided attention, for he looked unexpectedly splendid, having discarded his customary dusty coat for one of dark blue cloth. Instead of breeches he wore trousers, and his waistcoat was of cream gambroon. All in all he did not look at all like the Mr Dodswell she knew and she could not hide the surprise.

He smiled. 'The caterpillar is become a somewhat gaudy butterfly, I fear.'

'You look very handsome, sir.'

'In my youth I was considered presentable enough.'

'And still you are.'

'Thank you.'

'Have you seen who has come?' she asked anxiously. 'Is there anyone from outside the county?'

Augustine stood then. She was particularly beautiful, her hair peeping from beneath a frill of a day-cap, her tall figure swathed in folds of a creamy white muslin stitched with tiny blue stars. 'It will not matter how many come from outside the county,' she said coldly, 'for no one will help to destroy King's Cliff. They come merely to witness your disgrace, my *lady* and the ridicule which will be heaped upon you when this day's work proves an unmitigated disaster. Come, Mama.' She swept out into the sunshine, duly followed by her mother.

Laura glanced nervously at the agent. 'Do you think she is right?'

'They have come here to King's Cliff, my lady, and from that fact alone I take heart.'

'I am afraid to go out there.'

He took her hand and drew it through his arm. 'I will be with you. You should not be afraid at this eleventh hour, not when your undoubted courage has sustained you thus far. You have shown yourself to be, in my humble opinion, a very fine lady, with a strength which makes you so perfect for King's Cliff. I earnestly hope that you have reconsidered your decision to leave.'

She shook her head. 'No, Mr Dodswell, I have not.'

'Then I am very sad, Lady Grenville.'

They walked to the doors and out beneath the portico, but they had barely descended three steps when the arrival of another carriage caused a considerable stir among the crowd.

The costly, gleaming landau was drawn by six perfectly matched bays and was handled by postilions wearing very distinctive livery. The hoods of the carriage remained obstinately raised, concealing the identity of the occupants. A second coach followed it, a much plainer and less impressive drag that drew little attention from onlookers.

Mr Dodswell's lips parted with surprise when he saw the postilions. 'My lady,' he said softly, 'they wear royal livery.'

She stared as the landau came to a standstill at the foot of the steps.

The second carriage halted too and its door was opened to allow a very anxious, dapper gentleman in dull brown to climb out. He wore a very formal wig and carried a shining cane, which he used now to tap the arm of a nearby footman. He asked a question and the footman turned to indicate Laura.

The anxious man hurried up the steps toward her, sketching a swift, but excellent, bow. 'Lady Grenville?'

'Sir.'

'His Grace, the Duke of Gloucester, desires the hospitality of your house while the auction is in progress.'

'The Duke of Gloucester?' Her wide eyes went uncertainly to Mr Dodswell. What should she do? How should she act?

The anxious man waited, his cane swinging to and fro. 'Madam?'

'His Grace is of course most welcome to my husband's house, sir.'

He inclined his head and hurried back down the steps to the landau. Laura's mouth felt dry and her heart began to rush in her breast. She was glad of Mr Dodswell's presence, for without him she doubted if she could have said anything at all. She watched now as footmen flung open the doors of the landau.

A very stout young man climbed out. His body was supported by very spindly legs and his eyes were prominent. His face, while not exactly ugly, was far from being agreeable, and there was an expression upon it of great conceit and arrogance. His clothes were obviously stitched by the very finest tailor in Bond Street, although not even the greatest cutter and stitcher of cloth could make this gentleman a picture of sartorial elegance. Laura stared down at him. This was the man who was so soon to marry the Prince Regent's sister, Princess Mary, and who was himself a first cousin to both. To look at him was as repellent as looking at James Grenville, and Laura shuddered to think of him in the role of bridegroom.

Slowly he came up the steps toward her.

Chapter 33

She sank into a deep curtsy, remaining bowed before him for a long moment before rising. 'Welcome to King's Cliff, Your Grace.'

He grunted, flicking a kerchief fastidiously over his sleeve.

'W-will you honor my house by entering, Your Grace?' she went on, praying that she was behaving as protocol demanded, for she had no real idea of how to conduct herself before royalty.

He raised a quizzing glass to survey her for a moment, and then with a slight sniff he walked past her into the vestibule where the alert Hawkins had already assembled as many footmen and maids as possible. The duke stalked past them without a glance and Hawkins hurried to lead him up the staircase to the red saloon.

Laura looked momentarily at the watching crowds, catching a glimpse of Augustine's angry face for a moment before the anxious man at her side claimed her attention.

'I am His Grace's land agent, Lady Grenville, and I am to bid for the hounds on His Grace's behalf. While I am thus engaged, you must wait personally on His Grace.'

'*I* must?' she gasped, taken aback, 'Surely—'

'His Grace is most particular that great respect is paid to him. He will take coffee now and you must serve it yourself upon a silver salver. You must remain standing beside him while he drinks it and then instantly remove the empty cup and the tray when he has finished.'

She stared at him, and then at last found her tongue. 'Very well, sir, I will do what is expected of me. Mr Dodswell, you will have to commence the auction without me.'

'Of course, my lady.' The two agents walked down the steps together, and she turned to hurry into the house, seeing to her relief that Hawkins was descending the staircase after taking the duke to the saloon.

'Hawkins, bring coffee to the red saloon immediately, on a silver tray, and then allow me to serve it to His Grace.'

'You, my lady?' The butler's jaw dropped.

'The duke expects nothing less. Hurry now, for he does not appear to be a gentleman to brook delay of any kind.'

'Very well, my lady.'

'And see that Sir Nicholas is informed.'

The butler bowed and hurried away, and with great trepidation Laura mounted the staircase.

The duke was standing stiffly in the red saloon, his withering, superior glance taking in every item of furniture, every picture and the frame in which it was mounted. Without acknowledging her presence, he once again flicked his kerchief over his sleeve and then lowered his bulky person on to a sofa. He sat in the very center, his back straight, his whole mien one of self-importance and consciousness of his royal blood.

Nervously she approached him, praying that it was in order to do so. 'Your Grace, I have asked for some coffee to be prepared for you.'

He grunted again.

'May I be of service in any other way?'

'No, madam.'

She could think of nothing more to say. The seconds dragged like interminable hours and her nerve was beginning to desert her.

At that moment the doors were opened, and to her immense surprise and relief she saw that it was Nicholas, being helped by Henderson.

The duke rose to his feet. 'By gad, Grenville, you look done up.'

'Not too done up to forgo my duties as host, Your Grace. I pray you will allow me the honor of being seated in your presence.'

'Of course, my dear fellow.' The duke inclined his head graciously but made no move to assist as Henderson helped Nicholas to a nearby chair. Laura went to take his arm, and momentarily their eyes met before the duke claimed his attention again.

'Not a huntin' man then, eh, Grenville?'

'I fear not, Your Grace.'

'Damned anomaly, a King's Cliff Grenville who don't hunt.' The duke seated himself again, ignoring Laura, who alone remained standing as Henderson hurriedly bowed out of the room.

'Hounds are wasted upon me, Your Grace.'

'Damned if they'll be wasted on me.'

Nicholas was surprised. 'You are interested in them, sir?'

'I am – provided the price is right.'

'I trust that it will be, sir, for I can think of no finer fate for the hounds than to be in your ownership.'

The duke looked pleased, as Nicholas had intended he should. 'You don't come to Court now, Grenville. You should, they're a damned dull lot and need stimulating.'

'I'm something of a damp squib at the moment, Your Grace, and not stimulating company.'

'Damned odd affair. Venice. Fellow's a cad, of course, everyone knows that. Damned Austrian brigand. We thought you'd been finished, you know, it was all over Town. Your damned cousin behaved as if he'd inherited the lot.'

'So I understand.'

'Odious creature, James Grenville.'

'Yes, Your Grace.'

At last Hawkins brought the coffee, setting the silver salver on a table. On it stood a delicate cup of Sèvres porcelain. Taking a deep breath, Laura picked up the tray and conveyed it to the duke, sinking again into a deep curtsy. He hardly glanced at her as he took the cup and, with his little finger stiff, drained it all in one gulp. He replaced the cup on the tray and waved her away. She dutifully took the tray back to the waiting butler, who spirited it away again. She paused for a moment before returning to her place by Nicholas. She was very conscious of how all the ridiculous etiquette had reduced the situation to someting akin to a circus in which she had the part of performing monkey.

Nicholas addressed the duke again. 'May I be so bold as to congratulate you upon your recent betrothal to the Princess Mary? It is indeed a most fortunate match for England.'

Again the duke looked pleased. 'Damned good show,' he said. 'She's a fine gel. Quite suitable, of course.'

'Oh, of course.'

The duke looked up at Laura then. 'Damned handsome wench, Grenville. I see why you snapped her up now that I've clapped eyes on her. Damned uproar in Town, you know. The *monde* thought you'd tie a knot with the Townsend woman, and now you turn up with this filly. Mind you, never could stand the Townsend woman, damned cold armful if you ask me. And now that she's got her name connected with your damned cousin's. . . .'

Laura looked swiftly at Nicholas, but the duke's words seemed to have no effect.

The duke continued. 'Yes, you've chosen well this time, Grenville. Damned handsome wench.' He spoke all the time as if Laura was not present, or that at least she was stone deaf.

Nicholas smiled. 'The Venetian air, don't you know.'

The duke gave a loud guffaw. 'Damned fine! *Damned* fine! The Venetian *air*!

Outside the auction was well under way, and the rest of the conversation went over Laura's head as she gazed out of the window. Nearly everyone was gathered by the platform now and she could see the gentleman from Christie's conducting everything expertly. She watched his hammer come down as lot after lot was sold. Her eyes shone a little, for Augustine's prediction was obviously proving wrong. Maybe it was the Duke of Gloucester they had to thank, for his appearance had brought royal approval and had overruled any other considerations.

She had been standing there for over an hour when at last the duke's agent came to bow low before his royal master. 'Your Grace, the King's Cliff hounds are yours.'

Laura was conscious of great relief, for if the wretched creatures had gone elsewhere, it would have been decidedly embarrassing to face the duke. She glanced down at Nicholas and he gave her a brief smile. At that moment she knew that he was thinking exactly the same and probably had been from the outset.

The duke, however, frowned. 'King's Cliff? *King's Cliff*? Damn it, they're the *Bagshot* hounds now, and don't forget it.'

'No, Your Grace.'

The duke rose ponderously to his feet, obviously well pleased with the way things had gone. 'Damned good show, eh, Grenville? That's one in the eye for your wretch of a cousin! Ha! Ha, ha!' Still laughing, he moved heavily from the room.

Nicholas leaned back in his chair. 'You did excellently, Laura.'

'I can behave when I choose to.'

'I know. I assure you that I did not come to keep a wary eye on you, if that is what you think. I came to give you the support I knew you would need when confronted by the most arrogant and pompous princeling in the realm.'

'Is he always like that?'

'His – er, stateliness – is a byword, I fear. But you cannot afford to be stately, Laura; indeed you will need to be a hoyden once again if you are to successfully reach the door the necessary three paces behind His Grace.'

With a gasp she gathered her skirts and hurried out, just managing to achieve her correct position as the duke emerged from the house, regally accepting the cheers of the crowd as he descended to his waiting carriage.

The crowd followed the royal coach as it slowly left the steps, and as Laura watched, Mr Dodswell appeared at her side.

'Everything has gone excellently, my lady, as sweetly as Sir Nicholas could ever have wished.'

'So Miss Townsend was wrong.'

'I don't know, my lady, but I believe that the duke's presence swung the balance.'

She nodded. 'And so we indirectly have the Earl of Langford to thank.'

'My lady?'

'The duke came, I fancy, to annoy the earl. So, Mr Dodswell, everything has gone?'

'Lock, stock, and barrel. The duke even wishes to employ those at present responsible for the hounds – there will not be anyone from the kennels without a position at Bagshot. It has all worked out very well.'

'Except for those other servants here who have lost their positions and do not have a Duke of Gloucester to rescue them.'

'Aye, my lady, I fear you are right.'

'Ten people, Mr Dodswell, that is all. Surely King's Cliff will be able to absorb them?'

'That is a matter for Sir Nicholas.'

'I will ask him, of that you may be sure. I have given my word.'

A great many people still remained at King's Cliff at the end of the afternoon when at last the hounds were brought from their kennels for the last time. A silence fell over everyone as they emerged, under the strict control of the chief huntsman. Tails wagging, claws scrabbling, and tongues lolling, they milled around as they waited to be taken into the three large covered wagons the auctioneers had provided for their transportation to whoever their new owner might be.

At last they were all accounted for, and the lumbering wagons began to leave. Everyone watched, affected by the finality of the moment. Now King's Cliff was indeed less in stature. . . .

Laura stood with Mr Dodswell by the entrance of the now silent kennels, and then they began to walk back toward the portico. She was conscious of all eyes upon her, but no one said anything until she was at the foot of the steps, then a single word rang out.

'*Shame*!'

She halted, turning in the direction of the voice. She saw immediately to whom it belonged, for a tall dandy swaggered forward, very splendid and exaggerated in gray satin. He sketched a mocking bow, and drew a ripple of delighted laughter from the crowd. Laura had noticed him earlier, eating his fill of cold chicken and taking glass after glass of champagne. Even now he had a glass in his hand.

She turned to Mr Dodswell. 'I will not be a moment.'

'My lady—'

But she had gone, her face very cold as she approached the dandy. An expectant silence descended.

'I trust, sirrah,' she said in a voice as clear as his own had been, 'that you enjoyed the vast quantities of food and drink you partook today. I trust also that you will agree that you behave lamentably when you express a view so obviously at odds with those expressed by your host. You have enjoyed Sir Nicholas Grenville's hospitality, sirrah, and now you abuse it. That is not the behavior of a gentleman; it is the behavior of an oaf. And so I say to you – *shame*!'

He was silenced. She looked coldly at him once more, and then her glance swept over the crowd. Few met her eyes. She turned to walk back toward the house, and no further word was hurled after her as she went inside on Mr Dodswell's arm.

The crowd had gone when Augustine went to see Nicholas. She paused outside the door, rubbing her eyes for a moment until they watered, and then she went in. Her eyes seemed to shimmer with tears as she closed the door, leaning back on it as she looked at him. 'Oh, Nicholas—' Her voice broke, and she ran to him, slipping her arms around his neck and hiding her face against his shoulder.

'What is it, Augustine?'

'F-forgive me. I know I should not come weeping to you, you least of all, but suddenly it is all so final. The hounds have gone, and all that land has been sold. I am faced at last with the fact that King's Cliff will never be the same again.' Her voice was tremulous, hesitant, and designed to extract the maximum sympathy from him.

'No, King's Cliff will never be the same. It will be better.'

She said nothing to that, turning away and searching for her handker-chief. She wasn't sure of him, and she had come now to reassure herself that she still had a hold over him. 'I – I have been thinking that maybe I should go away from King's Cliff for a while, maybe go to Taunton and inspect the shops.' She smiled bravely through her tears. 'Is that not what is expected of ladies of quality, that they forget their sorrows by immersing themselves in the delights of feminine fripperies?'

He smiled. 'No doubt it is.'

'You will not mind if I go?'

'What right have I to mind where you go?'

She stared at him, for that was not the answer she sought. 'None, I suppose,' she replied.

'By all means go to Taunton, Augustine. I trust that the visit will have an appropriate effect.'

'Effect?'

'I hope that it will make you feel better.'

'Oh.' To hide the uncertainty she felt, she went to him again. 'Hold me, Nicholas, hold me close.'

'That is not easy with but one good arm,' he said, but he nonetheless slipped his arm around her waist. She tried to read his eyes as he kissed her, but they revealed nothing. She left him a little later, still uncertain. She did not wish to go to Taunton with James Grenville, but she was afraid not to. She also did not wish to go because she feared to leave Laura alone with Nicholas. Augustine knew in her heart that Laura was more of a rival for his love than Laura herself could possibly realize.

Chapter 34

In spite of the fact that his excellent green coat with its high collar was tossed casually over his shoulders, Nicholas still looked elegant, achieving that lazy gracefulness that is the aim of every gentleman of fashion. His arm was supported by a light sling and his full shirt looked very white indeed against his indigo waistcoat. A jeweled pin shone in the folds of his cravat, and the tassels of his Hessian boots swung as he crossed the library to where Laura sat waiting with Mr Dodswell. Briefly he took her hand and brought it to his lips, but it was merely a gesture of politeness, no more than that.

The agent lit his meerschaum pipe and the aroma of his tobacco mingled with the smell of coffee. Sunlight streamed into the room, dusty sunbeams dancing by the tall shelves of books, and there was a rustle of paper as Mr

Dodswell opened up the final account books of the auction. Laura sat back. It was good to be merely party to this meeting and not to have any responsibility, for Nicholas could take that for himself now. He had gained in strength and health, improving visibly over the past week. There was color in his cheeks once more and his lips were no longer so deathly pale. His eyes were brighter too, having lost the awful dullness that had glazed them for so very long now.

It was also good, as far as Laura was concerned, to be free of Augustine Townsend and her mother once again, for they had gone to Taunton – to meet the earl, as Laura knew full well. She glanced at Nicholas as he consulted with the agent. The Duke of Gloucester's remark about Augustine's name being connected with the Earl of Langford's had not had any apparent effect. Nicholas had not seemed surprised at the time, and he had made no mention of it to Augustine – at least, not when Laura had been present. Augustine had, of course, made a great thing of saying farewell to him, draping herself clingingly on his good arm and addressing him with a familiarity he did nothing to check. And yet Laura felt he was reticent, neither encouraging nor discouraging. Only one thing could explain his conduct: that since he loved her so very much, he was prepared to forgive and forget.

Charles Dodswell inspected his pipe, which was proving difficult to keep lit, and closed the final ledger. 'There you have it then, Sir Nicholas. The books balance most excellently, pleasing both the agent and the lawyer in me. The various diminutions resulting from the auction and other necessary sacrifices have had the beneficial effect you sought. With the marsh drained, King's Cliff will eventually be solvent again, and I foresee a goodly profit.'

Nicholas smiled knowingly at him. 'Provided I am intelligent enough to employ high farming methods.'

'Naturally.'

'I believe that when you die the words "high farming" will be found written across your heart.'

'I pray they are, for it is my most fervent belief that the future of estates such as this will depend upon such new ways.'

'I agree with you. Have you heard from Mr McDonald?'

'Only that he has received our communication and will come as soon as possible.' Mr Dodswell lit his recalcitrant pipe again, drawing heavily on to it so that a cloud of smoke surrounded him for a moment. 'At least local opinion will change when people realize that the marsh project will provide work for about five hundred men. All work is good work in these depressed times.'

'The Tibdales and their kind will not see it that way.'

'I for one will be delighted to see them forced to seek other means of supporting themselves than stealing that which does not belong to them.'

'Charles, whatever situation they find themselves in, they will survive by *illegal* means, if not poaching from King's Cliff, then poaching from someone else. Now, is there anything else we need to discuss now?'

Laura sat quickly forward. 'Yes, there is.'

He glanced at her. 'Yes?'

'It concerns those servants who still have not found positions elsewhere. There are only ten of them, Nicholas, and in view of everything having gone so well, I was wondering – hoping. . . . Could they not be taken on here again?'

He gave a slight nod. 'I see no reason why not. Ten will not put me back in penury.'

'Eight,' said Mr Dodswell. 'There are only eight, as I happen to know that two took the wagon to Taunton last week and have found employment there.'

Nicholas gave a short laugh. 'It seems the whole world converges on Taunton town!'

Laura was conscious of the irony of his statement. 'Yes,' she agreed quietly, 'even Baron Frederick von Marienfeld.'

Nicholas's eyes went swiftly to her face. 'I beg your pardon?'

'The baron. *He* once converged on Taunton too.'

'When?'

She was surprised by the interest her statement had obviously aroused. 'I don't know exactly; he merely told me that he had but recently visited Taunton. Why?'

'Idle curiosity,' he replied, but his eyes were lowered thoughtfully to the quill in his hand.

She was puzzled and so was Charles Dodswell, who watched him carefully for a moment before clearing his throat. 'We take the eight remaining servants on again then?'

'Yes. See to it, will you, Charles?'

Laura sat forward again. 'There is one I would like to inform myself, if that is in order. Frank Roberts.'

'Because he is your maid's father?'

'Partly.'

And partly because the road to his cottage passes the gates of Daniel Tregarron's house. . . . The accusation passed through Nicholas's head, but he merely nodded to her. 'Very well, tell him if you wish.'

'I will go directly,' she said, getting up.

The two men stood politely, but Nicholas made no move to open the door for her, leaving that task to Charles Dodswell. It was a deliberate and obvious omission and she could not help but notice it, although she gave no sign that she had.

Charles Dodswell could not fail to notice it either, and when she had gone he turned to Nicholas. 'It grieves me that you are so unhappy in your private life, Sir Nicholas.'

'And what makes you think I am unhappy?'

'It appears quite obvious to me.'

'All is not what it seems, Charles,' said Nicholas, going to pour himself a cognac. 'Will you join me?'

'Thank you. Maybe all is not what it seems, but I would like to tell you how it seems to me.'

'You intend doing that even if I forbid you,' replied Nicholas drily, smiling as he pushed a glass into the other's hand.

'It is a liberty I allow myself as your friend and mentor. I make no apology now for speaking frankly to you. I do not think you have even begun to realize yet how very hard your wife has labored on your behalf these past weeks. She faced great opposition from the outset and extreme unhelpfulness from many quarters – most particularly from those now absent in Taunton – as well as the earl, your cousin, to whom she stood up very sturdily. She took responsibilities few women would consider, and she shouldered them as gallantly as any man. She sat up night after night reading ledgers, going through ancient accounts, deeds, and agreements until I swear she must know as much, if not more, than I do about this estate. She rode out herself with - myself and Mr McDonald on his first survey, and she did not sit idly by but asked pertinent questions which much impressed Mr McDonald, for he told me as much.

'Furthermore she informed the servants herself that their numbers must be cut, and although this would normally be the duty of the lady of the house, I tell you of it because she found it particularly grueling, as she knew only too well how much losing their positions would mean to them. On their behalf she has done all she can to help, writing thankless letters to the gentry of the neighborhood, asking them to offer employment to those unfortunate enough to find their names on my cursed list. She did all this, Sir Nicholas, and you knew nothing because your precarious health caused your doctors to advise her against telling you anything which might cause you stress and which would then maybe impede your recovery. She is a very fine woman – beautiful, charming, and determined to at least *try* to do what she knows to be necessary. So, I am brought back to my opinion of what *seems*. She is admirably suited in every way to be your wife, she shares your humor and your thoughts, and she is more than a little desirable – which even a confirmed bachelor such as myself can acknowledge. In short, Sir Nicholas, you married her because you loved her, and any other reason you have given is only secondary to that. Now then, can you tell me that I am wrong?'

Nicholas was silent for a moment. 'I confess that I hadn't realized the extent of her labors here, but that cannot alter the fact that if I loved her once, I do not love her now.'

'Why?'

'You have many faults, Charles, but deafness to rumor is not one of them. Do you deny that you have heard whispers about my wife and Daniel Tregarron?'

The agent looked away. 'No,' he said at last, 'I do not deny that I have heard, but that is not to say I believe them.'

'I have evidence enough to know that they are lovers.'

'Evidence?'

'Her tale of her horse bolting and leaving her in Langford Woods where Tregarron happened to find her was merely to mask the fact that she went there solely to keep a meeting with him. One of my gamekeepers saw them lying in each other's arms – and they were not admiring the flora and fauna, I promise you! I need no further proof of her infidelity. I married her because I had fallen in love with her, but I know now that she has always regarded the match as purely one of convenience. There is no surer remedy for lovesickness, I do assure you, Charles.'

'Have you ever given her cause to believe the marriage was anything but a temporary affair as far as you were concerned? I believe the impression she has had all along was that it was at best a makeshift affair, which you would terminate when you saw fit, so that you could then marry the woman you really love – Miss Townsend. By your own actions you could have driven her to turn to Daniel Tregarron, who is a man of passion and whose desire for her I believe to have been aroused from the outset. When I first met her, Sir Nicholas, I would have sworn on a stack of Bibles that her heart was given to you and that she felt nothing beyond friendship for him.'

'Then it is obvious that her affections have undergone a considerable change, is it not? There is no mistaking her actions now and I find her sins quite unforgivable. She has committed adultery, not with a stranger but with the man I once thought of as my best friend. I cannot and will not forgive, and that must be the end of this discussion. I do not wish you to mention the subject of my marriage again, Charles.'

The agent reluctantly inclined his head. 'Very well, I will of course respect your wishes, but just one last thing I think I should tell you – I believe it is her intention to soon leave King's Cliff.'

Nicholas turned sharply away, his knuckles gleaming white as he clenched his glass. Bitter anger burned in his eyes. No doubt she was leaving with Daniel Tregarron. . . . God damn them both to hell! God *damn* them!

Slowly Charles Dodswell put down his own glass. 'If there is no other business to discuss, I will take my leave of you.'

Nicholas turned back again. 'No, Charles, there *is* something else I wish to speak of, something very important and nothing at all to do with what we have just finished speaking of. You may think me unhinged for what I am about to tell you, but I wish you to hear me out. Then I wish you to do what you can to find out if my surmise is correct. It will mean you leaving King's Cliff for a while, but it must be done.'

'I am at your disposal, Sir Nicholas, as always I am.'

'I am very much afraid that it concerns what almost befell me in Venice at the hands of a certain Austrian gentleman. . . .'

While Nicholas was speaking, Laura was in the landau heading toward Langford. The carriage moved swiftly past Daniel's house, but there was no thought in her head of visiting him, and the coachman tooled the team down the long hill towards the narrow bridge spanning the River Parrett.

It was a fine day and the hoods were down. Laura's parasol fringe trembled in the warm breeze, and the ribbons of her Leghorn bonnet streamed behind her. She wore a chestnut spencer and a walking dress of sea-green merino, and she smiled as she thought of Kitty's tearful delight on hearing the good news about her father.

The coachman's whip cracked and the team gathered speed. Laura gripped the side of the landau in sudden fear as the carriage rattled and swayed over the narrow bridge, reminding her that once before this same coachman had almost caused the wheels to touch the parapet, which would have caused a terrible accident. In a blur she noticed the faces of some men sitting on the bank by the bridge, among them the Tibdale brothers. But then the carriage was safely over and pulling up the hill toward the church where she had been subjected to such cruel snubs by the Countess of Bawton and her followers.

Frank Roberts's small cottage lay beyond the church. It was neatly whitewashed, its upper windows peeping out beneath a low thatch that had recently been repaired. A hedge surrounded the little front garden, rising to an arch above the gate, and from the gate a cinder path led to the porch, which was covered by a rambling rose of such splendor that she immediately guessed it had originally come from King's Cliff.

She alighted and walked up the narrow path, noticing the neat vegetables growing on one side and on the other the glorious display of Frank Roberts's brilliance – his flower garden. It was a riot of summer colors, and the air was heady with the perfume of pinks and sweet peas, while the tall spikes of lupins added their own peculiar grace to a garden which seemed to have been planted haphazardly but was in fact carefully laid out to achieve the finest show imaginable. Laura could understand only too well why the services of such a talented gardener had been so earnestly sought after by the Countess of Bawton.

The door was opened by a plump woman in a plain blue gown and crisp white apron. Frank Roberts's wife stared at her illustrious visitor, adjusting her clean mobcap before managing a belated curtsy. 'M-my lady?'

'Who is it, Ann?' A man's voice called from inside.

'It's Lady Grenville, Frank.'

'What? Then show her in, show her in, you daftie—!'

'P-please come in, my lady.'

Laura smiled. 'Thank you.'

She stepped into a low room that smelled faintly of paraffin, for Ann Roberts had only shortly before finished cleaning and polishing the little windows. Flowery curtains hung at those same windows, and the table in the center of the room was scrubbed so well that it was almost white. The floor was tiled in red and there were low beams on the ceiling, from which strings of onions, dried fruit, and bunches of herbs were suspended.

Frank Roberts sat before the oven, his broken leg stretched out carefully on a three-legged stool, and as he made to get to his feet Laura hastily stopped him. 'Please do not rise, Mr Roberts, for there is no need.'

He smiled. 'Thank you, Lady Grenville. I cannot offer you fine brandy or anything like it, but I can offer you some good elderberry wine.'

'Frank!' His wife felt uncomfortable, doubting very much whether a fine lady would enjoy such a country brew.

Laura smiled at her. 'I would very much like to taste your wine, for I am sure it is delicious.'

'It is,' said Frank. 'It certain sure is.'

Laura waited until the glasses had been carefully taken down from the corner cupboard where all the best china was carefully displayed, and when she had been given her wine, she told them why she had come.

'I will not delay a moment, Mr Roberts; I have come to tell you that you have no need to worry anymore – your post at King's Cliff awaits your return.'

He closed his eyes with obvious relief, and his wife's eyes filled with tears, which she dabbed with the corner of her apron.

'Lady Grenville,' he said at last, his voice shaking with emotion, 'you don't know how glad I am to hear those words.'

'Oh, I think I do know, Mr Roberts.'

'And to think that you should take the trouble to come here yourself—'

'I very much appreciated the tulips you gave me, Mr Roberts, and does not one good turn deserve another?' A movement caught her eye and she glanced toward a chair in a corner to see Kitty's little brother and sister peeping out at her, their eyes huge.

'Off with you now,' called their mother. 'You've your tasks to do and shall not be idle!'

Giggling, they scrambled to their feet, their little boots pattering on the tiled floor as they ran out into the garden.

'They are lovely children, Mrs Roberts,' said Laura. 'You must be proud of your family.'

The countrywoman swelled with delight. 'Oh, that I am, my lady. As proud as you'll be when you have children.' She immediately flushed then, for she knew from Kitty that all was far from well between Sir Nicholas Grenville and his wife.

Frank took a long breath. 'I'll be more than delighted to get back on my feet and back at King's Cliff, Lady Grenville. I had my doubts anyway about going to the countess. King's Cliff is where I belong. Mind, I'd thought I would be working indirectly for King's Cliff again soon anyway, when my leg's healed.'

'Indirectly?'

'On the gangs when the marsh is drained. It's to happen soon, isn't it?'

'It is, but I hadn't realized that word was out already. Mr Dodswell has only just heard from Mr McDonald.'

He smiled. 'Lady Grenville, the folks in Langford knew the moment a letter was sent to Mr McDonald in the first place and what it said in it. We've known that there's to be work for nigh on five hundred and it's news that has been greeted with great delight, I can tell you.'

'Except by them Tibdales,' said his wife. '*They* reckon on undoing all the work that's done each day on King's Cliff Moor once it starts. Got short shrift an' all. Folks want work, not starvation.'

Her husband nodded sagely. 'Reckon that the changes at King's Cliff didn't go down too well when they were first heard, but there's more who know it was right than there are those like the Tibdales who disagree. King's Cliff doing well can only be of benefit to the folks around here.' He raised his glass. 'Will you drink a toast with me, Lady Grenville?'

She smiled. 'Of course.'

'I say it as much for King's Cliff as for my own small dwelling. Here's to this old house: may the roof never fall in and those inside never fall out.'

Laura drank the wine, savoring its delicate and elusive flavor. In its way it was as fine as any grand vintage from the vineyards of France.

She left a little later, and as she went down the little path she noticed that there were some clouds in the sky now and the coachman had raised the landau's hood. She waved once to Ann Roberts, who stood by her gate, her two small children clinging to her apron as they watched the grand carriage draw away, wheels crunching and harness jingling, the teams' hooves striking sparks from the cobbled road.

Laura leaned her head back against the upholstery, gazing out at the passing buildings as the carriage moved down toward the bridge. How good it would be to spend the rest of her life in this part of England. If only Nicholas could love her as she loved him, then this would indeed by a heaven on earth. . . .

The coachman urged the team on to the bridge, gathering speed once again as he did so, and there was a sudden grating noise, a splintering crack, and the carriage was jerked violently sideways. Beyond her own scream she heard the team whinnying in terror and the coachman's frightened shouts. The world seemed to spin and everything went black.

Chapter 35

She could hear water gurgling very close by. Slowly she opened her eyes and found herself looking at the river, passing barely a feet few away directly below her, the long weeds waving seductively in the current. A cold fear touched her, for she was pressed against the door on the landau, and only the fact that the coachman had so providentially raised the hoods had saved her from certain death.

The carriage trembled slightly and she could hear men's voices nearby. Someone was by the other door, almost directly above her, and she stared up as the handle was moved and someone raised the door to look in. She almost wept with relief to see Daniel looking down at her.

'Laura, are you all right?'

'I think so,' she replied shakily.

'You've been unconscious for almost a quarter of an hour, but I did not dare to climb in to you. Whatever you do, don't move, for it will not take much to tip the carriage the final few feet into the river – only the strength of about ten Langford men has held it safe until now.'

Trembling with fear, she nodded. 'I won't move.'

'They will be able to hold it for a little longer, long enough for me to reach down to you. I want you to take my hand and let me draw you up. Don't struggle at all, just trust me.' He smiled at her.

'I've always trusted you, Daniel.'

Stretching in as far as he dared, he reached down to her, gripping her tightly around the wrist and pulling her steadily but surely toward him. She vaguely heard someone cheer as he lifted her out of the landau and then carried her to safety just as the men holding the vehicle could detain it no longer. With a shattering, splintering shudder, the landau slid into the river, striking the water with a great splash that scattered droplets over Laura as Daniel put his arms around her and held her close.

Men leaned over the bridge to watch as the river swamped the carriage, and the water, so clear a moment before, was now brown with mud stirred up from the bed.

Laura felt quite weak. 'What happened, Daniel? Did the wheel strike the bridge?'

'I am afraid that that was but part of it.'

'Part?'

'The main cause of the accident was the team being frightened by the two Tibdale brothers. It was a deliberate action, and they knew you were in the carriage.'

She stared at him as the full import of what he was saying was borne in on her. She had come so close to death and it had not been an accident?

'It was witnessed, Laura, and you now have friends enough here for the culprits to be apprehended. The parish constable is even now taking them to be locked up. They will not escape justice this time as they have escaped so many times in the past.'

Slowly she looked around: at the men who had held the carriage while she was rescued, at the anxious coachman who was struggling to control the nervous team, and at Daniel's carriage which had been fortunately coming in the opposite direction at the time of her accident. She felt quite numb, and Daniel took her arm gently, steering her toward his carriage. One of the men bent to pick up her reticule and parasol, which had fallen as she had been lifted down, and with his cap in his other hand he held them out to her now. In a daze she took them. 'Th-thank you.'

Her thoughts were confused as she let Daniel help her into his carriage, and she hardly noticed as he sat beside her and the door was closed. The carriage turned slowly in the road and began the long climb away from the bridge. Daniel's arm was around her and she was glad to have it there because she was still afraid.

The carriage turned into King's Cliff, and as it at last swayed to a standstill by the main steps Daniel put his hand briefly to her cheek. 'Tomorrow I must go to London for a day or so. I have to settle my affairs before leaving for America. On Thursday I will be back and I want you to meet me.'

'No.'

'I saved your life, Laura,' he pressed.

'That isn't fair,' she whispered.

'It was not meant to be. Meet me, Laura. I will be in the clearing where I found you before at three o'clock on Thursday afternoon.'

The carriage halted by the portico steps and she did not wait for the door to be opened, but thrust it open and jumped lightly down. She hurried up the wide steps without a backward glance.

Her steps echoed in the vestibule as she approached the staircase, but then something made her stop and look at the head of the stairs. Nicholas stood there. He said not a word as he gazed coldly down at her, and then he turned on his heel and walked away.

A great heaviness descended over her then and she slowly walked on to the foot of the staircase. He thought she had deliberately met Daniel Tregarron. The handrail was very cold to the touch and momentarily she could see the rushing waters that had so nearly claimed her moments before. Her whole body began to shake. A strange feeling of nonexistence seized her and she felt as if she was not really there but was somewhere else, where she was becoming weightless. The sunlight was fading sharply now and the columns at the head of the staircase lurched toward her. She began to slide to the floor, her legs could not support her, and the black and white tiles were suddenly very close. She tried to call out as everything went silent but for the gurgling and hissing of the river. So close, so close now. . . .

There seemed to be green and white flowers above her, and a refreshing coolness touched her forehead. She felt lethargic, deliciously so, and her limbs were warm and heavy. She had no strength, nor did she want any, for time was suspended and all cares had gone.

'My lady?' Kitty's anxious voice drew her inexorably back to reality as the maid pressed another cool cloth to her forehead.

'Kitty?' she whispered, looking up as the maid's face swam indistinctly before her.

Then Nicholas was there, leaning over to take her hand. 'Are you all right?'

'What happened?'

'You fainted. I heard you call me and I found you at the foot of the staircase.'

'I called you? I don't remember,' she murmured, but she could see again his cold face looking down those stairs at her. 'You walked away,' she whispered, beginning to remember.

'Forgive me, I did not know about the accident and I thought—'

The accident! Memory flooded back then and she struggled to get up, but he held her back.

'Be still now, you are quite safe, I promise you.'

'The river—'

'I know, the coachman returned a few minutes ago.'

'Daniel saved me.'

'I know that too.' He released her hand abruptly.

She was very conscious of his immediate withdrawal. 'I didn't do anything wrong,' she said, 'I swear to you that I didn't.'

Dear God, when she looked at him like that he wanted so much to confess to her, to tell her he loved her, but he knew that such confessions were the province of fools and would be the grave of what little pride he had left after she had destroyed his trust and love. But even though visions of her lying in Daniel Tregarron's arms hovered in the air between them, Nicholas could not totally reject her, for she had come so very close to death. He had nearly lost her completely, never to even touch her again. 'Perhaps,' he began hesitantly, 'if you are recovered a little later, we could dine together. *À deux*, as we did in Venice.'

'Without the Austrian band?' she asked with a glimmer of a smile.

She saw a momentary return of his old humor as he replied. 'Dear Lord, I sincerely hope so.'

Her pale blue silk gown was blushed to lilac by the rays of the setting sun as she approached the doors of the dining-room. The golden strings tying her sleeves touched her skin, making her shiver, and she drew her rich shawl more closely around her arms as the footmen opened the doors to admit her. She saw immediately that Nicholas had not yet come down.

The dining-room at King's Cliff was an impressive chamber, and although she had dined there on occasion since arriving, notably when Mr McDonald had been a guest, she had not really looked at it closely before. It was an almost masculine room with its dark green walls and strikingly intricate gilded plasterwork. Several white marble statues stood in niches and a magnificent collection of Chinese jade was displayed in large cabinets on either side of the tall fireplace. A Boulle marquetry clock stood on the mantelpiece, together with some large candlesticks and a clutter of statuettes. The room's glazed doors stood open on to the terrace and a lacquered screen shielded the table from any draught. But the evening was warm and the rain, which had threatened so briefly earlier in the day, had not come to anything.

The room was dominated by the long, rosewood table, which could seat thirty people, but which tonight was laid at one end for only two. It was covered by a starched white tablecloth, which almost touched the parquet floor, and an array of silver cutlery and cut-crystal glasses, in which napkins folded like fans had been tucked, was neatly set out for the master and mistress of the house. An epergne tumbling with clear green grapes presided in the center of the settings, and on either side of it were low bowls of pale pink roses. It was very gracious. And very remote.

Waiting for Nicholas, she went to examine the jade. How strange it would be to dine with him again. She had not dined in his company at all since entering this house and the only meals she had enjoyed had been those shared with Daniel Tregarron and those with Mr McDonald, during which the charming Scot had entertained her with his tales of the rivalry between those two eminent engineers, Mr Thomas Telford and Sir John Rennie.

The doors opened and Nicholas came in. He wore black velvet, his coat tossed casually over his shoulders because of his arm. The jeweled pin in his cravat flashed as it caught the sunlight.

'Good evening, Laura, I trust that I have not kept you waiting for long.'

'Good evening, Nicholas. No, I have not been here more than a minute.'

The customary words were polite and meaningless, for there were too many barriers.

'The room is a little large for just two, but I hope you will not mind.'

'Mind?'

He smiled a little. 'I understand you have been in the habit of taking your meals in the library.'

She flushed, for it was an indirect reference to Daniel and she knew it. 'I resorted to the library to escape Miss Townsend and her mother.'

'Yes, so I understand,' he said, taking her hand to escort her to the table. Hawkins seemed to appear from nowhere to draw out her chair for her.

She decided to choose a safe topic of conversation. 'I wonder if the *monde* will ride to the Bagshot hounds this coming season?'

'The duke will create a pretty scene if things are not ready in time.'

'Is he always as unpleasant as he was when he was here?'

'I'm afraid so. Prince William Frederick is guaranteed to empty a drawing-room within seconds.'

'I have never met royalty before.'

'Would you wish to again?'

She paused as Hawkins served the asparagus soup. 'No,' she said then, 'not if they are in any way like the Duke of Gloucester.'

'There are degrees. The Prince Regent is a very charming and entertaining fellow, his conversation is witty and interesting, and he can be excellent company.'

'Do you know him well?'

'Well enough.'

'I had not thought. . . .' Her voice died away.

'Thought what?'

'I feel very insignificant suddenly. You move in the highest circles in the land, and I am so very – well, ordinary.'

'That is not a word I would use to describe you.'

She looked up, but he did not meet her eyes.

'Besides,' he went on, 'if I once moved in Court circles, I certainly no longer do.'

'But I thought the duke expected you to return.'

'Possibly. I shall not, however.'

'Why?'

'Well, to begin with, such a life requires copious funds, which I do not have and which if I had I would not wish to squander on the foolishness of London Seasons. King's Cliff is too important to me for that.'

'Is it very exciting in London society?'

'It can be decidedly dull. All the masquerades, balls, assemblies, and routs may take place in different buildings each night, but the faces are all the same. It is one vast and exclusive club, and I have resigned my membership.'

'You are so disenchanted?'

'I have acquired a little wisdom. In my brief life, I have seen a great deal.

I enjoyed a wild and reckless youth which was abruptly brought to an end by fighting for my country against Bonaparte. I have wandered through many fashionable London drawing-rooms, attended many royal levees, and in the end known only boredom. I have therefore come to the conclusion that such a life is not for me.'

'My life, by comparison has been very uninteresting.'

'Would you have preferred to enjoy a wild and reckless youth, to have fought on Spanish battlefields – and so on?' He smiled a little. 'I think you would not. As to London life, well maybe that might hold some appeal for you, I don't really know. From what I know of you, however, I think it very unlikely that you would enjoy the empty life of a society belle, being trotted out in the marriage market day after day until a suitable match is made for you. A woman who throws caution to the winds and blues everything on Venice is too interesting for that.'

She said nothing as the soup course was removed and replaced by a beautifully garnished dish of pigeons wrapped in bacon. It proved as delicious as it looked.

'Laura,' said Nicholas after a while, 'I believe that I have shown myself to be ungrateful.'

'Ungrateful?'

'I was not aware of all you had done here while I was ill.'

'I did what I promised.'

He glanced away, remembering the last time she uttered those words to him. If only she had turned back to him then, maybe it could have been different. . . . Maybe. Maybe it was all too late anyway, for Daniel Tregarron had claimed her now.

She sensed that conversation had been dampened, and she knew in that moment that she must ask him about their future. 'Nicholas, what is to happen to us?'

A veil passed over his eyes. 'Happen?'

'You did not really wish to marry me, did you? We both know that you want Augustine as your wife.'

'I don't think this is the time or the place to discuss that, do you?' His tone was calculated to freeze her.

'I just want to know.'

'I have not even considered the matter,' he said shortly. He met her gaze without wavering. He believed she wanted to leave, to go with Daniel Tregarron, and he had no intention of making it any easier for her. Until that moment he had not faced the situation or made any decision, but now he did and he knew that he would never willingly release her from this marriage contract. She had betrayed him and taken a lover, but she was his and she would remain his.

But she could know nothing of his real thoughts; she could only hear a refusal to discuss something that was of the utmost importance and she could only see the coldness in his eyes. 'I don't understand,' she said at last.

'No? Then I suggest we leave the subject, don't you?'

She stiffened at his attitude then. 'Very well, if that is what you wish.'

'It is.'

She said nothing more, and the meal was completed in virtual silence. The pigeon was removed and replaced by a final course of nectarines and walnuts, eaten between sips of sweet liqueur.

After dinner, they walked for a while on the terrace, but there was no ease between them. She was close to tears, but he could not see that in the darkness. The sun had set now, leaving a jagged blaze of crimson low on the horizon beyond Sedgemoor.

He took his leave of her civilly enough, but that was all it was – civility. She remained alone on the terrace when he had gone. The candles in the dining-room threw a soft light across the flagstones and the night breeze whispered through the nearby trees. The tears were wet on her cheeks now. They had been alone and she was his wife, but he had not claimed her. One moment she felt closer to him, and then something seemed to harden him against her. It was all hopeless. If ever she had needed proof that he felt little or nothing for her, then she had been given that proof tonight.

She returned to her own room, giving the letter addressed to Lady Mountfort to Kitty, asking her to give it to the letter carrier in the morning. Sadly, Kitty accepted the letter, for she knew what it meant.

Chapter 36

Thursday came and went and Laura did not go to meet Daniel. Her relations with Nicholas remained cool and had not improved at all when Augustine and her mother returned from Taunton. Intent upon concealing his feelings from his wife, Nicholas immediately made his preference for his first love known, leaving Laura feeling more and more isolated. And more and more unhappy. Daily she waited for the letter carrier to arrive, although she knew that it was too soon to expect a reply from Lady Mountfort – if indeed she warranted a reply after having disappointed that lady earlier in the year. Laura told herself that she *would* receive a favorable reply, however, and that thought carried her through the days, although her nights were spent in tears. The moment the letter came from Lady Mountfort, she would face Nicholas, informing him that she was leaving. He may not have bothered to consider the matter of his futile marriage, but his unhappy, unwanted bride certainly had.

Sunday arrived, and the carriage came to the main steps to convey everyone to church. Laura stood in the vestibule drawing on her gloves and then
picking up her ivory-covered prayerbook. Mrs Townsend stood primly
nearby, her hands clasped neatly before her and her eyes deliberately
averted from all possibility of meeting Laura's glance. Nicholas and
Augustine had not come down, but already Laura could hear Augustine's
rippling laughter.

They descended the staircase together, Augustine leaning so close to him
that it was as if she would be part of him. Her beauty was breathtaking, and
Nicholas appeared to find her enchanting. She wore a striking pink pelisse
that should have clashed most dreadfully with her red hair but somehow
managed to look quite perfect. The tassels on her military-style hat trembled a little, and the military theme, so fashionable after Waterloo, was
echoed by the epaulets on her shoulders and the hussar braiding on the
bodice of her pelisse. But if she had chosen a martial theme in her clothing,
there was nothing martial in her demeanor; she was femine, adorable – and
adoring. Her hand rested lightly on Nicholas's sleeve and her whole body
seemed to curve against him. Laura turned away, feeling very drab in her
demure lilac pelisse. She was a moth compared with this entrancing butterfly.

Augustine kept up a gay rattle of conversation as the carriage drew
away from the house. Her arm was linked through Nicholas's and they sat
facing Laura and Mrs Townsend. Laura said nothing; indeed she had no
need, for Augustine had enough to say for all of them. Laura's face was a
mask to hide her innermost self during that short but dreadful journey,
and only when the carriage crossed the bridge over the River Parrett did
any emotion show briefly, an echo of that terrible fear. . . . But then the
bridge was behind them and they were driving up the long hill toward
Langford church, and another of Tobias Claverton's interminable, flat
sermons.

The carriage halted by the lych-gate and Nicholas handed the three ladies
down. Laura was last and he held her hand firmly, making her look at him.
'Have you nothing to say this morning?'

'I did not notice a suitable lull in the chatter.'

'There is no need to be sullen.'

She drew her hand away. 'And there is no need for her to be quite so
vulgarly obvious. It surprises me that you could find her to your taste – but
then I suppose you've revealed yourself to be most susceptible to flattery.'

His eyes were angry. 'This mood ill becomes you, madam.'

'Oh, forgive me,' she said acidly. 'I am so sorry that I do not find her as
enthralling as you do.' She walked past him, pushing open the lych-gate and
walking up the path. At the church porch she waited, however, for it would

not have done to go in alone. As Nicholas and Augustine strolled slowly along the path, Mrs Townsend following in their wake, Laura wondered if he would go so far as to enter the church with Augustine, leaving his wife to her own devices.

Augustine obviously wondered the same, and her eyes flashed angrily as he offered his arm to Laura. Slowly Laura slipped her hand over his sleeve, then he removed his hat, and they entered the cool mustiness of the church.

His appearance caused a stir in the congregation, for this was the first time that he had left King's Cliff since his return from Venice. The savage changes at King's Cliff were already fast becoming old news, and as few had suffered by them, most were only too prepared now to greet him with a polite nod of the head. There was curiosity too, of course, for everyone was still wondering about the rumors concerning Laura and Daniel Tregarron – rumors that were being whispered even now, for Daniel was in the congregation. He turned as Nicholas and Laura approached their pew, and he inclined his head only at Laura, winning a smile from her. That small exchange was witnessed by everyone in the church, including Nicholas.

They took their places in their pew. Across the aisle James Grenville sat stiffly in his own place. He ignored Nicholas and Laura, but smiled and bowed his head to Augustine and her mother. Laura knelt to pray, shutting everything out and retreating into her own little shell. It was her only defense.

She remembered little of the service, except that Tobias Claverton surpassed himself, droning on and on about a particularly obscure text that interested no one but himself – and, of course, his kinswoman, the Countess of Bawton. To everyone's disappointment, the Duke of Gloucester had returned to London, so Langford church was never honored with the royal presence – for which fact Laura did not think it had suffered in any way!

The sunshine was bright and dazzling after the dim atmosphere of the church, and Tobias duly waited at the porch to greet his departing flock. He swiftly engaged Nicholas, and therefore Augustine and her mother as well. Laura deliberately strolled slowly on, not wishing to join them, and it was then that she saw Daniel again. He stood in the shade of one of the large yew trees, and he smiled at her. She hesitated only a moment, for she knew that her next action would anger Nicholas greatly, but somehow after his conduct with Augustine, she did not really care. She went to Daniel.

He held her eyes for a long moment before speaking. 'I waited for you on Thursday.'

'I did not say that I would come.'

'No. But you considered, didn't you?'

She lowered her eyes. 'No.'

'I know a fib when I hear one,' he said softly. 'You considered closely, and you almost came. I watched you in church – you and he did not even exchange a glance, and yet he frequently leaned to whisper to Miss Townsend. He even sat closer to her than he did to you.'

'You tell me nothing I do not already know.'

'Maybe I don't, but you seem to need prompting to face it for what it means as far as you are concerned. He wants her, Laura, and he could not make it more plain to the world if he tried.'

'Please don't say any more.'

'I love you, Laura. I promised you that I would pursue you, and so I will. You defy him by speaking to me now, don't you?'

'Yes.'

'Then I will go on hoping that you come to me. I will go to Langford Woods each day at the same time from now until the day I leave for America, and one day you will be there too, I know that you will.'

She could see in his eyes all the love and warmth she so wished to see in Nicholas's eyes.

'Oh, Laura,' he whispered, 'if only you knew how I would like to take you in my arms now and kiss you and proclaim to them all that I love you.' He glanced beyond her then to where Nicholas stood watching. 'I will leave you now, before your husband feels he has cause to upbraid you publicly. But remember, Laura, I will be there every day. Just come to me; let me give you all my love. Let my love wash away all the hurt he has caused you.' He smiled just once more before taking his leave of her – a tall, elegant figure in mulberry coat and dark gray trousers.

Augustine watched, the satisfaction she felt showing only in the small curve on her lips. She no longer felt unsure of Nicholas as she had done before going to Taunton, for it was quite obvious that the distance between husband and wife was as great as before, if not greater. Since her return, Nicholas had been attentive, and he had virtually ignored Laura. He believed his wife committed adultery with Daniel Tregarron, and her present behavior did nothing to dispel that belief.

James Grenville emerged from the church, brushing so close that he almost touched Augustine's skirts, and her smile faded into fear as she met his eyes. Suspicion stared at her from his pudgy face, and she was afraid. She felt his web around her, forcing her now where once she played a clever game of her own, treading the delicate path between cousin and cousin, determined to gain everything she wanted. James Grenville was not a man to toy with; he was dangerous and capable of great evil. She shuddered a little, a shiver of revulsion as she remembered lying in his arms, submitting to his kiss in that hostelry in Taunton.

The pleasantries with Tobias Claverton were over at last, and Nicholas handed the ladies into the carriage once more. Again Laura was last, and he detained her, his fingers tightening roughly over hers, hurting just a little. 'I will see you when we return, madam!' he said icily. 'Alone!'

She snatched her hand away and climbed into the carriage without his help.

She faced him in the library.

'You deliberately disobeyed me this time, madam!' he snapped.

'At least he is able to be civil to me.'

'And I'm expected to believe that that is *all* he is to you?'

She stared at him. 'How dare you,' she whispered, her voice shaking. 'How *dare* you say that to me!'

'I have the right to say anything I wish to you, madam, and in any way I see fit!'

She struck him then, her fingers stinging bitterly across his cheek. He seized her wrist in an ironlike grip and a sob caught in her throat as she twisted to be free of him, pressing close momentarily in her efforts so that her face was close to his, their lips almost touching.

Very slowly he released her.

Her cheeks were wet with tears as she turned to run from the room. He stood dejectedly where he was, the jealousy and anger that had urged him on evaporating suddenly, leaving him feeling nothing but emptiness. He was struggling against the inevitable, for in the end she would go to Daniel. In the churchyard her face had been hidden, but Daniel's love for her had been written so very clearly on his.

That same unfortunate day Mr McDonald and his assistants returned to King's Cliff, bringing with them a train of heavy, lumbering wagons, which trundled through Langford and then along the lower road toward the Home Farm. They conveyed all manner of items, from spades to wood for shoring up the rhines, and their passage was greeted with great interest. Throughout the afternoon, more and more wagons arrived, regardless of the fact that it was the Sabbath, and toward nightfall great stacks of timber had appeared along the firm land edging the marsh. Word spread like wildfire throughout the neighborhood, for those who had not witnessed the convoys of wagons soon learned of what was happening when Mr McDonald sent out his men to begin taking on the necessary five hundred laborers. When darkness fell, Langford and the surrounding area buzzed with excitement, and many families prepared for their menfolk to go out to King's Cliff Moor the following morning.

Mr McDonald intended to lodge at the Home Farm, but as Mr Dodswell had still not returned from the secret business Nicholas had dispatched him to attend to, the Scot was only too pleased to accept when Nicholas invited him to dine at King's Cliff that night.

Laura could hardly be expected to look forward to the occasion. She had remained in her room after her violent confrontation with Nicholas, weeping long and hard, and not even Kitty's gentleness could soothe away the tears. At last, as darkness began to descend and the hour approached to dress for dinner, the weeping stopped, and she reluctantly allowed Kitty to dress her. This time she had to resort to a great deal of powder to hide her tear-stained eyes, but at least in candlelight it would not be quite so obvious. She dressed simply in her apricot lawn, choosing her favorite shawl and declining even to wear her black velvet ribbon at her throat. She was entirely unadorned, except for Nicholas's ring on her finger. As she slowly descended the staircase, however, her only thought was a fervent hope that in the morning the letter carrier would bring word from Lady Mountfort.

The dinner endured, there was a further ordeal for Laura in the music room. Augustine sang beautifully; her voice was light and melodic and there was not even the vaguest hint of an uncertain note. Her long, pale fingers moved effortlessly over the keys of the piano and the jewels in her hair sparkled in the flickering candlelight. The rest of the room was indistinct, the dusky blue curtains lost their color in the darkness, and the furniture cast long, black shadows over the floor.

Nicholas leaned on the piano watching her as she sang. She wore a gown so very *décolletée* that on most women it would have looked shameless, but as always with Augustine, it simply looked breathtaking. He gave her his undivided attention and there might as well have been no one else in the room but the two of them.

Laura sat on a sofa, her fan folded in her hands, her eyes downcast. He had not said more than two or three words to her throughout the evening, ignoring her so pointedly that even Mr McDonald was embarrassed. The engineer sat opposite to her now, fidgeting a great deal and now and then taking a surreptitious look at his watch. The candlelight picked out the red in his sandy hair, giving him a demonic look that did not go at all with his gentle character.

Mrs Townsend watched her daughter proudly. What mother could not be proud of such a beauty? Such talent, and looks so glorious that a brilliant painter would have begged for the privilege of committing her loveliness to canvas. Mrs Townsend's eyes glowed. How could she ever have doubted the wisdom of her daughter's conduct? She could not fail to achieve her ambition; she would have Nicholas Grenville, and through him the house she had craved all her life. And she would slip from the clutches of James Grenville, her character unblemished, her reputation untouched. Augustine was a true Townsend, unconquerable, and destined to achieve her heart's desire.

The last trilling note of the song died away and Augustine sat back, smiling up at Nicholas as he applauded her. Mrs Townsend rose to her feet, applauding rapturously, and Mr McDonald murmured some halfhearted words of praise that passed unnoticed. Laura didn't move a muscle, and Augustine threw her a scornful, triumphant glance.

Mr McDonald got up. 'I fear I must depart now, Sir Nicholas, for I must rise at dawn to commence work. Thank you for a most – enjoyable – evening.' He stumbled over the word 'enjoyable', for that it certainly had not been.

'I trust you will join us again, sir,' said Nicholas, walking with him to the door.

'Indeed. Indeed.' The young Scotsman turned in the door, bowing to Laura. 'Good night, Lady Grenville.' He smiled a little, and she knew that she had his sympathy for what she had endured that evening.

'Good night, Mr McDonald.'

Nicholas returned to the piano and Laura watched him for a moment. How very handsome he was; she doubted if there was another man the length and breadth of the kingdom who could hold a candle to him for excellence of face, figure, or dress.

He did not even notice when his wife left the music room. But Augustine saw and she exchanged a secret smile with her mother.

Nicholas was about to retire to his bed when Hawkins came to inform him that Mr Dodswell had returned at last and had been shown into the library.

The tired agent accepted gladly when Nicholas asked him to be seated. Neither man said anything as Nicholas poured some cognac, pushing a large glass into the other's hand. 'Well, Charles?' he asked at last.

'I am sad to tell you that it is as you suspected, Sir Nicholas. It was a devious and clever plot, and but for the grace of God would have succeeded.'

A nerve flickered briefly at Nicholas's temple where the baron's bullet still left a scar, and he slowly took a seat opposite the agent.

'I'm so sorry, Sir Nicholas, for I wish I could have come with any other answer than that.'

'You found someone with evidence, someone who is willing to stand up in court?'

'I believe so, but you must understand that it is a grave crime, and there is a certain amount of reluctance to become involved. I believe that you must see the woman I spoke with yourself.'

'If that is your advice.'

'It is. I am a lawyer and I was as persuasive as possible, but your presence would sway the issue with her. I am sure. You are after all a justice of the peace, and you have a title.' He smiled a little wryly.

Nicholas nodded. 'Very well, I will leave first thing in the morning.'

'Sir Nicholas, I would deem it an insult if you did not permit me to come with you. You know how close I feel in spirit to you, and more than anything else now, I wish to see this damned affair through to its foul conclusion.'

'You know that I wish you to be with me.'

The agent gazed at his cognac for a moment. 'Sir Nicholas, I think that one good thing at least must come out of this, and that is that you are forced at last to see the light about a certain lady whose name I choke to utter after what I have recently learned.'

'My dear Charles, do you not realize that I have long since seen that particular light? I first saw it in Venice.'

'Then do something about it!'

'It is too late, as I said before. Too much has been said and done.'

'Surely—'

'I think it best left. It was never meant to succeed.'

'I believe in fate. Fate decreed that you should live and fate has given you this chance now, but fate cannot anticipate the outcome, for that is in your hands.'

'Not only mine,' reminded Nicholas softly, 'not only mine.'

The agent declined to press further. He finished his glass and rose to his weary feet. 'If we are to leave early, I had best return to my bed—'

'You must rest here tonight, Charles. I will not hear anything to the contrary. I think you could do without the final short journey to the farm, don't you?'

Charles Dodswell smiled. 'I am too weary to do anything but accept your kind offer.'

A little later Nicholas was alone in the library. He poured himself a little more cognac and then went to the windows, flinging them open to let the cool night air in. From the marsh, hidden from the house, came the sound of fiddles playing and bursts of laughter as some of the laborers who had accompanied Mr McDonald and his assistants made merry prior to the hard work of the following morning. Through the trees Nicholas could see the faint flicker of their campfire on one of the causeways stretching out across King's Cliff Moor. The night was very still, the leaves hung motionless on the trees, and not a flower stirred.

He stared across the dark grounds, but it was a sunny morning in Venice that he saw, and the balcony of the Hotel Contarini. And Laura, forgetful of propriety as she stood there in her nightgown, her dark hair tumbling over her shoulders and her eyes shining with the sheer joy of being there.

Chapter 37

The following morning Laura was awoken when Kitty came to her, bringing the long-awaited letter from Lady Mountfort. Kitty bit her lip as she watched her mistress sit up in the immense bed, breaking the seal on the letter and unfolding it. Lady Mountfort was in a crusty mood, complaining that Laura lacked manners by not arriving at the appointed time and by not having had the decency to write sooner, but although the letter complained, in the end it conveyed to Laura that the position was indeed still open. Nothing was said of Laura's title or the interesting address where she could be reached, but she knew that Lady Mountfort could only be all agog to know the details.

Laura looked at Kitty. 'I have somewhere to go, Kitty.'

'Please don't leave King's Cliff, my lady.'

'I must, for there is no place for me here.'

'But you love Sir Nicholas—'

'A one-sided love.'

The maid lowered her eyes. 'My lady . . . I have another letter for you.' She held out another folded, sealed paper. 'It's from Dr Tregarron.'

'He gave it to you?'

'Yes, my lady. I wouldn't have taken it, but he said it was very urgent.'

'And he can twist you around his little finger, can't he?' said Laura with a smile.

Kitty flushed.

Laura broke the seal and read. *My dearest love, I must see you, for my plans have had to be brought forward and I must now leave within a few days. If you have any affection for me, any gentleness toward me as a friend, then I beg you to come where you know I will be waiting this afternoon. Daniel.*

Well, how could it be wrong to see him, for by then Nicholas would know that she intended to leave anyway. Nicholas. Thinking of him brought her back to what she must now do.

'Kitty, I must dress quickly, for I wish to see Sir Nicholas before breakfast.'

'Oh, but you can't, my lady, he's not here.'

'Not here?'

'He set off very early this morning in his carriage with Mr Dodswell. I think they are expected to return either tonight or tomorrow, but I don't know for sure.'

Laura's heart sank. The moment had come at last; she had screwed herself up to the necessary pitch – and now he had gone away and she could not see him. She must endure for at least another day. For a moment she contemplated leaving anyway, for what good would it serve to face him again? But almost immediately she discarded the notion, for she at least owed him an explanation of her decision. He was, after all, still her husband.

She had no intention of taking her breakfast with Augustine and her mother, and so ordered some coffee and toasted bread brought to her room. She was sitting in her favorite place, the window ledge, gazing over the park, when she heard the light steps and rustle of silk she had come to know only too well and to loathe greatly.

Augustine halted, glancing critically around the room, which was so much less grand than her own. 'Good morning, my *lady*.'

'Good morning.'

'I trust you slept well.'

Laura gave a thin smile. 'How kind of you to be concerned.'

'I also trust that you enjoyed yesterday evening.'

'You quite obviously did.'

'Admit defeat, my *lady*.' The primrose silk rustled again as she came a little closer. 'Have you no pride at all? I vow I would not humble myself so pathetically.'

'No?' Laura stood, shaking out her white muslin skirts. 'You surprise me, for that is exactly what I was under the impression you have been doing, Miss Townsend.'

'What can you possibly mean?'

'Oh, come now, I think we both know, so let us not pretend to wear kid gloves at this late stage of the game. You are soiled goods, Miss Townsend, for you have humbled yourself in the Earl of Langford's cheerless bed. Even a shabby, brazen little Nine Elms whore would think herself a lady compared with you.'

Augustine blanched, taken completely by surprise.

Laura laughed. 'Did you honestly think your sordid secret would remain undiscovered?'

'How dare you speak to me like this,' breathed Augustine, shaking a little.

'I dare because I no longer care two pence about you. As you say, Nicholas has made his choice quite obvious, and you waste your time coming here to taunt me. Your malice is water off the proverbial duck's back. I wish he was less blind where you are concerned, but I fear that that must be his misfortune, for there is obviously nothing I can do about it. He deserves better than you, and I would tell him the truth about you if I thought it would do any good. He is everything to me, everything in the world, but I must relinquish him to a malevolent *chienne* like you.'

Augustine recovered a little. Laura was not going to tell Nicholas. . . .

'You really do love him, don't you,' she asked at last, intent upon driving the final nail into Laura's coffin. 'You love him, but he despises you.'

'Please go.'

'He despises you and adores me. How very galling for you!'

'I asked you quite politely if you would go. Now I am telling you to get out of this room.'

'With pleasure.' Augustine turned and went out, leaving the door wide open so that Laura could hear her steps fading away along the passage.

To Laura's immense relief, Augustine and her mother drove to see the Countess of Bawton after luncheon, so there was no one to see her ride to meet Daniel in Langford Woods. She had no qualms about defying Nicholas, for it simply did not matter anymore. She had made her decision and was set upon her course, and that course did not touch upon either Nicholas Grenville or Daniel Tregarron. It was Laura Milbanke's course, and hers alone.

Daniel was waiting in the clearing and he smiled as she rode toward him. 'I knew that you would come,' he said, seizing the reins.

'Your letter made it hard for me to refuse.'

He reached up to help her dismount, and his hands remained on her waist, drawing her close, kissing her, but she drew away. 'No, Daniel.'

'But you have come to me—'

'I came because you asked me most urgently,' she reminded him. 'And I came to tell you that I am leaving Nicholas and going back to the life I should never have left in the first place.'

He stared at her. 'You're doing that? You're choosing a dreadful future as a lady's companion when you could come with me as my wife? I don't believe that you can be serious, Laura.'

'I am very serious, Daniel. I have said all I can say to you, including that in the end it would not work and you would be made very unhappy. It is best if I just step out of your life as swiftly as I entered it.'

'No,' he whispered, 'No, I will not let you go away like this—'

'I have decided.'

He saw that determination he knew so well, for it was the brave face on her heartbreak. He felt foolishly close to tears suddenly as he put his hand to her cheek. 'I love you, Laura,' he said softly, 'and I want to look after you – is that so very wrong? Is it truly so cursed and doomed to misery? I beseech you to think again. Promise me that you will think again.'

'Daniel—'

'Promise me, my love. I will not ask you to see me again, just that the day after tomorrow, no later than that, you send word to me of your final decision. I will abide by whatever you decide then, I promise you that I will.'

She stretched up to kiss him gently on the lips. 'Oh, Daniel,' she said softly, 'my poor Daniel. I know that my decision will not change. But I give you my word that I will think about it and weigh everything carefully.'

'If you do that,' he said, touching her face gently, 'then I know that you will see that you must be mine.'

The day turned cloudy as she rode back to King's Cliff, and it was raining heavily by the time she reached the house. The rain fell for the rest of the day, and at nightfall a bedraggled rider came from the Countess of Bawton to announce that Augustine and her mother would remain there overnight.

True to her word to Daniel, Laura did indeed think very hard about what she must do. He was so very persuasive, so convinced that he was right and that his love would prevail, that he made her doubt her plan to go to Lady Mountfort. Had it not been for the passionate love she had for Nicholas, she knew that she could have mistaken her feeling for Daniel as being true love, but that was not the case. She found him attractive and good company, but he had not engaged her innermost heart. Only Nicholas had done that.

She spent a very restless, sleepless night, going over and over in her mind the options that were open to her – going to Lady Mountfort, or casting her lot with Daniel. It was almost dawn before she fell asleep, her decision made. The past months must be wiped out completely. Laura, Lady Grenville, had never been; there was only Laura Milbanke, about to become companion to Lady Mountfort. . . .

Chapter 38

Rain was still falling the next morning, but after breakfast it became little more than a blustery drizzle and so Laura went for a walk. Her hood was raised over her head and her cloak flapped around her as she went past the silent, deserted kennels and down the hedged path to the copse on the edge of the escarpment. The wind moaned through the trees and the smell of damp moss and earth pricked her nostrils as she at last emerged from the small wood to gaze across the spectacle of Sedgemoor.

Gangs of men moved everywhere and she could hear the noise of their work, hammering and chanting in unison as they worked. Wisps of smoke from campfires were torn by the wind; gone forever was the peaceful serenity this place had once held.

For a long time she stood there just watching, and then at last the rain began to fall heavily again and she retraced her steps. As she came within sight of the house she saw that Nicholas and Mr Dodswell had returned, for the carriage was still by the portico steps. She saw them on the steps, Mr Dodswell obviously taking his leave to continue to the farm. Nicholas looked very tired; his face seemed almost gray and he had for the first time discarded the light sling. He flexed his wounded arm as he spoke to the agent, and then Mr Dodswell returned to the carriage and it drew away, passing Laura as she returned to the house.

Nicholas was in the library. He had poured himself a cognac but it was untouched. He leaned his head back against the chair, his eyes closed, but he heard Laura as soon as she entered.

'Nicholas?'

'Laura.'

'I must speak with you.'

He opened his eyes. 'What about?'

'Our marriage.'

Not now, please not now. . . . 'I still do not wish to speak of it,' he said curtly.

'I am afraid that you have no choice now, Nicholas, for I am leaving.'

Slowly he stood. 'No, Laura, I will never release you from those vows you made in Venice. You are my wife and I intend that you shall remain so.'

She stared at him. 'But why? *Why?*'

'Because that is how I wish it to be. You are Lady Grenville of King's Cliff and you will damned well stay in this house!'

'Remain here to be treated with contempt? To watch while you pay court to Augustine Townsend and humiliate me? Never!'

'You are my wife,' he repeated.

'In name only!' she cried.

His eyes were dark. 'Oh, believe me, Laura,' he said softly, 'I am quite prepared to rectify that state of affairs. Quite prepared.'

'You would not—'

'I am your husband. Laura, and your body is mine.' Suddenly he turned, dashing his glass into the empty grate. Fragments of crystal shivered over the smoke-blackened stone. 'Damn you. Laura, I will not let you go! Do you hear me? I have done parting with what belongs to me, from now on I will keep what is rightfully mine – and that includes you.'

She was shaken by the barely held fury of his outburst.

'Nicholas'?' She could only whisper his name in bewilderment.

He closed his eyes, passing a weary hand across his forehead before turning back to her, and for the first time she noticed how strained and tense he was. When he spoke, however, his voice was more rational. 'Forgive me, Laura, but I have a great deal on my mind again, and as you know so well, I am not renowned for my courtesy at such times. I promise you that I will speak to you about – about our marriage. But not now, I beg of you. Later today, maybe.'

'What's wrong, Nicholas? Is it the estate?'

'No, it isn't King's Cliff.'

'What then?'

'You will learn it all soon enough, but at the moment I am too weary, too damned drained, to talk clearly about it.'

'Is there anything I can do?'

'Oh, yes,' he said drily. 'You can make this most difficult of days for me go a little more easily by desisting from this talk of leaving, which presumably will eventually entail an annulment, until I have spoken to you again.' He looked at her for a long moment. 'Did you see Daniel Tregarron during my absence?'

She did not flinch from his gaze. 'Yes.'

'At least you are honest about it.'

'Nicholas, I have never been *dis*honest about anything.'

'No, perhaps not. Ours is, after all, a marriage of convenience, is it not? Or maybe it should be termed a marriage of inconvenience; there are no doubt erudite arguments in favor of both descriptions of the same empty contract.' He turned away again.

She said nothing more and it wasn't until she had returned to her own room that she realized she had not told him she was going to Lady Mountfort. She had said nothing at all beyond the fact that she was leaving King's Cliff.

Five minutes later Nicholas emerged from the library, calling for Hawkins as he descended the staircase.

'Yes, Sir Nicholas?'

'Have my curricle brought around immediately.'

'Yes, sir.'

'Has any further word been received from Miss Townsend?'

'No, Sir Nicholas. She and Mrs Townsend must have decided to spend today with the Countess of Bawton.'

'Are my orders being carried out?'

The butler faltered. 'Y-yes, Sir Nicholas, but—'

'Hawkins, everything is to be done as I commanded the moment I returned. I want those rooms cleared and packed as quickly as possible.'

'Yes, Sir Nicholas.'

'Well, jump to it, man, I don't wish to dally here all day!'

The unfortunate butler began to hurry away, but then halted again. 'Sir Nicholas, if Miss Townsend should return, where can you be found?'

'Dr Tregarron's house.'

Hawkins's eyes widened and then he hurried on to see about the curricle.

Mrs Thompson could not hide her nervousness as she asked Nicholas to step inside. The hall was filled with baggage and trunks, and two footmen were carrying another heavy trunk down the staircase as the housekeeper fled up to find Daniel.

Daniel was putting the phials in a traveling box as she showed Nicholas in a little later, and he did not bother to turn around when the door had closed behind her again. 'And what brings you here, Nicholas? Do you require a salve for your bruised pride?'

'You will require a wooden casket if you step near my wife again.'

Daniel turned at last. 'Do you threaten me?'

'I warn you.'

'And why should I pay heed?'

'You would be advised to. I may owe you my life, Daniel, but I will still deprive you of yours if you see Laura again.'

'If ever there was a dog sitting tight in its manger, it is you, Nicholas Grenville. You want that damned bitch Augustine Townsend, and you want to keep Laura as well. Why? Because your pride will not stand the shame of her leaving you? You don't want her, but I do. I love her and I know that she loves me.'

'I am not interested in your feelings—'

'I have possessed her Nicholas; she has lain in my arms and given to me that which you have chosen to ignore.'

'Have a care now, Daniel,' said Nicholas softly, 'for I am not a man to lightly suffer your taunts.'

Daniel looked away, not daring to go too far, for there was much to fear in Nicholas's cold, controlled anger.

'She is my wife, Daniel, and I fully intend keeping her. Because you were once my friend, and because I owe you my life, I give you this warning, but if I learn that you have so much as looked at her again, then so help me I will extinguish you. I do not toy with you, and I trust that you understand that fully.'

'And if she wishes to come to me – as I know she does?'

'She will not come.'

'She is coming to America with me, Nicholas. Hasn't she told you she is leaving King's Cliff?'

Nicholas said nothing.

'Face facts, Nicholas, your loss is my gain. Laura is mine.'

'I need face only one relevant fact, Daniel, and that is that I am prepared to kill you if you persist.' With a cold nod of his head, Nicholas turned and left.

Daniel leaned his hands on the table, his head bowed. Only a fool would not fear such a warning. And only a fool could fail to see that Nicholas behaved as he did because he loved his wife. Only a fool. Or poor, unhappy Laura, who believed he loathed her.

Slowly Daniel raised his head, glancing at his own reflection in a mirror that hung on the whitewashed wall. Guilt looked back at him from the dusty glass. He had broken a cardinal rule, for he had now openly lied and cheated to win her. He had stooped to a depth that only months earlier he would never have dreamed possible. But that had been before he had fallen under her spell. Love could steal the halo from a saint, and Daniel Tregarron had never been a saint. . . .

It was dark and Laura sat reading in the red saloon. Nicholas still had not come to speak to her, and Augustine and her mother had not returned from the Countess of Bawton's. She looked up from the book as she heard a sound. Puzzled, she went to the window, looking down at the main entrance where she saw a carriage being loaded with trunks. There was a great deal to be put on the vehicle and the sound she had heard was the footmen as they sought to shout up to their companion on top of the carriage. Arms gesticulated and fingers pointed urgently in differing directions, and the poor fellow looked quite perplexed by the light of the lanterns.

As she watched, another carriage arrived, this time approaching along the drive, and she recognized it as the one that had conveyed Augustine and her mother the day before.

The door of the second carriage was opened, and Augustine stepped down first. She turned as her mother alighted, and at first did not glance at the carriage that was being loaded, but when she did her whole body stiffened visibly as she stared. Her mother's hand crept to her throat. Augustine seemed to recover then, hurrying up into the house and out of Laura's sight.

Slowly, Laura returned to her seat and picked up her book, but she was no longer interested in the beauty of Shakespeare's writing; she was too preoccupied with the odd scene she had witnessed at the main entrance. What did it mean?

Then she heard Augustine's raised voice by the door of the red saloon and Nicholas's more quiet reply. He opened the door then and his voice became clear. 'I will not argue publicly with you, Augustine; nor will I be questioned in my own house. If you will step in here, I have a great deal to say to you.'

Augustine swept in. Spots of high color touched her cheeks and her eyes flashed angrily when she saw Laura. Mrs Townsend followed her in but said nothing at all. Her face was white and she twisted a handkerchief in her restless hands.

Augustine faced Nicholas imperiously. 'I will not discuss any of this in front of her.' She nodded briefly in Laura's direction.

'Laura remains here, for she is the mistress of this house – which you will never be, Augustine.'

Laura stared at him. Augustine's face was thunderstruck. 'You cannot mean that,' she breathed. 'Not after all you have said to me.'

'I have said very little – you have assumed a great deal. Does it not occur to you that I may be as consummate an actor as you are actress?'

'What do you mean? And why have you ordered that all my belongings and those of my mother should be removed?'

'It must be obvious that the answer to your second question is that you are soon to leave this house forever.'

'No!' she cried. 'No, you cannot mean that!'

'But I do. And you may be thankful that I am contenting myself with banishing you, not only from King's Cliff, but from England itself, for it could have been so much worse a fate for you, could it not?'

The color drained from her face. 'I don't understand.'

'No? Perhaps it would make things a little clearer to you if I told you that I have been making detailed inquiries at a certain King's Head hostelry in Taunton.'

Mrs Townsend gasped, weakly collapsing into a chair.

Laura put her book down completely now. What was behind all this? There was more to it than merely discovering that Augustine had been conducting an affair with James Grenville. Unbidden, a thought entered her head, a thought concerning the earl's secret, discovered and condoned by Augustine and her mother. . . .

Nicholas was contemptuous. 'Augustine, do not think that I am in the least concerned to know that you are my cousin's mistress, for your sexual proclivities are of absolutely no interest to me. You leave me quite unaroused, I promise you that.'

'I know that that is not true, Nicholas,' she replied softly.

'It suited me to encourage you and the actor in me was equal to the task. That is all there is to it.'

'You are only saying these things because you think I have been unfaithful to you.'

'I could not care less if you were unfaithful with the entire British cavalry!'

'I deny that I have ever been untrue to you, Nicholas,' cried Augustine. 'But even if I had, it is no reason to throw me out of my home. I am a free agent and do not need to seek your permission for anything. You married another, Nicholas, and you thereby relinquished any rights to interfere in my life!'

'You do not see, do you? My actions today have nothing whatsoever to do with your sordid affair with my cousin.'

Tears were pouring down Mrs Townsend's cheeks now and she was so distraught that she rocked herself backward and forward, moaning quietly.

Augustine threw her a furious look. 'Be silent, Mama!'

'But he knows, Augustine,' whispered her mother. 'Can't you see that he knows?'

'There is nothing to know.'

Nicholas smiled without humor or warmth. 'I fear there is no point in denying anything anymore, Augustine, for I have absolute proof of everything. At this moment my kinsman James Grenville languishes in Taunton jail, charged with plotting my murder, and he now awaits trial for his miserable life. You and your mother are as guilty as he is, for you discovered what had been done and chose to keep silent. You condoned my murder, Augustine.'

Laura rose unsteadily to her feet, shaken by the enormity of what she had heard. He glanced quickly at her and, seeing how pale her face was, held out his hand to her. He smiled just a little as his fingers closed reassuringly over hers, but she could see how harrowing and how very horrible he was finding this vile turn of events. She felt almost faint for a moment. She had been right; her instinct in Venice that the baron had deliberately forced the duel had been right. But oh, the reason, the cause behind it all. . . .

Augustine was staring at him, her own cheeks ashen now. 'I am innocent,' she whispered. 'I am innocent and so is my mother. We know nothing of what you say.'

'I am prepared to believe that originally you did not, but that state of innocence did not last for long, did it? I believe I can with great accuracy pinpoint the exact moment when you found out what he had done – it was that moment when your mother fainted in the dining-room at the King's Head. Am I right, Augustine?'

She did not answer.

'I have a witness,' he went on, 'who can reliably prove that in early January this year my cousin stayed at the King's Head, and at the same time a certain Baron Frederick von Marienfeld, an Austrian hussar officer, stayed at the same hostelry. Unfortunately for you, the baron has a predilection for pretty maidservants, but his boorish behavior did not make him friends among their ranks. So confident was he that when he met my cousin, he left a certain Jenny Hobson in the adjoining bedroom. She heard every word which passed between them and she is prepared to give evidence in a court of law. She heard my cousin require the baron to put an end to me in Venice, and he handed over half of a considerable sum of money for this service – the other half to be paid when the deed was done and I had been neatly consigned to my Maker. It was in order to receive this second sum that the baron sent false word to my cousin afterward, and his deceit paid dividends, for my cousin duly and gladly sent the outstanding money.'

'We know absolutely nothing of all this, Nicholas, I swear that we don't,' said Augustine, but her voice was wooden with fear.

'Nothing I have said has really been news to you, except the fact that the dealings between my cousin and the baron had been overheard. I *know* you are guilty of complicity. The proof of it all is there in the King's Head –

dates, witnesses, even the baron's signature on a letter he happened to leave behind. My cousin told you what he had done, and why he had done it – to gain King's Cliff and to persuade you to marry him. He judged you sweetly, my dear, for you decided to hold your tongue because of the glittering prize he held out to you, and the moment you made that decision you were in his hands.'

'But I love you, Nicholas, I have always loved you—'

'A washy emotion such as you are capable of, my dear Augustine, can hardly aspire to the name of love. If you love anyone, it is yourself, for in your opinion there is no one else worthy of you but your own self.'

'No—'

'I feel nothing but contempt for you, and I felt like that *before* I realized what you were guilty of. Once I was away from you, far away in Venice, I could see you in a clear light for the first time – and what I saw disgusted me. Never in your life had you done anything out of kindness, never had you thought of anyone but yourself, and never had your damned pride unbent sufficiently to make you even remotely lovable. You are very beautiful, dazzlingly so, but you are an empty shell, madam – if there is anything inside you, then it is stone.'

'No, Nicholas, please no . . . I love you.' Tears shone in Augustine's magnificent eyes, and Laura could see how she trembled from head to toe. But Laura felt no pity, no compassion at all.

'One circumstance and one alone makes me offer you a chance to escape the fate which will befall my cousin,' went on Nicholas, 'and that is that you did not know of the crime before it had been committed. That is my only reason for sparing you, Augustine.'

'I am innocent,' she repeated. 'Before God I swear I am innocent.'

'You will spend tonight in a room which has been prepared for you. It has no windows and its door will be guarded – you will have no chance to escape. In the morning you will be conveyed to Bristol where you will take a ship to whatever foreign destination you please – but you will never dare to return here, for the moment you have set sail. I shall report what I know to the necessary authorities. Set foot in England again, Augustine, and you and your mother will face arrest and trial for attempted murder.'

She flinched as if he had physically struck her. 'No,' she cried. 'No, this house is mine, I will not leave it!'

'You have no choice.'

'*She* has no right to this house!' breathed Augustine, pointing a quivering finger at Laura.

'I do not intend to speak further on the subject with you,' said Nicholas, going to the door and opening it to admit several footmen who had been waiting.

'I am innocent, Nicholas!' screamed Augustine then, sinking to her knees as the tears poured helplessly down her cheeks.

Her mother got up and went to her, putting a soothing hand on her trembling shoulder. 'Be done with denials, my love, and be thankful that we are to be spared. Come.'

Augustine resisted, still weeping bitterly, but gradually she allowed her mother to draw her to her feet once more. Mrs Townsend put her arm around her, looking at Nicholas. 'You have my gratitude, sir, for I know we do not deserve this leniency. We are guilty, but it was a tangled web. . . .' She gave a faint smile. 'Not that that excuses our crime.'

They went to the door then, and Nicholas made it plain that he intended to see them locked away safely for the night. He turned back to Laura before leaving the saloon. 'I will return in a moment. I promised that I would speak with you, and so I will.'

'After all that has been said here tonight, I am sure that our talk can be put off until tomorrow.'

He shook his head. 'No, Laura, I will have everything dealt with tonight.'

'Very well. I will wait here.'

Chapter 39

Alone in the red saloon again, she sat down on the sofa. Her thoughts went back to Venice. So much was explained now, from the strange interest the baron had shown in her from that very first morning, to the inevitability of the challenge. She had provided the baron with the means, and she had unwittingly done as he wished, involving Nicholas in her affairs and thus placing him in an impossible position when the baron chose to pounce.

But now it is done, in a few minutes it will all be over and my purpose completed – well, almost completed. . . . Even had you been as ugly as sin itself, Miss Milbanke, then I should still have come here now. Fortune, however, has smiled upon me and made you so very beautiful that my task will be sweetly accomplished. Oh, how sweetly. . . .

The baron's words were so clear it was almost as if he was in the room with her. She felt cold suddenly, and it was as it had been in Venice when he had always seemed to have stepped from sight but a moment before she looked around. His purpose was clear now, as it had been almost clear to her then.

Now too she understand the behavior of James Grenville, Augustine, and her mother that first time she had seen them, alighting from his carriage after attending a ball. James Grenville, so villainous and so triumphant that his evil plot had brought him everything he desired. Augustine, embarked upon her own scheme, prepared to accept the attentions of a man she loathed because he offered her the wealth, position, and the house she craved. Any lingering heartache for Nicholas had been buried beneath her all-consuming ambition, and only when Nicholas had returned from the dead had she realized that she felt more for him than she had known. Mrs Townsend, the sheep not the bellwether, prepared to go along with everything even though she, of the three of them, had a terrible conscience about what had been done.

Nicholas returned. 'In the morning they will be gone, and that part of it at least will be over.'

'I would not have spared them. They should face the law as well, for I believe them as guilty as the earl.'

He smiled. 'How hard your heart is, Laura.'

'Not hard – just. They laughed and made merry when they thought you had been murdered. *They* showed hardness. I feel that justice will only be really done when they appear in a court of law for what they did.'

He nodded. 'You are right, of course, but I just could not bring myself to have them arrested. Do you understand?'

'I understand, but that does not mean to say I agree.'

'Ah, that would appear to be you running true to form,' he said, remembering her arguments against the duel that had been the cornerstone of it all.

'I am right now and I was right then,' she said, knowing exactly what he was thinking. 'For so much of all this could have been avoided by simply refusing to be drawn by the baron.'

'Yes, Laura,' he said quietly, 'so much could have been avoided – including our marriage. Which brings us to the reason for this conversation now.'

She looked up at him. 'You would not have married me had you not thought you were dying, would you?'

'We will never know, for events overtook us. Laura, I will be blunt with you. I will never submit to the ignominy and scandal of an annulment on the grounds of nonconsummation, and as there are no other grounds, then an annulment can only be out of the question.'

'And what grounds there are can be readily removed, as you reminded me earlier. I am your wife and my body is yours.'

'I spoke in the heat of the moment.'

'But nevertheless, what you said was true, wasn't it? You would be prepared to do that in order to avoid such an annulment.' She looked up, trying to read his eyes.

'Laura, that is a question I would rather not answer.'

'So, what it comes to is that I am your chattel and you are going to keep me, for whatever reason.'

'Believe me, Laura, I do not mean it like that.'

'How else then?' She stared up at him, still bewildered by his apparent contrariness.

'I mean that I see no burning reason to end this marriage.' *Daniel Tregarron is not going to have you.* . . . But his face bore no expression that even remotely reflected his thoughts as he looked down at her.

'Do you then see a burning reason to keep it?'

'Our relationship may not be the stuff of dreams, but then neither is it a disagreeable nightmare. I know full well that you entered into the contract for reasons that were thrust upon you in the heat of the moment. You say that I would not have married you at all had it not been for the extenuating circumstances, but then exactly the same can be said of you. I am not the husband you would have chosen, am I? Nevertheless, I am your husband, and you are my wife. Tomorrow morning when Augustine and her mother depart, many of the reasons for your unhappiness here will be removed. I can offer you a comfortable life here; you will lack for nothing and you will certainly not be at the beck and call of a harridan like Lady Mountfort.'

'Those are reasons in my favor, Nicholas,' she said quietly. 'But what is in your favor? What will you gain if the marriage continues?'

'I will have a wife who has proved herself more than equal to the task of being mistress of this house. The arrangement works and will continue to work, to the detriment, as I see it, of neither side.'

She stared at him. Had he expressed an eagerness to part he could not have hurt her more. What he spoke of was still little more than the marriage of convenience it already was; it was a business agreement that had proved itself to be acceptable to him. There was no suggestion that he wished them to stay together because he felt affection for her – they merely did well together, no more. He said that she would lack for nothing – except the one thing she craved more than anything else – his love.

'That is how I feel about it, Laura,' he went on. 'But whatever my reasons, my wishes are plain enough – I will not agree to the ending of our marriage.' *You will not go to him, for you are mine, mine.* . . .

She felt close to tears suddenly. He would be her husband and yet he would not. It was everything – and nothing! Unable to bear being close to him, she got up, the book she had been reading earlier tumbling to the floor as she hurried from the room.

Her flight made the candles leap and dance, and Nicholas slowly bent to retrieve the book. Wearily he sat on the sofa, lounging back with seeming gracefulness, but really with no more than extreme weariness. This day had almost done with him now, and it had brought him to the limit of his endurance. The web of murder and intrigue that had surrounded him was almost too heinous to contemplate, but it was the thought of losing Laura that now preoccupied him and took him to the edge of that limit.

He glanced at the book she had been reading. *The Merchant of*

Venice. . . . But whose casket would this modern Portia choose? Her lover's? Or that of the husband whose damned pride prevented him from confessing his great love?

The sound of the carriage that would shortly convey Augustine and her mother away from King's Cliff for the last time aroused Laura from a shallow sleep. The gray of dawn filled the room as she sat up. The thoughts that had been with her when she had at last fallen asleep were with her again now. Where she had had two courses open to her, she now had three. She could go, as planned, to Lady Mountfort. She could decide in Daniel's favor. Or she could remain at King's Cliff with Nicholas. But now, with dawn, it was so much clearer to her. Life without Nicholas, knowing all the time that she could have stayed with him, could not easily be contemplated. Being with him was all that really mattered, even on the terms he had presented to her the night before.

She got out of the bed and drew on her wrap, her decision made once and for all. She would write to Daniel and tell him that she could not leave Nicholas. Maybe her decision would prove in the end to be the wrong one, for would she not find herself in the very thankless, untenable position she had described as Daniel's were she to go to him? She was now guilty of doing with Daniel exactly what Daniel had wished her to do with himself – but the loveless existence she chose was with Nicholas. Having a small portion of Nicholas was infinitely to be preferred to having nothing of him at all. Had the vibrancy of her love been directed at Daniel instead, how much happier the conclusion might have been, but that was not meant to be, and so she would settle for a lesser existence, so near to the object of her love, and yet so far away too.

She carried the lighted candlestick into the library and placed it upon the escritoire where over the past weeks she had sat for such long hours. The soft light glowed on the books and on the shadowy gallery above. She sat down, took a sheet of paper, and began to write.

Daniel. My life here can only be unrewarding in the way I seek most deeply, and yet I cannot come to you. My love remains true, as I have always told you. Laura.

She laid the quill down and read the letter. It was too distant, too impersonal, and she owed Daniel far more courtesy than that. Pushing the first letter aside, she took a fresh sheet and began again.

My dearest Daniel. I have considered most deeply what I must do and can come to only one conclusion. Life with Nicholas, no matter how unrewarding, is infinitely to be preferred to life without him. I can only love him with all my heart and soul, and so my words already must have informed you that I shall stay with him. I know that you love me, and I am honored, but my own honor would be removed if I went with you when my heart remains in this house with him. Forgive me, and try to understand. Make that new life for yourself, and you will find someone who will give you that which you deserve and which I can only deny you. God be with you. Laura.'

Augustine had been wandering slowly from room to room, still escorted by a footman, but at least Nicholas had relented enough to allow her to look one last time around the house that had meant everything to her. Her eyes were dry now; she could weep no more. She had tossed the dice and lost. A numb sense of disbelief still filled her. Only yesterday she had been sure of victory, and sure of Nicholas too, but now it was all gone, slipping through her helpless fingers like sand. Too late she had realized that she loved him, for that one enchanted day in Venice had seen his heart given to Laura. Augustine smiled ironically, for she had sadly underestimated her opponent. She had been cold, calculating, and cruel, and she had been so very blind. Ambition, greed, and vanity had ruled her, making her cleave unwillingly to James Grenville. The gaining of King's Cliff had taken precedence over all other considerations, and now she paid the heavy price of her sins.

She made hardly a sound as she walked, feasting her eyes on the beloved rooms and passages, consigning each gilded sun in splendor to her memory, for memories would be all she would have. Memories of the paintings that had been old Sir Jasper's pride and joy, memories of the chair where the Prince Regent had once fallen asleep after too much cherry brandy, and memories of the library where once Nicholas had asked her to consider being his wife. . . .

She stood by the door to the gallery now. It was ajar and she pushed it open, stepping silently inside to breathe the perfume of the books once more. The footman waited respectfully outside.

Augustine's hands rested on the balcony, and she looked down. Laura sat at the escritoire, looking at a letter she had just completed. It was a short letter and was obviously not satisfactory, for it was discarded and another begun in its place. Augustine stood there in absolute silence, watching the woman she hated more than anyone else in the world. She watched Laura at last complete her letter to Daniel, sadly fold it, hold the sealing wax to the flame, and seal it. Her skirts rustled a little as she got up and left the library.

Augustine glanced out at the footman, but his attention was distracted by one of the prettier maids. Augustine did not hesitate; she descended the spiral staircase and sat immediately at the escritoire, taking up the quill as if she was about to write. Should the unwary footman realize his mistake, he would see only that she had apparently decided to write a farewell note. In reality, however, she was intent upon reading Laura's discarded letter, for she had seen to whom the other letter had been addressed – Daniel Tregarron. Seeing Laura again had, in the end, sent all thought of accepting the blame for her own misdeeds fleeing from Augustine's head. It was all

Laura's fault; *she* was the cause of everything going wrong; *she* had somehow won those things which Augustine had sought so urgently for herself –
this house and its master.

Now Augustine read the short note, wanting more than anything to find
that it could be used as the final weapon to drive Nicholas apart from his
wife. Her eyes began to gleam in that malevolent way Laura would have
recognized only too well. Her gaze was concentrated on seven words in
particular: *and yet I cannot come to you.* How simply those words could be
altered, giving them the opposite meaning. Dipping the quill carefully in the
ink, she dropped two blobs on the paper. Now it read: *and I can come to
you.*

Satisfied, she read the whole letter again. Yes, now it appeared that Laura
fully intended to go to Daniel Tregarron, and that was exactly what
Nicholas would think if he read it. She folded it and held the sealing wax to
the candle Laura had unwittingly left behind.

The footman ran on to the gallery, a surge of relief passing over him as
he saw his charge addressing a letter. She smiled innocently up at him. 'I
have written a farewell message to Sir Nicholas. Would you be so kind as to
give it to him when I have left?'

He descended the staircase and took the letter.

'Remember now,' she said, 'When I have left, not before.'

'Yes, Miss Townsend.'

A cruelly short time later, Augustine and her mother emerged from the
house and descended the steps to the waiting carriage. There were no lines
of servants to watch their departure; there was no ceremony at all.
Augustine climbed into the carriage and sat next to her white-faced mother.
The door was slammed on them. She gazed out at King's Cliff, struggling
with the tumultuous grief that engulfed her now that the final moment was
upon her. King's Cliff. Her house. *Her* house. The whip cracked and the
carriage drew away.

Daniel took the letter Mrs Thompson held out to him. 'It's just been
brought from King's Cliff, Doctor,' she said, glancing curiously at it and
wishing she could know what it contained.

'Thank you, Mrs Thompson.' He waited until she had gone before breaking the seal, and he needed only to read a few words to know that he had
failed to win her. *Oh, Laura, my love, my dearest and only love. . . .* He
closed his eyes, crushing the paper slowly and letting it fall to the floor.

'You won after all, Nicholas,' he murmured, 'You won.'

Laura sat before the dressing table, her hair crackling as Kitty drew the
brush through it. The running footman had taken the letter to Daniel over
an hour earlier and he would have received it by now. She had chosen her

destiny. Soon she would dress to go down to the first breakfast of her new life, the first of many such meals taken in the company of the man she longed for but who wished only to have a business arrangement with her. She gazed at her reflection in the mirror, but there was no joy in the pale face that looked back at her.

Suddenly the door was flung open and Nicholas entered the room. His eyes were bright and there was a bitter rage in his every gesture as he peremptorily ordered Kitty from the room. The frightened maid did not hesitate to obey, closing the door quickly behind her.

Slowly Laura rose to her feet, her eyes wide. 'Nicholas?'

'You seem to be under the misapprehension that you can still do as you please! You are to remain here, and it is time you accepted that fact!'

'I don't understand—'

'You are not going to your damned lover! Tregarron will not have you!'

'Daniel isn't my lover!' she cried, her own anger stirring now. 'He never has been and he never will be!'

'Allow me a little more intelligence than that, madam! You and he have been lovers almost since your arrival here – the whole of Somerset rings with it.'

'Then the whole of Somerset is wrong!'

'Do you deny that he wishes you to go to America with him?'

'No.'

'Do you deny that he wishes you to become his wife?'

'No.'

'Then he must have some cause to expect your compliance, madam. You and he are lovers; you have been seen together in circumstances which were incriminating to say the least!'

'Incriminating?'

'Lying in each other's arms in Langford Woods!'

She stared at him. 'That was not what it appeared, Nicholas. I swear to you that it wasn't.'

'Next you will tell me that this letter is not what it appears to be, a *billet-doux* from you to your lover!'

She looked at the letter he held out to her. 'I – I do not deny that I wrote it, but I would have thought its meaning was quite obvious. I do not intend to go to Daniel, even though I admit that he wishes me to. He loves me but I do not return that love.'

'Dear *God*, you astound me! Am I supposed to be half-witted? The letter is perfectly plain to me; it expresses your intention to go to him.'

Slowly she took it from him, lowering her eyes to the familiar writing. She saw immediately what had been done and she knew whose hand lay behind it. She looked at him for a long moment, trying to understand his motives, but there were too many contradictions. 'Nicholas,' she said at last,

'How long have you believed that Daniel has been my lover?'

'What has that to do with it?'

'To me a great deal.'

'A matter of weeks.'

'*Weeks*? And believing that you still wish me to remain your wife? Last night you spoke of an arrangement between us, which can only be described as a business contract. I am a business partner you believe to have dishonored you, to have betrayed you in such a way that it is simply not logical to wish to maintain that contract. Why do you not gladly cast me off, Nicholas?'

He looked away, still unable to tell her the truth.

'Nicholas, I spoke the truth when I said that Daniel had never been my lover but he would have been had he had his way.'

'He told me quite frankly that he had.'

She stared at him. 'Then he told you a lie. Oh, Nicholas, why are you so willing to believe ill of me? I have never deserved it, for I have never failed you in anything except that I could not make you love me.'

He looked swiftly at her, his eyes changing, but she did not see, for she had decided at last to confess everything to him. She walked away, standing by the window to look out over the park toward Sedgemoor.

'I wrote that letter to Daniel, but then thought it too brief and distant. Whatever you may think of him, *I* have a fondness for him, in spite of the fact that I now realize he was guilty of allowing certain untruths to occur. He alone made my days here pleasant, for he was charming, attentive, good company, and above all he could make me smile when but for his presence I would have wept. The letter has been tampered with; I suspect by Augustine, for she alone would have good reason to wish to make its meaning change. And you do exactly as she wishes, Nicholas, for you believe what is there now, not what I originally wrote. My life here with you *will* be unrewarding for me in the way which means most to me, for I will always be denied your love. I want a marriage of desire and passion, I want to be your sweetheart and your mistress as well as your wife. I want to fall asleep each night in your arms and wake up there in the mornings. I want all of you, Nicholas, not just an empty contract which places me beneath your roof but not in your bed. I want to bear your children, not content myself with inspecting estate ledgers. I married you because I loved you, you were always the husband I would have chosen for myself, and it is because I still love you that I decided to accept what you offered yesterday, hollow though that cheerless offer was. But now, after you have misunderstood that letter and once again chosen to think the very worst of me, I cannot face going on with this marriage without telling you the whole truth and risking your undoubted scorn. Everything must be stated here and now – you must face the fact that I love you and wish to be far, far more than the woman who just happens to bear your name due to a quirk of fate in Venice.'

It was as if his ears deceived him, for she was saying the words he had so longed to hear. He gazed at her as she stood by the window, her long dark hair falling around her shoulders, the silhouette of her slender figure visible through the flimsy wrap. 'Oh, Laura,' he whispered, 'If only you knew . . .'

She turned. 'After all I've said, do you still wish me to remain here?'

He saw the unshed tears in her eyes as he went to her, taking her face gently in his hands and brushing his lips over hers. 'Can't you see?' he whispered. 'Can't you understand why I will not let you go? I want you to stay because I love you, and I have loved you since that day in Venice. I have hurt you because I believed you hurt me. I was consumed with jealousy and bruised pride because I believed you gave to Daniel Tregarron that which I so craved myself. I cannot bear to think of life without you, and I feel for you all the desire and passion you say you seek.'

An unbelievable joy sang through her. Her lips moved to say his name, but she could not speak, and then his arms were around her, holding her close as he kissed her, and the kiss was no gentle brushing of his lips over hers; it burned with all the emotion that had been pent up for so long and that now found so sweet a release. . . .

There were tears on her cheeks, but they were tears of happiness. His eyes were dark as he looked at her. 'I have been a tardy bridegroom, my love,' he said softly. 'But I am about to put that failing right. This marriage is no makeshift affair, no mere business contract, I promise you. It is a love match, as I shall prove to you now. By *God* shall I prove it to you!'